serenity

serenity

JANET
NISSENSON

Dedicated to our soulmates, to second chances, and, of course, to true serenity for all beings.

prologue

June – Napa Valley

MATTHEW BENNETT MOTIONED TO THE bartender, who was enjoying something of a lull in the action for the first time that night.

"Can I get a refill on this?" he asked, sliding his glass across the bar.

"Sure thing, sir. Masterson's, right?"

Matthew nodded at the mention of the ten year old bourbon he'd been drinking for most of the evening. "Good memory."

The twenty-something bartender grinned good-naturedly as he poured Matthew's drink. "Not much call for bourbon this evening, what with all these British folks floating around. I don't think I've mixed so many martinis, or gone through this much single malt Scotch in two months combined. So when someone asks for a bourbon I tend to remember. Or the line of Patron shots that this very attractive lady keeps coming back for. Except I think her husband just cut her off."

Matthew offered the bartender up a smile, plus a ten dollar bill in the tip jar, as he picked up the cut crystal glass that held his drink. "I think I know who that lady is. If it's the same person I'm thinking of, her twin sister is the matron of honor. And from what I recall from the bachelor party I

1

attended last week, that lady can drink most grown men under the table."

The red-headed bartender sighed. "Not anymore, apparently. Her husband grabbed the last shot right out of her hand and drank it down himself. She was just about to give him hell for it when he kissed her instead. That seemed to shut her up."

Matthew laughed, but any reply he might have made was cut off when a couple walked up to the bar and ordered a martini and a glass of Glenlivet. The bartender gave Matthew an "I told you so" eye roll before efficiently mixing up the drinks.

Ian and Tessa's wedding had been every bit as lavish and wonderful as Matthew would have expected, knowing quite well what a stickler for detail his friend could be. He also knew how devoted Ian was to Tessa, and that no expense had been spared to give her the sort of wedding most women could only dream of. It was a stark contrast to the simple, budget-conscious event that was all he and Lindsey had been able to afford sixteen years ago. But given the way Lindsey spent money like a drunken sailor these days, it seemed at times that she was hell-bent on making up for all those lean years when they'd lived paycheck to paycheck, and would have never been able to stay at a posh, exclusive resort hotel like this one.

Matthew grimaced as he noticed his wife dancing with yet another partner this evening, this one fortunately nowhere near as young as some of the others she had gravitated to earlier. As usual, Lindsey was doing her damndest to circulate the room, flirting rather outrageously with every good looking man at the wedding, and more or less ignoring the fact that she had a husband of her own present. And she'd dressed once again with the sole purpose in mind of attracting as much attention as possible, especially since she had known all eyes would be focused on the bride tonight. Lindsey was wearing a short, tight cocktail dress of shimmery gold brocade, along with gold metallic stilettos that were so high she'd almost tripped over her own feet several times already. Never one for subtlety, she was practically dripping in jewels - necklace, bracelets, long chandelier earrings, and of course the enormous diamond solitaire ring that she'd insisted he buy her a few years ago to replace the tiny little stone that had been all he'd been able to afford way back when.

She did look good, he admitted, and nearly ten years younger than her actual age of forty-one. But, as Lindsey was so fond of saying these days, having plenty of money certainly helped a person age well, and she spent a considerable sum on a regular basis taking care of herself - hair cuts and color, facials, massages, spray-on tans, pedicures, and a whole lot of fancy spa treatments that he'd never heard of before. She also worked out like a fiend, spending hours each day at the gym or doing Pilates, and watched what she ate like a hawk. The result was a sleek, toned, and tanned figure that would make a girl of twenty jealous, and Matthew conceded that all of her hard work had definitely achieved results. With the exception, of course, of the overly large breast implants she'd had done over a year ago without his consent or approval, and most certainly not with his own pleasure in mind. Like most everything else she did nowadays, having the implants done had been strictly

3

for Lindsey's own personal satisfaction.

He shrugged and turned his back to the dance floor, not particularly eager to watch his wife make a fool of herself over some stranger who was probably wondering why this woman wasn't dancing with her own husband. Matthew wondered that himself, until he realized rather starkly that he didn't especially give a damn about Lindsey's reasons any longer. What he couldn't remember, though, was exactly how long it had been since he had stopped caring.

He drained his whiskey in one neat swallow, and was about to order another - mindful of the fact that they were staying overnight in Napa, which meant he didn't have to worry about driving - when a melodious, innately feminine voice sounded to his right.

"I don't suppose you have a pot of hot water back there, do you?"

The woman's question sounded hopeful, and Matthew glanced in her direction, curious as to who would be asking for hot water rather than alcohol at this hour. It was one of Tessa's bridesmaids - the slightly taller one with the really remarkable head of naturally curly hair that was half a dozen different shades of blonde. He didn't know her name, but it occurred to him all of a sudden where he'd seen her before - just a week ago at Ian and Tessa's joint bachelor/bachelorette party. Curlylocks hadn't been wearing an elegant, blue strapless gown like she had on this evening, though. Instead, she'd worn some sort of vividly printed cotton dress in yellows and oranges that had twirled and whirled as she and her date had treated the guests to an impromptu salsa dance. Lindsey had made some disparaging comment about the colorful dress, wondering snidely what vintage store or flea market it had been found at. But Matthew knew the real reason for his wife's cattiness was because Curlylocks's very attractive date hadn't paid Lindsey the slightest bit of attention, despite her rather pathetic attempts to flirt with him.

The bartender nodded. "Sure do. Can I get you anything else to go with that, like a tea bag or something?" he offered as he lifted a glass carafe filled with water from a hot plate.

Curlylocks shook her head, causing those amazing curls to bounce riotously, and laughingly held out her palm to display a little packet. "I brought my own, thanks."

Matthew regarded the woman curiously as she dunked the tea bag into the hot water to let it seep. It wasn't like him to strike up a conversation with a woman he didn't really know, but there was something about this particular female that suddenly seemed oddly fascinating.

"I'm pretty sure they have tea here," he joked. "And given how much this shindig must be costing Ian, you didn't need to bring your own drink."

She glanced up at him, as though startled that someone was actually speaking to her. Matthew sucked in a breath as the full impact of her green-gold eyes hit him. Coupled with the warm olive tones of her flawless skin, and that wild mane of multi-hued curls, she reminded him of a lioness. And when her mouth quirked up in a smile, he felt something he hadn't experienced in a very long time - desire.

"Of course they have tea here," she replied in that calm, melodious voice. "At least a dozen different blends if I recall correctly from the breakfast we had this morning. But, you see, this is a very special blend that I'm drinking now. It's made with turmeric, lemongrass, ginger, and licorice, and it's very beneficial in countering the effects of alcohol. Not that I've had very much to drink," she added as she removed the tea bag, "but since I typically don't drink alcohol at all I thought it best to take preventive measures."

Matthew stared at her. "I don't even know what some of that stuff is you just mentioned," he admitted.

She smiled at him serenely as she took a sip of her tea. "You should try it sometime, then. Especially if you've been drinking that nasty stuff all night." She gestured toward his empty glass of whiskey.

"Hey," he protested half-seriously. "That nasty stuff, as you just called it, costs seventy five dollars a bottle."

Curlylocks picked up his empty glass and gave it a dainty sniff before wrinkling her small, straight nose in distaste. "At least vodka or tequila barely has an odor. What is this exactly - bourbon or scotch? Either way, it smells horrid. And I'll spare you the lecture, but what this poison is doing to your insides - well, you don't want to think about that right now. I won't spoil your evening for you."

Matthew sighed. "Too late for that, I'm afraid. By the way, we haven't been formally introduced, but I'm Matthew Bennett - Matt, to my friends. I, uh, saw you doing that dance thing at the party last weekend."

She laughed, a tinkling, musical laugh that reminded him of bells or wind chimes. "I'm guessing you know as little about dancing as you do about herbal tea," she teased. "And, yes, that was me dancing. My partner and I were doing the salsa, and then later a rhumba. And I'm Sasha.

Sasha Fonseca. A pleasure to meet you, Matthew."

Sasha extended a hand towards him, and he gripped it in his automatically, pleased to discover how smooth and soft her skin was. He wondered what it was she did for a living to have hands like that. And it also pleased him that she'd addressed him by his full name. Most people, including Lindsey, called him Matt, but he really preferred Matthew. Especially the way Sasha pronounced it in that soft, almost hypnotic voice.

He released her hand after belatedly realizing he'd been gripping it for long seconds. "I didn't see the two of you out on the dance floor tonight," he commented. "Though I'm not sure this band would be able to play anything that, uh, festive."

"Doubtful," she agreed placidly. "But a fancy wedding isn't exactly the right setting for something as earthy as salsa music. And you haven't seen me out there dancing with my partner because Miguel isn't here this evening. He flew back to Los Angeles a few days ago, and is probably out dancing at some club right now. With his new boyfriend."

"Oh." Matthew wasn't exactly sure why Sasha had thrown that last bit in, but for some bizarre reason he was glad she had clarified that the hot Spaniard she'd danced so sultrily with last week was actually gay. Not that it was any of his business, of course. "So you're here alone tonight?"

She nodded, taking another careful drink of her tea, as though she was savoring each sip. "I figured that any date I could round up wouldn't know a soul here. And since I'd be occupied doing, well, bridesmaid-like things, it wouldn't be fair to just abandon him to sit with a tableful of strangers.

Plus," she added with a twinkle in those huge, curly lashed cat eyes, "most of the guys I tend to date would stick out like a sore thumb in a place this fancy."

Now Matthew was really intrigued, finding this woman with her wild curls and tiger eyes the most unusual, fascinating person he'd met in a very long time. "And what sort of guys would those be?" he asked, chuckling.

Sasha smiled, and that small movement lit up her radiant features, enough for Matthew to realize that Tessa's bridesmaid was seriously gorgeous.

"Oh, you probably couldn't begin to imagine," she began. "I mean, if you're one of Ian's friends, I'm guessing you're on the straight-laced side like he is. And he's such a kind man, a real gentleman, but I'm well aware that certain aspects of my, ah, lifestyle are pretty far removed from black tie dinners and mansions and five star resorts. Most people would call me a hippie just for starters, but it goes well beyond something that simple."

He glanced at her beautiful blue gown, silver high-heeled sandals, and the dainty diamond and sapphire pendant that hung around her slender neck - a bridesmaid's gift, he guessed, from Tessa. "You don't look anything like any hippie I've ever seen," he stated firmly. "You just look - lovely."

The look of pleasure on her animated face made him instantly and uncomfortably hard, and Matthew wondered what in hell had brought on *that* sort of reaction. He didn't know anything about this woman, had barely exchanged a few sentences with her, but apparently his dick didn't care. And evidently that particular part of his anatomy also didn't mind that he was a married man, one who definitely should not be reacting this way to a woman who wasn't his wife - no matter how pretty or interesting she was. His unwilling attraction to Sasha made him realize just how long it had been since he'd enjoyed sex with Lindsey - *really* enjoyed it, and not just gone through the motions.

"Well, thank you," replied Sasha charmingly. "But this isn't the way I usually dress. Not by a long shot. I did this to please Tessa, to make her happy. Because she's been a very good friend to me, and she and Ian are two of the best people I know."

The bartender caught Matthew's eye then, motioning to his empty glass and silently asking if he wanted a refill. It was on the tip of his tongue to say yes, but then he glanced at Sasha as she continue to sip her tea. He sighed, and asked the bartender for a bottle of mineral water instead.

She nodded in approval as he uncapped the bottle. "A much better choice than bourbon. Stick to water for the rest of the night, and it will help flush out the alcohol."

He regarded her curiously. "Are you a doctor in addition to a dancer?"

Sasha laughed again, and this time it definitely sounded like bells tinkling. "Neither one, actually. I'm a yoga teacher and masseuse mostly, but I've done some training as an herbalist as well. Not enough to get licensed, but I know quite a bit about the practice."

"Wow." Matthew shook his head. "I mean, we have masseuses at the health club I belong to, but they're these big, beefy guys. You're, well, less than half their size."

She shrugged. "It isn't always about raw strength, you know. And there are many different types of massage. Some

9

have more benefits than others, and it all depends on the client and their particular needs. Ian was skeptical at first, too, convinced that someone he outweighed by more than eighty pounds wouldn't be able to dig deep enough to make him flinch." Her eyes twinkled with a mischievous gleam. "The first time I had him on the massage table I found a sore spot between his shoulder blades he didn't know was there. And all I did was press on it with my thumb and he yelled so loud the table shook."

Matthew guffawed, unable to imagine his buff, fitness fanatic friend at the mercy of this slender, graceful young woman. "So *you're* the masseuse he always raves about," he mused. "Hmm, maybe I should set up an appointment with you myself. I, uh, have a pretty stressful job, and massage seems to help with that from time to time."

"Of course," agreed Sasha placidly. "I'm afraid I don't have a business card with me, but you can just ask Tessa or Ian for my contact info. *After* they get back from their honeymoon, that is."

"I'll do that."

Sasha set her tea mug down on the bar. "I should be getting back now. You're not here alone, are you, Matthew?"

He quickly decided that he loved the way she said his name - almost like a musical note. "No. My wife and I are here together. Though it seems like she's ditched me for a different dance partner," he joked, trying to sound carefree. "Several different ones actually."

Sasha frowned. "Why in the world would she do that? I mean, don't married couples typically hang out together at events like this one? And dance together?"

Matthew tried again to laugh the matter off. "I'm a terrible dancer," he admitted. "Two left feet, and all that. And Lindsey loves to dance, so it's better for both of us if she finds another partner. That way neither of us is miserable."

Sasha shook her head, causing those curls to bounce endearingly. "I don't believe you're a terrible dancer," she declared firmly. "Not for a minute. You hold yourself very well, have excellent posture, and seem extremely fit. If you can't dance well it's probably because you haven't had the right teachers. Come with me. I'll show you."

"But - honestly, I don't think.." stammered Matthew, as she took him firmly by the hand and led him out to the crowded dance floor.

"Relax," she assured him, patting him on the shoulder as though he was a small child she was comforting. "The band has just switched to a slow number, so all you have to do is move your feet a little."

Before he could protest further, Sasha had placed one of her hands on his shoulder and picked up his hand with the other. Automatically, Matthew's arm banded about her slender waist, holding her a respectable distance from his body. It was, he thought absently, a far cry from the way he'd seen Lindsey almost dry humping one of her dance partners a little while ago.

And surprisingly, with Sasha's softly murmured instructions, he found himself moving her around to the music, not stepping on her dainty toes even once. He gazed down at her, the top of her curly head barely reaching his chin, and realized he hadn't felt this sense of calm in a very, very long time.

"You're doing great," she assured him. "See, I told

you. Anyone can dance provided they receive the proper instruction. However," she added more severely, "you weren't kidding before when you said you needed a massage. You've got knots in your shoulder that a Shibari master wouldn't be able to untie."

"What exactly is a Shibari master?" he inquired, unfamiliar with the term.

"Oh, just someone who's skilled with tying patterns and shapes with rope," she replied hastily. "It's, ah, usually for bondage purposes. You know, like in BDSM."

Matthew coughed. "Are you into that stuff?" he wheezed. "Is that what you meant earlier about having weird boyfriends?"

Sasha laughed delightedly. "I never said they were weird. Just that they wouldn't necessarily fit into a fancy society event like this. And, no. I'm not into 'that stuff'. But I do appreciate all different art forms, and I saw a photography exhibit of Shibari last year. It's actually quite beautiful, very intricate. You should look it up sometime."

"Yeah, maybe."

A sudden, unbidden image of the graceful, lovely Sasha bound up in intricately knotted silk ropes made him hard again, and he was thankful that several inches still separated their bodies. By the time the song ended a minute or so later, he'd brought his unexpected erection back under control, and led her off the dance floor with a hand lightly resting on her elbow.

"Well, thank you for the dance," Sasha told him. "And I do hope you'll get in touch. For that massage I mentioned, of course. I could feel all the tension in your body just now.

And if your neck and upper back are anywhere near as tight as your shoulder feels, you need a massage urgently. So even if you forget to ask Tessa for my contact info, or just prefer to go to someone else, please make sure you get that massage soon, Matthew." She took a step back and frowned a little as she studied his face. "You have a very unsettling aura about you. Oh, I'm sure you think all of that stuff is for quacks and weirdos. Don't worry, most people feel the same way. But believe it or not, I do have something of a gift for reading peoples' emotional states. And yours - well, you don't seem like a very happy man, Matthew. And that's a shame, because you're also one of the kindest people I've ever met. So please take care of yourself, hmm?"

She touched his cheek briefly, softly, but for long minutes after she disappeared back into the throngs of guests, Matthew felt the imprint of her hand on his skin as though he'd been branded. And the way she'd so swiftly and neatly summed up his emotions was almost frighteningly accurate - because it had been a long, long time since he'd been truly happy.

chapter one

July – San Francisco

MATTHEW HAD SPENT A GOOD part of his life being called a nerd. Or a dweeb. Or a braniac. As a boy he'd been far more interested in reading a book or performing experiments with his chemistry set than playing sports. And as a teen and young man, he'd spent way more time writing computer code and designing software programs than pursuing members of the opposite sex.

But his continued fascination with academics, science, and computers didn't mean that he wasn't also very much a man - a man with the same sort of physical needs and desires as others of his gender. A man who got turned on by the sight of a beautiful, sexy woman, or who wouldn't necessarily look the other way if he accidentally stumbled across a couple locked in a passionate embrace or an even more intimate situation.

However, when the female of the said couple happened to be his own wife - a wife who was even now moaning in pleasure as her young, buff lover was fucking her with great enthusiasm - and in Matthew's own bed, to boot - he didn't find the sight the least bit arousing. By rights he should be furious right now, should be yelling at the top of his lungs, shoving his fist into the face of the arrogant prick who was

- well, ramming his prick into Matthew's eager, willing wife. But, as he continued to watch their frantic coupling with an odd sense of detachment, the only rational thought that crossed his mind was that now he was going to have to get rid of that bed. And what a inconvenience that was going to be.

"Do you think you two could finish this up soon?" he drawled in a weary voice. "I've got the flu and can barely stay on my feet. And as loud as you're being right now, I'll be able to hear you clear across the other side of the condo."

Lindsey Bennett froze in place, not an easy feat considering how hard her eager young lover was screwing her from behind. She was on all fours facing the foot of the bed, her long, dark brown hair half covering her face as her oblivious companion continued to shove his cock in and out of her all-too-willing body. Those ridiculously overlarge breasts of hers - as fake as a three dollar bill - barely jiggled an inch no matter how hard her paramour thrust his hips against her buttocks . Her dark green eyes were wide with shock, her mouth falling open in stunned silence as she met her husband's narrowed gaze.

"Matt. Oh, God," she croaked, trying desperately to ease herself away from the man who was still embedded inside her body. "Will you *stop* already?" she screeched, slapping the leanly muscled flank of her lover. "Jesse, for Christ's sake, stop! We're not alone, you idiot."

"Huh? Whatsa matter - oh, shit."

As Jesse - the flirtatious, egotistical personal trainer who worked at the exclusive private health club that the Bennetts belonged to - recognized Matthew, he visibly paled, then gulped, before gingerly withdrawing his still-engorged penis

15

from Lindsey's body. Lindsey wasted no time in springing from the bed, not bothering with clothes, and frantically grabbed hold of Matthew's arm.

Her green eyes were still wild with shock, her normally perfectly groomed hair a careless tumble about her shoulders. "Matt. *Matt.* For God's sakes, you've got to listen to me," she babbled, not bothering to disguise the panic in her voice. "This - this isn't what it looks like, I swear it."

Matthew glanced down at his wife's hand clasped almost desperately around his bicep. As usual, Lindsey's nails were long and perfectly manicured, covered in a shiny scarlet polish. Her wedding rings were almost garishly large, the ostentatious stones far too big for her small fingers.

She didn't seem in the least bit concerned that she was buck naked at the moment, but then Lindsey took great pride in that slim, tight body of hers and enjoyed showing it off. Privately, Matthew considered his wife too skinny with her boyishly slim hips, and practically no curve to her buttocks, and he could practically count each of her ribs right now. And of course those godawful breast implants threw her entire frame way off balance. She was too petite and small boned to be able to carry off such large boobs, and half the time Matthew was afraid she was going to topple over as a result of being so top-heavy.

He wrinkled his nose in distaste, the odor of sweat and semen and sex that clung to her naked body unmistakable. Evidently she and Jesse had been at this for some time before his untimely arrival.

"Really, Linz?" he asked sarcastically. "What exactly is it supposed to look like? Because from where I was just standing it sure looked to me like you and Jesse were having a real good time. And in my bed, to boot. Now, I know that just because I've got a genius I.Q. that doesn't always translate to street smarts, but even someone as naïve as you seem to think I am can see for myself exactly what's been going on here. And I also know that Jesse is just the latest in a very long line of your, er, playmates."

Lindsey's pretty mouth gaped open in shock, evidently too flabbergasted by this unexpected revelation to offer up a protest. Taking advantage of her momentary silence, Matthew grabbed up a handful of her discarded clothing and shoved it into her arms.

"Get dressed," he told her harshly. "And make it quick, because I wasn't kidding about having the flu. I want you and Lover Boy out of here within the next five minutes or I'll call security to have you both tossed out."

"You can't do that!" protested Lindsey wildly, even as she clumsily pulled on her lingerie. "You can't have me thrown out of my own house!"

Matthew made a noise that resembled a snort. "But it's not your house, sweetheart," he reminded her snidely. "The condo technically belongs to the business. The fact that you've chosen to use it for your little love nest whenever you feel the urge - which is pretty fucking often, according to all the reports I've received - doesn't make it half yours. Neither does the fact that you've seen fit to leave more and more of your things here. So get yourself dressed - *fast* - and get the hell out so I can get some sleep. And that goes double for you, jackass," he told Jesse, pointing a threatening finger at the trainer.

17

Jesse, to his credit, had begun to dress the moment he'd recognized Matthew, and was even now shoving his feet into his Nikes. "Mr. - Mr. Bennett," he stammered. "I - I'm sorry as hell about this, really I am. And - and I wouldn't blame you in the least if you punched my lights out right about now. In fact, I probably deserve it. So go ahead - do your worst."

Matthew regarded Jesse with undisguised distaste. "Yeah, you'd probably like that, wouldn't you?" he taunted. "You'd like it if I roughed you up a little, left a few bruises, maybe even a broken rib or two. That way you could sue me for assault, maybe come out of this fiasco with a nice settlement." He shook his head. "Forget it. As I just mentioned, I'm a pretty smart guy, way too smart to fall for a set up like that. And at this point, as sick as I feel, I'm way more likely to barf all over you than I am to land a punch or two. But mostly, I just don't care enough, Jesse. It really doesn't bother me all that much that I just caught you in the act with my wife. It *does* bother me, however, that now I'm going to have to replace that bed. I *liked* that bed, damn it."

Jesse stared at Matthew in disbelief. "You - you're just going to let me off the hook that easy? Just let me walk out of here like nothing ever happened?"

Matthew gave the much younger man an evil grin. "Oh, I didn't say that, Lover Boy," he drawled. "But there are far more effective methods of getting revenge than physical violence. I figure all it will take is a quick phone call to the owner of the club, and you'll be out on your tight cheeked ass. Especially if Ian Gregson also calls, as he's been threatening to do ever since you stupidly propositioned his new wife. You might be interested to know that *I* was the one who convinced him to keep it under wraps. But no longer, Jesse. Did I mention how much I like this bed? Or used to like it, I should say."

Jesse looked sick to his stomach, as though he'd suddenly contracted the same nasty flu bug that Matthew had been fighting off all morning. Wisely, though, he chose not to make matters worse by arguing his case, and merely strode out of the bedroom as though the place was on fire. Moments later the sound of the front door slamming shut echoed through the spacious condo, and Matthew turned to face his wife, wondering with a rather devious sense of satisfaction how the hell she thought she was going to charm her way out of this mess.

He held up a hand to forestall whatever lame-ass excuse had been about to pass through her lying mouth. The very same mouth that had more than likely been wrapped around Jesse's cock less than an hour ago, the same one that had without question given dozens of different men a very eager blow job over the past few years.

"I don't want to hear it, Linz," he told her, fighting off the waves of dizziness that were threatening to make his legs give out from under him. "I might be sick but I'm sure as hell not delirious, so there's no way I just imagined what I saw. And you can protest and whine and deny your life away, but it's been obvious to me for a long time now that you've been humping every hot young stud who crosses your path. Unfortunately for you, your nerdy, naïve husband wasn't born yesterday after all. I've had a private detective trailing you for almost two years now, and even *he* was shocked by how much action you've been getting. So don't bother lying,

19

because you'll just make a fool of yourself, hmm?"

Lindsey's green eyes were practically spitting fire at the revelation that her amorous activities hadn't been nearly as secret as she'd assured herself. "I wouldn't have to look for *action* as you so crudely put it," she spat, stepping into a towering pair of red Louboutin stilettos, "if you were at home more than a few hours a week. You might as well be married to your fucking job, Matt, considering how little the kids and I see of you these days."

Matthew felt the room spin sickeningly around him, the sensation almost as bad as the churning in his stomach. He slapped a hand against the door jamb to hold himself upright, and just hoped he wouldn't pass out - or throw up - before he could toss Lindsey out of here on those ridiculously high heels. "I'm too sick - and way too disgusted with you - right now to have this conversation," he replied wearily. "Except to say that I warned you about all of this - many, many times - when you pushed and coerced and begged me to take the company public. You knew what you were getting into, Lindsey, so don't use my job as an excuse for why you can't keep your legs closed. Now, would you please leave? I really am sick and I need to take a nap. Which is going to have to be in one of the guest rooms now, since there's no way I'm ever sleeping in this bed again."

"Fine," she acquiesced huffily. "Take your stupid nap. We'll talk when you get home tonight."

He shook his head. "I won't be coming home. Not tonight or any other night. This is it, Linz. I've held on as long as I could because of the kids, but I just realized I can't take any more of your antics. Our marriage has been over for a good long time, and I'm finally ready to deal with that. I'll be calling my lawyer just as soon as I get a few hours sleep. In the meanwhile, I suggest you get your own lawyer so we can hash all this out as quickly as possible. I'll call the kids tonight or tomorrow at the latest to break the news. Or if I'm feeling better I'll arrange to pick them both up from school tomorrow and tell them face to face."

Lindsey stared at him in horror. "You can't be serious," she whispered huskily. "Come on, Matt, it was just a harmless little fling. Nothing to get all upset over. And definitely nothing important enough to start talking about a divorce over."

He sighed tiredly, running a hand through his sweat dampened hair. In addition to the fatigue, dizziness, and nausea that had been plaguing him all morning, he was pretty sure he was also running a fever. His PA - a stern but frighteningly organized woman named Elena Ordenes - had nagged him all morning about going home or seeing the doctor - not necessarily in that order. In the end, he'd acquiesced to her orders, and agreed to nap for a few hours in the company-owned condo located just two short blocks from the office. What he certainly hadn't anticipated was that Lindsey would be using the place for one of her sordid little assignations.

But her ill-advised little "afternoon delight" was proving to be the catalyst Matthew had needed for a long time now to make some much-needed changes in his life - a life that he hadn't been happy in for long months, if not years. And for once he wasn't going to let her pleas and tears and empty promises sway a decision he should have made a long time ago.

21

"Actually, I've been thinking about filing for divorce for awhile now," he admitted. "Even before I knew for sure that you were fucking every hot young stud you could coerce into your bed. And you do like them young, don't you, Linz? At least Jesse's closer to thirty, not like that college football player you banged last month. Jesus, you're old enough to be his mother."

Lindsey opened her mouth to protest, before giving a resigned little shrug. "I've got a problem," she acknowledged in a small voice. "I probably need counseling. *We* need counseling, Matt. So before you even start mentioning the word divorce we should definitely see a marriage counselor. I'm sure after just a few sessions it will all work out. In fact, I can ask Holly for the name of the person she and Phil saw when they were having problems last year. She swore the sessions did wonders for them, that their marriage is better than ever, and I know it can be the same for us. In fact, let me call her right now and - "

"No." Matthew shook his head emphatically. "Do not call Holly. Do not call a marriage counselor. I fully agree that you've got problems - not the least of which is a condition known as nymphomania. But I have no intention of seeing a counselor, and no interest in saving this farce of a marriage. It's over, Lindsey, and probably should have been four or five years ago. Now, please leave so I can get some rest before I collapse right here. And if I have to sleep in this room - where I'm guessing you've brought more than a few of your fuck buddies - I'm really, really going to be sick. I'll have all your things packed up and sent to you at the house, though considering how much crap you've managed to accumulate here that might take a couple of days. Now, get out before I have you escorted out."

She glared at him as she picked up her Hermes satchel. "If you think for one minute that this is even close to being over," she hissed, "then you're stupider and more naïve than I've ever imagined. There's not going to be a divorce, Matt. Not now and not ever. And as soon as you get over this little hissy fit you're having, you'll apologize for all the horrible things you've just said and beg me to forgive you. Just like old times."

Lindsey stormed out of the condo, slamming the front door behind her for emphasis. Matthew wearily made his way to one of the guest rooms, toeing off his shoes and pulling back the covers. But just before he collapsed onto the mattress and let sleep take him over, he had just enough presence of mind left to pick up the telephone and press the number for the building's concierge.

"Xavier? Hey, sorry to bother you, man, but I really need a couple of urgent favors. Yeah, I've got the flu, feel like three day old crap right now. No, no. I don't need a doctor or anything from the pharmacy, just some sleep. Listen, this is what I need you to do, okay? First is to change my access codes to the building, including the one for the garage. And don't let anyone else know what the new codes are, got it? Especially Mrs. Bennett. Next, I need a locksmith up here ASAP to change the front door lock. Yep, that's it for now. Thanks, buddy, you're the best."

As his head hit the pillow and he found some much needed solace in slumber, Matthew sleepily figured he could deal with replacing the bed in the master bedroom tomorrow.

chapter two

Two weeks later

IAN GREGSON ARCHED A BROW observantly from where he sat across the table. "Perhaps you should have ordered a second entrée, Matthew. It looks like you haven't had a square meal in awhile."

Matthew gave his friend a sheepish grin as he popped another French fry in his mouth. "You may be right. Ever since Lindsey and I separated I've been subsisting on takeout food most nights. Fortunately, Elena has always been a bossy little thing, and she makes sure I have something for breakfast and lunch so I don't waste away to nothing, as she's so fond of saying. I keep insisting that she's got a Jewish mother somewhere in her background, even though she swears she's a hundred percent Latina, going back several generations."

Ian chuckled, taking a modest bite of his grilled halibut. "You're lucky to have an assistant like her to look after you. As exemplary as Andrew has always been at his job, I can't recall a single incident where he ever actually *fussed* over me."

Matthew gave a small shudder, not able to imagine Ian's stuffy, by-the-book PA ever fussing over anything. In fact, he couldn't recall ever seeing the serious, bespectacled young man even cracking a smile during the few times they had met. "No, that's for sure," he agreed readily. "Elena is more than happy to look out for me, though, especially since both of her boys are doing out-of-state internships this summer and she can only boss them so much from long distance."

Matthew's PA was a single mother who'd raised her two sons practically single-handedly, and bullied, pushed, and guided them into getting accepted to highly rated universities. Her eldest – Jaime - would be a senior at Duke this fall, while her younger son – Diego - would be starting his second year at Purdue. Seeing her boys excelling in school, and being presented with the sort of opportunities that Elena herself had never known growing up as one of six children born to poor Mexican immigrants, was by far her proudest achievement. Keeping Matthew organized at the office was a close second. And in the weeks since he'd separated from Lindsey, Elena had been fussing over him and keeping him in line more than ever.

This time it was Ian's turn to shudder at the mention of Matthew's ferociously protective PA. "Your Elena is more like a mama shark than a mama bear, I'm afraid," he pointed out. "But you need someone like her in your life, Matthew. Especially since - well, you know."

Matthew nodded, taking a generous bite of his triple-decker club sandwich. "Since I've been living on my own," he acknowledged. "She's been great, no doubt about it - not just with making sure I don't starve to death but taking care of all sorts of little details that sure as hell aren't part of her job description - the dry cleaning, banking, grocery shopping. She even took care of having my old bed hauled away - including all the bedding - and ordering a new one to replace it."

Ian frowned. "Why in the world did you need a new - ah,

never mind."

A few days after the scene in the condo where he'd caught Lindsey and Jesse in the act, Matthew had told Ian most of the gory details. Predictably, Ian had been extremely supportive of Matthew's decision to seek out a divorce under the circumstances, and had also encouraged him to call the owner of their health club to file a complaint against Jesse.

"If you don't I sure as hell will," Ian had declared. "I caught that horny little bastard with his hand on Tessa's backside the other day. I was just about to break his jaw when my beautiful bride took care of the problem for me."

Matthew had chuckled in spite of how lousy he'd been feeling. "Tessa punched that jackass in the face?"

"Not quite. But judging by how loudly he yelped when she bent his little finger backwards I'd say he got the message loud and clear to fuck off."

Ian's encouragement had been all Matthew needed to make that phone call, and just like that Jesse was gone. There was no possible way that the owner of their club was going to piss off either the CEO of a hugely successful software firm, or one of the heirs to the top luxury hotel chain in the world.

Word around the club, however, was that Jesse had left voluntarily to "pursue other opportunities", and Matthew hadn't been anxious to correct this misrepresentation of the facts. Despite his resolve to pursue a divorce, he wasn't willing to let it be known that his wife had banged one of the personal trainers - among a long list of others. A man was entitled to some semblance of pride, after all, even if his had been badly torn to shreds these last few years.

Matthew cleaned his plate, after having already polished off a bowl of clam chowder, and asked the waiter to bring over the dessert menu. At Ian's look of surprise, he gave him a wry grin in response.

"This is the first meal I've eaten in two weeks that hasn't come out of a takeout container," he explained. "So I plan on enjoying every bite."

Ian grinned, but only asked for a pot of tea when Matthew ordered a piece of peach pie. "Tessa and I will have to have you over for dinner one evening soon, then," he assured him. "She's already mentioned it to me a couple of times. And my wife loves nothing better than to fuss over me, so you can be sure she'll do the same to you. Probably even send you home with plates of leftovers."

Matthew gave a sigh of utter bliss. "I can't tell you how great that sounds, Ian. I'm pretty sure the last time I sat down to a home-cooked meal was the last time I was at your house for dinner. Lindsey was never much of a cook, and especially not in the last few years since we were able to hire domestic help. Not to mention the fact that her diet mostly consists of salads and protein shakes these days. You're a lucky, lucky man to have a wife like Tessa, that's for sure."

Ian smiled. "I won't argue with you about that. Every man should be so fortunate to have someone like her in their life. But she also happens to be one in a million, so I realize just how lucky I am. I'm just sorry your own marriage isn't as blissful as mine is already proving to be, Matthew. Do you think there's a chance that you and Lindsey can work things out? Especially considering the children."

Matthew shook his head. "The kids are the only reason I've stuck it out this long. And even if Lindsey hadn't slept with a few dozen men - and those are just the ones I know about - I would have initiated a divorce sooner than later. We've drifted apart, no longer want the same things from life, and, well, she's like a completely different person than the woman I married all those years ago. It's said that money changes a person, and in Lindsey's case that hasn't been a positive change."

"Hmm." Ian took a sip of his tea. "You've been married how long?"

"Sixteen years. We got married just a few months before our daughter was born. And, yes, before you ask," added Matthew, "Lindsey's pregnancy was why we got married in the first place. I doubt if she would have agreed to marry me otherwise. And considering I was immersed in my doctorate program at the time, getting married wasn't exactly at the top of my list back then, either." He shoved a piece of pie into his mouth, then washed it down with coffee. "But, hey, that was a long time ago, and it sure as hell feels like we were two completely different people back then. At least Lindsey was. Deep down, I'm still the nerdy computer geek I was when she met me."

Ian looked dubiously at Matthew's expensive Italian suit, silk tie, and expertly cut hair. "You look nothing like any geek I've ever known."

Matthew grinned. "You should have seen me in college - skinny, awkward, wire-rimmed glasses that had probably gone out of style a dozen years earlier. And I'm pretty sure my jeans were always a few inches too short. I've undergone something of a makeover during the last decade or so, I guess. Though I still prefer wearing jeans and a T-shirt to a Brioni suit any day of the week."

"So there's no chance then of a reconciliation?" inquired Ian.

"Not as far as I'm concerned," declared Matthew. "I filed for a legal separation within a week after moving out, and my attorney sent the divorce papers to Lindsey's a few days ago. But even though the terms call for giving her half of everything, plus continuing to contribute to the trust funds we have set up for the kids, I know she'll balk and try to hold out for even more."

"Half?" asked Ian incredulously. "Good Lord, that's a bloody fortune, Matthew! I take it you didn't have a pre-nup in place?"

Matthew gave a hoot of laughter. "Considering that when we got married I had less than four thousand dollars in the bank, drove a ten-year old Toyota, and about the only thing of value I owned were my three computers, a pre-nup would have been a moot point, don't you think? And while I certainly had plans to become successful, I would have never imagined getting to this level. Not to mention the fact that I naively thought our marriage would last forever. I assume Tessa signed a pre-nup?"

"No." Ian gave a firm shake of his dark head. "She offered to, practically insisted, but I was the one who refused to even consider the idea. I know that she'll always be the only one for me, Matthew, and that our marriage will last a lifetime. Some things you just know, and I've always had very good instincts about people. Besides, Tessa is the least greedy person I've ever known, has never asked me for a thing, and rarely spends any money."

Matthew grimaced. "The polar opposite of Lindsey, in other words. In a lot of ways. For one thing, as crazy as the two of you are about each other, there's just no way I could ever see Tessa flirting with another man."

"You're damned right she wouldn't," retorted Ian fiercely. "And not just because I'd break a few of the bastard's bones. Tessa is too fine of a woman to even think of doing something like that, too good a person. She's kind and considerate and hates the very thought of hurting someone's feelings. The fact that she's also madly in love with me helps, too, of course."

"Yeah, that's for sure." Matthew finished off his pie. "I know Lindsey tried like hell to flirt with you over the years, Ian. She'd come right out and tell me to my face that she thought you were hot stuff. And I'm also well aware that you went out of your way to discourage her, all while continuing to act like the gentleman you are."

"Married women have always been off-limits to me," declared Ian. "That's why I had to keep my feelings for Tessa such a carefully guarded secret for over two years, until she told me she and her husband had split up. And I definitely wouldn't have flirted with the wife of one of my closest friends, no matter how persistent she might have been. Plus, overly-aggressive women are a huge turn-off for me."

"Well, Lindsey certainly fits that description to a tee," acknowledged Matthew. "But now that we're divorcing she can flirt with - and fuck - anyone she wants to. Just as long as it doesn't involve the kids, of course. At least she's always had the decency - if one can think of serial cheating as something decent - to have her little flings outside of the house. According to her credit card bills, which she evidently thought I never bothered to check, she certainly made the rounds of most of the hotels here in the city. Including yours, I'm afraid."

Ian winced. "Sorry about that. I'm happy to call the manager there, ask him to flag Lindsey's name so they won't let her stay there in the future."

"Nah." Matthew waved a hand in dismissal. "As long as she leaves my children out of it, I don't especially give a damn who she screws - or where - any longer."

"Speaking of the children, how are they dealing with this whole situation?"

Matthew gave a small shrug. "Better than I expected, actually. Casey is a pretty cool kid, not much rattles him, you know? He's not even fourteen yet but he's so mature for his age that it freaks me out sometimes. He told me that he understands, that he just wants Lindsey and me to be happy. And frankly he and I probably talk and text and Facetime more often now then when I was living at home. As for my daughter - well, she's a typical sixteen year old girl. Too caught up in herself and her own little world to show much emotion about anything else. Overall, the kids are far more accepting of the idea than their mother has been so far. Getting Lindsey to sign those divorce papers is not going to be an easy feat."

Ian arched a brow in surprise. "I happen to know you cracked the top forty names on the latest Fortune 400 list, and even half of that sort of net worth seems like more money than one person could spend in ten lifetimes. What else could Lindsey possibly want?"

"You haven't seen the way she can spend money," declared Matthew. "I'm guessing she'd probably prefer to receive monthly payments over the course of her life. Getting a lump sum like that would be too much temptation, and God knows she has no concept of how to manage money. There's a real possibility that she could blow through that much in a decade or two. And if she took a lump sum she wouldn't be able to squeeze any more from me if she spent it all. But the money is only part of it. Lindsey also loves all the attention she gets as my wife - attending the social events, meeting important people, getting her picture in the newspaper and magazines. All of the stuff I despise the most about this job. She must hate the idea of giving all that up."

"She has no idea that you've thought about selling the company, then?"

Matthew shook his head. "You're the only person I've ever discussed that with, Ian. And as tempting as the idea is most days, it's complicated, as I'm sure you can imagine."

Ian nodded. "Of course. You have a great many people depending on you, Matthew - employees, a board of directors, investors, shareholders, the public. Not to mention your family. But also a tremendous amount of responsibility and stress. I can certainly understand the temptation to just say to hell with it all."

Matthew blew out a breath, as though he had a huge weight resting on his chest. "You have no idea how close I come to doing just that almost every day of the week," he admitted. "But then I think about all the people counting on me, like you said, and I realize I can't just walk away. I am definitely a victim of my own success, aren't I?"

"There's a solution to everything, you know," reminded Ian gently. "It may not be quick or simple, but if you're that miserable I'm sure you'll find a way out of it somehow."

Matthew gave a short, ironic laugh. "Hell of a time to get serious about it, though, considering the fact that I'm in the process of getting a divorce and living apart from my kids. At least working so many hours helps keeps me busy. Going home alone to the condo every night isn't exactly something I look forward to."

"I know that feeling all too well. Before I had Tessa in my life I used to joke to my family that I was married to my job," admitted Ian. "But ever since she and I have been together I've been gradually spending less time at the office, learning to delegate more, and not worry so much about constantly being in control."

Matthew grinned. "Well, if I had a wife like Tessa waiting at home for me I'd find every excuse in the book to leave work early. Or take a very long vacation."

Ian's hazel eyes twinkled. "My thoughts exactly. In fact, after our lunch I'm going to surprise my new bride by arriving home very early today."

"You smug bastard," chided Matthew with a chuckle. "It's not very considerate of you to rub salt into the wound, you know. I mean, it's bad enough that I'm divorcing my wife after getting fed up with her constant cheating. But to know that you're going home to your really hot bride after this and have afternoon sex is bordering on cruelty, Ian. Do you have any idea when the last time I had spontaneous sex with Lindsey was? Jesus, come to think of it, I'm not sure I can remember the last time I had any sort of sex with her."

"I apologize," Ian told him, though he couldn't hide the admittedly smug expression on his face, and his tone of voice didn't sound in the least contrite. "Perhaps you should, ah, remedy that situation sooner than later. Though not, of course, with Lindsey, considering the circumstances."

Matthew shuddered. "You got that right. Even though she had her tubes tied after Casey was born, I started using condoms once I suspected she was sleeping around. No way was I taking a chance at catching some STD from one of her bed partners. As far as scratching that particular inch with someone else - well, I confess to being way, way out of practice in that regard. Lindsey was really the only serious girlfriend I ever had. I'm not sure I'd even know how to begin to go about - uh, *remedying* the situation."

Ian withdrew his wallet from his jacket pocket and extracted a credit card. The two friends took turns treating the other to lunch when they met once a month. "I'm happy to ask Tessa if she could introduce you to someone," he offered. "She's made several friends at her yoga studio and at college."

"Thanks for the offer, but I don't think I'm anywhere near ready for that," admitted Matthew. "Despite the way we've drifted apart, and all of Lindsey's infidelities, it's going to take a little time for me to get used to the fact that I'm not a married man any longer. And that status has nothing to do with legalities or a piece of paper. I haven't felt truly married to Lindsey for a long time, and my moving out just validated what I've been feeling all along. And, well, at this point I think sleeping with some random woman I was set up with would just smack of a revenge fuck. I've gone without sex for weeks and months at a time before, and I can definitely do it now."

The two friends walked out of the restaurant together, pausing when they reached the sidewalk outside. Ian clapped Matthew on the back reassuringly.

"You'll get through this," assured Ian. "And you can always count on me for support, hmm? I'll chat with Tessa this evening about having you over for dinner, and text you with a few different dates. Now, not to rub salt in the wound as you so wrongfully accused me of, but I - er, am rather *anxious* to head home."

Matthew laughed as they exchanged a hearty handshake. "You *are* a smug bastard, Ian! And one with an evil streak as well. Get along with you then. And thanks for being such a good sounding board."

He was still chuckling as he walked the three blocks back to his office building, his mood far better than it had been over the past few weeks. Actually, if he was being completely honest with himself, while he wouldn't describe his mood as being actually *happy* right now, he did feel oddly content. He missed his kids something fierce, but was continually trying to assuage his guilt on that matter by keeping in frequent contact with them. At least he did with Casey, since Hayley didn't seem particularly distressed at his absence. Nor could she bother to spend more than a couple of minutes chatting on the phone with him before ringing off to talk to one of her friends instead. Matthew wondered vaguely when his little girl - the one he'd taken to soccer matches and the playground and Disneyland - had morphed into the slightly sullen, completely disinterested teenager she was

35

now. It had probably, he thought with a sigh of resignation, been around the same time that his marriage had started to crumble into tiny pieces.

The executive floor was its usual beehive of activity as he walked briskly towards his private, expansive office suite, being stopped half a dozen times en route by one of the many employees who worked on this floor. MBI Solutions - an acronym for Matthew Bennett Incorporated - occupied an even dozen floors of this high-rise building in San Francisco's trendy Mission Bay area. He liked the fact that the office wasn't located in the claustrophobic Financial District, that he had an unobstructed view of the bay from his office, and that the company-owned condo that he was currently making his home was less than a ten minute walk from here.

It took him a good twenty minutes to finally arrive at his office after all the interruptions, and he heaved a sigh of relief as he approached his PA's desk. Elena had her own office situated just outside of his own space, perfectly situated so that no one dared to get past her unless they had both an appointment and her permission. One of his management staff had once groused that Elena was like a really scary combination of a dragon, a hellhound, and the school secretary. And while that description was definitely an exaggeration, there was no denying that she guarded him like a hawk, and kept everyone in this place - Matthew included - on the very tips of their toes on a consistent basis.

The fiery, forty-something Latina was petite and full-figured, but rather than minimize her ample curves by wearing dark, conservative clothing, Elena could usually be found wearing bright, vivid colors, often in bold prints and patterns, and always wore four-inch heels, even on "casual Fridays". Today's outfit was one of her most eye-popping - a tomato red pencil skirt, yellow silk top, and a multi-hued, floral print jacket. The heels were of a shiny yellow patent leather, her chunky jewelry as flamboyant as the rest of her outfit.

A couple of the more conservative board members had mentioned to Matthew on more than one occasion that perhaps his assistant should think about "toning down" her office wardrobe, and wearing more subdued outfits. But Matthew had very firmly set his foot down on that particular subject, declaring that he found his PA's choice in clothing to be both cheerful and soothing, oftentimes the only bright spot in his otherwise hectic, stressful days. He hadn't bothered to admit to the board members that the very thought of approaching his ferocious PA on the matter of her wardrobe was more than a little terrifying.

Elena eyed him dubiously as he drew closer. "I see that you had lunch," she commented. "I'd guess Manhattan clam chowder, something with a lot of grease, probably bacon, and apple - no, make that peach pie."

Matthew stared at her gap-jawed. "How the hell did you guess all of that? Are you calling restaurants now to make sure I ate all my food like a good little boy?"

Elena snickered. "Even I'm not that anal. No, I can tell from the food stains on your shirt, tie, and lapel. And before you ask, the stain remover wipes are in your middle drawer, left hand side."

He grinned. "What the hell would I do without you, Elena?"

She smirked knowingly. "Starve to death, forget to attend meetings, have no idea where to find anything, and work eighteen hours a day. So you'd better never fire my ass, boss, because you'd be up a creek without a paddle for damned sure."

"You know that's never going to happen," he assured her gently. "You're of more value to this company than I am."

She gave a very unladylike snort. "You don't need to lay on the BS this thick, boss. It doesn't work with me, as you should have learned by now. Hey, it's my job to look after you, a job I like and that you pay me really, really well for. And you've sort of grown on me after all this time. Not to mention the fact that I can't abandon you now, can I? Not under the circumstances."

Matthew's expression sobered. "No, that's for sure. In fact, I don't know how I would have coped these past few weeks without your help. Not just here at the office but with all the domestic stuff, too. I'm still not sure I know the difference between the washing machine and the dryer."

Elena gave him a severe look. "You sound just like my boys did when I shipped them off to college for the first time. I'll tell you the same thing I told them - you're smart boys, smart enough to get into a good college. And if you can figure out stuff like calculus and physics you can damned sure learn how to operate a washing machine or an oven. And since you're supposed to be some sort of genius with - how high is your I.Q.?"

He shrugged. "Depends what sort of scale or test you're referring to. On the Stanford-Binet scale, I'm a 150. But if you use a different method, then the numbers could range anywhere from - "

Elena waved a hand impatiently in dismissal. "Yeah, yeah. You're super smart, I get that. My point is if you're that smart you ought to be able to operate something as simple as a microwave or a coffeemaker."

He grinned. "You'd think so, huh? But some wise-ass Latina once told me that brain smarts doesn't always mean common sense smarts."

"And she was right. As always," retorted Elena. "Now, quit wasting my time, boss, and let me get back to work. You've got a conference call in twenty minutes, so you'd better get ready for it."

"I'm on it." He paused before heading inside his office, gazing down fondly at the fiercely efficient woman who more than earned her very generous salary keeping him organized. "I really did mean what I said before, Elena. I'm not sure how I'd be getting through everything right now without your help."

"I'm happy to do it," she assured him somberly. "I've been through a divorce myself, you know, and it was pure hell. Which is exactly where I hope that *bastardo* ex of mine is rotting at this very moment."

She didn't add that in her opinion Lindsey should be residing in the same location as her despised ex-husband. Elena was probably the most candid, outspoken person Matthew had ever met, but she had just enough diplomacy to know when to keep her mouth shut. In the years she'd been working for Matthew, Elena had never once badmouthed or complained about Lindsey, even though he was convinced his wife had frequently treated his PA like she was the hired help.

39

But Elena had never needed to come right out and say anything after she'd taken a phone call from Lindsey, or left Matthew a message from her. It had been very obvious from the scowl on her face or the ferocious expression in her dark eyes that she was good and pissed off. And when he had confided in Elena about his separation and imminent divorce from Lindsey, the fiery Latina had nodded and mumbled something in Spanish that he was pretty sure meant "well, it's about fucking time".

As he went over his scribbled, barely decipherable notes for his upcoming conference call, Matthew heaved a disgruntled sigh, wondering for at least the tenth time since he'd tossed Lindsey out of the condo where and when everything had started falling apart so epically.

chapter three

HIS BROTHER PATRICK HAD OFTEN liked to joke that the two of them - along with their younger sister Jackie - had been destined even before they were born to become nerds. After all, both of their parents had chosen career paths that were generally considered to be on the nerdish side - their father Wade was a tenured, highly regarded professor of advanced mathematics at the University of Wisconsin, while their mother Maureen also worked at the university as a research scientist in Biophysics. With both parents possessing IQ's in the highest levels, the likelihood of all three Bennett children also having the potential to be geniuses had been exceptionally high.

And while attention to their studies had certainly been a requirement in the Bennett household, Wade and Maureen had also recognized the need for their children to have interests outside of the classroom. Growing up in Wisconsin had provided a variety of outdoor activities - sailing and swimming during the summer months, hiking in the fall and spring, skiing and snow shoeing in the winter. But for Matthew at least that had pretty much been the extent of any physical activity, and it wasn't until his freshman year at MIT that he'd ever completed a single chin-up or lifted anything heavier than his laptop.

It had been his college roommate Jeff, a member of the university wrestling team, who'd more or less strong armed Matthew into the school's fitness center for the first time. It had been Jeff's rather twisted way of repaying Matthew for tutoring him in both math and science, classes he would have flunked out of otherwise and been kicked off the wrestling team as a result. Jeff had taken one look at Matthew's tall but admittedly scrawny frame, and had vowed that by the end of the school year he would totally transform him.

In the end, it had only taken a few months to see real results, and by that time Matthew had felt like gagging every time Jeff had forced him to down a protein shake, or eat half a dozen eggs for breakfast. Admittedly, though, eating the extra protein and committing to a regular weight lifting regime had done the trick in filling out his previously skinny body, and developing a bonafide six-pack. He'd started swimming laps on a regular basis as well, which had helped to add additional muscle to his six foot frame.

And it had also been Jeff who'd dragged him away from his books and papers and computers once in awhile to go to a party or the movies or a campus event, declaring that all work and no play made Matt an even bigger nerd than he already was. Jeff was appalled to realize that Matthew was still a virgin, and had made it his mission to remedy that sad truth as quickly as possible. But after a few very awkward, uncomfortable sexual experiences, Matthew had shied away from any future hook-ups that Jeff tried to arrange for him, claiming that he was far too busy with his studies to deal with any sort of relationships at the moment. Jeff had eventually given up on him, and the following school year he'd decided to share a house off-campus with several of his wrestling teammates. Matthew's new roommate was an organic chemistry major from India who was an even bigger nerd than he was.

Matthew had devoted himself to his studies, taking on a heavier than usual course load, and had obtained both his bachelors and Masters degrees in computer science by the ripe old age of twenty-three. After being accepted into the highly competitive doctorate program at Stanford, he'd moved out to California and had become instantly enamored of the area. He enjoyed the mild winters, warm summers, and the close proximity to the booming Silicon Valley. During his spare time - which didn't amount to a whole lot - he'd continued to design software programs, and dream of the day when he would start his own company.

The demands of the PhD program left precious little time to socialize or relax, and Matthew's small circle of friends seemed to consist largely of his fellow doctoral candidates. Every so often, though, the stress of the program got to be more than even a dedicated scholar like himself could handle, and he allowed himself to be persuaded into going out to dinner or to a bar for a few beers.

It was on one of those rare occasions when he'd seen Lindsey for the first time, and he had been instantly and surprisingly attracted. She certainly hadn't been his usual type - though, technically, he hadn't really *had* a type, given his rather pathetic dating record. But Lindsey had definitely been the prettiest, sexiest, and most vivacious girl he'd ever met, and shockingly enough she seemed to take an instant liking to him. Several beers and a couple of hours later,

43

they'd wound up in bed at his studio apartment, and what he had lacked in experience and technique he'd more than made up for in enthusiasm.

Despite the fact that they were polar opposites in so many ways - he was introverted, brainy, destined to remain a hopeless nerd, while Lindsey was flitting her way through community college, outgoing, and an admitted party girl - they nonetheless seemed to click in an odd sort of way. They dated casually for several months, though most of their time together seemed to be spent in bed. And while Lindsey was always quick to assure him that she understood his doctoral studies had to take precedence over his personal life, and that she really didn't mind when he couldn't see her as often as he would have liked, Matthew always wondered if she was telling the truth. After all, it was hard to imagine a pretty, fun-loving girl like Lindsey just staying at home on a Saturday night. And as much as she enjoyed sex, he wasn't quite certain she was remaining celibate during the days and sometimes weeks in between their dates.

But she was certainly the most exciting thing that had ever happened to him, and he enjoyed the distraction she provided from the tedious hours of studying and doing research for his dissertation. He was probably still a few years away from even thinking about getting married, settling down, starting a family, and it was a relief that Lindsey seemed more than content with the casual, no-strings-attached relationship that they enjoyed.

It was a huge shock, therefore, when she showed up at his apartment one evening in tears, nearly hysterical as she told him about her unplanned pregnancy. He had been relieved to leave the matter of birth control up to Lindsey, who was admittedly far more experienced with such things than he was. She'd confessed to having missed several days of birth control pills last month when she'd had a bad cold, and been too strung out on Nyquil to remember to take them.

And despite the fact that he had no real financial means to support a wife and baby, no way to afford anything bigger than the studio apartment he was currently living in, Matthew had found himself asking Lindsey to marry him, and vowing to raise their unborn child together. Lindsey had resisted at first - for a couple of weeks, actually - not at all sure she wanted to settle down just yet, and definitely not sure she wanted to become a mother at this stage of her life. And when she'd fully realized what a limited budget they would have to live on until Matthew finished his PhD and got a full time job, she balked even more at the idea of getting married and having the baby.

But the more Matthew thought about it the more he knew he wouldn't have been able to live with himself if he'd allowed Lindsey to terminate the pregnancy. His family had never been especially religious, but they had certainly been very morally upright, and responsible for their actions. And while he had always viewed the idea of abortion from a somewhat scientific, clinical perspective, he found when it came to his own child that his point of view was definitely skewed in the opposite direction.

So he'd put the pressure on Lindsey to go through with the pregnancy and marry him, vowing that he would be finished with his dissertation in just over a year's time. After that, he'd more or less have his pick of good, high-paying jobs in Silicon Valley, and would be able to provide her and their child with a much better lifestyle than what he could offer now.

His parents - God bless them - had insisted on not only throwing them a small wedding, but also loaning them the money to move into a larger apartment and buy the things they would need for the baby. And for the next year they'd continued to send him some money each month to help pay the bills, since Matthew's stipend would only stretch so far. Lindsey hadn't returned to work, since what she'd be able to earn waiting tables or being a sales clerk - the only sort of jobs she'd really been qualified for at the time - would more than be eaten up paying for childcare.

And he'd learned, somewhat after the fact, that Lindsey certainly wouldn't be able to count on her own family for any sort of support - financial or otherwise - since she was estranged from both her mother and her sister. Her father had died when she'd been in high school, and from that point on her relationships with other family members had begun to fracture and disintegrate.

Matthew had known without having to ask that his parents weren't particularly happy about the situation he'd landed himself in. It hadn't been about the money, especially since they could easily afford what they insisted on giving him, and since Matthew had initially resisted their efforts to help as a matter of pride. Instead, it had been about wanting to see him in a better set of circumstances - his PhD complete, gainfully employed in a solid, well-paying job, dating a woman who had more in common with him, and was of a similar intellect and background. Wade and Maureen weren't snobs, not by

46

a long shot, and while they were comfortably off now both had come from distinctly middle class upbringings.

It had been more a question of Lindsey not seeming especially bright or ambitious or the least bit eager to improve herself. Matthew knew without having to ask that if she hadn't become pregnant so unexpectedly his new wife would have continued on happily with her party girl ways for several more years, and that the two of them would have more than likely ended their relationship sooner than later. They were most definitely opposites, with only their sexual chemistry and now their unborn child in common.

That first year had been one of the most difficult times of Matthew's life, especially after his daughter had been born. He'd struggled to balance the demands of his PhD program with his own research, and at the same time help out as much as possible with taking care of the baby and the household chores.

But survive he did, and at the end of the year he'd received his doctorate, along with multiple job offers - all of them lucrative and all with the promise of rapid advancement. With the substantial signing bonus he'd been given they were able to make a down payment on a modest condo, even though Lindsey had pushed him to buy a single family house instead. Right from the beginning of their marriage, it was readily apparent to Matthew that his wife had no concept about managing money or living on a budget. He'd had to take over paying the bills himself, and making sure Lindsey understood the need to take things one step at a time.

By the time she'd become pregnant with Casey, however, Matthew had moved on to an even better paying job and was able to afford the four-bedroom house she picked out in an upscale community. He often worked long hours, creating increasingly brilliant and more complex computer programs, and making a real name for himself in the industry. But he had always made time for his family, making sure he attended Hayley's soccer games and dance recitals, and taught Casey how to swim and play baseball. They took several family vacations together each year, going to Hawaii or Disney World or visiting his parents back in Wisconsin. Life had been busy but good, and Matthew had known both happiness and contentment.

Everything had started to change, however, when a group of investors had approached him with the idea of starting his own business. It had actually been a long unrealized dream of his to be the CEO of a company, where his computer programs could be developed and marketed according to his very exacting standards. Lindsey, of course, had been ecstatic at the idea, and had strongly encouraged him to take the investment group up on their offer, including their suggestion that he establish the company headquarters in San Francisco rather than the ultra-competitive Silicon Valley.

The business had taken off immediately, and their fortunes had literally multiplied overnight. They'd moved to the exclusive suburb of Hillsborough, where everyone was a millionaire, and the schools the children attended were among the highest ranked in the entire state of California. Matthew was busier than ever, but at least living closer to San Francisco meant a shorter commute, and he was still able to fit in family time, though nowhere near enough for his liking.

But it was when his board of directors pushed him into taking the company public that he'd ceased feeling in control of his life. He'd resisted the idea for almost a year, knowing the demands it would make on his already overtaxed schedule, but also realizing the company needed the additional capital to continue with their research and development. And when Lindsey caught wind of the idea, she had kept at him on pretty much a daily basis to go along with the board's idea. She had recognized that such a move would catapult them from being millionaires to billionaires, and the dollar signs in her eyes had more or less blinded her to anything else at that point.

Oh, Matthew had tried - multiple times - to remind her how many more hours he'd have to spend at the office and traveling on business, and that it would cut down even more on the limited time he had to spend with her and the kids. But Lindsey had countered back that the additional money would set the kids up for life, and that Matthew owed it to all of them to improve their lifestyle. He'd argued that they already had plenty of money, already enjoyed a very extravagant way of life. But it hadn't been enough for her, not by a longshot, and so between the twin influences of his ambitious board of directors and his avaricious wife, Matthew had reluctantly acquiesced to their demands and taken the company public.

It hadn't taken very long for the changes in their lifestyle to become apparent. As expected, he was busier than ever, constantly attending staff meetings or overseeing presentations to clients or being a guest speaker at one tech conference or another. He traveled a week to ten days - and often more - out of every month, and twelve to fourteen hour workdays became the norm rather than the exception. He'd rather quickly found himself spending a couple of nights a week at the condo the board had advised him to buy soon after taking the company public. Matthew had hated spending even more time away from his family, but he had often been so tired from his workday that driving back to Hillsborough at midnight had been outright dangerous.

And Lindsey hadn't wasted a moment in taking full advantage of their vastly improved financial status. She'd found an even larger and more elegant home in Hillsborough, one with a ridiculous amount of square footage that included a pool, tennis courts, servants quarters, a guest house, and a six car garage. She had spent a virtual fortune redecorating and remodeling the place, even though she spent little time there herself. Lindsey managed to keep herself very busy between visits to the gym and Pilates studio, the various department stores and designer shops where she made frequent additions to her vast wardrobe, and the salon where she was either having her hair cut, her nails done, or some sort of exotic skincare treatment or massage.

Against Matthew's express wishes, she had also hired a full-time nanny to help out with the kids, even though Hayley and Casey were both a little too old to need one. The various nannies they'd had over the past few years - none of whom seemed to get along with Lindsey for very long - had largely been responsible for taking the kids to and from school and supervising their after-school activities. When Matthew had rather tactfully pointed out that Lindsey - who'd been a stay-at-home mom since before Hayley's birth - could very easily perform these tasks, she'd blown up at him, declaring that she deserved some alone time each day after devoting herself to the kids for so many years.

Even with more money than they could possibly spend in ten lifetimes, however, Lindsey still wasn't happy or satisfied. As predicted, it hadn't taken her very long at all to start complaining when Matthew wasn't around very much, exactly what he'd cautioned her about all the times she'd pushed him to take the company public. He carved out as much time as he possibly could for his family, even when it meant getting by on three or four hours sleep a night, and rarely having a leisurely hour or so to himself. He took Lindsey and the kids on luxurious vacations several times a year, though they were more often than not working vacations for him. His stress level was higher than it had ever been, he was usually always exhausted, and his eating habits were bordering on unhealthy. He sorely regretted not just taking the company public, but even starting his own business in the first place. He longed to return to a simpler way of life, to sell the business and invest the money, and then just take an occasional consulting job when the whim suited him to do so.

But he knew that such a move would have a whole string of repercussions, ones he wasn't ready to deal with at this point in his life, so he kept his wishes to himself and soldiered on as best he could with all of the responsibilities and demands and stresses in his life.

As busy as he was, however, Matthew wasn't so immersed in the daily grind that he didn't notice how much his wife flirted openly with other men. It didn't seem to matter much where they were - at a restaurant, a party, the gym, on vacation. Lindsey always seemed to find a good-looking guy - and nearly always one who was considerably younger than she was - to flirt with. The first few times it happened he'd confronted her, telling her that he was well aware the flirtations were a way of getting his attention. And Lindsey had initially apologized, assuring him that it was just a bit of harmless fun, and that she hadn't meant to upset him or hurt his feelings. But as the flirtations continued and became increasingly more blatant, Matthew had realized that it didn't really matter all that much to him - largely because his marriage no longer mattered very much to him.

Quietly, he'd contacted a very discreet private investigator who specialized in such cases to keep occasional tabs on Lindsey. And when he'd first been presented with the cold, hard facts that she was in fact having a series of affairs, his natural instinct had been to confront her about it. But he had resisted, not at all sure how such a confrontation would affect their marriage - and therefore their kids - and he sure as hell didn't have the emotional energy at the time to deal with that kind of fallout.

So he'd kept the knowledge to himself that his wife was fucking one hot, young stud after another, even stopped looking over the reports that the investigator continued to compile after awhile. He also stopped sleeping with Lindsey, the idea of having sex with her more than a little stomach-turning after realizing how many other men she'd been with. The fact that she had never once questioned him about their total lack of a sex life had been a clear signal to him that she no longer loved him, if she ever really had. She liked the money and the extravagant lifestyle it afforded her, liked the prestige and modicum of fame she enjoyed being Mrs. Matthew Bennett, but he didn't think she actually liked *him*.

And it was when he finally admitted the latter fact to himself that he'd decided it was time to end things between them. Catching her in the act with that randy bastard Jesse had simply been a handy excuse for filing for the divorce he should have sought out a long time ago.

chapter four

Early August

"THANK YOU ALL FOR SHARING your practice with me on this beautiful summer morning. I hope you enjoy the rest of your day and that I see you again soon. *Namaste.*"

The fifty or so students gathered in the studio all bowed their heads respectfully, hands folded at their hearts in a prayer-like gesture, and replied as one voice, "*Namaste.*"

Sasha Fonseca smiled at the crowd of happy, flushed, and visibly sweaty faces of the students she'd just guided - and occasionally prodded - through a very vigorous ninety minute yoga class. Her Sunday morning class had gained itself a reputation as being one of the most hardcore, kick-ass classes in the entire city of San Francisco, and the room was always filled to capacity with practitioners who wanted a challenge, and a teacher who would inspire them to attain the next level in their yoga practice.

She made her way over to the petite, tawny-haired woman in the front row, squatting down easily in front of a three-months pregnant Julia Atwood. Sasha placed a hand on her longtime student's - and friend's - arm.

"You doing okay there?" she asked in concern. "You need to make sure you're staying hydrated more than ever, Julia. And I see your water bottle is only half-empty."

Somewhat guiltily, a rosy-cheeked Julia gulped down the rest of the water in a few swallows. "Sorry," she offered with a sunny smile. "I get so caught up in the poses and the flow that I forget to drink as much as I should. But I'll do better in the future. I promise."

Sasha gave her friend a look of mock severity. "You'd better," she cautioned with a twinkle in her green-gold eyes. "Otherwise, no more heated classes for you. You'll be restricted to the pre-natal or restorative classes only."

Julia scowled as she finished rolling up her mat. "You wouldn't do that to me, would you?" she begged. "I mean, given that I'm carrying twins I'm going to get huge sooner than later, so I won't have a choice at some point. But not yet, please? Yoga is one of the very few things that seems to help with my morning sickness. Which, by the way, is also noon and night sickness."

"Ginger tea," reminded Sasha. "Or raspberry leaf. And I know you're a coffee person, but that's not going to help with your nausea."

Julia made a rather horrible face but then gave a resigned shrug. "You're right. I'll give up my cappuccinos and café au laits for the time being and switch to tea. As long as you don't ban me from your class."

Sasha laughed, and gave her friend a quick hug. "As long as *you* work harder at staying hydrated during class," she replied firmly. "It's tough enough on the average person to sweat through ninety minutes of strenuous yoga in ninety-five degree heat. But for a pregnant woman - especially one who's pregnant with twins - the risks are that much higher. So be warned, Julia. I'll be keeping a very close eye on you and make sure you're drinking a ton of water. And if you look the least bit overheated or winded, I'll make you take a rest or even leave class. You need to take very good care of yourself and these two little ones inside of you."

She gave Julia's gently rounded tummy a gentle pat. "Now, go home, have a warm bath, a nice cup of ginger tea, and something nourishing to eat. *Not* one of those disgusting breakfast pastries you're so fond of. Boil a couple of eggs or make some oatmeal."

Julia sighed in surrender. "Fine. First my coffee goes, now my chocolate croissants. These girls better appreciate the sacrifices their mommy is already making for them."

Sasha eyed Julia's barely visible baby bump quizzically. "Don't be so sure you're having girls," she cautioned. "It's a little too soon for me to tell for sure, but I'm sensing a very masculine aura around these babies right now."

Julia's green eyes widened in horror. "Oh, God, don't say that, please! I really, really want the twins to be girls. Or at least one of them. You've been wrong before about your hunches, haven't you?"

Sasha tapped a finger against her lips as she studied Julia a little more intently. "Hardly ever," she replied calmly. "I actually have an excellent track record when it comes to predicting the gender of a baby. Though I usually don't try to sense that sort of thing until the pregnancy is further along. I'll re-assess in another couple of months."

"Well, until then, I'm going to wear nothing but pink every single day," declared Julia. "That way I can trick my aura into thinking I'm going to have girls."

Sasha laughed in delight. "It doesn't work that way, Julia,

and you know it."

"What doesn't work what way?" chimed in Tessa Gregson as she sidled up beside the two women.

The tall, beautiful blonde was a newlywed of less than two months - both Sasha and Julia had been bridesmaids at her fairytale wedding - and the glow on her face probably had less to do with the rigorous yoga class she'd just finished than it did the lusty sex she'd undoubtedly engaged in with her hunky husband earlier this morning. Sasha tried not to feel envious, given that it had been a seriously long time since she'd had sex at all - much less really *good* sex.

Julia stuck out her bottom lip in a pronounced pout. "Sasha is pretty sure she's sensing a masculine aura around the twins," she told her friend. "And I told her I don't believe her, not even a little. At least one of them has to be a girl. I mean, boys are no fun at all to dress, are they?"

Sasha and Tessa exchanged a knowing look. Julia was a veritable fashionista, always dressed to kill, and with a wardrobe that any model or actress would envy. She was also the epitome of femininity, and about the only time she didn't wear a dress or skirt was here in yoga class. And even then she managed to look feminine and fashionable, her exercise clothing perfectly color-coordinated and stylish.

Tessa jabbed Julia in the ribs good-naturedly, mindful of her baby bump, and gave her a naughty wink. "But they're awfully fun to *un*-dress," she snickered. "In fact, I've got a male waiting for me outside who happens to look amazing without his clothes on. So, sorry to rush out like this, but Ian is taking me out to brunch. And after that - well, that's the part where the undressing is going to happen."

57

Julia rolled her eyes. "Honestly, Tessa? Didn't you guys already go at it this morning before class? You're going to wear the man out, honey."

Tessa's blue eyes widened, and she blushed furiously. "How did you know that?" she whispered urgently.

Sasha smiled indulgently. "You, ah, have a certain look in your eyes at times, Tessa. It's always been rather obvious to me what - or who - put that particular look there."

"Yeah," chimed in Julia. "We know the real reason you're always one of the last ones to arrive here on Sunday mornings. So stop blaming nonexistent traffic, and just fess up to the fact that you and your hot hubby like starting your day off with a bang. Literally, in this case."

Tessa's cheeks flushed an even deeper shade of pink as she hastily stuffed her yoga mat into its carrying bag. "Oh, God," she muttered, half to herself. "Guess I'd better start setting my alarm a few minutes earlier on Sundays."

Sasha winked at her knowingly. "Hey, don't knock it. I mean, you're definitely still a newlywed so we'd be shocked if you weren't having lots and lots of great sex. And I'm trying my best not to feel jealous about that right now. I'm, ah, in the middle of what you might call a dry spell right about now."

"Anything we can do to help you out with that?" offered Julia mischievously. "Nathan's friend Jonathan asks about you all the time, ever since he met you at our pool party over Memorial Day weekend."

Sasha didn't bother to hide her distaste. "You mean the guy who arrived with a redhead but left with a brunette and tried to hit on every other female there in between? Thank you for thinking of me, Julia, but I don't date players."

Tessa sighed. "Well, forget my idea, then. I was going to suggest setting you up with Jordan Reeves, my OB/GYN. He's incredibly sweet and really good looking, but he does tend to, um, get around a lot."

Julia rolled her eyes. "And as usual, Tessa, you forgot to mention that your hot doctor has the hots for *you*. Though he does look like he could show a girl a good time, Sasha. Especially one who's in the middle of a dry spell."

Sasha shook her head, causing a couple of corkscrew curls to escape from the messy knot she'd unsuccessfully tried to contain them in. Most days it seemed that her wild, untamed curls had a mind of their own, and attempting to style them in any sort of way was usually an exercise in futility.

"Thank you both - I think - for offering to fix me up with your husbands' manwhore friends," she replied drily. "But I'd prefer to find my own man, actually. And this certainly isn't the first time in my life that I've been celibate for a long stretch. Relationships can be complicated, after all, and I've made it one of my goals to live as uncomplicated a life as possible."

Sasha continued to reflect on that statement as she chatted briefly with a few other students, then made sure the studio was neat and tidy for the next class that would be starting in less than a half hour. As she exited the practice room - the largest of the three here at SF Flow, the most popular yoga studio in San Francisco - she noted that students were already assembling out in the lobby for the next class. Weekend mornings were especially busy here at the studio, though nearly all of the classes were well attended and often filled to capacity.

Callista, who worked the front desk on weekends, was busy checking in students but took a moment to smile at Sasha as she approached.

"Well, from the way half your students were practically crawling out of here a few minutes ago, I'd guess you gave them all a good ass kicking this morning," drawled Callista.

Sasha laughed softly. "Nothing they can't handle," she assured. "Hey, I know you're busy, I just wanted to see if Studio Three was empty for awhile."

"It's all yours," replied Callista. "Nobody's got anything scheduled in there at all today. So have at it."

"Thanks." Sasha gave the clerk a grateful little pat on the shoulder.

Unlike a few of the other teachers here at the studio, who tended to treat the support staff like - well, *support* staff - Sasha was always mindful of treating everyone with kindness and appreciation. It was just one of the reasons that she was not only the most popular teacher among her students but among the staff as well.

Studio Three was the smallest of the trio of practice spaces here at SF Flow, designed to hold no more than twenty students. The room was used mostly for private and semi-private sessions that some of the teachers offered, as well as the workshops and lectures that were presented on a regular basis at the studio.

And it was where Sasha often retreated for her own personal yoga practice, a place where she could easily spend two to three hours at a time. During the classes she taught, she actually spent very little time actually practicing yoga herself, except to demonstrate a pose here and then. Most of the time she was busy making her way around the crowded room, ensuring that her students were doing the poses correctly, and making adjustments to their alignments as necessary.

These sessions served a dual purpose - not only allowing her to enjoy her own practice, but also to plan out sequences for future classes. Her bedroom at the multi-level Victorian home that she shared with four other roommates was much too compact for the space she needed to do her practice. And there was no other suitable space in the old house, considering that her landlords - married couple Chad and Julio (for whom she'd also been a member of their wedding party) - subscribed to the belief that more must always be better. As a result, nearly every room of the historic old Victorian was crammed full of furniture, mirrors, paintings, and a great deal of assorted bric-a-brac.

And these private sessions were also a time when she could completely immerse herself in the beauty and flow of the ancient practice she'd devoted her life to, accompanied by an inspiring music track.

Sasha would be the first to admit that she was both technologically challenged, and rather hopelessly detached from much of mainstream society. She didn't own a computer, and barely knew how to send and receive emails on the cell phone she mainly used to store her extensive music files. She disliked most television shows, and the only time she went to the movie theater was to see a documentary or occasionally a classic film. She preferred reading or listening to music or attending art exhibits, in addition to taking long walks and hikes.

As the daughter of a musician - her father Enzo was a member of one of Brazil's most popular samba groups - Sasha had both music and dance running through her veins. For her yoga classes, she was known to play an extremely eclectic variety of music - everything from Indian classical to jazz to reggae and rock - and her students constantly pleaded with her to post the diverse playlists on her Facebook page or website. Problem was Sasha had neither a Facebook account nor a website, and zero desire to create either one. But she was always happy to share her music with her students and other teachers, and pleased that they enjoyed the variety of genres as much as she did.

As her limber, slender body - toned and strong and leanly muscled from so many years of both yoga and dance training - began to move through the physically demanding practice, she lost herself in the music as one track segued into the next. Anoushka Shankar gave way to Jason Mraz, then to the Gipsy Kings and Stevie Ray Vaughn. And, of course, the tracks were peppered here and there with selections from her father's vast catalog of songs that he and his band had recorded over the past three and a half decades. She was half-Brazilian, after all, and had spent a good part of her life in South America, so the music was in her blood.

The practice she put herself through was much more difficult and demanding than anything she would actually teach to a class. The arm balances, handstands, intricate twisting and binding poses, and the complex choreography of the flow were all very advanced postures, ones that only a very skilled practitioner could hope to achieve. She preferred

62

to practice with others, thriving on the energy that could only be generated by the shared breath and movement of other practitioners. But since she rarely had time nowadays to attend a class taught by one of her old teachers, or even attend a training workshop, these solitary sessions had to suffice.

A little over two hours later, Sasha was tired, sore, and dripping in sweat, but feeling both exhilarated and blissful. She'd felt the exact same way after finishing her very first yoga class as a girl of fifteen, and more than a dozen years later her practice still felt like the place she had always been meant to be. It fulfilled her in different but equally important ways - physically, emotionally, spiritually, artistically. Considering her background - the gypsy-like existence she'd been compelled to accept until she'd finally rebelled against it as a teenager - yoga had provided a haven, a place where she belonged, something that would always be constant in a life that had never been stable or the same for very long.

She was walking past Studio One, the largest of the three and where all of her own classes were taught, when Micah Walters waved at her from the open doorway. Micah taught the eleven a.m. class on Sunday mornings, and while his class was nearly as popular as Sasha's, the major difference was in the rather noticeable gender imbalance among his students. All but a handful of Micah's students were female, most of them young, attractive, and all too eager to flirt and giggle with the handsome, buff yoga teacher. Even now he was surrounded by half a dozen females, all of them wide-eyed and adoring as they vied for his attention. He was admittedly a good-looking guy, not especially tall but extremely fit and leanly muscled. Micah rarely if ever had a shirt on inside the studio, and was more often than not garbed solely in a pair of short, close-fitting athletic briefs. He was tanned and sported more than a dozen colorful tattoos along his back, arms, and torso, a small gold hoop pierced his left lobe, and his dirty blond hair was clubbed into a short ponytail at his nape.

Ever since Micah had joined the teaching staff here at SF Flow a little over a year ago, he'd been trying almost nonstop to get into Sasha's pants. The fact that she continued to gently but firmly rebuff him only seemed to make him more determined. He didn't accept her excuse that the owners of the studio frowned on co-workers dating. And while that particular excuse was indeed a real one, the main reason that Sasha hadn't taken her fellow teacher up on his multiple and very aggressive offers to go on a date was because guys like him immediately turned her off. Micah was too sure of himself, too vain and egotistical, and way, way too much of a playboy for her liking. She didn't expect a commitment from a guy, especially on the first few dates, but she also refused to simply be another notch on his bedpost, one more female for him to fuck and then forget.

But there was no polite way to avoid Micah at this moment, not when he was making a big show of calling her over. He bid good-by to several more of his overeager "groupies" - as one of the other teachers here had teasingly dubbed his smitten students - and then slid an arm around Sasha's shoulder, pulling her in close for a hug.

"How's my favorite goddess on this beautiful summer day?" he murmured in her ear.

Sasha forced herself not to cringe at the combined odors

of garlic and sweat that emanated from Micah's body. She knew that he took garlic supplements as part of his fitness regime, and while she certainly appreciated the various health benefits of garlic, she also knew better than to ingest the capsules before teaching a class of several dozen students all packed into the same heated studio. One of the negative side effects of taking garlic supplements was the way the odor could emanate through one's pores and sweat glands, and for that reason it was a bad idea for someone in Micah's profession to use them on a regular basis.

"I'm good," was all she told him in reply, offering up one of her usual serene smiles. "But I'm pretty wiped out after teaching class and then doing two hours of my own practice, so I'm anxious to head home and relax for awhile."

Micah gave her a mock scowl. "Ah, and just when I was going to try and convince you to let me buy you lunch. One of these days, sweet Sasha, you're going to give in and say yes. I'm not going to keep buying that line about management frowning on co-workers seeing each other outside of business hours."

She shrugged, using the opportunity to slip out from under his forced embrace. "You're more than welcome to discuss the matter with Serge or Morgana. Though you might want to hold off on that chat for a bit. I understand they're still peeved at you about that incident with one of your students."

Serge and Morgana were the married couple who owned SF Flow. Serge still taught classes occasionally, though he devoted most of his time nowadays to his massage practice. In addition to handling all of the bookkeeping and personnel matters, Morgana taught pre-natal yoga and offered monthly workshops for expectant mothers. And while they were two of the most down-to-earth and open-minded people Sasha had ever known, they drew a hard line with any of their teachers dating their own students. Micah usually got around that particular problem by slyly suggesting to whatever pretty student who caught his eye that she should quietly start attending a different class. Sasha had lost count months ago of how many of Micah's former students had wound up in one of her classes - and how many of them he'd pissed off when things had ended rather abruptly between them.

Micah had the good graces to look sheepish at the reminder. "Yeah, guess I'd better lay low for awhile, huh? No sense rocking the boat. But I'm not the sort who gives up easily, as you know. So, one of these days, Goddess Sasha, you'll give into me. I had a sixth sense about you from the very first time we met, and those vibes have only gotten stronger over time. It's fate, sweet Sasha, that we'll be together one day."

Sasha resisted the urge to roll her green-gold eyes. It had been very obvious to *her* from the first time she'd met Micah that he was something of a poser - a spiritual wannabe, in so many words. He'd only been practicing yoga about six years, and while he more or less had the physical aspect of the practice down, he had a long way to go before he fully understood all of the other facets. But he liked to put on certain airs, was wont to talk in New-Age terms, and acted like some sort of modern-day guru at times. To someone like Sasha, who'd not only studied many of those other facets in depth for more than a decade but had *lived* them as well,

66

Micah's put-on airs were both comical and mildly insulting.

"Well," she told him with a mischievous grin, "*my* sixth sense is telling me that you might have gone a wee bit overboard on the garlic supplements this morning. You might want to abstain for twenty four hours before you teach a class from now on. See you later, Micah."

As she passed by the front desk, Sasha caught Callista's eye, knowing that the receptionist would have just overheard the conversation with Micah, and the two women exchanged a knowing grin. As she waited for the bus that would bring her home a few minutes later, Sasha was still chuckling under her breath at the shocked expression in Micah's light blue eyes at her admonition.

'That was just a tiny bit evil, you know,' she scolded herself. 'And not very kind. But, boy, did he ever deserve it! Maybe now he'll stop asking you out every time you cross paths.'

But Sasha doubted this would be the end of Micah's attempts to ask her out on a date, given his massive ego and not especially bright intellect. However, he certainly wasn't anything she couldn't handle easily, and she dismissed the incident from her thoughts during the bus ride home.

A couple of blocks from home, the cell phone that she rarely used pinged, signaling a voice mail. Sasha sighed, knowing before she looked at the screen that the call would have been from her mother. These Sunday calls were pretty much a regular thing, unless of course Katya was preoccupied with something related to business, or had to head in for a last minute rehearsal or costume fitting.

Katya Veselov was one of the professional ballroom dancers on the long running TV show *Beyond Ballroom*. The immensely popular reality show paired professional dancers with celebrity partners, most of whom had little to no dance training, and who were quite often something of a train wreck to actually watch. Sasha's mother had been with the show nearly from its beginning a decade earlier, and was now quite the celebrity herself. Katya was close to fifty years old now, though she was as toned and fit and stunning as she'd been as a young ballroom protégé in communist Russia. Still, the show's producers had begun assigning her partners who were closer to her own age as of late, something that Katya frequently raged about. Not, thought Sasha wryly, that her fiery-tempered mother ever lacked something or other to get into a rage about.

During Sasha's bohemian, nomadic-like childhood and adolescence, the most frequent subject of Katya's rages had been Enzo - her on-again, off-again lover, and the father of her child. Enzo was every bit as fiery and passionate as Katya, and during the times they'd been together it had always been unclear what was more fervent - their epic screaming matches or their wild bouts of lovemaking. Sasha had often thought that her parents went together like fire and ice, and that the day they had first met must have triggered either an earthquake, a hurricane, or a tsunami somewhere in the world.

They had met in Paris, the city where Katya had defected from her home country. She'd been near desperate to escape not just the oppressive communist regime that had governed Russia at the time, but also her abusive, domineering mother who had pushed Katya into the world of competitive ballroom dance at a very young age. And while she had grown to love dance and competitions and performances, she hated the restrictions placed on her by both the government and her overbearing mother.

The dance troupe that she belonged to was rarely allowed to travel outside of Russia, so when Katya learned about the trip to a competition in Paris she knew this could be her one and only chance to escape. Fortunately, her older sister had herself defected to Paris several years ago and Katya had been able to hide out with Polina until the troupe returned to Russia without her. Katya had been barely twenty years old at the time, but still possessed of a steely determination to make a better life for herself, a life where *she* and no one else could make her decisions.

She'd been working as a waitress at a neighborhood café, struggling with both the unfamiliar work and her limited command of the French language, when she'd met Enzo Fonseca for the first time. He had been in town with his group for a series of performances, and they stopped in at the café for a late lunch. The attraction between them had been both instantaneous and explosive, and would be the first of many such encounters between them over the next three decades.

Sasha couldn't recall a time when her parents had actually lived together for more than a few weeks at a time, until one of them stormed out of whatever city they happened to be residing in at the moment in a fit of anger. As her father was fond of saying, he and Katya loved as fiercely as they fought, and at times it was difficult to draw a line between love and hate where they were concerned.

They had never married, of course, even though Enzo had proposed multiple times once Katya had fallen pregnant and given birth to Sasha. Katya had remarked scathingly many times over the years that the two best decisions she'd ever made in her life had been to leave Russia and to remain single. And neither parent, it seemed, was capable of remaining faithful to the other during the times they were apart. Though they had both been discreet when Sasha was around, she'd been well aware from an early age that her parents each had lovers. And because she'd never really known the stability of a normal, two-parent household, or had a real house to call a home, Sasha had never considered the whole situation to be even the least bit odd.

She had lived the life of a gypsy from infancy, especially after her mother took a job with a ballroom dance company based out of New York City. Sasha would spend part of the year in Paris living with her Aunt Polina and her husband Maxim, another few months in Sao Paolo with Enzo's family, and time in New York with Katya, as well as traveling with each parent during their dance and band tours. She attended schools in three different cities, often during the same calendar year, and had to make the switch between French, Portuguese, and English each time. No place ever truly felt like home, and she learned quickly not to get too attached to a particular place or person, or to accumulate too many belongings because she would more than likely have to leave some of them behind.

Sasha had always been a quiet, placid child, a stark contrast to her explosive, intense parents, and in some ways she had acted as a calming influence on the two of them. She'd gone along with their wishes, never complaining when she was uprooted yet again, or when she spent weeks on the road with one or the other on a tour.

But all of that changed when she turned fifteen, and had quite firmly set her foot down about the nomadic existence that had been forced on her. Katya and Enzo had been startled when their obedient child had spoken up for herself for the first time, but neither had argued the point for too long when she'd calmly announced that she was going to live with her aunt Linda in northern California full time. And while her mother had grudgingly accepted her decision, Sasha sensed that Katya had never really forgiven her for it.

Knowing that a phone call from her mother meant twenty minutes *minimum* of lots of drama and heavy sighs, Sasha wisely waited until she arrived home before returning the call. She'd made the mistake once or twice of taking Katya's calls on the bus, and cringed as she recalled the odd looks directed her way from other passengers as her mother's very loud voice chattering away in rapid Russian had carried over the phone.

The house was quiet as Sasha let herself in, and she assumed her other roommates were either out or closeted up in their rooms. Chad and Julio, who owned the house, were almost certainly out somewhere on this sunny summer day. They had a wide circle of friends, both gay and straight, and were constantly being invited to picnics, brunches, parties, and other social doings. They also did their fair share of hosting parties here at the house, and Sasha wasn't in the least fazed to arrive home to find forty or fifty people milling about with cocktails in hand and music blaring from the sound system.

Her other two roommates were Elliott, a nerdy computer

programmer whose bedroom was a semi-shrine to all things *Star Wars*, and Sadie, who was working on her PhD in Genetics while moonlighting as an exotic dancer to help pay the bills. It was, for sure, a rather odd household, but everyone got along extremely well, and Sasha was more than content with her somewhat unorthodox living arrangements.

She made a comfortable enough living now, between teaching yoga and doing massage, that she could have afforded to live alone, albeit in a tiny studio apartment given how high rents were going for these days in San Francisco. But Sasha had never lived alone in her entire life, had always been surrounded by people - often strangers - and wasn't at all sure that she'd like having her own place.

She took a leisurely shower, ate a bowl of Greek yogurt, fresh berries, and granola, then brewed a cup of tea before finally – reluctantly - returning her mother's call. As she carried her steaming cup of herbal tea out to the small but sunny backyard of the house, Sasha hoped she wouldn't feel the need to drink something a whole lot stronger than tea after the phone call with Katya. She seldom indulged in alcohol, but there had certainly been occasions after a conversation with her fiery mother that she'd wished for a glass of wine - followed by several shots of pure Russian vodka.

Sasha usually had a pretty good idea of what her mother's current mood was depending on the language she began the conversation with. If Katya was in good spirits, more or less content with the way her day was going, then she'd speak in English. But if she was upset about something - which she frequently was - then the conversation would begin in rapid, agitated Russian. Sasha kept her fingers crossed as her mother answered the call that it would be the former rather than the latter.

"Aleksandra. What took you so long to call your mother back?"

Sasha sighed. Not only was Katya speaking Russian but she was also calling Sasha by her full name, a sure sign that she was upset about something.

"I'm sorry, Mama," replied Sasha with a long-practiced calm. "I stayed at the studio after class to work on my own practice. And you know I hate calling you from the bus. Is everything all right?"

"Yes, yes," assured Katya impatiently. Then, with a little sniff, she added, "All this time you spend doing the yoga you could be dancing instead. If you practiced your dance even a little, Aleksandra, you could be on the show with me. You're so much better than all of these silly little American girls, or the one from Australia who is nowhere near as good as she thinks she is. I mentioned the idea to the producer once, and he thought it would be wonderful to have a mother and daughter both on the show. Though if that happened everyone would know how old I am so perhaps not."

"Mama, you know that's not going to happen anyway," Sasha pointed out gently, her Russian every bit as fluent as her mother's. "My competitive dancing days are long over. That's not the sort of life I want for myself."

"Hmmpf." Katya made a small sound of disgust. "None of these other girls would ever be able to compete in an actual ballroom competition. You could dance circles around them even now. But I know better than to convince you to resume your training. You choose the yoga and living like a hippie over the kind of life you could have down here."

Katya had been living full time in Los Angeles for nearly ten years now, and had taken to the glitzy lifestyle like a duck to water. Sasha paid her mother a very reluctant visit twice a year, and couldn't wait to return back to San Francisco each time, the crowds and traffic in L.A. more than a little claustrophobic.

"How are things going at the studio, Mama?" asked Sasha, smoothly changing the subject.

In addition to appearing on *Beyond Ballroom*, Katya owned a popular dance studio in Los Angeles. The studio specialized in ballroom, of course, but also offered classes in ballet, jazz, hip hop, and theater dance. The place had been bankrolled a few years back by one of Katya's celebrity partners on the show - an older restaurant magnate who'd been more than a little enamored of his fiery Russian partner. When Sasha had quizzed her mother about whether she'd actually had a fling with the man, Katya had coyly changed the subject, but the implication had been rather glaring.

"Good, good. A little slow right now since it's the summer, but once the show starts up again next month the students will come back from their vacations. I hired a new teacher - a nice Russian boy, one who trained with one of my old teachers. Next time you come to visit I'll introduce you to him, Aleksandra. You'll be thirty soon, and it's time you started thinking about settling down. And Pasha is a very handsome young man, a fantastic dancer. The two of you would make a beautiful couple."

Sasha rolled her eyes. This was far from the first time her mother had tried to fix her up with someone, or hinted about

74

her "advanced" age. Sasha resisted the impulse to remind Katya that *she* had never married, as that particular topic typically sent her off on a rant of some sort about Enzo.

"His name is Pasha?" she asked instead. "Wouldn't that be adorable - Pasha and Sasha. But I'll pass on meeting your newest protégé, Mama, thanks all the same."

"Yes, I'm sure you're dating some hippie who also teaches the yoga. Or does the massaging. How does he expect to support a wife and children doing those things?" asked Katya scathingly.

With Katya, it was always "the" yoga or "the" massage, as though she found both professions equally distasteful. But Sasha knew better than to argue with her mother on the matter, and simply changed the subject.

"Do you know yet who your new partner is going to be for the fall season?" she asked, knowing how much her mother adored talking about the TV show.

"Pah!" Katya spat out in disgust. "That is why I called you, Aleksandra. Can you believe they want me to dance with this fat old man? They tell me he used to be on the television a long time ago, some program where he was some sort of policeman. Or detective, I don't remember which one. But he's at least seventy years old now, out of shape, losing his hair. Ugh. He looks *nothing* like the photograph they showed me of him when he was on the television. I can already tell he's going to be clumsy as an ox, and he's going to get us voted off the show within the first two weeks."

Sasha tucked her bare feet under her as she settled more deeply into the padded outdoor lounge chair, and merely continued to sip her tea calmly as Katya went on and on

75

about her new partner. It was very obvious to Sasha that the real reason her mother was upset was because she was ultra-sensitive about her own age. *Beyond Ballroom* liked to rotate their professional dancers in and out of the lineup, introducing new faces and sitting out some of the older ones for a season in order to keep things fresh. And each time a pretty twenty-something female dancer was brought on board, Katya's hackles went up, for she feared it would only be a matter of time before the show's producers decided she was too old now to compete.

Fortunately, Katya was extremely popular among the viewers, for they liked her feisty, bossy Russian temperament, and she had a way of bringing out the best from her partners. Sasha had little doubt that the fat, balding seventy year old would *not* be voted off the show within the first two weeks, and would actually wind up staying on much longer than anyone would initially predict.

Half an hour later, Katya had finally exhausted her supply of insults, and had begun instead to think of ways she could possibly make something of her partner. She bade Sasha good-bye, but not before chastising her one more time about her lack of a boyfriend, and urged her to come visit soon.

"If you don't want to meet Pasha, I can maybe introduce you to one of the new celebrities on the show. Don't you dare tell anyone," cautioned Katya dramatically, "but I just learned that Rafe Constantine is going to be on the show this season. Why I couldn't have had *him* for a partner I have no idea. But I could set you up with him, Sasha, if you're interested. He's very successful, you know, not like the yoga or the massage people you date."

Sasha didn't bother telling her mother that not only did she have zero idea who this Rafe Constantine was, but that she rarely ever dated fellow yoga teachers or massage therapists. The former admission would trigger a shocked reaction from Katya that Sasha didn't know who this supposedly famous person was, while denying the latter would be met with disbelief.

Still, as she ended the call and sat quietly for a few more minutes enjoying the warm summer sunshine, Sasha was honest enough to admit to herself that there was in fact *something* missing from her life. She had good friends and a loving family, even if some of the latter drove her to distraction at times; adored the work that she did and felt fulfilled by it every single day; lived in a warm, friendly household with an interesting assortment of roommates. She resided in what she considered one of the most beautiful, fascinating cities in the world, and was young, healthy, and vibrant.

But there was no denying that there were gaps in her life here and there, ones that had been made more evident over the past year when two of her closest friends - Julia and Tessa - had both fallen in love and gotten married. And while Sasha had never been the sort of woman who needed or wanted a man for the sole purpose of defining who she was, there were definitely times when she thought it would be nice to have someone special in her life.

'It will happen one of these days,' she told herself with a calm confidence. 'And most likely when you're least expecting it to do so.'

chapter five

September

"THAT WAS ONE OF THE best meals I've ever had in my life, Tessa. And I'm not just saying that because I haven't had an actual home-cooked meal in longer than I can remember," added Matthew teasingly.

Tessa Gregson smiled warmly at her dinner guest. "I'm glad you enjoyed it, Matthew," she told him softly. "And I'm so sorry that we haven't managed to have you over before now. Between business trips and our vacation with Ian's family in Tuscany last month, it's been an incredibly hectic summer."

"Not to worry," he assured her. "Besides, that meal was worth waiting for. I understand now why Ian works out so often and so intensely if you cook for him like this every night."

Ian grinned, giving his dark head a brief shake. "Not every night, no. At least not a feast like this. I'd easily be twenty pounds heavier if my bride cooked this way all the time. But she does adore taking care of me, and insists on cooking almost every night of the week despite how busy she is."

Tessa shrugged, taking a sip of the very expensive Chardonnay that Matthew had brought as his contribution to dinner. "I'm not that busy," she demurred. "Not like you and Matthew are. And I like to cook. Besides, Ian's right. We usually have a very simple meal most evenings - just some fish or chicken with vegetables or a salad."

"Well, I certainly wouldn't call tonight's dinner simple," declared Matthew, indicating the array of serving dishes and bowls that were spread out on the glass-topped patio table. "You definitely outdid yourself, Tessa. And my stomach and I are very, very appreciative!"

The weather had been unseasonably hot in San Francisco today, hovering in the low nineties, and it was still quite warm at seven-thirty in the evening. Tessa had chosen to serve dinner on the spacious, flagstone courtyard located just outside the French doors leading to the kitchen. Matthew liked the quiet intimacy of the Gregsons' outdoor space, vastly preferring it to the sprawling grounds of the Hillsborough estate that had never truly felt like a home to him.

And he'd sure as hell never enjoyed a home-cooked meal like the one Ian's wife had just prepared for them – a perfectly seasoned and grilled surf and turf combination of juicy Chateaubriand and tiger prawns, accompanied by a wedge salad, saffron risotto, fresh vegetables, and soft, buttery rolls. And when both men had stuffed themselves of the delicious meal until they were groaning a bit, Tessa had laughingly warned them to find a bit of room for dessert – an apricot tart she'd made from scratch, using fruit she had just picked up this morning at the farmers market.

Matthew patted his very full belly. "I might need to wait a bit before I can do that tart justice," he cautioned.

"There's no rush," replied Ian, as he topped off their wine glasses. "Unless, of course, you plan on working when you return home tonight."

Matthew shook his head. "I promised myself not to even think about work tonight. I've been putting in way too much time lately, both at the office and after hours as well. I fell asleep in my office yesterday, literally face planted right on my desk. Elena swore I'd been out for over half an hour when she found me that way." He winced, rubbing his nape. "Guess that's why I can barely move my neck today."

"You need a massage," declared Tessa. "And not just because you have a sore neck. I'm guessing with everything you're going through right now that your stress level is off the charts."

Matthew grimaced. "That's probably the understatement of the century, Tessa. And a massage would definitely do me wonders right now. I'll ask Elena to call the health club tomorrow and try to set something up with one of their therapists."

Tessa shook her blonde head. "Don't bother with one of those guys," she told him. "From what I've heard they're all brute strength and zero finesse. If you want a real therapeutic massage, you need to call Sasha. When she lays her hands on you for the first time, you'll melt right there on the massage table."

Matthew frowned. "Sasha? Why does that name sound so familiar? I – oh, now I remember. She was one of your bridesmaids, wasn't she? The one with all that curly hair who was dancing up a storm at the pre-wedding party. And - God, I forgot all about this until now. I ended up talking to her at the wedding for a little while. I was at the bar belting back another bourbon when she came up and asked the bartender for hot water so she could brew some sort of tea

80

she'd brought along with her."

Ian rolled his eyes. "Yes, that definitely sounds like something Sasha would do. I always considered my diet to be extremely healthy until she told me I was missing at least a dozen different nutrients and vitamins, and wrote up a list of supplements I should be taking. But she does knows her stuff, Matthew. And she's definitely the best masseuse I've ever had. You wouldn't imagine that someone as slim as she is could also be so strong, but she's made me yelp more than a few times."

Matthew groaned. "And I also just remembered that she encouraged me to get a massage. She, uh, sort of strong-armed me into dancing with her, and could tell how tense I was just from that contact. I was supposed to ask one of you for her business card after you got back from your honeymoon, but, well, it's sort of been a hell of a summer, you know?"

"We get it," assured Tessa gently, patting him on the arm. "You've had a lot on your plate with the separation and work and your children. Let me go find one of her business cards for you now, Matthew. Be right back."

Matthew didn't miss the possessive way Ian watched his wife as she hurried through the French doors inside the house, and smiled a little wistfully. Had he ever felt that way about Lindsey, even when they'd been newlyweds? It was extremely obvious to even a casual observer that Ian and Tessa were both madly in love, and also enjoyed a deeply passionate relationship.

"I envy you, Ian," he admitted with a sigh. "In the nearly twenty years that Lindsey and I were together, I'm not sure she ever once looked at me the way your wife's been staring at you all evening. Then again, I'm not sure I've met any couple who seem as crazy about each other as you and Tessa do. Not to repeat myself, but you're a very, very lucky man."

Ian smiled. "I am lucky. And I'm the first to admit it. And, yes, I realize that what Tessa and I have together is very rare, very special. I just wish that you had known that sort of love in your own marriage, at least for a time. Or that at the very least you might be able to have that sort of relationship with someone else one of these days."

Matthew gave a little snort of derision. "That's probably the farthest thing from my mind these days, what with all the pressures at work and trying to fit in enough time to see my kids. Not to mention the twice weekly phone calls from my divorce attorney updating me on the progress with the proceedings. And before you ask, the progress has pretty much come to a grinding halt. Lindsey refuses to even consider looking at the divorce papers unless I change the terms. Her latest demand is that she still gets half of everything, *plus* receive a very sizeable monthly payment for the next twenty years. I told my attorney I wasn't quite that desperate yet."

"Good. You're being far more than generous with your offer, Matthew. I just can't imagine someone being offered such a staggering sum of money and still wanting more." Ian shook his head in disbelief. "Is Lindsey doing this out of greed or spite?"

"Probably both," replied Matthew. "My attorney wants me to use all the reports the private investigator compiled about her infidelities as leverage. But that would be hard to keep quiet, and I don't want the kids to know. Though there may come a time when I don't have a choice any longer."

The topic was swiftly dropped as Tessa returned to the table, and handed Matthew a business card printed in sage green and tan. It bore the name, address, and telephone number of a yoga studio here in San Francisco, along with *Sasha Fonseca/LMT*.

"She works out of the yoga studio?" inquired Matthew as he tucked the card inside his wallet.

Tessa nodded. "Most of the time. She sees some clients at their home, like me and Ian, but that's only because we have a massage table and the other supplies she needs here. She doesn't own a car, and it's a little tough to cart a folding table around on the bus. But the studio has several massage rooms, and I've had sessions with Sasha there before. Be warned, though. It might take you a couple of weeks or longer before you can snag an appointment with her. She's very in demand. In fact, maybe I should call her for you and set something up. Her evening class should be ending soon, so I can try calling her in a few minutes."

"If you don't mind, that would be awesome," Matthew told her gratefully. "The more I think about it, the more the idea of a massage sounds miraculous. With each passing minute, it feels like another muscle or joint is aching."

"I don't mind at all," assured Tessa. "I just hope she has her phone turned on. She, ah, isn't very big on technology, which is why I never text or email her. In fact, I'm not even sure she has an email account."

Matthew, who was considered one of the modern day kings of technology, was more than a little appalled at that revelation. But he was greatly relieved a few minutes later when Tessa was able to reach Sasha on her cell phone, and set up an appointment for Matthew the following afternoon.

"She's basically fitting you in between other appointments," explained Tessa. "As something of a favor to me. So you'd better give her a really big tip!" she added teasingly.

Matthew chuckled. "No worries there. And if she's as good as you and Ian insist she is, it will probably be the biggest tip she's ever received before. I can barely move my neck at all right now. Thank you, Tessa, I really appreciate it."

"No problem. I think – well, you'll figure it out for yourself pretty quickly, but Sasha is a very special person. She's not just a great massage therapist, but she has a very calming, grounding presence about her as well. I think she could be very good for you in more ways than one, Matthew," commented Tessa. "She's helped me through some difficult times, and maybe she can do the same for you."

Matthew regarded her quizzically. "How so exactly?"

But Tessa merely gave him a mysterious little smile before replying, "You'll see for yourself soon enough."

"HAVE I TOLD YOU YET today that you're really the perfect husband? I mean, not only are you gorgeous and sexy and really, really amazing in bed, but you help with the dishes, too. What else could a girl ask for?"

Ian laughed at his wife's teasing inquiry, and bent to kiss her cheek. "The least I could do, darling, considering how much effort you put into cooking such a wonderful dinner this evening. And I know Matthew appreciated it very much

– especially the plates of leftovers you sent him home with."

Tessa smiled as she placed the last glass in the dishwasher, popped a detergent pod inside the appliance, and started the wash cycle. "I'm sure it must be tough on him getting takeout almost every night," she sympathized. "And he's admittedly not much of a cook. Besides, I doubt he'd have time to cook given all of the demands on his time. Don't you think the CEO of a company would be able to delegate a little more of his work?"

Ian shook his head. "Matthew is something of a control freak from what I've observed. And since he's still deeply involved in the design and development process of the software programs his company produces, it's not always possible for him to delegate certain aspects of the job. He's a genius, you know. Literally. His IQ is someplace in the stratosphere. So it's doubtful that too many people would be able to do some of the things he does."

"Well, I'm just glad he was able to join us for dinner tonight," declared Tessa. "We'll have to make it a point to have him over more often. And I'm so pleased that Sasha was able to fit him in for a massage tomorrow. I think she'll do him a world of good."

Ian looked at his wife quizzically as they began to make their way upstairs to their bedroom. "You are just referring to the massage, aren't you? Tessa, please tell me that you aren't trying to do a bit of matchmaking here."

She gave a careless little shrug. "That certainly wasn't my intent, no. But the more I think about it the more I like the idea. Strange as it may sound, I think Sasha might be exactly what Matthew needs in his life right now."

85

"They're absolutely nothing alike," pointed out Ian as he began to undress. "Matthew's the CEO of a multi-billion dollar corporation, lives in a penthouse, wears eight thousand dollar suits, and drives a top of the line Tesla – which is just one of the cars he owns. Sasha teaches yoga and does massage for a living, rents a single room in someone else's house, take the bus or walks everywhere, and the only time I've seen her wear anything but yoga clothes was at our wedding."

Tessa tapped him on the nose with her index finger. "Snob," she taunted teasingly, just before presenting him with her back so he could lower the zipper of her dress.

Ian chuckled, even as he sucked in a breath at the sight of her semi-nude body. He wasn't certain he'd ever stop feeling like an adolescent schoolboy in the presence of his young, sexy wife, and especially not when she was almost naked, clad in just a lacy bra and thong set of pale pink lace.

"It has nothing to do with the differences in their financial status," he clarified, even as he hooked an arm around her waist and pulled her flush against his bare chest. "In spite of his wealth, Matthew is a very down-to-earth person, and not in the least bit snobbish. It's more a case of he and Sasha having different interests, and very different lifestyles. He's probably the most tech savvy person I've ever known, while I believe you've told me that Sasha doesn't even own a computer. And try as I might, I simply can't envision Matthew attempting a yoga class. Or meditating."

Tessa shrugged, running her hands up and down her husband's heavily muscled arms, her lips hovering around the hollow at the base of his throat. "Hmm. But maybe both of those things – yoga and meditation – are exactly what he needs right now to help relieve his stress. And you're right – the two of them are very different from each other. But you know the saying – opposites attract. It will be interesting to see if anything, ah, develops after his appointment tomorrow. And before you say anything, Ian, I am *not* trying to matchmake. Just trying to help out a friend in need is all."

"Speaking of needs," he whispered wickedly in her ear. He grabbed hold of her hand and brought it to his crotch, where his cock was already hard and fully erect. "As you can tell, love, I'm very, *very* needy for you this evening."

"I can tell," she purred, her slender hand stroking him up and down with slow, deliberate movements, the way she knew all too well drove him crazy with lust. But when her hand slid further back to gently squeeze his swollen testicles, he clamped his fingers around her wrist, stilling her movements.

"I'll come in your hand in about ten seconds if you keep doing that," panted Ian. "And I would much rather come inside of *you*.'

Tessa squealed in surprise as he swooped her into his arms, tossed her on their enormous king-sized bed, pulled off her barely there thong, and then thrust fully inside of her – all within a matter of seconds. As controlled and disciplined as Ian was about most aspects of his life – including their lovemaking – he could just as easily turn into a wild man in the bedroom with very little encouragement. This, evidently, was going to be one of those times.

"**SASHA WILL BE RIGHT WITH** you, Matthew. Are you sure I can't offer you some water or tea?"

Matthew smiled at the perky front desk clerk. "No, thank you. And here's the form you asked me to fill out. I don't think I missed anything."

"Oh, thanks."

He handed the clipboard and pen, along with the client information form and waiver he'd just completed, across the counter to the young girl who'd introduced herself as Willow upon his arrival. She was nearly as thin as the tree she shared a name with, almost waifishly so, with shoulder length black hair that had been dyed purple at the tips. Like everyone else he'd seen walk through the yoga studio since his arrival five minutes ago, Willow was casually dressed in cropped yoga pants, a floaty tunic, and flip flops. Matthew silently cursed himself for not having taken the time to change clothes before leaving the office, since his Dior suit, Brooks Brothers tie, and Prada oxfords were very sadly out of place here.

Truth be told, he'd never felt entirely comfortable wearing a suit and tie, or any other sort of expensive designer clothing. He missed the early days of his career, when he could get away with wearing jeans and a T-shirt to the office and no one would blink an eye. And even on the casual Fridays he'd insisted on implementing at MBI, he hesitated at presenting too casual of an image and usually wore pressed khakis and an open-necked shirt.

Unlike the handful of men he'd seen in the studio since walking through the front door. They had all been wearing loose fitting shorts or nylon track pants, T-shirts or tanks, and either sandals, sneakers, or no shoes at all. Self-consciously, he undid the top two buttons of his shirt and loosened his tie, wondering if he should just dispense with the latter altogether and stuff it in his pocket. He –

"Matthew. It's a pleasure to see you again. Even if you're several months later than expected."

He glanced up at the sound of that soft, melodious voice, his gaze colliding with those mysterious green-gold eyes that had reminded him of a lioness's the first time they had met. Sasha was smiling at him with that particular air of serenity that seemed to envelop her like a cloud, and he stared at her for long seconds as though awestruck. And while her attire of slim fitting dark gray yoga pants and a midnight blue tank top was at the very opposite end of the scale from the formal bridesmaid's gown she'd been wearing at Tessa and Ian's wedding, Matthew thought vaguely that he preferred her this way. He didn't think he'd ever met anyone who seemed as comfortable in their own skin as Sasha did, and he knew without being told that she wasn't a woman who fussed over her appearance.

She also, he noted with an unexpected surge of lust, had a rather amazing figure – slender and graceful, with leanly muscled arms and legs, and narrow hips and shoulders. Her breasts were on the small side but looked firm and nicely shaped, and their size was in perfect balance with the rest of her body. She looked like a dancer, and he could still visualize the impromptu little ballroom dance performance she and her date had given at the Gregsons' joint bachelor/bachelorette party. Her bare feet were as slim and dainty as the rest of her body, the toenails unpolished.

89

As she continued to gaze at him expectantly, Matthew rather clumsily reached out a hand in her direction. "It's - it's good to see you, Sasha," he replied, his voice cracking just a little. "And I'm, uh, sorry for not making an appointment until now. Life has been - well, let's call it complicated as of late."

She shook her head, causing that untamable mane of corkscrew curls to bounce endearingly. At the same time she clasped his hand in her much smaller one, giving his a reassuring little squeeze. "No need to apologize," she replied softly. "And I hope that your being here will help make things a little less complicated for you. Come, follow me."

During the brief walk down a short hallway that had several rooms on each side, Matthew tried like hell not to let his lecherous gaze drift past the graceful curve of Sasha's spine. But it was damned near impossible to ignore the way those form fitting yoga pants cupped the firm curves of her ass, and he was able to sneak in a quick, furtive peek before she stopped in front of one of the doors.

"Here we are," she announced as she opened the door and ushered him inside. If she'd been aware of his hot gaze on her butt, she was evidently too discreet to make mention of it. Matthew just guessed that he was far from the first male yoga student or massage client to take note of the fact, however.

The room Sasha had brought him to was small but had obviously been decorated with comfort and calm in mind. The walls were painted a soothing shade of blue-gray, and a soft area rug covered the wood floor. The lighting was muted, and there was a minimum of furniture in the room, with the massage table taking up most of the space. An aromatherapy diffuser was emitting a subtle scent of peppermint oil, and New Age music was being piped discreetly through small, wall-mounted speakers.

"You can leave your things on the chair in the corner," Sasha told him as he finished his brief inspection of the room. "Or hang them on one of the hooks."

"My things?" he quizzed, turning to face her.

She smiled before replying calmly, "Your clothes. All of them. And, yes, before you ask, that includes your underwear."

Unwittingly, he felt his cheeks grow hot and was grateful for the dim lightning of the room. "Oh. Um, yeah, sure. What – whatever you prefer."

Sasha's smiled deepened but her voice was reassuring. "Don't worry, you'll be covered the entire time with a sheet. Plus, I can assure you that you don't have any body parts I haven't seen many times before. I'll give you a few minutes to undress and get under the covers. Face down to start, please. I'll knock before I entering."

The door clicked shut quietly as she left, and Matthew quickly began to disrobe. He hung his suit jacket on a wall hook, but took less care with his shirt, tie, and trousers, draping them casually over the chair. After removing his shoes and socks, he stood in the middle of the small room wearing just his dark blue briefs, wondering vaguely if he really needed to take *everything* off. After all, he reasoned, it was mostly just his neck and shoulders and upper back muscles that needed attention, so why did he have to take off his Calvins?

But he didn't want to displease Sasha by going against

her wishes, so he quickly shucked the cotton underwear and shoved it under the other clothes on the chair. He had just stretched out on the massage table and pulled the top sheet up to cover his bare ass before a soft knock sounded on the door.

"Uh, yeah. Come in."

Sasha's bare feet didn't make a sound as she entered the room, only the slight click of the door behind her signaling her arrival. Wordlessly, she pulled the butter soft cotton sheet and lightweight blanket all the way up to his neck. Beneath the bottom sheet was some sort of heated pad that felt so fantastic against his bare skin it made him want to close his eyes and take a really long nap.

But it was the first touch of Sasha's long, elegant fingers on the back of his neck that caused him to actually groan out loud, the sound escaping his throat involuntarily.

"My God, that feels good," he sighed, his voice muffled by the fabric covering the face rest.

She chuckled softly as her hands began to knead a little more forcefully along his shoulder blades. "I barely touched you," she pointed out. "But I can already tell that we've got a lot of work to do here. Your muscles are about as tense as I've ever felt. I'm afraid it's going to take several sessions before you feel any significant improvement. How long has it been since your last massage?"

Matthew gave a little shrug, closing his eyes in half-bliss, half-pain as she began to dig a little more deeply into his knotted muscles. "Months. Maybe closer to a year. I'm not good at taking care of myself, unfortunately. I get pretty wrapped up in my job, work really long hours, travel a lot.

And then, well, I assume Tessa has told you about my family situation. My wife and I are, uh, in the process of getting a divorce."

Sasha's hands stilled momentarily, and she didn't offer up a reply for several seconds. "She didn't tell me, no. Knowing Tessa as well as I do, I assume she withheld that information because she respects your privacy. When she called me last evening to book this appointment, she simply said that you've had a great deal of stress to cope with lately and really needed a massage."

"Yeah, that sounds like Tessa. She's a great girl. Ian is just about the luckiest man in San Francisco to have a wife like her," murmured Matthew.

"They're both lovely people," agreed Sasha. "Tessa in particular is very nurturing, very caring. I'm grateful to have her as a friend."

He grunted as she located a particularly tight spot, but then let out another sigh of relief as she began to work out the knot. "Jesus, you really do have a knack for finding all the sore spots, don't you?" he asked half-jokingly. "Ian has been singing your praises to me, but I admit to being skeptical when I walked in here. But you do, uh, have magic fingers."

Sasha laughed this time, the sound reminding him of tinkling bells. "I do my best," she assured him. "It's more difficult with bodies like yours and Ian's, though, considering how much muscle mass you have. I have to dig a little deeper sometimes."

Matthew grit his teeth, determined not to cry out in pain when she definitely dug in deeper as she moved to his shoulders. "I, um, don't have anywhere near as much muscle mass as Ian, though," he pointed out. "The guy could be a linebacker or a tight end on any professional football team. Though considering he's British I guess he'd be the prop or a flanker on a rugby team."

"I'm afraid I don't know much about professional sports, American or otherwise," admitted Sasha. "But while you may be a bit leaner than Ian, you're still very muscular, very strong. And very, very tense. I could spend the entire hour on just your neck and shoulder blades. Did you fall asleep in an awkward position or something?"

Sheepishly, he told her about slumping face first onto his desk the previous day. "I guess all of the stress is starting to catch up with me," he acknowledged. "It's been a rough few months all around."

Unbidden, Matthew found himself telling her about the nasty, contentious divorce proceedings and how uncooperative Lindsey was being; how difficult it had been on him not to see his children as often as he would have liked; how his responsibilities at work seemed to be mounting at an alarming rate, and how he rarely seemed to have a minute to himself these days.

Throughout the one-sided conversation, Sasha didn't comment or offer up any sort of opinion or feedback. Occasionally she'd make some small sound of acknowledgment or sympathy, but mostly she just continued with the massage, her slim, capable hands working out knots and tension and soreness that he hadn't even known existed in certain spots.

At some point he ceased talking, far too relaxed by now to do anything but close his eyes and enjoy the pure indulgence of the massage. Sasha was rubbing some sort of lotion into his skin, and the subtle scent was both pleasant and vaguely stimulating. And, as her hands gradually moved to his lower back, hip flexors, and hamstrings, Matthew unwittingly became aware that other parts of his body were also feeling, well – *stimulated.* Perhaps it was simply because it had been so long since a woman had touched him in any manner – sexually or otherwise – but his body was definitely reacting to Sasha's soothing, knowing touch. Combined with the scents of the massage lotion and aromatherapy oil, the strains of the hypnotic violin music playing through the speakers, and the cocoon-like warmth of the heated pad beneath his naked body, Matthew felt surrounded by sensations, all of them pleasant, almost hedonistic. And with each stroke of Sasha's expert hands on his muscles, his erection seemed to grow another inch, until it was almost painfully swollen.

He bit down on the fabric covering the face rest, determined not to emit the slightest sound that might betray his growing arousal. He shifted around a bit awkwardly, trying to find a position to more comfortably accommodate his rapidly hardening cock. Sasha merely rested a hand in the middle of his back, stilling him, and he obeyed despite the overwhelming urge to do otherwise.

But it was when she murmured to him softly, "Time to turn over", that he had to fight off a sense of panic. There was no way, *no* way, to disguise the fact that he had a rather obvious hard-on. But there was also no easy way to refuse Sasha's instructions, so Matthew rather gingerly eased himself onto his back, willing his cock – which seemed to have a mind of its own at the moment – back into compliance.

95

Sasha spent a couple of minutes pulling and readjusting the sheet and blanket, making sure he was adequately covered, and if she noticed his rather conspicuous erection she was far too discreet and professional to acknowledge the fact.

It was with equal parts relief and dismay when she only spent a few minutes working on the front side of his body, mostly focused on his shoulders and neck. He figured that the hour was nearly over, and marveled that sixty minutes could go by that quickly. She gently massaged his temples and forehead, soothing away the tension headache that was almost always with him nowadays. She lifted his head very slightly off the table, her fingers threading through his scalp for a few seconds, before she carefully set his head back down. Matthew wanted to moan – or purr – from the sheer pleasure of it all, and couldn't help feeling dismayed when Sasha stepped away from the table, quietly signaling the end of the session.

"Take a few minutes, hmm?" she murmured softly. "I'll be back in just a bit with some water for you."

She exited the room as quietly as she'd entered an hour earlier, and Matthew could no longer hold back the groan of mingled pleasure and mortification that escaped his lips.

'Jesus, please do not have let her noticed the fact that my cock was just tenting this sheet a few minutes ago,' he begged silently. 'It has obviously been *way* too long since you've had any action, Bennett. Maybe you should make sure you jack off before your next massage. Otherwise, you're really going to embarrass yourself."

The temptation was strong to just keep his eyes closed and

drift off to sleep at this moment. He hadn't felt this relaxed and warm and content in a very long time, and the stress that was his constant companion these days seemed to have taken a temporary leave of absence. He stretched his arms and legs in opposite directions before slowly, reluctantly, easing his body off the table.

He dressed quickly, oddly reluctant to have Sasha catch him in the act of putting his clothes on, even though he'd just been naked as a jaybird in her presence for the last hour. True to her word, though, she had kept all the private parts of his body well covered at all times, and he hadn't felt the least bit awkward or embarrassed as he'd initially feared he might.

He was just pulling on his socks when she knocked gently on the door, entering at his bidding. She crossed over to where he sat on the chair, a glass of lemon and orange infused water in her hand. Matthew marveled yet again at how easily she moved, how light and graceful she was on her feet, and wondered aloud how many years she'd trained as a dancer.

Sasha smiled at his somewhat absentminded inquiry. "All my life, actually," she replied. "Since the time I was a very young girl right up until today. Oh, I don't do any formal dance training or classes these days, but dance certainly factors into my yoga practice. A lot of the yoga poses I do in my own practice and the classes I teach are influenced by dance."

"Do you miss the training?" he inquired casually, taking a long sip of the cool, refreshing water.

Her smile quickly vanished, replaced by a look of mingled annoyance and irritation, two emotions that he would have never attributed to the calm, even-tempered Sasha.

"No," was all she said in reply. "Those particular memories are not the most pleasant. So, how do you feel now? Are those shoulder and neck muscles a little looser?"

He allowed her to change the subject abruptly, having quickly picked up on the fact that her past dance training was not something she enjoyed discussing. He rolled his neck from side to side experimentally, and was pleasantly surprised to find how much looser it felt.

"I'd say so, yes," he replied, grinning broadly. "You've definitely got some magic in those fingers of yours."

Sasha laughed, her good humor quickly restored. "I do my best. Now, I'd like you to finish the whole glass of water, and then promise me you'll drink at least two or three more glasses this afternoon. Hydration is very important, and especially after a massage."

Dutifully, he downed the rest of the glass and nodded. "Okay, I promise."

She held out a sheet of paper to him. "Now, you can choose to do this or not, it's entirely up to you. But I took the liberty of writing down several types of vitamins and supplements that I think you should consider taking. Some help with stress, others with muscle recovery, and most are just for overall good health. I also included the names and addresses of a few different health food stores where you can pick these up if you decide to try them. Again, it's completely your decision, Matthew, but I do think taking these would do you a world of good."

He grinned, taking the sheet from her, and quickly scanning over what she'd written in a neat, artistic hand. "Ian warned me that you'd probably do this," he replied teasingly.

Sasha arched a dark blonde brow. "Did he now? Well, you see, Ian is a prime example of someone who just assumed he was getting plenty of vitamins and minerals from his daily diet and the generic supplements he was taking. It was something of an eye opener for him to realize that his regime wasn't quite as healthy as he'd always assumed. And I'm going to guess that your own diet isn't as disciplined as his – given what you just told me about your current lifestyle."

Matthew sighed, and folded the paper in half before tucking it inside his jacket pocket. "My diet can only be described as appalling right now," he admitted. "I think the only time I eat vegetables are when there's lettuce and tomato on my burger or club sandwich. And since I already know how you feel about drinking alcohol, I won't freak you out by admitting how many glasses of whisky I put away every night."

She shook her head. "I'm not here to lecture you, Matthew," she told him gently. "That's not my place, after all. But if you'd ever like advice about changing your diet and other habits I would be more than happy to help you with that. You know how to get in touch with me now."

"Speaking of which, I definitely want to set up another appointment. As soon as you can fit me in. Do you have your appointment book nearby?"

"The front desk handles all of that," she corrected. "On your way out you can have Willow check to see when my next open time slot is. I'm guessing not until sometime next week, unless there's been a cancellation. And I'm glad that you've decided to book another session. As I mentioned, it's probably going to take several appointments before I can really make some progress. You've got some real tough knots there."

He gave her a lopsided smile. "Think we'll have to call that Shibari master in to get them untied?"

Sasha laughed in delight, her green-gold eyes sparkling. "You remembered that from the wedding, did you? But, no, I think I can handle these particular knots on my own. Now, please take good care of yourself until our next appointment, hmm? Try to eat a real vegetable or two, drink some nice cold-pressed juices, and maybe cut back just a little on the whiskey. I understand that this is a very stressful time for you, but there are many other methods beside alcohol that can help relieve that."

Matthew bit his lip, forcing himself not to utter the very suggestive phrase "You mean like sex" in response. Instead, he merely nodded and held out a hand to her.

"Thanks again for fitting me in today," he told her earnestly, then had to fight off the really dirty image of how snugly his cock might fit inside that taut, slim-hipped body of hers. "I didn't realize how badly I needed that massage until I arrived."

She smiled as she gave his hand a brief, reassuring squeeze. "Most people don't. And even though you're a few months late, I'm very, very glad that you came in today, Matthew. You've taken the first step in helping yourself get through this difficult time in your life, and I hope that you'll continue to take better care of yourself. Starting immediately. FYI, one of those health food stores I recommended is just across the street."

The urge to pull her into his arms and give her a quick hug was strong, and he guessed that she wouldn't resist such a gesture. She was by nature a very nurturing person, caring and compassionate, but in the end he fought off the temptation - largely because his motivation in holding her in his arms had absolutely nothing to do with comfort and instead everything to do with sexual attraction.

chapter six

Early October, Marin County

"**WANT TO TALK ABOUT IT,** niná? And before you try and bullshit your Tia Linda that it's nothing, forget about it. I can always tell when something's going on in that pretty head of yours."

Sasha smiled at the woman who sat in the chair to her right. "Of course you can. And I wouldn't dream of denying it. You were the one who taught me how to pick up on that sort of thing, after all. As for what's on my mind this afternoon... would you believe me if I confessed that it was a man?"

Linda Vargas gave a hoot of laughter. "I'd believe you, niná, but only because I know you never lie about anything. But I will admit to being surprised. Who is this mystery man responsible for that very intense expression on your face?"

Sasha took a sip of the herbal tea that her aunt had brewed just a few minutes ago, then set the hand painted ceramic mug - one of Linda's creations - on a low table. "A friend of a friend. And also one of my massage clients."

Linda made a clucking sound of disapproval. "Sasha, you aren't sleeping with a client, are you? Not that I'm a prude by any stretch of the imagination, but that's a bit on the unethical side."

"I'm not sleeping with him, Tia," she replied. "You know

me better than that. But that doesn't mean I haven't thought about it. He's - well, not exactly my type, but that doesn't seem to matter much where my hormones are concerned. The first time I met him I felt this sort of connection with him. Even though he happened to be a married man at the time. Still is, legally."

Linda's scowl was positively ferocious. "So not only is he a client, but a married one as well? Sasha, you are a beautiful, accomplished young woman. You could have most any man you wanted. So why are you craving the forbidden all of a sudden?"

Sasha smiled and patted her aunt on the forearm reassuringly. "You should know better than anyone, Tia, that you can't control the way you feel about someone. And even though nothing has happened between us, Matthew is technically single nowadays. He filed for divorce a few months ago and moved out on his own. And to hear him talk about it - which he seems to do every single time he comes in for a massage - he considers his marriage to be over."

"Hmm." Linda still looked skeptical. "Does he have kids?"

"Yes. A boy and a girl. Both in their teens, so not all that young. He's a good father, too, calls them almost every night and sees them as often as possible. And I can tell he misses them a lot, given how much he talks about them during our sessions."

Linda took a long, thoughtful sip from her tea. "You need to tread carefully here, niná," she cautioned. "Dating a man with children - even a man who's in the process of getting a divorce - is always tricky. Because he will almost always choose his children over anything, and especially if he's as devoted to them as you describe. And you're too good a person, Sasha, to have your heart broken."

Sasha waved a hand in dismissal. "I think it's a little premature to start talking about broken hearts here. After all, he's just one of my clients at the moment. And he hasn't said or done anything to indicate that he's interested in a relationship with me."

Linda quirked a brow at her much-loved niece. "Really? Because it's hard to imagine you being attracted to a man if he hasn't given you some sort of signal that he feels the same way."

Sasha's cheeks flushed beneath her pale gold skin, and she grinned at her aunt. "He hasn't said anything directly, or asked me out on a date or anything. And I suppose it's just normal physical reactions, certainly not the first time that a male client has, er, been *stimulated* during a massage, but..."

Linda returned her niece's grin, though her expression was far naughtier. "He's had a boner, has he?" she joked. "Well, if he's been separated from his wife for a few months that could explain things, especially if he hasn't been seeing anyone else. But my guess is that he'd react that way to you regardless, niná. You've always been a very sensual woman, very attuned to sensation and emotion, and I'm guessing your Matthew can't help but respond to that."

"He isn't my Matthew," corrected Sasha as she picked up her mug. "And even if he is attracted to me, you were right earlier - it would be incredibly unprofessional to have any sort of relationship with him under the circumstances."

Linda shrugged. "Two ways to handle that one. One is you find him another masseuse. Or the second is you continue to give him massages, just as long as you don't do it at the studio and you don't charge him for it. I fail to see the conflict of interest under those circumstances."

Sasha nodded. "I thought about that. Silly of me, I know, given that Matthew hasn't even asked me out for a cup of coffee yet. I do think, though, more like *sense*, that he's attracted to me as well. And it's not just the, ah, obvious physical reaction. The way he smiles at me, or touches my hand, the sorts of things he confides in me about. And I know he's incredibly rich - my friend Tessa told me he's the CEO of some big computer company - so maybe he just treats everyone this way, but the tips he leaves for me are more than the cost of the massage."

Linda's eyes widened. "Maybe you shouldn't ditch him as a client after all. But that would mean you couldn't sleep with him, either."

"You know the money means nothing to me," pointed out Sasha. "In fact, I've been meaning to tell him that the tips are too much. And if Matthew is actually interested in me, then there's really no choice to make. He's - well, I think he would be good for me, Tia. And I know exactly what you mean about the complications with his children. But I'm talking about going out once in awhile, enjoying his company, not moving in with him. I'm not sure long-term relationships are ever going to be my thing."

"Well, God knows you've never had a good example of one to follow," commiserated Linda. "Between the disaster of my marriage to your uncle, and whatever passes for a relationship between your crazy parents, it's a wonder you'd ever want to date anyone. The most stable marriage you've ever witnessed is probably your gay roommates'."

Sasha's green-gold eyes twinkled. "Chad and Julio are certainly devoted to each other, but that doesn't mean they haven't had their fair share of knock-down, dragged-out fights. Unlike my parents, however, one of them doesn't storm out of the house and catch the first flight out of the country after an argument."

"How are Katya and Enzo, by the way? I haven't spoken to either of them in months."

Sasha rolled her eyes. "Mama is a bigger drama queen than ever, but what else is new. Though with the new season of the show in full swing, she's too busy to call very often. Dad's on another tour, this time in eastern Europe. Both of them are threatening to visit me around Christmas, unless I can think of a reason to keep them away. I'd like to have a peaceful holiday for once in my life."

"That may not be possible, niná, given that you've got two hotheads for parents. But they do love you very much, you know that, hmm? They may have odd ways of showing it, but I happen to know that you're the single most important thing to your mother and father."

"I know," sighed Sasha. "And even though they drive me crazy at times, I love them, too. I'm just not sure I'm emotionally up for dealing with both of them at the same time, and especially at Christmas. I've spent too many years of my life playing peacemaker between those two."

Linda gave her niece a sympathetic look. "I know, niná. You had to grow up far too quickly with those parents of yours, particularly when they acted like children so often. But you've made a good life for yourself, Sasha, despite spending your first fifteen years living like a gypsy."

Sasha nodded. "I love my life," she agreed. "And if it hadn't been for you, Tia, I might never have had the chance to live a normal life."

She had come to stay with her aunt Linda, the divorced wife of her uncle Joaquim - Enzo's older brother - for what was supposed to have been just a few weeks one summer. Sasha had been weary of following one or the other of her parents on whatever tour they'd been on, and when the offer had come from Linda to stay with her for a time she'd eagerly accepted.

Sasha had been entranced with both Linda's brightly painted cottage, and the coastal community of Stinson Beach where her aunt had taken up residence after the tempestuous divorce from Joaquim. It was peaceful there, despite the influx of weekend visitors to the beach, and Sasha knew within days of her arrival that she didn't want to leave anytime soon. Linda had filled the whimsically decorated cottage with the various forms of art she produced for a living - paintings, sculptures, pottery - as well as a veritable menagerie of animals, most of them rescues. Dogs and cats cohabited with birds and fish, and outside in the little garden was a small chicken coop and a rabbit hutch. Linda also grew vegetables and herbs, and canned her own fruit. She lived a simple, peaceful existence, far removed from the hectic, unceasing weeks Sasha spent traveling around the globe. Linda's cottage had felt like home the first time Sasha had stepped through the doorway, and when the invitation had come to remain there after her visit was supposed to be over, she had jumped at the chance.

Enzo hadn't put up much of a fight when Sasha had broached the subject of living permanently with Linda, but then again he had always been something of a pushover when it came to his daughter. Katya, however, had been quite another matter, and she'd screamed and cursed and threatened when Sasha had quietly insisted on staying put. In the end, it had been Enzo who'd convinced his fiery sometime-lover to acquiesce to their daughter's wishes, but Katya had been so hurt and angry that she had refused to speak to Sasha for almost three full months. And it hadn't simply been Sasha's desire to stay put and live in one place for a few years that had created such a rift between her and Katya. Rather, it had been Sasha's decision to quit dance that had really sent her mother over the edge.

But they had eventually made up, even if Katya had never really forgiven her daughter for abandoning the career as a ballroom dancer that she'd always envisioned for Sasha. And when Sasha had decided to become a yoga teacher, and then a masseuse as well, Katya's ire had been stoked anew. Katya strongly believed that Sasha was wasting her time and God given talents on something as frivolous as yoga, and that she could have had a very successful career as one of the professional dancers on *Beyond Ballroom*. The fact that Sasha had grown to hate all of the pageantry, costumes, and cattiness involved in competing and performing hadn't seemed to matter to Katya. All she saw was a wasted opportunity, and that her only child had elected to live like a hippie instead of a celebrity.

Sasha idly stroked the fur of one of Linda's cats - a fat orange marmalade named OJ. "I should be heading back soon," she told her aunt regretfully. "Even though it's in the opposite commute direction, there's always plenty of traffic heading into the city."

Sasha didn't own a car, but Chad or Julio were always happy to loan her one of their vehicles when she needed to go somewhere. She didn't particularly like to drive, but always made it a point to visit her aunt at least once or twice a month. Linda was the only family she had in northern California, and frankly the only family member she could turn to when she needed advice.

"It was good to see you as always, niná," replied Linda. "And I appreciate your driving all the way out here on your day off."

Friday was the one day of the week when Sasha didn't teach a yoga class or schedule any massage appointments. Instead, she spent the day sleeping in a bit, going for long walks, running errands, and seeing Linda, either here in Stinson Beach or in San Francisco for brunch or dinner.

Sasha reached over to give her aunt a hug. "You know I always love coming out here. And that I still consider this place home, even though I moved out a long time ago."

"It will always be your home, Sasha," assured Linda. "But before you go, tell me. What are you planning to do about this new man in your life, hmm?"

Sasha sighed. "I wish I knew. Like I told you, I'm not even sure he's interested in me. We're nothing alike, live in two totally different worlds. I don't know anything about fashion or designer clothes, but even I can tell that his suits and shoes must be horrendously expensive. And when I mentioned where Matthew lives to Chad, he told me all of those condos cost big bucks, like five million dollars for the smallest ones."

Linda regarded her niece curiously. "And how do you know where he lives?"

Sasha bit her bottom lip uncertainly. "He, ah, might have arranged for me to do an in-home massage on Monday. He's a very busy man, you see, and has to travel a lot on business. So he asked if I could possibly work around his schedule every so often."

Linda grinned. "And you still think he's not interested in you that way, niná?"

Sasha gave her aunt a mock glare. "You know very well that I have several clients that I see at their homes. Tessa and Ian are two that come to mind, and I have a few others as well."

"Ah, but are those clients as *stimulated* as your Matthew gets during a massage? And do any of them tip you more than a hundred dollars each time?" asked Linda pointedly. "He might be as busy as he says, but I guarantee you that he's got other motives behind asking you to do an in-home appointment. I have a feeling that come Monday you're going to discover that your Matthew is very, *very* interested in you, Sasha. And not just as his massage therapist."

"LINDSEY, FOR WHAT IS PROBABLY the fiftieth time, no. I am not interested in seeing a marriage counselor with you. In order for counseling sessions to do any good, both parties in the marriage have to actually *want* for things to improve. And even though you insist that's what you want, I'm having a real tough time believing that. Why? Maybe

110

because despite all your claims that you love me and want me back, I happen to know you're still intent on sleeping your way through all seven Bay Area counties before the year is up. And stop trying to deny it, Linz. I can give you names, dates, times, and hotel room numbers, and probably what color shoes you were wearing each time. Yes, my P.I. is very, very thorough. The best in the business from what I'm told."

"I can't believe you're still having me followed around like that," hissed Lindsey. "Especially since you're the one who moved out on me. What do you care what I do any longer, so long as the kids aren't involved?"

"I don't give a damn who you fuck," he replied calmly. "But I do care about those divorce papers, the ones you keep refusing to sign. So, yes, I am still having you followed, Linz, in case I have to resort to using that information one of these days to force your hand."

She gasped. "You wouldn't dare, you bastard! You wouldn't dare make that information public, or risk letting the kids find out. What sort of man are you, Matt?"

"The sort who wants this marriage over with once and for all," he retorted. "And you're right - I don't want the kids to know that their mother is a whore. But if you keep up this bullshit about not signing the papers, things might have to get ugly. And if a judge learned about all of your little flings, it's pretty much a given that I'd get full custody of Hayley and Casey, too. So you should give your lawyer a call, Linz, and tell her you're finally ready to end this thing."

"Screw you!" she spat out. "You don't have the guts to use that information against me, wouldn't risk hurting the kids that way. And even a man as nerdy and sexless as you

111

wouldn't want the word to get out that his wife had to find satisfaction somewhere else. Maybe if you'd been a better lover I wouldn't have had to scratch my itch with other men. And I'm not signing those goddamned papers. Not now and not ever!"

She disconnected the call abruptly, leaving Matthew to glare darkly at the phone in his hand. He was sorely tempted to fling the device clear across the room and watch it shatter into a hundred pieces.

Instead, he set the phone down on his desk, closed his eyes, and began to take deep, calming breaths - just the way Sasha had been teaching him. It was only one of the ways she was helping him to combat his sky high stress levels.

Quickly realizing that a scant hour was nowhere near enough time for his massage sessions with her, Matthew had bumped them up to ninety minutes. Sasha would spend a brief part of each session teaching him breathing and meditation techniques, and had encouraged him to take a few minutes out of each day to practice them.

She'd seemed inordinately pleased when he had told her that after their very first appointment he had gone out and bought all of the supplements and vitamins she had suggested, and even more so when he'd acknowledged that they already seemed to be having results. He was sleeping better at night, had more energy during the day, and more endurance during the workouts he was able to squeeze in. But when he had begun to ask her for advice on changes he should consider making to his diet, Sasha had hesitated.

"I don't want to sound like some sort of dictator, Matthew," she'd told him. "I'm the first to admit that I keep to a very rigid diet – no meat, chicken, or fish, very little dairy, lots of organic fruits and vegetables, and practically no processed foods. And I rarely drink any alcohol. I realize that it's unrealistic to expect most people to adhere to that sort of diet, so I generally don't try and impose my standards on others."

"But you're not dictating to me," he'd pointed out. "I'm the one asking you for advice, and I think I know you well enough by now to realize that you'd never try to impose your will on someone else. And while I may not be ready to go to the same extremes you've done, I know that I need to make some changes to what I'm currently doing. I don't feel healthy right now, so give me a few ideas to help me start changing that."

And thus, little by little, he'd begun to make those subtle changes to his diet and lifestyle over the past few weeks. Ian had nodded his approval at lunch last week when Matthew had ordered grilled salmon instead of his usual cheeseburger. Though Elena had stared at him in disbelief when he'd asked her to get him some herbal tea instead of coffee.

"You sick or something, boss?" she'd queried sarcastically. "Because I can't think of any other reason why you'd drink chamomile tea instead of your usual triple espresso."

Matthew had grinned. "Maybe I finally figured out all that caffeine is bad for my stress level. By the way, hold all

113

my calls for the next fifteen minutes, would you? It's time for my morning meditation."

Elena had felt his forehead then, convinced he was burning up with fever. But when his skin had been cool to the touch, she'd merely shaken her head and walked away, muttering something under her breath in rapid fire Spanish. All he had been able to decipher had been "ese hombre está loco", which he figured meant something like "that guy is crazy".

But cutting back on his caffeine intake, eating less red meat and fried foods, and limiting himself to one beer or glass of whiskey a day had already begun to have positive effects. He'd lost a few pounds, especially around his mid-section, and the dark circles under his eyes had faded. He was overall in a better, happier, and calmer mood, and had more patience when confronted with problems at the office.

Dealing with his hopefully soon to be ex-wife, however, was still every bit as vexing as always. And, unfortunately, getting Lindsey to agree to the divorce was not going to be nearly as easy as cutting back on caffeine or alcohol or giving up triple bacon cheeseburgers. Feeling his fists begin to clench tightly in irritation, Matthew took another of those deep, soothing breaths, holding it in at the top for several seconds, and then expelled it slowly. He repeated this action several more times before he felt a sense of calm begin to wash through his senses.

'Forget about Lindsey for now,' he told himself. 'You've got more important things to deal with today. Not to mention something to look forward to this evening.'

He was booked for a ninety minute massage with Sasha, and while he always anticipated those appointments with an inexplicable sense of excitement, he was looking forward to tonight's more than usual - most likely because the appointment would be taking place at his condo for the first time.

After he'd discovered that Sasha always administered Ian and Tessa's massages at their home, he had asked her if she might also be able to offer the same sort of service to him. She had hesitated briefly before informing him that yes, she did do in-home massage for a few of her clients, but only those who could provide a massage table and the other equipment she'd need.

"I don't own a car, you see," she'd explained, "and it isn't always possible for me to borrow one to get to appointments. And since it would be a little tricky to cart a table and my other equipment on the bus, the only way I can offer in-home services is if the client has all of that available."

He'd instantly asked her for a list of what she would need, and then hadn't wasted any time in ordering a top of the line table, sheets, heating pad, plus the various oils and creams she used. He had set everything up in the room he utilized as his home office, including a portable sound system, and had even downloaded a relaxation playlist to the iPod. Shy of painting the walls a more relaxing color, Matthew was pretty sure he had done all he could to replicate the room at the studio where he normally received his massages, and hoped that Sasha would approve.

It had become important to him over these past few weeks to gain her approval, and even more so to please her. The desire to make her happy had been the main reason why he'd been so quick to comply with all of her suggestions about his diet and health, and each time she had smiled approvingly at him Matthew had felt as though he was on top of the world. And he had been so grateful for all of her advice, for her kindness, and nurturing, that he had shown his appreciation in the only way he knew how - with money.

He had always been a generous tipper, even in the days when he'd had precious little money of his own. And since his fortunes had multiplied so significantly over this past decade, he hadn't hesitated to share his wealth with those less fortunate. Lindsey had always chided him about how much he would tip a waiter or a bellhop, or complain about the amount of money he insisted on donating to various charities. But he'd ignored her, going so far at times to remind her that it was *his* money after all, and he certainly gave her plenty of it to lavish on herself. Giving a hard working, low paid waitress a hefty tip would hardly make a dent in their finances.

Sasha had told him very little about herself, and then only because he'd asked her some very specific questions. He knew that she didn't own a car or a computer - the latter fact in particular having appalled him. She rented a single room in an old Victorian house in the city's Mission district, and seemed perfectly content with the simple lifestyle she'd adopted. She didn't wear any jewelry or makeup, left her nails unpolished, and dressed in either yoga apparel or on

116

occasion a long, floaty skirt and cotton tank top. It was fairly obvious to Matthew that she didn't have a lot of money, and his natural reaction had been to rather extravagantly over-tip her each time he'd had a massage. Since he left the money for her in an envelope with the front desk clerk after paying for the massage, he had never presented her with the tip personally. He suspected that if he had done so, however, that she would find some way of gently refusing it.

He wasn't sure why he was quite this anxious about her being at his condo this evening, but it had been practically all he'd been able to think about all day. After all, he scolded himself, it wasn't like a date or anything. Sasha was simply his masseuse, and to some extent his friend. At least, it pleased him to think of her that way, and hoped that she considered him as more than just a client.

And, if he was being completely honest with himself, he would have to admit that lately he was thinking about Sasha more and more, and in ways that had nothing to do with her being either his masseuse or his friend. He was attracted to her, very much so, both physically and emotionally. Each time she touched him, even when it was to work out a particularly nasty knot in his neck or upper back, he had to fight back the growing arousal he experienced in her presence. And it was downright impossible to suppress the erections that occurred almost automatically during the massage sessions. Sasha was still tactful enough not to mention his physical reactions, but Matthew knew damned well that she had noticed them each and every time. And later that day, in the privacy of his walk-in shower, he'd found himself jerking off each and every time, his eyes closed in ecstasy as he imagined it was Sasha's smooth, soft hand stroking his cock instead of his own.

He was drawn to her, he acknowledged now. Drawn to her kindness and compassion, and the way she expressed concern for his wellbeing. It had been a long, long time since anyone had gone out of their way to take care of him, to encourage him to think about himself, and to forget about the rest of the world for a little while. God knew that Lindsey was probably the least nurturing person in the world, and she had always assumed he would take care of everything when it came to the house and their finances and even the children. Hayley was unfortunately evolving into a mini-me of her mother, and was completely caught up in her own teenaged universe at the moment. Casey continued to be a great kid, the one person who made life worth living most days, but he wasn't even a teenager quite yet and couldn't be expected to shoulder too much responsibility at this point in his life. Elena looked out for him, of course, but Matthew was never quite sure if most of that was because she considered it the chief responsibility of her very well-paid job - and also because she was just bossy by nature. The rest of his staff - including managers, board members, and investors - were all quick to make multiple demands on his time, but rarely if ever asked if *he* needed anything.

He didn't think - or, more accurately, didn't *know* - if Sasha was attracted to him as well. He might have been forty years old, and married for nearly half that time, but he was admittedly still naïve when it came to the opposite sex. Of course, it had been a hell of a long time since he'd dated or even thought about another woman, and he had zero idea at the moment about the best way to pursue his attraction to Sasha. Nor did he have any friends he could consult, with the exception perhaps of Ian. But Ian seemed rather protective of Sasha, likely because of her close friendship with Tessa, and Matthew wasn't at all sure that he would approve of his interest in her.

As the day wore on, Matthew decided the best course of action would simply be to let things unfold naturally. Whether that resulted in things remaining status quo, or with him simply asking Sasha out for coffee or dinner, or wound up with the two of them in bed, he was content to let nature take its course.

Of course, he mused, it probably wouldn't hurt if he left the office a little early today just to make sure the condo was tidied up in anticipation of Sasha's arrival this evening. He'd make sure there was plenty of herbal tea on hand, maybe chill a bottle of wine, and have some fresh fruit available as well. As he jotted down a list, he wondered if buying a bouquet of flowers would be considered overkill.

chapter seven

Sᴀsʜᴀ ᴛʀɪᴇᴅ ʜᴇʀ ʙᴇsᴛ ɴᴏᴛ to feel intimidated upon entering the lobby of Matthew's condo building, telling herself that he was far from her only client who was wealthy and lived in luxurious accommodations. The Gregson's house, for example, was a veritable mansion, three stories high and surrounded by a security gate. But as lavish as Ian and Tessa's home was, it still felt warm and welcoming every time Sasha set foot inside the door, and she had never once felt out of place there. Unlike, for example, the way she was beginning to feel right now in this high-ceilinged, discreetly lit lobby with its white marble floors and walls, and the dark-haired, bespectacled concierge who was regarding her suspiciously from behind his desk.

"May I help you, madam?" he inquired in a snooty voice, the accent sounding vaguely British or perhaps Australian.

"Yes, please," replied Sasha in the sort of soothing tone she used to calm particularly stressed out clients. "I'm here to see Mr. Bennett. Can you please let him know that Ms. Fonseca has arrived?"

The concierge gave her a look of disbelief, as though he couldn't comprehend why this woman who resembled a gypsy was asking to see the building's wealthiest resident. Sasha sighed, wondering if she should have taken Chad's fashion advice after all and worn something besides the batik printed peasant skirt and hip length cotton sweater that she'd selected. Trouble was, she thought, that this was actually one of the nicer outfits in her limited wardrobe. And Sasha highly doubted that any of her clothing would have met with the approval of the uptight young man who was still regarding her warily. Now *here*, she thought rather meanly, was someone who was in dire need of a relaxing massage, and whose jaw muscles probably ached constantly from maintaining that stiff upper-lipped expression of disapproval.

"I'll inform Mr. Bennett of your arrival," he informed her disdainfully. "Please have a seat."

He motioned to a trio of plush white leather sofas that had been arranged around a low, glass-topped table. Sasha hid a smile as she took a seat, thinking that the concierge was probably afraid she'd dirty something. With a rare display of devilry, she plunked her oversized brown and gold brocade shoulder bag on top of the table, watching with ill disguised glee as the concierge was unable to hide his horror. She briefly considered stretching her legs out and resting her espadrille shod feet on the table, but too many years of being forced to abide by her mother's rules about ladylike behavior stopped her just in time.

As she waited to be granted admittance to Matthew's condo, Sasha fretted yet again about whether this had been a wise decision or not. There had really only been a couple of occasions in the past when male clients had tried to cross a line with her or outright proposition her, and neither of those times had occurred during an in-home appointment. But she had always been very attuned to things like emotions and feelings, and had even attended a few workshops and read several books about reading the auras of others. It was how she'd known that Julia's unborn twins were going to be boys, and how she'd sensed from the first moment after meeting Matthew at the Gregsons' wedding last June that he was unhappy.

And now, after having had several massage sessions with Matthew, she was quite sure that he was attracted to her, both physically and emotionally. Small wonder, she supposed, given the fact that he'd been living apart from his wife and children for months and was obviously lonely. Sasha was used to her clients confiding in her about a wide variety of things during their massages - not unlike what you'd tell your hairdresser or manicurist, Julia had joked once. And Matthew had been no exception, freely expressing his frustrations about work and family during their sessions.

But he had also made it a point to ask her personal questions, to engage her in conversation, and at times it almost felt to Sasha that he was flirting with her just a little. Not that she was an expert on that sort of thing, however, but enough men had tried to hit on her during her twenty-eight years that she could recognize the signs. And while Matthew himself seemed more than a little awkward and definitely out of practice, she was pretty sure that he'd begun to lay the groundwork for putting the moves on her. And it was that particular realization that made her wonder for perhaps the tenth time since agreeing to this in-home appointment if her being here this evening was the right thing to do. In fact, maybe she should just tell Matthew she wasn't feeling well and that they needed to re-schedule. She could ask the concierge to -

"Sasha. It's so great to see you. I really, really appreciate your agreeing to come over here this evening."

She glanced up to find Matthew smiling down at her, and looking far more casual and relaxed than she was used to seeing him. Instead of his usual suit and tie he was wearing jeans and a plain gray T-shirt, with a pair of Adidas trainers on his feet.

Sasha took the hand he extended towards her as he helped her to stand. "It's no problem at all," she assured him, even though she felt less than confident in her own words. "I understand how busy you are, that you can't always make it into the studio."

He kept a hand on her elbow as they began to walk towards the elevators, but paused as they reached the concierge desk. The dark-haired man who'd been so snooty towards Sasha was all smiles now as Matthew approached.

"Yes, Mr. Bennett. What can I do for you this evening?" he practically cooed.

Matthew's gaze narrowed, and he did not return the concierge's smile. "When Ms. Fonseca visits again in the future, you're to allow her right up. No need to call and get my approval next time. And if you could please let Xavier and the rest of the concierge staff know, I'd appreciate it. Thank you, Gareth."

Gareth looked visibly stunned at this instruction, but was evidently too well-trained and well-mannered to offer up any sort of protest. Instead, he merely stammered, "Of - of course, Mr. Bennett. I'll make a note of it immediately. And please let me know if there's ever anything I can do to offer assistance when you visit, Ms. Fonseca. The concierge staff prides itself on taking very good care of our residents and their guests."

Sasha didn't really have it in her to be mean or catty to anyone, and the smile she offered Gareth was sincere. "I appreciate that, Gareth."

"Let's head upstairs," urged Matthew as he steered her towards the elevator. He took a key card out of his back pocket and inserted it into a slot at the top of the panel of floor buttons.

At Sasha's quizzical look, he grinned a bit sheepishly and put the card back in his pocket.

"I've got one of the penthouse units," he explained. "The elevator only stops at that floor if you use this access card. Not really my idea to buy such a big place, by the way. When my board of directors suggested the company acquire a condo near the office to use for visitors, I envisioned something a little more on the compact side. But it was definitely convenient to have this place available when I filed for divorce, even if it's not exactly my style. Ah, here we are."

The sleek, ultra-modern elevator had zoomed up thirty-six floors in what felt like a matter of seconds, and Sasha was glad that she didn't suffer from either motion sickness or fear of heights. Still cupping her elbow in his hand, Matthew ushered her to the right at they exited the elevator.

"There are only four penthouse units in the entire building," he explained as he opened a set of wide double doors. "Two on each of the top floors. I've got a view of the bay from mine, while the other has a city view."

And what a view it was, thought Sasha in awe as she walked

slowly inside the spacious, light-filled condo. She ignored the polished wood floors, sleek cream and gray furnishings, and the various paintings and sculptures that hung from the walls or rested on tabletops as she glided over to the closest window. The sun was just beginning to set on this balmy October evening, and the view of San Francisco Bay was indeed breathtaking. She stared out at the cityscape in awe, mesmerized by how tiny everything looked from this height, and enchanted by so many bright lights. She was sorely tempted to fling open the door that led out to a spacious balcony in order to get an even closer view, but somewhat belatedly recalled why she was really here this evening.

"Sorry," she apologized as Matthew appeared at her side. "I didn't mean to space out that way. But this view is really spectacular. I can understand why your company wanted this particular unit."

He nodded. "It's a pretty special place, that's for sure. And surprisingly quiet given the location. There's another balcony that you access through the master bedroom, and that one is even more private. I've, uh, got all the equipment set up in my home office, though. Would you - should we go take a look?"

"Yes, of course."

En route, Matthew gave her a quick tour of the spacious condo, which consisted of a living room, dining room, enormous eat-in kitchen, a family room, home office, three bedrooms, and three and a half baths. The décor throughout the unit was sleek, cool, and modern, not at all what Sasha normally liked, but even so she could appreciate the clean, simple lines of the furniture, and admired the pieces of modern art that had been hung at strategic locations.

"Here we are. I hope I got everything you'll need. And that all of it's okay."

Matthew sounded so anxious, almost apprehensive, that she gave him a reassuring smile even before entering the room he used for his office. But upon seeing the top of the line massage table that had been set up in the middle of the room, Sasha couldn't stop herself from gasping in surprise.

"Wow." She ran a hand almost reverently over the sturdy oak frame, and the exquisitely soft sheets that covered the thick table pads. "You might have gone a little overboard here, Matthew. The tables we have at the studio aren't half this nice. Same with the sheets."

"That's just part of it. Look."

He hurried to show her the rest - the half-dozen Jo Malone bergamot scented candles that he began to light; the tray of assorted massage creams, oils, and ointments; the iPod in its docking station that began to play some soft, relaxing music at the touch of a button. The room was lit only by a fabric covered floor lamp in one corner, but the lights from the city, not to mention the magnificent blaze of the sunset, nearly flooded the room with brightness.

She was deeply touched that he had gone to so much trouble, far more so than any of her other clients had ever done, and she knew without having to ask that he had ordered all of this himself, hadn't delegated the task to his assistant or another staff member.

"It's lovely. Just lovely," she told him earnestly, placing a hand lightly on his forearm. "Thank you for arranging for all of this so quickly, Matthew. But these weren't on the list I gave you."

Sasha took a deep, appreciative sniff of the lavish bouquet of autumn flowers that had been expertly arranged in a hammered bronze bowl - tiger lilies, chrysanthemums, daisies, roses, all in shades of bronze and gold and burgundy.

"No." He looked down at his feet a bit uncertainly. "Those - those are just for you. As a way to thank you for coming here this evening. I hope I'm not keeping you from something important, that you didn't have to cancel plans or re-schedule something."

"I didn't," she told him gently. "And there's no place I'd rather be this evening than right here in this beautiful room with the amazing view and gorgeous flowers and my favorite client. Speaking of which, I'll leave you to get ready, hmm? I need to wash my hands. I'll just use the bathroom we passed out in the hall, if that's all right."

Matthew's eyes had widened when she'd referred to him as her favorite client, and the smile that lit up his face made something in her tummy begin to flutter with - what? Nerves? Anticipation? Desire? Or maybe a little bit of each. Sasha beat a hasty retreat, closing the door after her, as she struggled to bring her wayward emotions under control.

'You've got to remember that he's just a client,' she told herself sternly as she washed her hands in the elegantly appointed bathroom. She was pretty sure the bathroom was larger than the bedroom she occupied at Chad and Julio's. 'A really good looking, and really sweet one, but a client just the same. Act like a professional, Sasha. And no more giving him compliments, understand? The poor man obviously needs a boost to his ego, but that's really not your responsibility, is it?'

She took a minute or two to run through a few deep breathing exercises of her own, something she often did when she needed to focus for an extended period of time. When she knocked on the bedroom door a moment later, Sasha felt much more in control of herself, with renewed determination to keep this evening's session strictly professional.

But as the next hour progressed, she found it increasingly more difficult to remind herself that Matthew was simply her client - not her boyfriend and definitely not her lover. He seemed to be extra responsive this evening, groaning and grunting a bit louder than usual when she found a sore spot or dug a little deeper into a knotted muscle. Or moaning in pleasure when she soothed away the tension he always seemed to hold in his neck and upper back.

Maybe it was the fact that they were all alone up here in his penthouse condo instead of back at the yoga studio, where there were always other people close by. Or it could have been the sensuous, musky scent of the candles as they continued to burn, combined with the hypnotic strains of the violin piece that was currently playing on the iPod. All of those factors combined to make Sasha hyper-aware of the smooth, leanly muscled masculine flesh beneath her hands, and of the clean, fresh scent of his skin, as though he'd showered just before her arrival this evening. Several times during the massage she had to pause and take a few more of those deep, calming breaths, feeling the need to continually re-focus her energy and attention on what she was doing.

She was also reminded - reluctantly so - of exactly how long it had been since *she'd* had sex. Long months, maybe closer to a year, she figured, and gave her head a little shake in bemusement. She had never been one to sleep around, or feel that she desperately needed a man in her life. Too many years spent watching one or the other of her parents with their current paramour had turned her off the concept of casual, meaningless sex. And while she had never actually been in a long-term, committed relationship, at the same time she had always *liked* the men she'd slept with, had had something in common with them, and for the most part had remained friends with them after the physical part of the relationship had fizzled out.

Her aunt Linda had been accurate in her description of Sasha during their most recent visit. Sasha was very much a creature of sensation and emotion, had always been comfortable in her body, and while her attitude about sex was nowhere near as carefree and relaxed as that of her parents', she was honest enough to admit that she liked sex, enjoyed being intimate with a man, and had missed sharing a bed with one.

Which was very likely why she was becoming increasingly aroused with each passing minute, why her hands seemed to linger as if with a will of their own on Matthew's lower back, his biceps, his calves. It was true that he wasn't as muscular as Tessa's husband - Matthew was a few inches shorter, about twenty five pounds lighter, and built along leaner lines than Ian, who had the powerful physique of a professional bodybuilder. But Sasha had never been attracted to imposingly muscular men, had always felt a little intimidated in their presence, perhaps because she herself was of only medium height and a slight build. Matthew's form, on the other hand, reminded her of an athlete's - similar to a triathlete who'd been a client of hers once, or a swimmer she'd worked with a few times.

"Time to turn over," she murmured softly, as she placed a hand gently on his shoulder.

She kept her eyes averted as he slowly shifted onto his back, focusing her attention on rearranging the top sheet so that his lower body remained covered at all times. But once Matthew had settled himself, she couldn't help from sneaking a quick, furtive peek, and had to bite her bottom lip to stifle a gasp at the sight of his impressive erection tenting the sheet. And then, for some unknown reason, instead of glancing away again she found herself meeting his very intense, very hot gaze.

This time Sasha wasn't able to suppress her gasp of mingled surprise and alarm when Matthew grasped her wrist and pulled her close enough that her hip collided with the massage table. Her eyes widened in shock as he swung his legs over the side of the table, shoving the covers off of his body at the same time – his very naked and very, very aroused body.

She tried to pull her wrist out of his grasp, while at the same time finding it impossible to tear her eyes away from his proudly erect penis. "Matthew, what are you - this can't be happening. I - "

"Please." The single word escaped his lips in a husky whisper. "God, it's been such a long time, Sasha. I've wanted this, wanted you, since the first time I felt your hands on me. And I'm not talking about the first time you gave me a massage. I meant when you and I danced together at Ian and Tessa's wedding back in June. I thought then that you were the loveliest woman I'd ever met, and even though I was still a married man I knew I wanted you. So, please. Don't deny me. You have no idea how much I need this."

Sasha nearly recoiled in shock as he brought her hand to his cock, and especially when she felt how hard he was, how his hot flesh was pulsing beneath her fingers. "We can't do this," she whispered urgently, even as she began to stroke his cock with long, slow strokes. "I mean, you're my client, and this is really crossing a line."

He groaned his pleasure as her hand continued to pump his cock, his breathing becoming uneven. "If - if that's the only issue," he panted, "then consider yourself fired."

Before she could think up a retort, he'd literally scooped her up onto his lap, then threaded a hand into her curls to hold her head still. In the next second his mouth was on hers, kissing her like a starving man, and with a sigh of surrender she began to kiss him back.

Matthew's kisses were rough, a little clumsy even, and completely lacking in any sort of finesse, but none of that mattered to Sasha. She could sense his overwhelming need for her, for this sort of physical closeness and connection that he'd been missing, and she willingly gave herself over to him. She ran her palms over his bare chest and upper back, caressingly this time instead of in her usual clinical manner, and could clearly feel the press of his erection against her backside.

And then Matthew proved just how strong and fit he really was by lifting her into his arms and carrying her to the other side of the condo into his bedroom, their lips still tightly

131

fused in one hungry kiss after the other. He'd left a lamp on, bathing the room in a soft golden glow, and carefully set her on her feet by the side of the king-sized platform bed.

"Can - can I undress you?" he murmured hesitantly. "Or, um, would you rather do it yourself?"

She smiled at him, finding his uncertainty and fumbling incredibly endearing, even arousing, and cupped his cheek tenderly. "I'd like you to do it. Please."

Matthew hands were visibly shaking as he grasped the hem of her lightweight sweater and began to pull it up over her head. He stared for long seconds at the sight of her torso clad only in a cream lace bra before his palms skimmed lightly up the sides of her ribcage. Clumsily, he unhooked the bra, baring her small, firm breasts.

"You're so beautiful," he marveled as he cupped her breasts reverently. "So perfect."

When he'd fumbled three times with the hook and zipper of her skirt, Sasha took pity on him and unfastened it herself, letting the garment drop soundlessly to the floor. She'd removed her shoes upon entering the condo, since she always preferred to be barefoot, and was now clothed in just a skimpy pair of panties that matched the bra. Matthew's hot gaze burned a path down her belly and hips all the way to her toes.

Then he shocked her again by dropping to his knees in front of her, practically tearing the fragile scrap of lace from her body before burying his face between her legs. Sasha cried out in surprise as he nuzzled his nose against the damp golden brown curls there, her hands tangling in his hair as she bucked her pelvis up against his mouth.

"I love that you left this natural," he rasped, his thumb brushing softly through her pubic hair. "And I love how good you smell. And especially how good you taste."

"Ohhh."

Her head fell back in rapture as his tongue flicked briefly over her clitoris before plunging deep inside her wet slit. It didn't matter to her in the least that he seemed as lacking in finesse with oral sex as he did with French kissing, and she thought somewhat incoherently that she liked his overeager attempts to give her pleasure, that she preferred his wildness and lack of control over what a more practiced lover might have done. Especially when he added his fingers to the mix, and the result was a really fantastic orgasm, one of the best she'd ever had.

Matthew was staring up at her, as though unable to believe he'd brought her to climax quite that easily. "Did you - I mean, was that real? Did I really - "

Sasha laughed huskily, running a finger over his lips that were shiny with her juices. "Uh, huh. You sure did. And it was amazing. Really, really amazing."

He looked both dazed and joyous at the same time, and didn't resist as she pulled back the duvet and then tugged him onto the bed with her.

"Your turn now," she whispered, just before sliding down his body sinuously and taking his throbbing cock into her mouth with one motion.

"Ah, fuck!" he cried, his lower body bucking up off the mattress as she took long, slow pulls of his penis with her lips, taking him as deep inside of her mouth as she could manage.

Sasha knew he wouldn't last long this first time, not when he was so obviously aroused and needy, and when he likely hadn't had sex in months. He began to move in sync with the pull of her mouth, thrusting his hips eagerly as she focused on intensifying his pleasure.

She slid a hand back to very gently squeeze his balls, and that was all he needed to come, spilling himself uncontrollably inside her eager, welcoming mouth. Matthew emitted a long, drawn out groan, his body shuddering in release, and then flopped back weakly against the mattress.

Sasha curled up against his side, her fingers tracing a delicate pattern over his bare chest and abs, her lips pressed against his shoulder as his breathing slowly returned to normal. He took her hand in his, then brought it to his lips.

"That was - unbelievable," he told her hoarsely, and she was startled to glimpse a sheen of tears in his eyes. "If I told you how long it's been since I've felt that good, you probably wouldn't believe it. In fact, I'm pretty sure I've *never* felt that good. Thank you, Sasha."

"Shh." She placed a finger over his lips. "Silly man. Don't ever thank me for something like that. Especially when you were enough of a gentleman to take care of me first."

He grinned. "Yeah, but that was really for me, too. You've got such a beautiful body, Sasha. I just couldn't help myself."

She laughed softly before snuggling up against his body, pulling his arm a little tighter around her shoulders. "I'm not sure anyone has ever had that sort of instant reaction around me before. But thank you, Matthew. Both for the compliment and the orgasm." Her voice turned sober as she asked him quietly, "How long had it been for you?"

134

"Since I had sex?" he asked, with a half-smile. "Or since I had a blow job? The answer to the first part is several months, certainly awhile before I filed for divorce. As for the latter - well, years is the answer. I'd have to do some real thinking before I could remember exactly how many."

Sasha frowned, interlacing her fingers with his. "Didn't your wife like oral sex? I mean, I know it's not for everyone."

Matthew gave a short, sardonic laugh. "Oh, I'm sure she likes it well enough. Just not necessarily with me. In fact, the straw that broke the camel's back in terms of my filing for divorce was when I wandered in on her with another guy."

She gasped in dismay. "Oh, God, Matthew. I'm so sorry. I had no idea. You've never talked about what specifically broke the two of you up. It must have been so upsetting for you to discover she was having an affair."

He shook his head. "Not by that point, no. Lindsey - well, she's been having a series of little flings for some time now, going back more than a couple of years. When I first figured it out, I was upset, wanted nothing more than to confront her and demand it stop. But I blamed myself, you see. Because I was working so many hours, was away from home so often, I rationalized it away as her being lonely and feeling neglected."

"No." Sasha was emphatic in her denial. "That's not an excuse, not even a little. She should have talked to you, worked things out, instead of setting out to hurt you."

Matthew cupped her cheek tenderly. "I should have expected a reaction like that from you. But not everyone is as kind as you are, Sasha. Or as considerate of someone's feelings. And that turned out to be just the beginning of

Lindsey's serial cheating. I put a private detective on her, pretty much knew every move she made for over a year. But I never confronted her about it, never let on that I so much as suspected. Part of that was because I didn't want a showdown, didn't want to have my kids hurt by the fallout. But over time I came to realize that it was also because I'd stopped caring about her. Or about our marriage. I just lacked the motivation to do anything about it. Until I walked inside this very room and literally caught her in the act."

"Here? It was in this room that you saw her?" asked Sasha, not bothering to hide her revolt.

"Yup. But don't worry. One of the first things I did after kicking her out and calling my lawyer was to replace the bed, and every piece of bedding. The only person who's ever slept on this mattress or these sheets has been me. At least until now."

"That was a smart move on your part," she agreed. "Though I'm guessing getting rid of the bed was a lot easier than wiping out the bad memories you must have associated with this room."

Matthew startled her anew by swiftly rolling her under his body, his leanly muscled thighs straddling her hips. "Well, if you're willing, I can think of at least one way to wipe out the bad memories. And replace them with some very, very good ones."

"Mmm."

Sasha wound her arms around his neck as he claimed her lips in a deep, searching kiss, their tongues tangling almost frantically. His hands roamed over her nude body, touching her everywhere - squeezing her breasts, skimming over her hips, cupping her ass. He drew a long, low moan from her lips as he thrust two long fingers deep inside her vagina, where she was still wet from her previous climax.

"I want you again," he rasped against her ear.

She reached down between their bodies and grasped his fully erect cock, stroking him persuasively. "Yes," she whispered. "Make love to me, Matthew."

He was almost comically uncoordinated as he fumbled inside a nightstand drawer for a condom, and then cursed vividly when he had trouble tearing it open. Calmly, Sasha extracted the packet from his fingers and opened it easily, then just as smoothly rolled the latex over his penis.

"Thanks," he mumbled, looking more than a little embarrassed. "Guess I'm a little out of practice."

She shook her head, brushing a stray lock of hair from his forehead that was beaded with sweat. "My hands are just smaller, that's all," she soothed. "And it's been quite awhile for me, too, by the way."

Matthew looked like he was ready to debate that point, at least until Sasha positioned the tip of his cock between her thighs, and he quickly seemed to forget about anything else except burying himself as deeply inside of her as possible.

"Ah, God, you feel so good," he rasped, burying his face against the side of her neck, his tongue tracing the small shell of her earlobe. His thrusts were slow and controlled, but she could tell by the tightly bunched muscles of his biceps that he was deliberately holding back. "It's been so long since anything felt this good."

She wrapped her legs around his waist, then cupped his cheeks between her hands and kissed him with mingled

137

tenderness and passion. "It's the same for me," she whispered. "Don't hold back, Matthew. Let yourself enjoy this."

He groaned, shutting his eyes tightly, and gritting his teeth. "I don't want this to end," he protested weakly. "I'm half-afraid that if I let myself go it will all be over with too soon. And that nothing will ever feel this good again."

Her hands slid to the tight curves of his ass, her nails digging slightly into the flesh as she silently urged him to go faster. "It will always feel this good," she told him fiercely. "And I'll be here for as long as you want me. So don't be afraid of anything when we're together. And don't ever, ever hold back."

Her words acted like a sort of trigger for Matthew, causing the very last of his self-control to snap, and then he was like a madman, pounding into her welcoming body as though he was starved for affection, for intimacy. Sasha bit down on his shoulder to stifle a tiny cry of alarm as the sex quickly became wild, almost savage, and more than a little dirty. He was alternately groaning and grunting, cursing and then calling out her name, and the whole time he kept increasing the rapidity and force of his thrusts, until she was very nearly seeing stars each time the broad head of his cock rammed against the tip of her cervix.

It wasn't always easy for Sasha to orgasm vaginally, and she typically needed to have her clit stimulated at the same time before she could climax. But as the wild, frantic fucking continued, she felt the orgasm approaching, her hands by now clutching fistfuls of the bedsheets for leverage, as Matthew had most definitely stopped holding back and was taking her on the ride of her life.

When it hit, the orgasm stunned her, causing her mouth to fall open in a wide "O", and the tight walls of her vagina to convulse around his cock. Mere seconds later, he was following her over, shouting out incoherent phrases, his body shaking uncontrollably as he found his release.

They both remained motionless for several minutes, their sweat-slicked bodies still joined together, as their breathing gradually returned to normal. Sasha was more than content to remain exactly that way, not speaking or moving, simply reveling in the sensations that were still humming through her body. But at Matthew's next hoarsely murmured words, she rose up on an elbow to gaze at him tenderly.

"That," he began haltingly, "was absolutely the most incredible experience of my life. And I - well, not surprisingly I haven't felt like much of a man these past couple of years, ever since I discovered that my wife was so dissatisfied with me as a husband and a lover that she had to try for the world record in bed hopping. You - well, let's just say that I've never felt as much like a man as I do right now. Thank you for giving me that, Sasha. For giving me my dignity back. Not to mention the best orgasm I've ever had."

She felt tears begin to well in her eyes at the heartfelt sadness and honesty of his words, and gave a small shake of her head. "Same here," she replied softly. "You're a wonderful lover, Matthew, in spite of any doubts your wife might have given you. You're passionate and uninhibited and giving. And you've pleased me very, very well. So don't ever think less of yourself as a man ever again, because you're the best man I've ever met."

He pulled her into his arms fiercely, as though afraid she'd slip away if he didn't hold on tight. "You know," he admitted in a sheepish voice, "when Tessa first encouraged me to set up a massage appointment with you, she said that you would be good for me in more ways than one. I'm not sure if this was exactly what she had in mind when she said that, but she was definitely right."

Sasha laughed softly. "Tessa is very much a romantic. And I think since she's living her very own fairytale these days with Ian, she wishes everyone could be as happy as the two of them are. But I'm glad that I've been able to help you, Matthew. Because like I told you at the wedding back in June, you're much too kind of a man to ever be unhappy."

"Speaking of making me happy." He brought one of her hands to his lips, pressing a kiss to the palm. "It would make me very, very happy if you'd agree to spend the night. I'll drive you home in the morning, whatever time you might need to be somewhere."

She hesitated. "I don't teach class until late afternoon, but I do have an early massage appointment scheduled at the studio. But I don't know, Matthew. Sleepovers aren't usually my thing."

"Please?" He pretended to beg, giving her his best puppy dog eyes, until she couldn't help herself from laughing.

"It depends," she teased. "I can't start the day without a cup of herbal tea, so if you don't have any on hand, the deal is off."

Matthew grinned enthusiastically. "I've got about a dozen different varieties, actually. They're, uh, for you. Not that I expected this to happen," he explained anxiously. "I just thought you might have wanted a cup after the massage."

"That was really sweet of you," she assured him, cupping his cheek in her hand. "And speaking of the massage, we need to talk about that for a minute. Given what just happened here, there's no possible way we can continue to have both a professional and a personal relationship. That is, assuming you want to continue to have a personal relationship with me."

"God, yes!" he was quick to exclaim. "I mean, you aren't seeing anyone else at the moment, are you?"

"No." She hesitated a moment before explaining, "I don't really do relationships per se, I'm not sure I really know how to. But I do like you, Matthew. A lot. And I like the idea of spending time with you, getting to know you better. I have no idea how long it will last, or where it's going to go, but I'm open to figuring that out. However," she added a bit sternly, "I can't continue to have you as a client and a lover at the same time. So this is how it's going to go. One, I either refer you to another massage therapist - and I know several who'd do a great job for you. Or, two, I can continue to do your massages but only here in your home. And without any sort of payment. There's no possible way I can ever take money from you again. Including tonight's appointment."

Matthew frowned. "But that hardly seems fair. I mean, you'd be out the income for that ninety minutes you'd be spending on me each time."

She shrugged. "I can afford it. Otherwise, if it bothers you that much, you can use another masseuse."

"No." He shook his head. "You're by far the best masseuse I've ever had. I don't want anyone else. So, fine. We'll do it your way." He waggled his eyebrows at her lasciviously. "I'll

141

just have to think of some inventive ways of paying you back. Now, what's your decision about spending the night? Yes or no?"

Sasha glanced at the huge, king-sized bed and the ultra-lux Egyptian cotton sheets longingly. Her own, much smaller bed back in her room was nowhere near as comfortable, and much lonelier to boot. But it had been a long time since she'd spent the entire night with a man, and her long-honed tendencies to shy away from commitment were tough to break.

"I don't know, Matthew," she fretted. "It might be a little too soon for that. Everything is happening so fast."

But he was evidently too stubborn to give up without a fight. He took her by the hand and urged her along with him until they were standing in the doorway of his en-suite bathroom.

"Remember you told me that I should buy those bath salts? The ones you swore would relieve my stress?" he inquired.

Sasha nodded. "The ones with lavender and clary sage? What about them?"

He pressed a switch, turning on the muted overhead lighting. "What say we try them out?"

She gasped audibly at her first sight of the enormous whirlpool bathtub, more than large enough for two people, and so tempting that she heaved a little sigh of surrender, giving him a mock glare.

"You can play dirty at times, can't you?" she scolded. "You knew somehow that I wouldn't be able to resist the thought of soaking in this tub. Fine. You win. I'll stay the night. Though I might fall asleep in that tub."

Matthew came up behind her, wrapping his arms around her waist as he nuzzled the side of her neck. "You can sleep wherever you like," he murmured seductively. "Just as long as it's next to me."

chapter eight

Early November

MATTHEW RESISTED THE URGE TO run his hand along the gentle curve of Sasha's bare hip as she continued to doze lightly. In the month since they'd become lovers, he had yet to stop marveling at the perfection of her lithe, graceful body. He loved the smoothness of her pale gold skin, the concave tautness of her belly, the lean muscles of her arms and legs. She was strong and toned and extremely fit, and she'd come by all of that without ever having lifted a single weight or using any cardio equipment at a gym.

He had watched her go through her yoga practice a few times, having moved several pieces of furniture aside in his seldom used living room so that she would have enough space, and had been in awe at just how flexible and skilled she was. Just the other night, in fact, he'd stared in disbelief as she had executed a series of poses that he would have sworn only a performer from Cirque du Soleil would have been capable of doing - like kicking up smoothly into a handstand, then bending her legs over her head until her toes touched her forehead into a pose she'd called Scorpion. She'd finished the sequence by lowering her feet all the way to the floor into a backbend. And that had been just one of the mind boggling poses she'd twisted, bended, and otherwise contorted her limber, toned body into over the course of an hour or so. It had also been very obvious during her practice that she was a trained dancer, her movements so graceful and in sync with the accompanying music that he had felt he was watching a dance performance of some sort.

Naturally, he'd quickly grown aroused watching her, especially considering how closely her yoga pants and tank top clung to her curves. It didn't matter in the slightest to Matthew that her breasts were on the small side, especially since they were perfectly shaped and very firm. He found them far sexier than the ridiculously large implants that Lindsey strutted around with.

In general, he considered Sasha a much sexier, and far more sensual woman, than his soon to be ex-wife could ever aspire to be. Despite the fact that she didn't wear makeup or paint her nails and was more often than not barefoot, Sasha's sensuality couldn't be denied, and was simply a part of who she was. She was earthy and natural and entirely comfortable in her skin, and he'd never met anyone who turned him on the way she did.

Matthew glanced at the digital bedside clock and sighed. It was Saturday morning, and Sasha would need to be at the yoga studio sooner than later. Fortunately, the class she taught today didn't begin until eleven a.m., a full two hours later than tomorrow's start time, but she also had three massage appointments scheduled this afternoon. Syncing their schedules had been a little frustrating for him, especially on weekends like this one when he didn't have Hayley and Casey. He didn't get to see nearly as much of Sasha as he would have liked, given his own packed schedule at work,

145

but recognized that it would hardly be fair to expect her to cancel client appointments simply to accommodate him.

And she remained steadfast in her resolve not to accept a penny from him for the massages she gave him on a weekly basis. He felt badly that she was losing potential income from the times she devoted to him, but that didn't seem to bother Sasha. He'd never come right out and asked her how much money she made, or if she had any savings. They hadn't been together nearly long enough for her to confide such things in him, and he already knew how fiercely she cherished her independence and self-reliance.

And she had no idea, none at all, about just how much he was worth. She had asked him about his work and the company, and confessed that she knew practically nothing about computers or electronics in general. She'd seemed a little taken aback to learn that he owned four cars, each one a top of the line luxury model. He had taken her out to dinner several times, though the fact that she was a vegetarian had limited some of his choices in restaurants, further complicated by the fact that she had seemed a bit uncomfortable at a couple of the fancier places he'd chosen.

But Matthew knew instinctively that even if he told her exactly how much money he had, down to the last penny, that her attitude towards him wouldn't change a lick. She would still be the same easygoing, down to earth woman that she always was, the sort who would never ask him for a thing, or expect anything from him. It seemed that all she really wanted was to enjoy the times they spent together, whether that was watching a movie, going for a long walk, or making love.

And the sex had been truly amazing between them, certainly the best he'd ever known. Sasha was a quiet lover, not feeling the need to talk very much during their lovemaking, but she was adept all the same at communicating her feelings - with a caress, a kiss, a low moan of pleasure. He knew without having to ask that he pleased her, and that she enjoyed their encounters every bit as much as he did. And she had made him feel good about himself again, had given his male ego a much needed boost after it had taken a severe beating after Lindsey's complete disregard for his feelings. Matthew felt much more confident about himself as a lover, even after a scant month with Sasha, and found that she'd awakened a passion within himself that he would have never suspected he possessed.

His stress level continued to dissipate as well, and with the subtle changes he was still making to his diet, he felt healthier and more vital than he had in years. Sasha had shown him how to make green smoothies, and he drank one nearly every day now before leaving for work. Elena had given him a skeptical look when he'd asked her to stop bringing him breakfast pastries or bagels in the morning, requesting yogurt parfaits or protein bars instead. He'd cut his coffee intake - which had begun approaching the eight cup a day tally - to no more than two cups, and drank green tea most of the time. And he found himself ordering vegetarian entrees more and more frequently when he ate out with Sasha - not because she encouraged him to do so, but because whatever she selected always seemed to look more appetizing than the meat or chicken he would have normally chosen.

Being with her simply made him happy, he realized, as he gave in to temptation and ran a finger down the curve of her hip and thigh, smiling as she wiggled her bottom slightly in protest. She never fussed or complained, never demanded anything from him or argued, and was always understanding and supportive if he had to cancel a date or was running an hour late. Unlike Lindsey, he thought with a scowl, who would have a fit if he had to back out of a party she wanted to attend at the neighbors, or if he was more than five minutes late meeting her for lunch.

Sasha's cell phone pinged from where she'd left it on the nightstand with an incoming voice mail. Matthew, who made it a point to always own the very latest, most high tech models of cell phones, tablets, and computers, had been visibly appalled at how outdated and simplistic her phone was. She'd shrugged it off, admitting that she rarely used the phone and barely knew how to send a text message. And then she had really shocked him with the fact that she didn't own a computer of her own, just borrowed one of her roommates' from time to time to download music tracks that she used for her yoga classes.

"You do understand what it is I do for a living, right?" he'd asked incredulously. "And that I have four - no, make that five - computers just here at the condo? I used to build computers from scratch when I was in high school. So my life has basically revolved around them for more than twenty years, and my business is completely dependent on them. I guess given all of that it's tough for me to understand that not only don't you have one of your

148

own, but don't seem to care very much about having one, either."

Sasha had given a little shrug. "Not really, no. I've already told you that I prefer to read a book or listen to music as opposed to using a computer or watching TV. But I realize that computers are very important to you, to your business, so it doesn't bother me in the least if you use yours when we're together. Correction - if you use one of the five you apparently own."

She had laughed when he'd threatened to not only upgrade her phone but to give her one of his laptops as well, probably figuring that he was just joking. But Matthew was completely serious about the matter, and planned to do something about the situation sooner than later.

Sasha began to stir and stretch, having been woken either by his teasing caresses or the sound of her phone pinging. She opened her eyes and smiled up at him drowsily, pulling his head down to hers for a lazy good morning kiss.

"Mmm, what time is it?" she drawled sleepily, stretching her arms and legs in opposite directions, completely unselfconscious of her nudity.

"Around eight-thirty," he told her, bending to nuzzle the side of her neck. "You've still got plenty of time before you need to be at the studio."

She made a sound that was half-groan, half-chuckle. "Except that on Saturdays I usually spend a couple of hours before class starts doing my own practice. Guess I'll be giving that a miss today."

"I'm sorry," he replied somewhat guiltily. "I should have

149

set an alarm for you. But we, uh, were up pretty late last night so I figured you needed your rest."

"It's fine," assured Sasha, cupping his stubbled cheek in one hand. "It won't kill me to miss a day once in awhile. And it did feel nice to sleep in for once. Did I hear my phone buzz or was that a dream?"

Matthew shook his head and handed her the phone. "A call just came in a couple of minutes ago."

She propped herself up against the pillows, seeming not to notice when his gaze dropped automatically to the proud thrust of her breasts, and sighed anew when she checked her messages. "My mother, of course. And given that she's calling this early must mean she's wound up about something."

He dropped a kiss on the top of her curly head. "Tell you what. I'll go fix you a cup of tea while you call her back. Should I bring you a protein bar, or just some fruit?"

Sasha beamed at him, her green-gold eyes shining. "Hey, aren't you the CEO of some multi-billion dollar company? You're not supposed to be waiting on me. In fact, I've always wondered why you didn't have live-in help, someone who's always ready to wait on you at the drop of a hat."

Matthew rolled his eyes. "Please. I might be rich but I've never been pretentious. Plus, I like my privacy so no live-in help ever. I'll go get your tea. And since you couldn't decide, I'll bring you a bar *and* a bowl of fruit."

She blew him a kiss and then frowned as she began to call her mother back. When he returned a few minutes later, she was speaking in rapid, fluent Russian, and looking more than a little irritated - something he'd never seen her do before.

Sasha took the steaming mug of tea from him with a grateful smile, and then took a deep, appreciative sip of her favorite herbal brew. Matthew could hear her mother speaking quite clearly on the other end of the line, and without having any clue what the woman was saying, he winced at the mere sound of her angry, increasingly loud voice.

Sasha merely gave a little shrug and rolled her eyes, as though this was a regular occurrence with her mother. She replied in Russian, though her tone was far calmer and quieter than her mother's.

He'd already known, of course, that she spoke several languages, not just her mother's native Russian and the Portuguese she'd learned from infancy from her father. She was also fluent in both French and Spanish, the former from the times she'd lived with her aunt and uncle in Paris, and the latter from traveling extensively through South and Central America with her father. Matthew had joked that the only languages he knew besides English were Java, PHP, and CSS - all of which, of course, were computer programming languages - but he had been incredibly impressed by Sasha's own foreign language skills. For someone who had never attended college, except for an eighteen month stint when she had taken courses at a holistic medical school, she continued to amaze him with how intelligent and well read she was, as well as her ability to converse on a wide and diverse number of topics.

Sasha ended the call looking both exhausted and dazed, and peered into her mug of tea before taking a long drink.

"Why is it that every time I get a call from my mother I feel in need of a good stiff drink afterwards?" she mused. "And definitely something stronger than oolong."

Matthew grinned. "I could mix you up a killer tequila sunrise, if you'd like."

She returned his smile. "Don't tempt me. But if anyone could drive a person to drink, it would be my mother. Or, on occasion, my father. And when the two of them are in the same room - even the same city - for too long, it's a wonder I don't spend the entire visit drunk."

Over the past few weeks, he'd coaxed little bits and pieces of information from her about her parents, and what it had been like growing up while following one or the other of them around the globe.

"I guess most people, and children in particular, would think it was fun and exciting," she had told him. "Never staying in one place very long, seeing different cities and countries and cultures, basically living in hotel rooms or tour buses or trains. I switched schools several times a year, or occasionally had tutors. I didn't have a regular bedtime, pretty much got to eat whatever I wanted, and life was basically one ongoing adventure. Until I grew up and realized how much I hated living that way, how all I really wanted was a normal family, and to sleep in the same bed every night. That's when I set my foot down and went to live with Tia Linda."

It had been her aunt who'd first introduced Sasha to yoga, and she had known immediately after that first class that this was what she had always been meant to do. During high school, she'd worked part-time jobs after school and on

152

weekends, mostly waiting tables or being a receptionist at a couple of different yoga studios, and had saved as much money as possible. After graduation, she'd immediately enrolled in a yoga teacher training program, and had then begun the slow, often frustrating process of getting classes assigned to her and growing her student base. At one point in those early years, she had taught classes at five different studios and substituted for other teachers whenever possible.

Becoming a massage therapist had quickly become her next ambition, and she'd scrimped and saved even more diligently to afford the fees involved. But now, a full ten years after she'd begun the journey, Sasha was one of the most popular, well liked yoga teachers in San Francisco, and her classes were always filled to capacity. And getting a massage appointment with her often took weeks. Matthew had secretly read reviews from both her yoga students and massage clients on Yelp, and had been immensely proud to learn how highly each and every one of them regarded her.

At the same time he envied her, too. She might not have chosen a high-paying profession, but she was definitely living her dream and doing what made her happy. And Matthew hadn't been able to truthfully say the same for himself for a long time now.

"Your mom sounded a little upset there," commiserated Matthew. "I couldn't understand a word of what she said, of course, but she seemed pretty agitated."

Sasha shrugged, unconcerned, as she speared a slice of honeydew melon from the bowl of fruit he had brought for her. "My mother spends her life in some form of agitation," she mused. "I've tried more times than I can recall to get her to relax, tried to teach her how to meditate and do some deep breathing." She shook her head, causing her curls to bounce. "Never going to happen. She's the most hyperactive person I've ever met, and it's exhausting to be around her for more than an hour or so at a time. One of the reasons I don't see her all that often."

"Hmm." Matthew took a drink of his coffee, a habit he still wasn't quite willing to give up entirely. "I take that to mean there are other reasons."

"Yes." Sasha gazed out the bedroom window, where the sun was shining brightly on what promised to be a cool but clear autumn day. "My mother is also incredibly stubborn, and doesn't give up easily when she gets an idea in her head. Apparently she's still determined to convince me to take up dancing again, specifically so that I can join the cast of that TV show she's on, and the producers can work the angle of having mother and daughter working together. There are only so many ways you can tell a person "never in this lifetime", and I'm pretty sure I've tried them all."

Matthew seldom had time nowadays to watch TV, and when he did reality shows tended to be at the bottom of the list. But he knew that both Lindsey and Hayley were big fans of *Beyond Ballroom*, and they had coerced him a few times to watch the show with him. He'd been incredulous to learn that Katya Veselov, one of the most popular professional dancers on the show, was actually Sasha's mother. The two women didn't resemble each other all that much, especially considering the amount of makeup and the glitzy costumes Katya wore, and he would have never made the connection if Sasha hadn't mentioned it.

He frowned. "How long has it been since you danced? Not counting the party before Ian and Tessa's wedding, that is."

"I stopped training and competing when I was fifteen," she replied solemnly. "Which not coincidentally was the exact same time I chose to live with my aunt. I'd had enough of that whole world by then, couldn't stand the thought of entering one more competition, or spending four hours or more at a time in a dance studio. But even though it's been more than a dozen years since I quit, my mother has never really let me live my decision down."

"Did you ever enjoy it? The competition, that is."

Sasha nodded. "Of course. I mean, I can't think of too many little girls who wouldn't love the idea of putting on pretty dresses and makeup and having their hair done, and then going out on a stage to perform. I entered my first ballroom dance competition when I was six years old, and it was pretty much nonstop after that. Everything revolved around training and competing, even dictating the times I was able to see my father and his family in Brazil. By the time I turned twelve, I had already started to resent it, and was trying to figure a way out. My dad knew I was unhappy, and tried to persuade my mother that I needed a break, but even he wasn't a match for her when she really set her mind to something."

"I imagine she was pretty pissed off when you finally set your foot down," commiserated Matthew.

She gave him a wry smile and speared a chunk of pineapple. "My dad was there when I broke the news to her, and afterwards he confessed that he would never have been able to find the nerve to do what I did. To say that she was angry would barely begin to describe the fallout. She refused to speak to me for months afterwards, and it took years before we could have an actual conversation. And while she's mostly forgiven me, she has definitely not forgotten. Which is why she keeps pushing me to resume my training and join the show - "Aleksandra, you could dance circles around these stupid, lazy cows. The American girls have no passion, no talent. You would be the best dancer on the show." I hear something like that almost every time we talk."

He chuckled as she gave what he assumed was a perfect imitation of her mother's heavily accented voice. "I didn't know that your real name was Aleksandra."

Sasha popped a grape in her mouth. "Uh, huh. Sasha is a nickname, though my mother prefers to use my full name. My dad always calls me Sasha, though, says that Aleksandra sounds like a grouchy old Russian lady. It's just one of the many things the two of them disagree on."

"Are you ever tempted?" asked Matthew. "I mean, to take your mother up on her offer and go back to dancing? She's right, you know, that you'd be great on that show."

She didn't even attempt to suppress a shudder. "God, no. I mean, I do miss dancing. That was never the issue. It's the competing, and the performing that I hate. Can you even imagine me with false eyelashes, a spray tan, and an itty bitty costume covered in sequins? That's what I used to have to do when I competed, even at the age of eleven. My mother would insist that all my curls ruined the image, so I either had to spend over an hour flat ironing my hair or wear a wig."

He rumpled her curls affectionately. "I love your hair just the way it is," he assured her. "I think one day I counted six different shades of blonde and light brown. I like that everything about you is natural, Sasha - your hair, your body, *you*. So don't ever feel the need to be something you aren't, or change who you are to please someone else. Because you please me very, very well, and I would never ask you to change."

She set the bowl of fruit down on the nightstand, then placed her hands on either side of his face before giving him a quick kiss. "Thank you," she whispered. "I know I'm nothing like most of the people you interact with on a regular basis - your employees and clients and friends - and sometimes I can't help but think that being with me is just something of a novelty for you."

"God, no," he assured her fervently. "Being you with is the only thing that keeps me sane some days. And listening to your story - how you found the courage to stand up to your mother and chose to live your life your way - well, I can't tell you how proud that makes me feel. Proud and more than a little envious at the same time."

She looked at him quizzically. "Envious? Of me? Might I remind you that you're the billionaire CEO while I teach yoga and do massage?"

"Money isn't everything," replied Matthew quietly. "And like the saying goes, it sure as hell doesn't buy happiness. I'm envious because it's very obvious that you love what you do, Sasha. I'm not sure I've ever met anyone who's as content and at peace with their life as you are. And I would give up almost everything I owned to know that same sort of serenity. If it was up to me, I'd quit my job, sell the company, buy a sailboat, and travel around the world for a couple of years."

Sasha opened the wrapper of the protein bar he'd brought in for her and took a bite. "So what's to keep you from doing exactly that?" she asked matter-of-factly. "Oh, I realize it wouldn't be quite that easy, and that it wouldn't happen overnight. But you should be able to do exactly what you want with your life, Matthew, provided that you do it responsibly. Like making sure your employees are taken care of, and that your relationship with your children remains stable. Otherwise, if what you're doing doesn't make you happy, then you should stop doing it."

He tumbled her back onto the pillows, causing her to emit a little squeal of surprise. "I'll tell you what *does* make me happy," he told her ardently. "*You.* You make me happy, Sasha. Being with you this last month has made me happier than I've felt in a very long time."

"Matthew, I…"

Whatever she might have been about to say next was cut off by the hungry, demanding pressure of his lips on hers, his tongue taking possession of her mouth. He was fully aroused within seconds, as he usually was when she was close by, and the feel of her small, perfect breasts pressing against his bare chest only increased his need for her. Roughly, he palmed one firm mound, his fingers teasing the nipple until she was groaning beneath his kiss. He slid further down her body until his mouth was at the same level as her breasts, and he could run his tongue over her taut, dark red nipples.

158

At the same time one of his hands delved between her thighs, where she was already wet and squirming impatiently for his touch.

"Do we - do we have enough time for this?" he murmured in concern, even as he thrust two fingers inside her tight pussy, his thumb whisking over her clit.

Sasha gasped, her pelvis arching up from the mattress as she simultaneously reached for his cock. "We'll *always* have enough time for this," she whispered, as she took him inside of her.

He had stopped using condoms a couple of weeks ago, after he'd learned she got Depo-Provera shots every three months, and after both of them had tested negative for any and all sorts of communicable disease. The first time he'd fucked her bare he had almost come on the spot, it had felt that incredible. Fortunately, with Sasha's guidance these past few weeks, he had learned to control himself and prolong their lovemaking, and not worry about climaxing too soon. Having regular sex had also helped in that regard, and he knew he'd never been so physically satisfied in his life. Given, however, that the bulk of his sexual experiences had been with Lindsey - who had always been focused on her own pleasure and had rarely bothered tending to his needs - it wasn't at all surprising that having someone as giving and unselfish as Sasha for his lover had changed all of that.

As he thrust deep inside her warm, welcoming body, he thought wildly that nothing had ever felt so good, that no other woman had ever made him feel so much like a man, and that he never, ever wanted to let her go.

chapter nine

Late November

FOR WHAT WAS PROBABLY THE third or fourth time already this evening, Sasha offered up silent thanks that she had taken so many workshops over the years on meditation, and had spent so many hours working on her own deep breathing techniques. Because for the better part of the past ninety minutes, she'd found herself utilizing nearly every method she knew of to control her nearly nonexistent temper, and to restrain herself from giving the teenaged girl sitting across the table from her a good hard smack.

Matthew had been so excited at the prospect of finally introducing Sasha to his children that she hadn't had the heart to dissuade him. It wasn't that she didn't like kids, not that she'd had much experience with them over the years. She had dated a guy a couple of years back who had two small children, and the relationship had fizzled out pretty quickly when he realized that Sasha had no intention of settling down anytime soon. It hadn't taken a rocket scientist to figure out that he had really been looking for a stepmother for his kids, especially since he had primary custody of them. Since then she had more or less kept her distance from guys with kids from previous relationships, not wanting to be thrust into the unwelcome role of surrogate mom at this stage of her life.

At least Matthew's kids were older - sixteen and thirteen - and both of them seemed self-sufficient and mature. Though given the snooty way his daughter had been acting all evening, Sasha thought dourly that her behavior was more like that of a spoiled little girl than a teenager.

Hayley had been in a sullen, withdrawn mood from the moment Sasha had arrived to meet her, Matthew, and Casey for dinner at this trendy restaurant. The girl had barely acknowledged Sasha, and the replies she'd made thus far to any questions posed to her had been short and grudgingly given. She had spent the better part of the meal practically glued to her smartphone, texting back and forth with several friends, or checking her email. None of Matthew's admonitions to put the phone down and join in the conversation had had any sort of effect, and considering the angry, irritated expression on his face, it seemed that he was giving up on things improving anytime soon.

Casey, on the other hand, was friendly and easy to engage, and seemed more than eager to talk about school, sports, and whatever else Sasha asked him about. He was a very likeable, entirely genuine kid, and seemed almost grateful for the attention she was paying him. Unlike his brat of an older sister, who had just rolled her eyes when Sasha had politely inquired if she had begun to think about what colleges she might want to attend.

It was pretty darned obvious that Hayley wasn't happy about having her father's new girlfriend along for dinner, a possibility that Sasha had cautioned Matthew about more than once. But he'd dismissed her concerns, stating firmly that his daughter wasn't a little girl any longer, and that she needed to accept the fact that her parents weren't getting back together.

Sasha, however, didn't think that was the real motive behind Hayley's unfriendly behavior this evening. The girl paid her father scant attention, and seemed completely bored at having to spend time with him. She had barely touched her food, even though she'd apparently insisted on going to this particular restaurant, and had ordered one of the most expensive items on the menu. There had been another eye roll from her, accompanied by a look of scorn, when Sasha had ordered the only vegetarian entrée on the menu, followed up by a look of complete shock when Matthew had also ordered the same dish.

And when the delicious Moroccan vegetable tangine that they ordered had arrived, Hayley had made a huge production number of turning up her nose in disgust and telling her father in disdain, "I can't believe you're actually going to eat that, Dad. It looks like someone puked up their guts. And it smells awful."

Matthew had quietly rebuked Hayley for her comments, but the girl had just shrugged and resumed texting, more or less ignoring the very costly steak she had ordered.

Sasha glanced across the table discreetly at Hayley, who hadn't glanced up from her phone or said a word for at least ten minutes. She tried to imagine her own mother tolerating such rude behavior for even a minute, and shook her head with a wry smile. Katya might be short-tempered, impatient, and outspoken, but she had raised Sasha with very strict standards of behavior, had taught her from a very young age how to act like a lady and always mind her manners. Katya wouldn't have hesitated even for a second to rip the phone from Hayley's hand and refuse to give it back until the girl showed some respect to her father and the others at the table. Sasha's own hand itched to do just that, but she would never be as bold and confrontational as her mother, so she kept her mouth shut. Besides, she reasoned, Hayley was Matthew's daughter, not hers, and it wasn't any of her business how the girl behaved.

She was a very pretty girl, acknowledged Sasha, though she wore far too much makeup for a sixteen-year-old. The girl's eyebrows had been professionally waxed and shaped, and her nails recently manicured. Hayley was wearing skintight designer jeans, a low-cut black cashmere sweater, and a fitted black leather jacket. Knee high black leather boots with a spiky heel completed the outfit that Sasha privately considered a tad too provocative for a girl still in high school. Hayley's dark brown hair was long, shiny, and stick straight, and Sasha guessed it took frequent visits to a very expensive hair salon to keep it looking that way. The black leather handbag Hayley had plunked on the table bore a Prada label, and even though Sasha eschewed designer styles herself she was still familiar with the name of the high end brand, and just assumed that the bag had cost a considerable amount of money.

And Sasha hadn't missed the scornful way Hayley had glanced at her own outfit this evening - a long skirt of taupe wool, a cream cotton peasant blouse, and the faux-suede tan ankle boots that she'd bought nearly a decade ago in Brazil. Combined with Sasha's wild curls, lack of makeup, and a matching set of drop earrings and bangle bracelets made of amber and copper, she was the image of boho chic - a style that Hayley evidently was not impressed with.

If she had to venture a guess, Sasha would assume that Hayley had been pampered and indulged for years - largely by her mother, since Matthew seemed far more down-to-earth - and got whatever she wanted - the designer clothes and purse; eating out at expensive, exclusive restaurants; salon treatments. For her recent sixteenth birthday, Matthew had bought Hayley a brand new car, along with the phone that never seemed to leave her hand, and Sasha assumed that hadn't been all of her gift.

It didn't bother her in the least that Matthew indulged his children. They were his kids, after all, and he was perfectly entitled to buy them whatever he desired. Sasha just wished - for Matthew's sake - that his daughter might appear to be a little bit grateful for the very posh lifestyle she enjoyed. Instead, from what she'd been able to determine, Hayley just expected these things, had grown used to getting whatever she wanted, and didn't feel the need to express her gratitude. Matthew deserved better than that from his daughter, and Sasha continued to bite her tongue to keep herself from saying exactly that out loud.

Fortunately, Casey was the polar opposite of his surly, snooty sister, and joked and conversed easily with his father. The boy resembled his father greatly, from the color of his hair and eyes, to the slight cleft of his chin. He was also extremely intelligent, evidenced by the in-depth questions he asked Matthew about computers and the newest software MBI was designing. It was obvious from the way he beamed with approval at everything he said that Casey was Matthew's pride and joy, and Sasha's heart ached a little to think of how badly father and son must miss each other. As opposed to Hayley, who more or less continued to ignore her father as the evening progressed.

Matthew made yet another attempt to engage his disinterested daughter in conversation. "Hayley, did I ever tell you that Sasha's mother is one of the dancers on that show you and your mom like so much - uh, what's it called? Ballroom something or other."

Hayley rolled her eyes - Sasha estimated this had to be at least the tenth time tonight - and replied wearily, "*Beyond Ballroom*, Dad. How come you can never remember stuff like that but you can't shut up about all your computer stuff?"

Matthew grinned. "Because I'm a geek. Always have been, always will. So, isn't that exciting news about Sasha's mom?"

Hayley gave a little shrug. "Yeah, I guess so. Which one is your mom?" she asked Sasha reluctantly.

"Katya Veselov. She's been on the show since almost the first season," replied Sasha. "If you're a fan of the show, I'm sure you know who she is."

"Oh. The old one. Yeah, I know who she is. My favorite is actually Amber, though. She's an *amazing* dancer!" declared Hayley.

"Hayley," chided Matthew, not bothering to hide his growing irritation with his daughter. "Where the hell are your manners this evening? Sasha's mother is probably only a few years old than your mother and I, and I know you wouldn't dare to call your mom old."

Sasha bit her tongue yet again, restraining herself from mentioning that she was pretty sure Amber was the girl Katya had been ranting and raving about just last week.

"She's a terrible, terrible dancer, Aleksandra," Katya had railed. "Can you believe she doesn't even know how to do a proper jive? The producers asked me to work with her for a couple of days, and it was like starting from scratch. But, you know, she's what the producers like these days - all big hair and fake breasts and phony smiles. Ack! Why do I stay with this stupid show and humiliate myself year after year? This isn't real dancing we do on the show, nothing like what you and I did when we were competing. These girls, like this stupid, clumsy Amber, they wouldn't even be allowed to compete in a big time competition. Or if they were they would be dead last, lowest scores of anyone."

"I haven't really watched the show for the last couple of seasons," admitted Sasha. "But while my mother might be the oldest one on the show, she's definitely the most experienced dancer. And she always seems to get results with whoever her partner is each season. When I spoke with her this past weekend, she told me she made the semifinals again."

Hayley didn't reply, merely taking a sip of her drink before picking up her phone yet again. Sasha half-wished her fiery, fearsome mother was actually here right now. Not only would Katya have made Hayley sorely regret the sly crack about her age, but she would have definitely put the snotty teenager in her place and insisted she put the damned phone away.

There were times, thought Sasha reluctantly, that a girl really needed her mother, even a mother as unpredictable and slightly crazed as her own.

The awkward and at times uncomfortable dinner drew to a close soon thereafter, but not before Hayley got in one more dig, this one nowhere near as sly. Matthew had just paid the check, and glanced around the table to make sure everyone was finished with their food.

"Everyone set to go?" he asked in a deliberately cheery voice. "If so, we ought to head out so we can drop Sasha off at her place. She's got an early class to teach tomorrow. Hayley, you should go to one of her classes soon. Sasha is the best yoga teacher in San Francisco."

Sasha gave him a quizzical look. "Ah, and how do you know that? Given that *you've* never taken a yoga class in your life, much less one of mine."

He grinned teasingly, brushing his knuckles across her cheek. "Oh, I've read all the reviews on Yelp and Google. You've got five star averages on both, by the way."

Hayley scowled, clearly displeased by the attention her father was showering on his new girlfriend. "I don't like yoga," she muttered sullenly. "Too boring. Pilates is way better."

Matthew shook his head. "I've watched Sasha go through her practice several times, and there's nothing boring about it. You should see some of the stuff she can do, Hayley. Amazing. Here, let me show you."

He took out his phone and started scrolling through it at a dizzying speed. Before he could hand it across the table to Hayley, Sasha glimpsed a photo of herself that he'd evidently taken in secret, where she was in full splits and bending backwards over her leg, her hands wrapped around the ankle. The pose wasn't all that difficult or challenging, but it required tremendous flexibility, especially in the back and hamstrings.

But Hayley, unsurprisingly, wasn't impressed, and merely shrugged at the half dozen or so photos Matthew showed her. Casey, on the other hand, was practically agog and studied each photo with enthusiasm, which only further annoyed his sister.

"We should go," offered Sasha diplomatically as she reached for her bag, the one of brown and gold brocade she carried with her almost everywhere. It had probably cost less than the zipper on Hayley's pricey Prada purse, but Sasha wouldn't trade it for the world. Her father had bought the bag for her during a trip to Morocco, and it was one of her most treasured possessions.

Matthew hurried to pull the chair out for her, earning yet another dark glower from Hayley, but Sasha ignored the girl for once and smiled her thanks at him.

The drive back to her place was fairly quick, and made mostly in silence, with Sasha all too aware of the animosity being directed her way from the back seat. When Matthew got out of the car to open Sasha's door for her, Hayley muttered something beneath her breath that was indecipherable but undoubtedly rude. But when Matthew would have walked her to the front door, Sasha placed a hand on his forearm and shook her head.

"It's okay," she assured him. "I think your daughter is annoyed enough with the two of us for one evening. You don't need to stir the pot any longer. Besides, Chad and

Julio are hosting a little soiree this evening, so unless you want them to drag you inside, it's probably best if you let me go in alone."

Matthew couldn't suppress a small shudder. He'd met her affable, sociable landlords on more than one occasion, and had even agreed to join a couple of their parties. He had been the only straight man present both times, and Sasha had taken pity on him after an even dozen of Chad and Julio's friends had tried to flirt with him.

"You've convinced me," he replied dryly. "And I'm sorry about tonight. Unfortunately, Hayley's manners have become even worse since I moved out, and I'm guessing Lindsey pretty much lets her and Casey do whatever they please. I'll have a talk with her tonight, let her know that I won't tolerate her being that rude to you ever again."

"Please don't," requested Sasha quietly. "I think perhaps you'd only make things worse if you did. And I don't believe it's just me that she dislikes. Hayley would probably feel that way about any woman you dated."

Matthew shook his head. "I won't say anything tonight, but in future she needs to know that her behavior is unacceptable. She's a spoiled brat, but I'm afraid I need to take the blame for at least part of that." He glanced over at the car. "Look, I'd better get going, but is it okay if I call you in an hour or so? We didn't get to talk much tonight given the circumstances."

"Of course. And thank you for dinner. In spite of what Hayley thought, it was actually delicious," she told him with a little wink.

He laughed, then quickly bent down and gave her a long,

deep kiss before she could protest. She was breathless by the time he lifted his head, and he grinned down at her mischievously.

"*That*," he confided in a conspiratorial tone, "probably really pissed Hayley off. But it was worth it. Talk to you in just a bit."

Sasha was still chuckling to herself when she walked inside the brightly lit house, filled with the sounds of music and laughter and the scents of what she quickly determined to be Chinese food. But any hopes she might have harbored about quietly tiptoeing through the entryway and up the stairs to her own room without being noticed ended almost immediately as Julio spotted her and waved almost fanatically.

"Hey, where do you think you're going?" he demanded. "We're all dying to know how dinner out with Mr. CEO and his offspring went. So don't be thinking you're going to sneak off to your room without spilling, *querida*."

Sasha always had to bite her tongue when Julio attempted to speak Spanish around her. Despite his given name, he wasn't even Latino. Rather, he was a mix of Filipino, Irish, Italian, and Japanese. But he liked to throw around the few Spanish words and phrases he knew, even though his pronunciation was usually way off.

Julio, who was on the short side, a bit plump, and favored vividly colored, attention grabbing clothing, made a beeline for Sasha, clasping her around the forearm. "Please come over for a few minutes," he whispered urgently. "Chad invited his co-workers over tonight, and you know how dull they are. I've had two cups of coffee already just to keep from yawning. Anymore and I'll never sleep. So you have to save me, *querida*. Ten minutes is all, I promise."

Sasha gave him a look of mock severity. "I'll literally be counting those ten minutes," she warned him. "I have to get up early tomorrow you know."

Julio kissed her on the cheek. "I owe you one," he promised. "In fact, I'll even get up extra early and drive you to the studio in the morning. Just bail me out here for a bit, please?"

"Fine." Sasha sighed, and allowed her landlord/roommate to lead her into the living room where the guests were gathered.

Chad, a tall, slender African American with an impeccable fashion sense, glanced up from the conversation he'd been having with the eight or so other occupants of the room, and smiled warmly at Sasha.

"You're home early," he said by way of greeting. "Please, join us. Can I get you anything? A glass of wine? Some tea? And there's leftover food in the kitchen if you're hungry."

She shook her head as she perched on the arm of the burgundy and cream striped satin sofa. "I'm good, thanks. I just finished dinner less than an hour ago."

Chad introduced her to everyone, though Sasha had met at least two or three of the guests before. They were admittedly a quiet, reserved group, all of them fellow attorneys who worked with Chad, and a mix of men and women, gay and straight. And if they had been talking business most of the evening, as Sasha suspected, it was little wonder that Julio - who was far more outgoing and sociable than his spouse - was desperate to change the subject.

At Julio's prodding, she gave a quick recap of her evening out, describing the restaurant and what she'd ordered, which led to a discussion of what everyone's favorite dining establishment was.

"But you haven't told us what I'm really dying to know," protested Julio. "How did his kids like you? More importantly, how did you like them?"

Sasha hesitated, not wanting to say too much in front of virtual strangers, and also wishing she'd taken Chad up on his earlier offer of a glass of wine - or something stronger. "The kids were fine," she offered up diplomatically. "Matthew's son is a sweetie, just like his dad. His daughter is incredibly pretty, dresses to kill. Chad will be proud of me since I recognized her handbag as a Prada."

Chad let out a low whistle. "This girl is *how* old? And she's carting a two thousand dollar bag around town? Wow, somebody's mommy and daddy sure love her a whole lot."

Sasha was aghast that one small purse could possibly cost that much, but didn't comment further. "Well, I'm guessing they can afford it, given Matthew's profession."

She glanced pointedly at the huge wall clock mounted over the fireplace. The gilt framed clock was an antique according to Julio, who'd found it at an estate sale, but to Sasha it just look old fashioned. And really, really ugly.

"I, ah, hate to duck out on everyone like this," she ventured, "but I've got to get up early in the morning. Please, enjoy the rest of your evening."

"Hey!" protested Julio. "You didn't finish telling us about Mr. CEO's daughter. Was she a sweetie like her brother?"

Sasha couldn't hold back the urge to roll her eyes. "Not

exactly, no. She was - well, I guess a typical teenaged girl, is all. Spent most of the night glued to her phone."

That began a whole new debate, with one person bemoaning how rude everyone had become and how no one actually *talked* to each other these days, while someone else defended their frequent use of a phone in a public place, claiming it was for business purposes. No one noticed when Sasha very quietly stood and left the room - except, of course, for Julio, who caught up with her just as she was about to ascend the stairs.

"Traitor!" he hissed. "You were supposed to bail me out."

She shrugged. "We agreed on ten minutes," she reminded him. "It's been almost thirty. Besides, they're not talking about work right now, so I did what you asked. And Matthew is supposed to call me in a few minutes, so I need to go. Okay?"

Julio sighed and gave her a quick hug. "Okay. Though I know there's more to the story about Ms. Prada. I'm willing to bet she was a Class A royal bitch to you."

"Yeah, sort of," acknowledged Sasha wearily. She gave him the basics, including the offhand remark Hayley had made about Katya.

"Omigod, she did *not* call your mother 'The Old One'!" gasped Julio. "That little bitch! Oooh, if your mother had heard that she would have stomped all over little Ms. Prada with her high heeled dancing shoes. For starters."

Sasha laughed. "I would never dare repeat that comment to my mother. She'd insist I stop seeing Matthew immediately, ask why I would want to date someone who had such a rude child. But since I haven't actually told either of my parents that I'm dating anyone, I guess it's a moot point."

Julio frowned. "Why haven't you said anything? You've been seeing Mr. CEO for what - two months now?"

"About that, yes. And you know exactly why I haven't told them, especially my mother. You know what they're both like, Julio. If my mother knew I was seeing Matthew she'd demand to know everything about him. And if she learned he was rich, she'd be calling me every single day and asking all sorts of questions, pushing me to settle down. My dad wouldn't be much better. Besides, the two of them certainly don't tell me about the latest person they're sleeping with. Not that I want to know," she added hastily. "Or that I'd be able to keep track, given how much they both like to sleep around. But don't say anything to them, please? I'll tell them when the time is right."

Julio and Chad had met both Katya and Enzo on several occasions when they had come to town to visit Sasha, and at times she thought that her landlords got along better with her parents than she did. Julio in particular adored Katya, watched every episode of *Beyond Ballroom*, and was even Facebook friends with her.

"Well, my lips shall remain sealed," declared Julio. "And I'll be up bright and early as promised to drive you to the studio. A deal is a deal after all."

Sasha bid him good night and was halfway up the stairs when he called out her name, causing her to turn around.

"Don't let the little witch get you down, hmm?" advised Julio. "I can tell Matthew really likes you, so don't let one bad dinner with his kids spoil things. She'll come around eventually. I mean, how could she not love you?"

174

She blew him a grateful kiss and continued up the stairs to her room.

But as she waited for Matthew to call, she recalled the warning her aunt Linda had given her last month - about how a man would nearly always choose his children over the new woman in his life. She just hoped that Hayley's animosity towards her wouldn't force Matthew to one day have to make such a choice.

"SO HOW WAS YOUR WEEKEND with your father?"

Lindsey had waited barely ten minutes after the kids arrived home to quiz her daughter about the last two days they had spent with Matt. She knew getting any real information out of Casey was useless, since he still hero worshipped his father and would never dream of betraying any confidences or secrets they might have shared. Hayley, on the other hand, was growing up to be very much her mother's daughter, and would be Lindsey's best ally in getting this ridiculous divorce called off.

Hayley shrugged, not even looking up from the text she was sending to her best friend Sierra at her mother's question. "Boring as usual. Especially when Dad and Casey start talking all that computer geek stuff. Ugh. Do I really have to go visit him every other weekend? Sierra said I missed an awesome party at Angelica's last night. Instead of having fun with my friends, I had to sit through some dull dinner with Dad and his new girlfriend."

"What? Your father has a girlfriend?" Lindsey was incredulous at this revelation. "When did this start? And when the hell were you planning to tell me about it?"

Hayley waved a hand in dismissal. "What do you care? It's not like you've been sitting home knitting since you and Dad broke up. Or before then, for that matter."

Lindsey's cheeks grew red as she attempted to deny the accusation. "Don't be ridiculous," she replied in a huff. "I have never been unfaithful to your father. And how could I possibly even think of dating anyone now when all I want is for us to be a family again?"

Hayley laughed out loud, the most emotion Lindsey had seen her express in months. "Oh, Mom, that's a good one! Come on, it's no secret that you've been seeing other guys since Dad moved out. Sierra said her parents saw you at some restaurant in Palo Alto a few weeks ago, and that you were practically sitting in your date's lap. And Libby's older sister ran into you at that new dance club in San Francisco. Apparently the guy you were with works in the same office as Libby's sister. Ugh, Mom. Just how young was *that* one?"

Lindsey was speechless with shock at these revelations. "Your friends must be mistaken," she insisted. "Or they had a little too much to drink and didn't know what they were seeing."

Hayley smirked in response to her mother's false bravado. "Actually, it sounds like *you* were the one who had too much to drink. Both times. But, hey, I'm not judging you, Mom. If you want to go out and have some fun, go ahead. It's not like I really care all that much. And apparently Dad doesn't care at all."

Lindsey's green eyes narrowed angrily. "Watch your mouth, little girl. You're getting way too cheeky these days.

But speaking of your father - what's the deal with this new girlfriend of his? Who is she - some nerdy little computer tech who works in his office?"

Hayley scoffed. "Not exactly. She teaches yoga, and looks more like a hippie than a nerd. I guess she's pretty in a way. Her name is Sasha. Oh, and turns out her mom is one of the dancers on *Beyond Ballroom*. The older Russian one you like."

"Katya?" asked Lindsey in surprise. "I didn't know she had a daughter. She can't be all that old. My God, is your father dating a teenager?"

Hayley rolled her eyes, already weary of her mother's constant dramatics. "No, Sasha is not a teenager, Mom. Geez, you make it sound like Dad's some sort of pervert. I'd guess she's in her twenties, maybe closer to thirty. She's - oh, fuck. I really don't want to keep talking about this, you know? But Casey the Dweeb made me take a picture of him with Dad and Sasha. Just let me find it."

Lindsey stared in dismay at the photo of Matthew and Casey gathered around an admittedly stunning woman. Matt's new girlfriend wasn't quite as young as she had initially feared - late twenties, most likely - but still a good ten to twelve years younger than Lindsey. She scowled to notice the woman's smooth, flawless skin, her sparkling smile, and headful of multi-hued curls. Her clothes did look a bit on the bohemian side, and were certainly not what Lindsey would ever be caught dead wearing, but they seemed to suit her.

But what really pissed Lindsey off was seeing how happy and relaxed her husband looked in this woman's presence. She hadn't actually seen Matt in person for almost three months, since he never came inside the house when he

177

picked up or dropped off the kids, despite the list of excuses she'd conjured up to get him to do so. If something needed to be repaired, he had told her to notify their gardener/ handyman. If there was a bill or some other document she wanted him to look over, he told her to scan it and email it over to him. He was curt and to the point when she called or emailed, and had made it very, very clear that he considered their marriage over, a mere legal formality that would end just as soon as she signed those goddamned divorce papers.

"Do you think he's serious about her?" asked Lindsey, not bothering to disguise the panic in her voice.

"Jesus, Mom." Hayley shook her sleek, dark head in disbelief. "I have no idea. It's not like I came out and actually asked Dad. I mean, he seems to like her a lot, and they were all smiling and happy during dinner, but they weren't making out or anything like that."

"Did she spend the night at the condo?" Lindsey prodded. "I swear, if he's sleeping with that bitch with my kids present, I'll have his visitation rights taken away."

Hayley gave her mother a look of disgust. "Seriously, Mom? Come on, it's not like Casey and I are toddlers. But, no, she did not spend the night. Dad dropped her off wherever it is she lives, some old house in the city. And before you ask, no. We did not see her again today."

Hayley turned her attention back to her phone, busily tapping out yet another text, but Lindsey was far from finished in her quest for information about this mystery woman.

"She's a yoga teacher?" she inquired in disbelief. "Where the hell did Matt meet someone like that? And if you tell me

178

he's started taking yoga classes, I will *not* believe you!"

"I truly doubt that," replied Hayley dryly. "Dad is one of the clumsiest people I've ever seen, so I really can't see him doing yoga. He *is* eating differently, though. At dinner last night he actually ordered some sort of gross vegetarian entrée. Probably because *she's* a vegetarian. And he had herbal tea with dessert instead of coffee. Weird."

Weird wasn't the word Lindsey would have used to describe the situation. More like troubling. Matt should be miserable right about now, missing his wife and kids and house, and wanting nothing more but to resume his old life. Instead, he looked younger and happier than he had in a long time, and perfectly content with his current lifestyle.

"Your father looks good," she admitted grudgingly. "A little thinner. Is he - does he seem happy to you?"

Hayley sighed again, obviously growing impatient with this persistent line of questioning. "I guess, yeah. He's not all mopey and depressed or anything. Oh, and I think maybe he met Sasha through some friend of hers. Tessa or Tess, someone like that."

"Tessa Gregson." Lindsey almost spat out the name. She had heartily disliked the beautiful blonde the first time Ian had proudly introduced her to all of his friends at a benefit ball a year and a half ago. Ian, who had coldly rebuffed any of Lindsey's attempts to flirt with him over the years, hadn't bothered to hide the fact that he was completely infatuated with Tessa. And every time she and Matt had socialized with the Gregsons, Tessa had always been polite to her but never friendly. It was little wonder, thought Lindsey angrily, that the snooty Mrs. Gregson hadn't wasted any time in fixing poor, lonely Matt up with one of her friends. Tessa and Ian, in fact, were probably rejoicing in the fact that Matt had filed for divorce, had even encouraged him to do so.

'Well, it's not going to be that easy,' she thought angrily. 'I'm not about to sign those stupid divorce papers. Not now, not ever! And I'll be damned if I'm going to let some funky yoga teacher steal my husband. But I will have to figure out a way to get Matt to come back to me. And sooner than later, by the sound of it.'

"Do you like her?" ventured Lindsey. "I mean, is she a nice person?"

Irritably, Hayley tossed her phone onto her bed and glared at her mother. "I guess she's nice enough. And I have no idea if I like her since I barely know her. Are you finished asking me dumb questions now? I want to call Sierra and find out more about this awesome party I missed last night."

Lindsey sniffled, and made a little show out of brushing a nonexistent tear from her eye. "I - I guess so. It just upset me to learn about your father's new girlfriend. It hurts to realize he's moved on so easily."

"Oh, brother." Hayley shook her head in disbelief. "I'm not buying the fake tears and hurt feelings, Mom, so save it. Look, if it makes you feel any better, even if Dad wasn't seeing someone, I don't think it would make any difference in terms of the divorce. One way or the other, he's not coming back."

Lindsey lifted her chin stubbornly. "Then I guess I'll need to find a way to make him change his mind, won't I? I don't suppose you'd care to help me? It might be worth your while, Hayley. Like, for example, that Piaget watch you've been wanting. With a two week trip to Ibiza next summer thrown in as a bonus."

"Hmm." Hayley tapped her index finger against her lip. "Maybe. What did you have in mind?"

Triumphantly, Lindsey plopped down on the bed. "That's the problem. I haven't been able to think up anything just yet. But I'll bet if the two of us work together, we can dream something up. So put your thinking cap on, sweetie. Between the two of us, we'll figure out a way to get your father to move back in. And ditch the yoga teacher in the process."

chapter ten

December

"IT WAS SO SWEET OF you to serve a vegetarian entrée tonight, Tessa," said Sasha to their hostess. "But you really didn't have to do anything special."

Tessa waved a hand in dismissal. "Don't be silly, it wasn't any trouble at all. And vegetable moussaka is one of my favorite dishes to make."

Julia, whose twin-sized baby bump was extremely noticeable at nearly the seven month mark, swallowed another forkful of the eggplant and mushroom laden dish. "Mmm, and it's *sooo* good, Tessa! I definitely don't miss the meat."

Julia's husband Nathan grinned at her good naturedly. "I guess since you're eating for three it's acceptable to have seconds. Though I honestly don't know how you've got room in there any longer."

He patted her burgeoning belly affectionately, then planted a kiss on her cheek after she gave him a mock glare.

"You're right," sighed Julia. "Your sons are taking up most of the space down here. I can usually only eat a little bit at a time or it's uncomfortable. They aren't even born yet and already I'm making all these sacrifices for them. When Tessa and I went out for lunch earlier this week, I was way too full to even think of eating dessert."

Nathan arched a brow in her direction. "Would that particular dessert have been the giant lemon bar that you were snacking on in the middle of the night?"

Julia exchanged a quick look with Tessa before shrugging. "Guilty as charged. Hey, I might have been too full at lunch but no way was I passing up on that lemon bar. I've been craving sour stuff like crazy the last couple of months."

"Which is why I made a key lime cheesecake for dessert," announced Tessa. "So hopefully you'll save a little room for it."

Even Sasha, who wasn't overly fond of sweets, made a little "mmm" of pleasure at the mention of the dessert Tessa had planned. She took a small sip of the one glass of red wine she'd indulged in this evening, smiling at Matthew as their eyes met.

This intimate dinner party at the Gregsons' had been one of the most enjoyable evenings Sasha had experienced in a long time. Given that she had spent the first fifteen years of her life constantly packing up and traveling from one place to another, Sasha had never been able to make close friends. And even after she'd come to live with Linda, and then later as an adult, she'd found it difficult to form lasting friendships.

But Julia and Tessa had quite firmly brought her into their small but close knit circle, one that also included Julia's friend Angela and occasionally her twin sister Lauren, in addition to some of Julia's co-workers. And while Sasha mostly eschewed girly activities like shopping or spa visits, she liked having brunch with Julia after yoga class, or going on a strenuous hike with Tessa. She'd also helped Tessa plan a baby shower for Julia to be held right after New Year's, admitting that it would be the first such event she'd be attending.

And once she'd finally fessed up to both of them that she and Matthew were in a relationship, Tessa and Julia had squealed excitedly like little girls. Tessa in particular had been elated to hear the news, and assured Sasha that she was exactly the sort of woman Matthew needed in his life.

"I don't know all the details, of course, about why he and Lindsey split up," Tessa had confided. "But I can tell you that she was never very nice to him, took him for granted most of the time. Any woman who can blatantly flirt with another man right in front of her husband - especially with a husband like Matthew, who's just about the nicest person I know - doesn't deserve someone like him. I'm just glad that he finally decided to do something about it, because he should have the chance to be happy. And I'm doubly glad that he has you in his life, Sasha. You're two of the kindest people I've ever met, and I hope that things keep working out for you."

Sasha had been touched by Tessa's ardent declaration, but had also been quick to downplay her relationship with Matthew. "It's pretty casual between us, you know. We really only get to see each other once a week, maybe twice, since he travels so much or is busy at work. And then of course he has his children every other weekend, and tries to see them at least once during the week, too."

"How are you getting along with his kids? They're both teenagers, correct?"

Sasha had given a nod. "Hayley is sixteen, and Casey turns fourteen in February. As for getting along - well, I'm afraid Hayley doesn't like me very much, not so surprising under the circumstances. Casey on the other hand is a great kid, very kind and friendly like Matthew. I actually haven't spent all that much time with them, since it's important for Matthew to have time alone with his children."

"Hmm." Tessa had looked pensive. "My guess is that the daughter is taking her mother's side in this divorce. Like you said, not all that surprising. When are all the legalities supposed to be finalized anyway?"

Sasha had hesitated a moment before replying. "Lindsey apparently is playing hardball with Matthew and refusing to sign the papers. He's supposed to meet with his lawyer again before the end of the month and see if they can force her hand. But I don't really discuss it all with him very often. Frankly, the whole situation makes me feel a little guilty at times."

Tessa's blue eyes had widened in surprise. "Why on earth would you feel guilty?" she asked in astonishment. "It's not like you broke up their marriage, after all. From what I've been able to figure out, Lindsey sort of destroyed things all by herself."

"He's still legally married, Tessa," Sasha had pointed out quietly.

Tessa had given a shake of her head. "Not in any way that matters. He and Lindsey haven't lived together for almost half a year, and Matthew has told Ian more than once that for all intents and purposes he considers himself a single man. Look at it this way, Sasha. If you weren't in a relationship with him, would Matthew be even thinking of going back to Lindsey?"

"No," Sasha had admitted. "He's told me the same thing several times - that he already considers his marriage to be long over, and that it's simply a matter of Lindsey signing the forms to make it official."

"Then you have nothing to feel guilty about," Tessa had assured her. "Especially since she treated Matthew so horribly. He has a right to find some happiness, you know. And I'm so pleased that the two of you are making each other happy. You both deserve it more than anyone else I know."

Tessa's assurances had made Sasha feel much better about the situation, and appeased the guilt that she still experienced from time to time. Matthew had told her more or less the same things as Tessa, that he considered his marriage as good as over, and that there was zero chance he would ever contemplate reconciling with Lindsey.

"I can't believe that it's already the fourth of December," declared Julia. "And thank goodness Nathan and I don't have to travel very far for Christmas, just down to my parents' place in Carmel. The flight we just took home from Michigan on Thanksgiving weekend is going to be my final one for awhile."

"When are the two of you heading over to England?" Nathan asked Ian.

Ian refilled his wine glass, then passed the bottle to Matthew. "On the seventeenth, I believe, returning about ten days later."

Julia glanced across the table inquiringly at Sasha and Matthew. "What about you two? Any plans for Christmas and New Year's?"

Matthew hesitated before giving a brief shrug. "Still working all that out, I'm afraid. Things are a tad complicated this year under the circumstances. Normally we head back to Wisconsin and spend Christmas with my family, but I'm still, ah, negotiating all that."

Sasha somewhat belatedly realized that she and Matthew had yet to discuss the upcoming holidays, and she told herself sternly that she was being silly to feel even the tiniest bit hurt or left out that he hadn't brought the subject up until now.

"It sounds like both of my parents are coming for a quick visit," she offered up. "At the same time. Which means the decibel level in San Francisco is bound to rise up pretty high. Fortunately, my landlords always host a big open house on Christmas Eve, so that will help diffuse the situation with my parents a bit since there'll be so many other people around. However, I'm afraid on Christmas Day I'll be stuck going out to dinner with them. And playing peacekeeper the entire time, I'm sure."

She smiled reassuringly at Matthew, who was looking a bit guilty, as though he'd just realized the subject of the holidays hadn't been brought up prior to this evening. Ian, who'd undoubtedly picked up on the awkwardness between them, smoothly changed the subject, for which Sasha was overwhelmingly grateful.

But less than five minutes after they left the Gregsons', Matthew broached the matter in a tentative voice.

"I'm sorry if things got a little awkward during dinner," he told her regretfully. "About the holidays, that is. I know we haven't talked about it at all, mostly because I've been busier than usual at work but also because - well, Lindsey is being incredibly difficult about it."

Sasha patted his thigh reassuringly. "It's all right, Matthew," she replied softly. "I know it's not an easy situation with your children, and especially not at the holidays. I wasn't expecting that you and I would be spending Christmas together, if that's what's worrying you. And since I'm definitely not going to be alone then, you don't have to be concerned about that, either."

He sighed, running a hand through his close cropped hair. "Believe me, Sasha. I would *love* to spend Christmas with you. More than anything. But it's one of the few times each year that I get to see my parents and the rest of my family, so I've got to go to Wisconsin. And I'd invite you to come along, except that Lindsey is already kicking up a fuss about my taking Hayley and Casey with me. If she knew you were coming too, I think a small war might break out."

She shook her head. "No. Don't make things worse, Matthew. You deserve to see your family and have your children along with you, spend some quality time together. Besides, I think bringing your new girlfriend along with you at the holidays isn't really, well, *proper*. Especially under the circumstances."

He frowned, giving her a sideways glance. "What circumstances would those be?"

Sasha shrugged. "You *are* still legally married. And I'm just afraid that your parents and the rest of your family would consider it in bad taste for you to bring another woman along when your divorce is still up in the air."

"Sasha." He took her hand in his, bringing it to his lips

188

while he drove with the other hand. His voice was gentle, tender even, as he asked, "Is that what *you* think? Does it bother you that technically I'm still bound to Lindsey by a piece of paper? Because I'll swear to you once more that the *only* thing that binds me to her is that pesky legality. In every other way that matters, she is no longer my wife and hasn't been for some time."

She entwined her fingers with his, resting their clasped hands on her lap. "I know that," she replied somberly. "And I know that your relationship with me has no bearing on your marriage. But can you honestly say that other people will view the situation in the same way? That your family wouldn't think it's morally wrong to bring another woman into their home before your divorce is officially legal?"

Matthew chuckled. "My family is a bunch of scientists and college professors and engineers. Everyone is very forward thinking and progressive, and not a single one of them would judge you or think of you as the other woman. On the contrary, they'd welcome you into their homes with open arms. Especially since their relationship with Lindsey has always been more than a little strained. After I started my own company and made a whole lot of money, she'd resent pretty much anything I tried to do for my family - giving them gifts, offering to buy my parents a new home, treating them to a nice vacation. Even when we all went out to dinner, she'd complain afterwards that my family was taking advantage of me by letting me pick up the bill or that my father should at least have paid the tip. The fact that we had more money than we could spend in five lifetimes never mattered to her. She's greedy and selfish and my family actually welcomed

189

the news that I was divorcing her. So, no. My family would be very, very happy if I were to bring you home with me to meet them."

His words filled Sasha with an unexpected warmth, and she beamed at him gratefully. "Thank you for saying that," she murmured. "And I would love to meet your family at some point. But this first Christmas after you filed for divorce probably isn't the ideal time."

He sighed. "Yeah, I suppose not. But mostly because it would only make Lindsey fight me even harder than she already is about having the kids for a week. She was actually shocked when I told her she wouldn't be coming along with us this year, and needed to make other plans. Unbelievable."

Sasha frowned. "Doesn't she have family of her own to spend Christmas with?"

"Nope. Oh, she's got a mother and a sister, but they've all been on the outs with each other for as long as I've known Lindsey. I'm not sure she even knows where they live any longer. I've offered to pay for her and a friend to spend the week at a very expensive resort down in Mexico, an offer she's currently thinking about."

"What do the kids want to do?" asked Sasha tentatively.

"Casey wants to go back to Wisconsin, of course. He gets along great with my family, and loves to hang out with my brother's kids. Hayley - well, who really knows what she wants nowadays? All she seems to care about is texting with her friends, finding a good party to attend every weekend, and spending a whole lot of money. Wonder who she picked up that habit from." He released her hand in order to downshift the Tesla Model X that he was driving this evening. "But when push comes to shove, I'm betting she'll go with us to Wisconsin. Especially since she'd really put a cramp in Lindsey's style if she announced she was going to Mexico with her."

"I'm sorry Lindsey is being so difficult," she consoled. "Sounds to me like she could use a nice long massage to help relieve all of that tension."

Matthew gave a sardonic hoot of laughter. "Yeah, except that she'd insist on having the massage done by some buff guy ten to fifteen years younger than she is. Hey, maybe that idea would sell her on going to Mexico!"

They shared a laugh over that one before he asked her quietly, "You're sure that it's okay for me to go to Wisconsin with the kids? You won't feel left out or neglected?"

She gave him a look of mock sternness. "At last count Chad and Julio had invited over fifty people for their Christmas Eve gala, and they aren't finished yet. The place is going to be a madhouse, so much that I'll probably be tempted to barricade myself in my room after awhile. And in spite of how much they drive me nuts, I do enjoy spending time with my parents. So I will definitely not feel either left out or neglected. And I understand, Matthew. Truly I do. You need to be with your children and your family on Christmas, and I think it's wonderful. You're a great father, and I'm sure you're an amazing son and brother, too. And I realized the first time I met you that you were the best man I've ever known."

Matthew closed his eyes briefly at her heartfelt words, taking a long, deep breath before opening them again and staring at her with a sense of wonder in his eyes. "And I think the first time we met that I knew somehow you would be the one to save me," he whispered hoarsely. "The one who would help me find myself again after being lost for a long time. Thank you, Sasha. You're the only Christmas gift I want."

She reached over and pressed a kiss to his cheek, before murmuring seductively, "Well, then. I think as soon as we reach your place that you should start unwrapping your present. It's never too early to get in the holiday spirit, you know."

He gulped as her hand dropped to his thigh, giving the tightly bunched muscles there a gentle massage, before stepping on the gas a little bit harder.

New Year's Eve

"MORE CHAMPAGNE?"

Sasha shook her head. "No, thanks. At least not right now. I'm already way over the amount I usually limit myself to."

Matthew grinned devilishly. "Ah, but it's New Year's Eve, after all. And if I don't get you a little tipsy, it will be that much harder for me to have my wicked way with you later."

She set her champagne flute down and reached across the table to give him a long, deep kiss. "It will actually be the easiest thing you've ever done in your life," she whispered teasingly.

He made a sound deep in his throat that sounded an awful lot like a growl. "Don't tempt me, sweetheart," he warned. "We haven't been together in almost ten days, so I've had to restrain myself all during dinner to not pick you up and toss you on my bed."

Her green-gold eyes sparkled at him mischievously. "Hmm, well perhaps you shouldn't have ordered in quite so much food, then. Including three different desserts, I see. This is just a little over the top, don't you think?"

"Nope," he replied cheerfully. "After all, I didn't get to spend Christmas Eve or Day with you, so tonight's dinner is sort of a combination of all three holidays." He took her hand in his and gave it a squeeze. "I missed you a whole lot, Sasha. Wished like hell the entire trip that you had come along with me. Maybe next year."

She tried to quell the alarm those last three words provoked, especially since she'd never really contemplated her future with Matthew. As much as she enjoyed being with him, as happy as he'd made her these past few months, she still considered their relationship to be somewhat casual, and certainly one with no commitments or promises about the future.

But since it was the holiday season, and she knew how much trouble he'd gone to so they could have a special evening, Sasha tactfully didn't comment further, except to smile and say, "Maybe so."

He had given her the choice of either dining out this evening at whatever restaurant she liked, or having food delivered in. She had chosen the latter, partly because every restaurant in the city would be packed to overflowing with holiday celebrants, and also because she'd sensed that was Matthew's preference. He had just flown in this afternoon from Wisconsin, and had seemed both pleased and relieved at the prospect of spending New Year's Eve in the privacy and serenity of his condo.

"You're sure you don't mind staying home?" he asked somewhat anxiously. "I mean, we've still got plenty of time to go out and do something fun. There's dozens of bars and clubs in town, and I'm certain most of them will be having a celebration of one kind or another."

"I'm very happy to be staying in this evening," she assured him, linking their fingers together. "As you might have guessed, wild parties and big groups aren't my favorite thing. And if I had wanted that I would have just suggested we take Chad and Julio up on their offer and attend their party. They pull out all the stops on New Year's Eve, so I'm glad I had the excuse of coming here to your place."

Matthew looked relieved. "Okay, if you're positive. But I definitely owe you a long weekend away someplace. Even better, a whole week. Is there some place you've ever wanted to go but haven't been to? I know you've traveled all over Latin America and Europe, but where else would you want to go?"

Sasha gave him a wry smile. "Just to clear up any misconceptions you might have had about my world travels, it wasn't as glamorous or exciting as you might think. Both my father's band and my mother's dance troupe always seemed to operate on a shoestring budget, so there were a lot of cheap hotel rooms and bargain meals. It wasn't like staying at a Ritz Carlton or Gregson hotel, or eating at five star restaurants. But that never mattered to me when I was young. I was just happy to be with whatever parent had charge of me at the time, and doing as much sightseeing as possible in each city."

"Well, now you've got a boyfriend who can afford to

take you anywhere in the world, and stay at the best accommodations in town," declared Matthew. "So give that idea some thought, okay? I'm hoping to schedule some time off in the spring."

"I think someplace warm and sunny sounds like a wonderful idea right about now," she answered. "It's been so cold and rainy already and we're only a couple of weeks into winter. And I've never been to Hawaii or the Caribbean."

He grinned. "Consider it done. I'll work on clearing a week in my schedule and then make plans for a tropical getaway. And before you ask where, it's going to be a surprise. Speaking of which," he added mysteriously, "I still need to give you your Christmas presents. Do you want them now or after dessert?"

Sasha patted her belly. "After that amazing dinner I know I won't be able to eat anything else for at least a couple of hours. And I hope you didn't go overboard on the presents, Matthew. Like you did with the food tonight."

She'd been agog at the display of all the different dishes he'd ordered in from the elite catering company who handled a lot of events for MBI, a veritable smorgasbord of various cuisines - Japanese, Italian, Thai, Indian, Mexican, French, and more. Sasha couldn't recall the last time she had eaten quite so much, and regretted that she hadn't saved a bit more room for another helping of chile rellenos, one of her very favorite foods.

Matthew's grin only deepened. "Depends on what you consider going overboard. I can promise that I didn't buy you a car. Or a twenty thousand dollar watch. Not that I wouldn't be happy to get both of those for you, of course, but.."

"No." She shook her head vehemently. "And you can't possibly be serious that some company really makes a watch that costs so much money."

"Twenty thousand is actually at the lower end of the scale for luxury watches," he admitted. "One year for Valentine's Day Lindsey requested a Cartier watch that cost eighty thousand. And that was just one of her gifts."

Sasha stared at him in disbelief. "Eighty thousand," she whispered. "My God, I barely earn that much money in two years. Wow. I - I had no idea that you were quite that wealthy, Matthew."

"I thought you knew," he replied soberly. "I, um, was named one of the wealthiest men in America earlier this year."

He told her then what his approximate net worth was, and she couldn't even begin to think of a suitable reply. That sort of wealth - in the billions rather than simply the millions - was something she couldn't even begin to fathom. And Matthew - with his goofy grin, easygoing personality, and endearing clumsiness at times - was certainly the most unlikely billionaire she could have imagined.

"Well," she told him a bit shakily, "I'll go on record right now and tell you that the only thing I'd like for Valentine's Day is a bouquet of flowers. And maybe some really good Mexican food for dinner."

He laughed heartily as he pushed back his chair and walked over to her side of the table. "Come on," he urged. "I'll make a note of your wish list for Valentine's Day, but I'm afraid I've already gone a little overboard with your Christmas gifts."

Before she could protest, he was drawing her to her feet,

then leading her by the hand to the room that doubled as his office and the massage room.

"Did you buy a new massage table?" she joked. "Because I'm pretty sure the one you already have is the top of the line and - oh."

As he flicked on the overhead light, Sasha could only stare in wonder at the sight that greeted her - at least two dozen gifts of various shapes and sizes, all beautifully wrapped in striped satin paper and elaborately tied velvet bows. She thought in a near panic that he had probably spent more on just the wrapping paper and ribbon that she had on his entire gift.

But she wasn't able to resist running her palm over the gift nearest to her, enjoying the lush softness of the velvet ribbon beneath her fingers. She'd never experienced such extravagance in her life before, had never been showered with so many presents at once, or had someone like Matthew who treated her like a princess. And while she had never been deprived of anything, had always had everything she needed, neither had she ever really been indulged before. Neither of her parents had made much money during the gypsy days of her youth, and while they were both comfortably off now Sasha certainly wouldn't call either of them wealthy. She'd counted herself lucky as a child to receive half a dozen small gifts, and had cherished each and every one of them.

The lavish pile of presents that took up an entire corner of this room, however, was like something out of a fairy tale. She shook her head in mingled dismay and delight as she picked up a medium sized box.

"I - I don't know what to say," she began haltingly. "Or

197

where to begin."

Matthew grinned. "The one you're holding in your hands is a good place to start. Here, I'll tell you what. Take a seat in the desk chair and I'll bring the gifts over one at a time."

Nearly an hour later, Sasha was down to her last gift, and felt moved nearly to tears at all of the beautiful, thoughtful things Matthew had chosen for her. He knew quite well that she wouldn't have been impressed by expensive jewelry or designer handbags, and had instead gone out of his way to make each gift - large and small - something personal. Oh, not that some of the presents hadn't been on the extravagant side - like the brand new laptop and top of the line cell phone he'd insisted that she accept.

"Hey, I'm the CEO of one of the biggest software companies in the world," he had pointed out. "If word ever got out that my girlfriend didn't even own a computer, and that her phone was hopelessly out of date, I'd be a laughingstock. So you have to accept both of them, don't you see? In order to save my reputation, that is."

But most of his gifts had been small, thoughtful items - a bag of her favorite loose leaf tea; an exquisitely soft cashmere scarf; a CD by a sitar player that she liked; a pair of copper and jade earrings that he assured her were costume and not the real thing.

It was his final gift, though, that touched her the most - a small painting of a woodland fairy that she'd admired once in a gallery while window shopping with him after dinner one evening. She had completely forgotten about the painting, and marveled that he could be this thoughtful, this observant.

Sasha set the painting on his desk carefully before flinging herself into his arms, pressing a tender kiss to his cheek.

"Everything is perfect," she whispered tearfully. "Absolutely perfect. You are the kindest, most wonderful man I've ever known. Even if all of this is ridiculously over the top, far, far too extravagant. You went completely overboard, Matthew."

He buried his face against her curls, pulling her close against his body. "Not even close, sweetheart," he assured her. "If you could have seen some of the things I really wanted to buy you, well - you'd have set your foot down for sure." He lifted his head then, cupping her cheek tenderly in his hand. "You are the one person in my life who never asks me for a thing, who never expects stuff. Whether it's Lindsey or Hayley demanding a new pair of shoes or a luxury vacation somewhere, or one of my managers needing an hour of my time to go over a proposal, it feels like every day, every hour, someone wants or needs something from me. Except you. Rather than ask me for things, you give them instead. And in these few months we've been together, you've already given me so much, Sasha. Far, far more than any present I could give you in return."

Tears had begun to pool in her eyes at his impassioned words, and her lips were trembling as he claimed them in a slow, sweet kiss. The kiss quickly ignited, and turned hungry, passionate, in the blink of an eye. He scooped her up into his arms, and kicked away a wadded up pile of discarded wrapping paper as he carried her out of the room.

Once in the master bedroom, he laid her down on the bed with great care, as though she was a fragile, treasured piece of glass. With only the bright light of a nearly full moon to illuminate the room, Matthew began to undress her slowly, taking his time this evening instead of nearly tearing her clothes off with frantic lust as he so often did. She had dressed up for their special holiday dinner, in a flapper-style dress of ivory silk and lace that she'd unearthed in a vintage store. He slid the dainty spaghetti straps off her shoulders, then carefully worked the dress down past her narrow hips and off her legs.

"My God. Look at you."

His voice was hoarse as he stared down at her prone body with ill-disguised desire. For once she'd chosen a push-up bra, this one of cream silk with lace insets, and it made her breasts appear fuller, more voluptuous. His hot gaze continued its downward path, past her toned abs and concave belly, to the lacy garter belt and miniscule pair of panties that matched the provocative bra. Sheer silk stockings were attached to the garters, but she had ditched her high heeled ivory pumps not long after arriving this evening, preferring as usual to walk around barefoot.

It was a much sexier look than normal for her, and from the way he was reacting, it seemed that Matthew approved wholeheartedly of the switch up. He was breathing heavily as his lips touched the side of her neck just beneath her ear, then began to trace a slow, sensual path down her body. He unhooked the fragile bra deftly, tossing it over the side of the bed, as his hands cupped the small, firm mounds of her breasts. His tongue flicked over one small, dark red nipple before his mouth closed over the entire areola and sucked hard. Sasha gasped, her hands clasping his head closer to her, as her lower body arched off the mattress in reaction.

He was unhurried tonight, seeming intent on taking his time with her, a departure from the way he usually made love to her - oftentimes with a hungry desperation, an almost boyishly eager desire to please her, and even a shy hesitancy at times, as though he lacked confidence in his skills. But he was using every one of the erotic skills he possessed now, employing them masterfully as he kissed and caressed his way down her body.

Sasha was the impatient one this time around as he continued to arouse her unbearably, her pelvis rotating in a circular motion as she silently begged him to satisfy the need that was quickly heating up to the boiling point. But Matthew refused to be rushed, and even the simple act of removing her panties became a seduction, as he used his teeth to slowly tug them down her legs. Then and only then did he give her what she'd been craving all evening - the slow, deliberate thrust of his long fingers deep inside her vagina, where she was wet and needy and so aroused that it took just a few quick pumps before she climaxed.

He gave her no time to recover, sliding down the mattress until his head was positioned between her thighs, his hands spreading her legs apart to give him the access he wanted. Using his lips, tongue, and fingers, he focused solely on her pleasure, on making her writhe and moan and pant until she was consumed with the need to climax again. Matthew cleverly used all of the skills she'd helped him develop, with a whispered word of encouragement or a subtle instruction now and then. He bore no resemblance whatsoever to the rather clumsy, adorably eager lover he'd been during the early weeks of their relationship. For tonight, at least, he seemed to be thriving on acting the role of the dominant, the one who was in complete control of their lovemaking, and Sasha was deliriously happy to let him do whatever he desired.

She offered no resistance, therefore, when he flipped her over onto her belly, especially since her body was still shuddering in reaction to the orgasm he'd so cleverly coaxed from it. Except for a small gasp of surprise, she didn't react as he bent one of her legs at the knee, angling it slightly away from her body, and then smoothly thrust inside of her from behind. His chest was pressed closely against her back, effectively trapping her in place. With any of her previous lovers, Sasha would have resisted this particular sexual position, would have felt too dominated and helpless. But she trusted Matthew implicitly, knew that he simply didn't have it in him to hurt another being, whether intentionally or otherwise, and gave herself over to him completely.

He seemed to sense her surrender, her willingness to let him take her over, and that realization unleashed the wildness in him. His sensual, almost teasing lovemaking quickly gave way to hungry, unrestrained fucking, until both of them became lost in a haze of lust and need. Growling, he reared back onto his knees, his hands at her hips pulling her into a kneeling position, and Sasha cried out in mingled surprise and pleasure at how deeply he penetrated her from this angle. The heavy sac of his testicles slapped against her buttocks with each savage thrust, and she had to bite down on her lip more than once to stifle a little scream of half-pain/half-pleasure.

Bracing himself on the mattress with one arm, Matthew snaked the other around her waist, as his palm slid down over her quivering belly. At the first brush of his thumb over the swollen, tender nub of her clit, she came undone, the orgasm rendering her incapable of either speech or thought as her legs nearly gave way from under her. As the blood rushed through her ears, she was barely aware when Matthew, too, found his release, his body collapsing onto hers as he shuddered over and over again.

Sasha wasn't certain how long they remained in exactly that position, either half-asleep or lost in a haze. But it was the sound of fireworks in the distance, and the multi-colored glow that suddenly lit up the room, that eventually roused them. Groaning, Matthew eased himself off of her, rolling onto his side, and ran a hand soothingly down the length of her spine.

"Guess we missed midnight," he joked, his voice hoarse.

She snickered. "We were too busy setting off our own fireworks, I guess. But, come on. The fireworks show probably just got started. And since we have practically a front row seat out on your balcony, I don't want to miss this."

They quickly bundled themselves up into robes, with Sasha grabbing the brand new one of dark green cashmere that had been one of Matthew's many Christmas gifts, and hurried out onto the balcony. She shivered despite the warmth of her new robe, and he promptly cuddled her close against him to ward off the chill of the night air.

"Happy New Year, Sasha," he murmured against her curls

as they watched another glorious burst of color fill the sky.

She wrapped her arms around his waist, resting her head on his shoulder. "And a very Happy New Year to you, too," she replied. "I hope that this next year is a much happier one for you, Matthew."

"Well, it's definitely starting off a hell of a lot better than last year's did," he declared with a grin. "And I'm not even referring to the sex. Which, by the way, was awe inspiring. I'm not sure if those are the right words to use to describe it, but, hey, I write computer code not poetry, after all."

Sasha laughed. "Those are the exact right words," she assured him. "And it was the same for me."

They stood together quietly for several more minutes, content to watch the fireworks display being held along the San Francisco waterfront, until Sasha began to shiver from the cold.

"Inside with you," he insisted. "Besides, we've still got half a bottle of champagne to finish and dessert."

"And you have presents to open," she reminded him. "Though I'm a little reluctant to give them to you after everything you just lavished on me. It's nowhere near on the same scale, you know, not even close."

"Hey," scolded Matthew gently. "I already told you, Sasha. Having you in my life is all the Christmas present I need. What you've done for me in these past months can't be measured in terms of material things or monetary value. You didn't need to buy me a gift of any sort."

She retrieved two small packages from the living room where she'd left her bag earlier. They were simply wrapped in sage green paper and tied with a bit of burlap ribbon.

He lifted the larger of the two packages to his nose and took a sniff. "This smells like you," he told her with a smile. "I've never quite figured out what scent this is, or if it's soap or shampoo or just your skin. But it's a combination of lemon and maybe a bit of rosemary or sage, and to me it's way, way more appealing than any perfume I've ever smelled."

He carefully removed the paper from the first package, which turned out to be a collector's edition of *The Prophet* by Khalil Gibran. Matthew had a vague recollection of having read the book at some point during his college years, but was unable to recall any specific quotes or passages. Reverently, because he already knew that Sasha had chosen this gift for him with great care, he opened the book to a random page. The first quote that jumped out at him seemed unusually timely under the circumstances - "the greatest of wealth is the richness of the soul."

"It's one of my very favorite books," ventured Sasha as he continued to flip through the pages. "When I was training to be a yoga teacher, I had to read a number of books, some of them sacred texts, others handbooks on anatomy. And while *The Prophet* wasn't required reading, one of my teachers suggested it. I pick up my copy almost every day to read a particular passage. I hope that you can find some inspiration from it, Matthew. I know that I have many times."

Matthew set the book down carefully, and pressed a soft kiss to her lips. "Thank you, Sasha. I already know that I'll treasure it. Now, what do we have here?"

The second package revealed a small black velveteen drawstring bag, and from its depths he drew out a tubular shaped piece of what looked like onyx suspended from a long suede cord.

"It's actually black tourmaline," clarified Sasha before he could ask. "I'm sure you aren't familiar with all of the healing properties of crystals, and most people think all of that is just a bunch of nonsense. But this particular crystal is known for its grounding properties, and is used to combat stress and fatigue. I thought, well, that you might like to keep it with you at your office or when you travel. I know most men aren't really into jewelry so you don't have to actually wear it. You can just hold it in your palm for a few minutes, and keep it in your pocket or a desk drawer the rest of the time."

In reply, he pulled the cord over his head, then pressed the tourmaline into his bare skin for a moment.

"No," he replied firmly. "It stays right here. This is the most thoughtful gift anyone has ever given me."

She smiled, pleased that he seemed so touched by the present. "It's not very expensive, you know," she chided. "A close friend of mine owns a metaphysical shop in the Castro district and gave me a good deal on it."

Matthew shook his head. "You could have picked it out of a bubble gum machine for all I care. It doesn't matter in the least to me how much it cost, because the real value is the thought that went into it. I'll always treasure it, Sasha, because you gave it to me."

The look in his eyes as he gazed down at her was both tender and almost frighteningly intense at the same time, enough so that she glanced away quickly, not wanting to think about what that sort of look might really mean.

"Now, didn't you mention something about champagne and dessert?" she asked brightly, intentionally lightening up the very serious mood. "I seem to have worked up something of an appetite."

chapter eleven

Mid-January

"**YOU KNOW, WHEN I FIRST** saw that dress, I thought it might not be the right color for you, given that your hair and skin are close to the same shade. But I couldn't have been more wrong. It's perfect for you, Sasha. And I'm totally impressed that you found such a gorgeous dress in a consignment store. You've got great taste."

Sasha gave Julia a lopsided grin. "Well, I can't take all the credit, I'm afraid. I know how difficult it is for you to get around these days, and Tessa was busy with all the last minute details for your baby shower. So, since I didn't want to bother either of you, I took my landlords with me."

Tessa frowned. "Both of them? I thought you told me only one had good fashion sense."

Sasha's grin quickly changed to a grimace. "That would be Chad. The one who actually found this dress in the racks. The other one is Julio, who tried to help but unfortunately kept pulling out the most atrocious things I've ever seen. I can't believe anyone actually bought those dresses in the first place, and that now there's someone else willing to put out good money for them."

Julia wrinkled her nose, then winced when one or both of the twins gave her a kick, before rubbing her swollen belly

208

soothingly. "Ouch! These two devils are really active today. I hope they don't decide to kick me again when I'm in the middle of lining your eyes, Sasha. Otherwise, your makeup might turn out a little scary looking."

"You look gorgeous," Tessa told Sasha warmly. "Absolutely gorgeous. And that's without a lick of makeup or any accessories. Julia's right - that dress could have been made for you. You're lucky it didn't need any alterations."

Sasha shrugged. "Just a couple of minor things that I was able to do myself. I learned how to be handy with a needle and thread when I was still a young girl. There were always last minute repairs that had to be made to our costumes before a competition or performance."

She had told her two friends about the years she had competed in ballroom dance as a child and adolescent, relieved to discover that she could actually laugh about some of the experiences now.

"You know, we're still waiting to see pictures of you from back then," reminded Julia, who was sipping peppermint tea and nibbling on one of the snickerdoodle cookies that Tessa had baked that morning. "And don't try and lie and say you don't have any, because we won't believe you."

"Unfortunately, there may be a few tucked away in the deep, dark recesses of a bureau drawer somewhere," she admitted reluctantly. "I'll show them to you someday. But I'll warn you now, you probably won't even recognize me. I showed them to Julio once, and he said I was wearing more makeup than a female impersonator. He should know - apparently he was one at some really sordid point in his life that I don't think I want to hear about."

Tessa gave a delicate little shudder. "Agreed. But I'm with Julia - I *do* want to see those pictures one of these days. And we'll make sure to keep the makeup for tonight very light."

Julia nodded emphatically. "No one is going to mistake you for a dude trying to look like a woman. Now, go take the dress off for now so we can glam you up a bit."

Obediently Sasha walked out of Tessa's lavish master bathroom into the bedroom, and carefully shimmied out of the one-shouldered, pale gold silk Grecian-styled gown. Tessa had thoughtfully left a spare bathrobe on the bed for Sasha to wear while having her makeup and hair done, and she slipped into it after carefully hanging up the dress.

It had been Tessa's suggestion that Sasha get ready for tonight's event at the Gregson home, especially since Tessa and Ian were also attending the charity ball benefitting the local children's hospital. Sasha had gratefully accepted the offer, especially since she was still having all manner of doubts and uncertainties about attending the event as Matthew's guest.

He had tentatively brought the subject up to her a couple of weeks ago, and she had known from the way he'd stammered and stuttered that he was just a bit nervous about what he wanted to say to her.

"Uh, I, uh, need to ask you something," he'd mumbled. "And you can totally say no, I would definitely understand because I'm guessing it just isn't your sort of thing. Matter of fact, it's not really my favorite thing to do either, but my board of directors is really pushing me on this one, so I've got to attend. And I don't mind in the least going solo, the

last thing I want is for you to feel obligated to go - "

Sasha had placed a finger over his lips. "Shush. Stop stalling and just ask me, okay? Where exactly would you like me to go?"

"It's a dinner, more like a formal dress ball, actually. A charity fundraiser for the local children's hospital. And since MBI has very close affiliations with the hospital - we've pioneered some of our medical software programs there - it's pretty much expected that I should attend. Especially since I've been blowing off a number of similar events since I filed for divorce."

"Hmm." Sasha had pondered the matter briefly. "When you say formal, what do you mean exactly? Like a tuxedo for you and a long dress for me?"

He'd nodded. "Yes. And I know you probably hate getting dressed up that way, and I wouldn't even ask under normal circumstances. But this one dinner is particularly important, so - "

"Yes. I'll go with you," she'd interrupted before he could continue arguing his case. "It does sound like a very good cause, and if your firm is that involved with the hospital you should definitely be there. When is it?"

He had given her the details then - the date, time, location. The ball was being held at the Gregson Hotel on Nob Hill, and Sasha had been pleased to learn that Ian and Tessa would also be attending. Matthew had promised he would make the necessary arrangements so that the Gregsons would sit at their table, and had been so pleased at her consent that he'd given her a loud, smacking kiss square on the lips.

211

And he had also offered to take her shopping for a gown, shoes, and the other accessories she would need, but on this matter Sasha had remained adamant.

"No, Matthew. Thank you," she'd added graciously. "It's very kind of you to offer, but I'd prefer to buy my own dress. I can ask Tessa and Julia for advice on what would be appropriate."

But he had stubbornly continued to press the matter. "Sasha, I'm not sure you have any idea just how much a dress and shoes and whatnot cost. At least, the sort of outfit that all of the other women will be wearing."

Grinning, she'd chucked him on the chin playfully. "Don't worry," she had laughed. "I won't embarrass you and show up in one of my usual outfits. Or, like my mother calls them, "those hippie clothes". I attended both Tessa's and Julia's weddings, so I have a very good idea of what to wear."

Matthew had frowned. "But you can't afford something like that," he'd argued. "And since it's because of me that you'd be attending, the least you can let me do is buy you a dress. We can set a dollar limit, if you'd like."

She had given a firm shake of her head. "I can get my own dress," she insisted anew. "I'll take Chad or Tessa along with me. Julia would love nothing better than to go along, but she's having some issues getting around comfortably these days, with the twins due in less than two months."

To mollify him, Sasha had promised that if the outfit for the dinner turned out to be ridiculously out of her budget she would let him know.

She'd told Tessa about the situation the very next day, while the two of them were enjoying a cup of tea after yoga class. Tessa had immediately offered to loan Sasha a dress and pair of shoes, but that idea had been nixed upon calculating the nearly four inch difference in their height , and two size difference in shoes. A phone call to Julia hadn't provided a solution, either, because while she was much closer to Sasha in height, her pre-pregnancy figure was still a size or two larger.

Sasha had gently refused any further efforts on Tessa's part to find a dress to borrow, insisting that she could find her own. And when she'd approached Chad about the subject, her clothes-horse landlord had been delighted at the prospect of scouring the various consignment stores that he frequented to find her the perfect dress. Unfortunately, Julio had overheard their plans and invited himself along, a circumstance that only he had been happy about.

As luck would have it, Chad had found the perfect gown at the very first place they had visited, and the price had been surprisingly affordable given the excellent condition the garment was in and the high quality of the fabric. Her luck had continued when Julio had triumphantly unearthed a pair of gold, strappy high-heeled sandals in her size that had been marked down for final clearance. On their way home, Chad had assured her that she'd be a knock-out in this ensemble, fitting in easily with the other women attending the ball in their designer duds.

Sasha wasn't all that worried about how she would look this evening. Even though it had been more than a decade since she'd last competed in ballroom dance, the performance skills that had been drilled into her from a young age hadn't been completely forgotten. Dressing up for the part she would be expected to play this evening wasn't the concern so much as acting the role. Spending the evening drinking champagne and making polite small talk with a roomful of wealthy, sophisticated socialites wasn't exactly her idea of a fun time, and she had a feeling that she'd be practicing her calming, deep breathing techniques off and on all night.

'This is for Matthew,' she reminded herself sternly. 'To make him happy. And in the scheme of things, it's just a few hours out of time. So suck it up, smile, and do it for his sake. And maybe it won't be as bad as you think.'

But she had to keep reminding herself of the reason she'd agreed to do this, especially when she walked back inside the bathroom where Julia was busily arranging her makeup brushes, eyeshadow palettes, tubes and pencils, swabs and sponges. Even during her competition days, Sasha had never seen so many cosmetics assembled in one place. On the contrary, because their budget had always been so tight, she and her mother had usually shared supplies and made do with a bare minimum.

"Julia," reminded Sasha calmly. "You're only making up Tessa and me, not the entire cast of Cirque du Soleil."

Julia smiled impishly. "I have a weakness for makeup. Along with clothes and shoes and purses. So sue me. Now, let's do you first, Sasha, just in case you don't like what I've done. That way we can start over again if necessary. But I promise I'll take it easy."

Half an hour later, Sasha was pleased to see that Julia had

been true to her word. Sasha's pale gold skin glowed and virtually sparkled with the dusting of gold-flecked bronzer that Julia had applied discreetly. Her green-gold eyes looked larger and more mysterious with their subtle shading and soft lining, while her eyebrows had been lightly tweezed and groomed. For the lips, Julia had used a nude gloss with peachy undertones. Overall, the effect was low-key and natural, two elements that Sasha had stressed she wanted when she had agreed to let Julia do her makeup tonight.

"You look gorgeous," assured Tessa as she surveyed Julia's handiwork. "Julia is as much of an artist with makeup as she is with interior design."

Julia grinned as she waved around a thick blusher brush. "Some artists use their brushes to paint on canvas. I use mine to make beautiful women look even more so. Your turn now, Tessa."

An hour later both Sasha and Tessa were both dressed and ready, turning around slowly for a final inspection by Julia, who admittedly was living vicariously through them both this evening.

Julia sighed, sinking down onto the padded bench in front of the bathroom vanity, her hand splayed over her belly. "It seems like an eternity since I was getting dressed up for an evening out on the town," she fretted. "And it's going to be even longer before I lose all this baby weight and can wiggle back into any of my pretty things. I'm so big I can't even fit behind the wheel of my car any longer. And if I move the seat back too much then my legs are too short to reach the pedals. So I need to rely on Nathan to drive me everywhere."

Sasha rubbed Julia's midsection soothingly. "It's all right.

Because very soon you'll have your beautiful baby boys to love and cuddle. And all of this will be worth it. Tell you what. As a little thank you for helping me get ready tonight, I'll borrow a car and drive over to your place one day next week for a pre-natal massage since it's so difficult for you to get around."

Julia's face lit up. "You have no idea how amazing that sounds. Between my aching back and swollen ankles, not to mention how often these two kick me, I could definitely use a massage."

"Consider it done. I'll call you on Monday to set something up."

And then Ian, who had offered to get ready in one of the spare bedrooms, was calling out from the doorway, "Time to leave, ladies. The limo is waiting for us downstairs. And Nathan is here for you, Julia."

Tessa and Sasha insisted on carrying Julia's hefty makeup cases downstairs, while Ian gallantly offered an arm to assist the expectant mother. Sasha was so intent on not tripping over the hem of her long gown, or turning an ankle in the unfamiliar high heels, that she didn't notice the man who stood watching her progress down the winding staircase until he was standing right in front of her.

"Wow," breathed Matthew. "Just - wow. You look fantastic, Sasha. Absolutely stunning."

"Thank you," she replied, a bit overcome by the way he kept staring at her. "You look very handsome, Matthew. Even more so than usual."

He and Ian were both wearing tuxedos, though Matthew looked distinctly less at ease in the formalwear than Ian. Tessa had joked once that her husband had come out of the womb wearing a suit and tie, given how comfortable he felt in such attire. Matthew had also done something a bit different with his hair, slicking it back a bit so that it didn't stick up in that slightly spiky style she'd come to find so appealing.

He took her by the hand and guided her outside to the waiting limo. The driver had picked Matthew up at his place first before heading over to the Gregsons' to get the others. Once comfortably ensconced inside the limo, Sasha carefully rearranged the folds of her gown around her legs. Just before Ian and Tessa joined them, Matthew placed a hand on her thigh, causing her to glance up at him inquiringly.

"Thank you," he told her sincerely. "I know this isn't your thing, that you'd probably rather be reading poetry right now or practicing yoga. But I want you to know how much it means to me to have you along tonight. I'm not a fan of these sort of events, either, but this is probably the first time I'm looking forward to attending one."

She squeezed his hand. "I don't mind at all," she replied warmly. "And I have to confess that it was actually fun to get all dressed up like this for once. Though I can't promise to keep the shoes on all night."

They were sharing a laugh as Ian handed Tessa inside the limo, and the Gregsons regarded their companions quizzically.

"Private joke?" inquired Ian, as the limo began to pull away from the curb.

Sasha shook her head. "Not exactly. I was just expressing doubt that I'd be able to handle these high heels for the duration of the evening, given that my usual footwear is

217

none at all."

"You'll be fine," assured Tessa. "I'm predicting that all those years of ballroom dance training will kick in. You did wear heels when you competed, didn't you?"

"Not anywhere near this high," corrected Sasha. "And it's been more than a dozen years since that time in my life. I'm not sure muscle memory lasts quite that long."

Matthew brought her hand to his lips. "I don't really give a rat's ass if you keep the shoes on or not," he declared. "Either way, you'll be the most beautiful woman there tonight. Uh, one of the *two* most beautiful women, that is. You, uh, look gorgeous as usual, Tessa."

Tessa, who did indeed look breathtaking in a sleek black gown with long, close fitting lace sleeves and a scooped neckline, smiled her thanks at Matthew. "That's sweet of you to say. But you're right - Sasha looks incredibly lovely. More so than ever. So be prepared for all the attention you're bound to get tonight."

Sasha frowned. "What sort of attention? And why on earth would anyone notice me?"

"Because," explained Matthew drolly, "this is the first event I've attended with anyone but my soon-to-be-ex wife, and everyone will want to know who you are. Especially since Lindsey wasn't exactly well liked by most of these people. She was considered to be somewhat on the crass side. Not to mention she liked to flirt with as many other men as possible, so none of the wives or girlfriends could stand her."

Tessa nodded in agreement. "I can vouch for that. Except that Ian, of course, was always far too decent to respond to

218

her attempts." She reached over and kissed her husband on the cheek.

Ian smiled at his young wife adoringly, brushing a long blonde curl off her forehead. "Why would I ever flirt with another woman when I had you, darling? Not to mention that I consider Matthew one of my very closest friends. And flirting with another man's wife is definitely considered to be in very, very bad taste."

"You should remind your friend Dr. Reeves about that," muttered Matthew. "I guarantee if Jordan is here this evening he'll find his way over to Tessa's side as often as possible, despite whatever new female he's got clinging to his arm."

Ian scowled at this bit of unsolicited advice, while Tessa's cheeks flushed and she glanced down at her lap, clasping and unclasping her hands in agitation.

"He doesn't flirt with me, Matthew," she murmured uncertainly. "At least no more than he does with any other woman. That's just who Jordan is. I can guarantee you that he'll do the same with Sasha tonight."

"He'd better not," declared Matthew. "She is most definitely spoken for."

"And she can most definitely speak up for herself," admonished Sasha calmly. "I'll handle this overly-eager Dr. Reeves if he makes an appearance. And now I think we should change the subject. We're upsetting Tessa."

"I'm sorry, Tessa," Matthew told her gently. "Sasha's right. We're supposed to be having a fun time tonight, so let's make sure we enjoy every moment, hmm?"

Tessa gave Sasha a grateful look, then squeezed Ian's hand reassuringly, changing his dark scowl into a tender smile. Sasha guessed the subject of the flirtatious Dr. Reeves was a sensitive one between the married couple, and she made a mental note to quiz Matthew for more details at another time.

The limo pulled up a short while later in front of the elegant Gregson hotel, often cited as one of the most beautiful structures in San Francisco. Sasha had only been inside the grand hotel once before, to attend a bridal shower for Tessa the previous spring. And while she wasn't sure she would ever truly feel comfortable around so much lavish grandeur, she could still admire the hotel's architecture and décor, just as she did most things of great beauty.

Fighting off an odd, somewhat unsettling sensation of unease, Sasha was more than content to let Matthew guide her inside the hotel and up a long, majestic staircase to the mezzanine level where the ballroom was located. The venue was already more than half filled with guests, and she gulped, wondering how many curious, calculating glances would be directed her way throughout the evening.

"Forget them," murmured Matthew in her ear, as he grabbed two flutes of champagne from a waiter hovering close by. "All of these other people here tonight - none of them matter. Oh, unfortunately there are a few I'll have to smile at and make polite small talk with - local government officials, members of my board, people I do business with. But aside from saying hello, how are you, enjoy your evening, I don't plan on socializing with any of them."

Sasha took a brief sip of the champagne, recognizing it as a pricey brand even though she knew little about wine or alcohol. "Apparently Lindsey enjoyed doing so."

Matthew grimaced. "Too much so, unfortunately. She loved going to these events, would make it her business to find as many as possible for us to attend. Especially if she knew there was going to be a celebrity or athlete or some politician in attendance, and she'd always make sure we had our picture taken with them. I think after a time she considered herself something of a minor celebrity herself, like she and I were the local equivalents of Bill and Melinda Gates or something."

Sasha offered up a sympathetic smile. "I'll take it from your tone that you didn't share her love of socializing."

He made a sound of distaste. "That's the understatement of the century. It's not a coincidence that this is only the second event I've agreed to attend since I filed for divorce. And probably the last one I go to for several more months." He slid an arm around her waist. "I have to thank you again for coming with me tonight. You're the only thing that's going to make it bearable. Especially since I've cut way back on the alcohol, thanks to a certain someone's influence."

She deliberately let her eyes sparkle at him. "That was a good influence," she reminded him. "You admitted it yourself - you've lost that bit of a beer belly you were starting to accumulate, you don't have dark circles under your eyes any longer, and you sleep much better at night."

Teasingly, his hand slid down to her ass and gave it a squeeze. "Yes, but I get my very best sleep when you spend the night. Especially since you've usually worn me out by then."

Sasha gave him a look of mock outrage. "I think you're confusing who wears the other out," she replied with

221

a knowing grin. Then she reached up to kiss his cheek, whispering in his ear, "I sleep very well when I'm in your bed, too. And it's not just because the mattress is so comfy."

Matthew laughed out loud, and would have continued trading quips with her, but at that particular moment an older, well dressed couple approached them.

"Matt. I wasn't sure we'd get to see you this evening," the man offered in greeting as he shook Matthew's hand.

"I'm afraid I haven't been in the mood to socialize much these past few months," acknowledged Matthew. "But I'm pleased to report all of that is beginning to change for the better."

He introduced Sasha to the couple, both of whom appeared to be in their sixties, as Larry and Marie Hartman. "Larry and Marie are major shareholders in MBI," he explained to her.

Larry's eyes lit up with interest as he shook Sasha's hand, holding it a bit too tight for her liking. "A pleasure to make you acquaintance, Sasha. Fonseca - that's an Italian name, I believe."

Sasha shook her head, tactfully withdrawing her hand at the same time. "Portuguese, actually. My father is from Brazil."

Marie, who was wearing a tight-fitting, low-cut gown better suited to a woman two to three decades younger than herself, gave Sasha a somewhat disdainful inspection. "What is it that you do, dear? For a living, that is."

Sasha, who had grown used to dealing with well-heeled, and quite often uppity students at the studio over the years, merely smiled at Marie with well-rehearsed patience. "I teach yoga classes, Mrs. Hartman. And I'm also a massage therapist. Both jobs that I love dearly."

At the look of wide-eyed shock on Marie's face, Matthew was quick to join the conversation before the woman could say something offensive. "And Sasha used to be a competitive ballroom dancer, Marie," he blurted out, not bothering to add that the last time she'd competed had been as a young teenager. "Do you watch the show *Beyond Ballroom?*" At Marie's nod, he added, "Well, Sasha's mother is one of the professional dancers on the show – Katya Veselov."

The haughty look of disapproval on Marie's tightly stretched face - the result of a not particularly effective facelift - quickly morphed into a smile of delight. "My goodness, she's my absolute favorite!" she gushed. "I just love how feisty she is, how she always seems to find a way to whip her partners into shape. And especially how she shows up those young dancers on the show every week. She's a *real* dancer, you can tell."

For the next few minutes, Marie chatted amicably with Sasha about the TV show, Katya, and Sasha's own dancing, while Larry preferred to talk Matthew's ear off about some new tech company he was thinking of investing in. Fortunately, Matthew was able to diplomatically cut Larry off sooner than later, and smilingly whisked Sasha away.

"Sorry about that," he muttered as he ushered her towards their table.

"For what?" she asked calmly. "The fact that Marie was visibly horrified at my choice of profession? Or the way you sort of stretched the truth about exactly when I stopped competing in dance?"

Matthew's cheeks flushed, making him look endearingly

guilty. "Uh, both, I suppose. As you probably figured out by now, the Hartmans are sort of on the snobby side, especially Marie. And she always hated Lindsey, especially because my ex used to flirt pretty outrageously with old Larry - who did nothing to discourage it from happening. Marie probably took one look at you, figured you were a hell of a lot younger and prettier than Lindsey, and just assumed you'd put the moves on Larry, too."

Sasha wrinkled her nose in distaste. "No, thank you. I'm not the least bit attracted to men who are older than my own father. Or who reek of offensive cologne. Not to mention the fact that I'm perfectly happy with the man I'm here with this evening. I don't need to stroke my ego by flirting with other men in order to prove they find me attractive, and especially not when I have the handsomest man in the room right next to me."

He gave her one of those wide, goofy grins that always made her toes curl up a little and cause a warm feeling to spread through her midsection. "Really? Not one of the handsomest, but *the* handsomest?"

With the added height from her stilettos, she didn't have to reach up on tiptoes as she normally did in order to press a kiss to his cheek. "I never say anything I don't mean, Matthew," she reminded him, then looped her arm through his and steered him over to where the Gregsons were standing.

The call to dinner was made a few minutes later, and Sasha was grateful that Tessa had made the arrangements for the two couples to sit together. The other four people at their table were two of Ian's management team and their spouses, and she guessed that Tessa had hand selected them to make sure Sasha would feel at ease in their presence.

And it turned out to be a very pleasant dinner, far more so than Sasha had expected, and she was surprised to find that she was actually enjoying herself. Though she had never attended college, she was extremely well read and made sure to read at least one newspaper every day to keep up on current events. It was easy for her, therefore, to join in the conversation at the table, and every so often Matthew would catch her eye and beam his approval at her.

The only slightly tense moment came when their dinner entrees were served, and the waiter placed a plate of beef tenderloin at Sasha's place. She felt a bit sorry for the visibly harried waiter, and attempted to call him over discreetly to point out his error. Matthew, however, was nowhere near as tolerant and impatiently motioned the man over.

"This is the wrong order," he told him bluntly. "The lady is supposed to have a vegetarian entrée."

The waiter shook his head. "I don't think so, sir. I didn't see that on my list. And I don't even think we have a vegetarian option available for tonight."

Ian, who'd closely observed the goings-on, was about to intervene, but Matthew held up a hand to forestall him.

"Then I suggest you ask the chef to prepare one," he told the waiter in a not so pleasant tone. "And quickly. And if your boss gives you a bad time about it, you might want to mention that *his* boss is in attendance this evening and watching carefully to see how all of this plays out."

Matthew indicated his head in Ian's direction, and it was obvious from the way the waiter's eyes nearly bugged out of their sockets that he knew exactly who he was. The waiter nodded wordlessly, plucked up Sasha's plate, and practically jogged into the kitchen.

Matthew pulled back the cuff of his white dress shirt and checked his watch. "Want to make a bet on how long it'll take him to return with the right order?" he asked Ian, chuckling.

Ian grimaced. "If he knows what's good for him, the answer had best be ten minutes or less. I'm sorry about the confusion, Sasha. I will certainly be making a phone call to his supervisor about this."

"Please, that really isn't necessary," she protested. "This certainly isn't the first time I've received the wrong food at a restaurant or an event. I've come to accept over the years that mistakes of that sort will happen. It comes with being a vegetarian."

"Still, being a vegetarian is not that unusual nowadays, and especially in California," argued Matthew. "I guarantee that the chef prepared a vegetarian dish, and that our waiter just screwed up. I should - "

"Forget about it," finished Sasha. "Especially since he's already headed back this way with my food."

The waiter apologized profusely as he set the steaming plate of pasta primavera in front of Sasha, then continued to fuss over her for another minute or two, making sure that everything was to her liking and asking if there was anything else he could do for her. And even though she thanked him profusely, assured him that everything was fine, he still looked anxious as he moved to another table.

Fortunately, there were no other mishaps for the remainder of the evening, and Sasha couldn't recall the last time she'd enjoyed herself so much. Even the dreaded high heels proved to be more comfortable than she'd feared, and remained on her feet the whole night. At some point, a jazz ensemble began to play some soft music, and after the other three couples at their table left for the dance floor, Matthew turned to Sasha hesitantly.

"Uh, I'd ask if you'd like to dance, but I guess that's sort of a silly question," he quipped.

She laughed. "You know I love to dance, but I also know that it isn't necessarily your favorite thing. I'm fine with staying here at the table and just listening to the music."

In reply, he rose to his feet and held a hand out to her. "But I'm not. I have too many bad memories of watching Lindsey dance with dozens of other men at these events, and feeling sort of helpless to do anything about it. Or maybe helpless isn't the right word. More like apathetic. I don't want to feel that way about anything or anyone again. You've managed to make me feel ten years younger, and a whole lot happier, and I don't want to miss out on things anymore. So, please. Will you honor me with this dance?"

Sasha's heart felt like it was stuck in her throat as she let him draw her to her feet. "I have never felt more like dancing than I do right now," she whispered.

"Good," he replied, as he guided her out to the dance floor. "Because we're going to dance a lot tonight. Maybe you can teach me a few new moves. Not that I've got any old ones, that is."

Their combined laughter rang out happily as he drew her close against his chest.

227

SASHA COULDN'T SUPPRESS A YAWN as she snuggled into her pillow. "I don't mean to be rude, but I'm really tired," she told him regretfully. "It would be different if I didn't have to get up early to teach in the morning. I'm sorry."

Matthew kissed her naked shoulder. "Don't be. You have nothing to be sorry for. Especially since we've already had one really spectacular time tonight. I'm just getting greedy, I suppose."

His hand caressed the sleek curve of her hip, before pulling the duvet up over her nude body. After arriving home from the party more than an hour ago, they had instantly fallen into bed, their lovemaking a little lustier than usual since they had both been a bit tipsy. But Matthew was hungrier than ever for her, and even after a tumultuous orgasm he was still semi-aroused.

Sasha was clearly exhausted, though, and he put a damper on his raging libido, even though he wasn't feeling in the least bit gentlemanly at the moment. But he sighed, and settled for a sweet good-night kiss, instead of the second round of lovemaking he really craved.

"Good night," she murmured sleepily. "Tonight was actually fun. More fun than I expected. So I'd be okay with going to more events with you in the future. That is, if you want me to."

He caressed her cheek tenderly. "Of course I want you to," he whispered. "Don't you know by now that I want you with me all the time? Or that I'm pretty sure I've fallen in love with you?"

228

But as he waited with bated breath for her reply or reaction, all he got in return was a faint snore, and he realized with a frustrated grin that she'd already fallen asleep.

chapter twelve

February

"**WOW, YOU REALLY WEREN'T EXAGGERATING** about those two. Do they always bicker this much?"

Sasha smiled faintly at Matthew's urgently whispered question. "This is actually pretty tame for them. When my mother starts looking for sharp objects to throw at my dad, that's the time to quietly duck out of the room and leave them to it."

Matthew grinned in spite of the increasingly loud and heated argument that was going on in his living room. "What is it exactly that they're arguing about anyway? Kind of hard to tell, given that they keep switching languages."

Katya and Enzo seemed to be arguing back and forth in either English or French, languages that they were both fluent in, and then occasionally would revert to their respective native tongues. And Matthew was just guessing that the Russian and Portuguese words they were flinging at each other weren't especially complimentary.

"Who really knows at this point?" asked Sasha tiredly. "I'm not even sure *they* remember what started this particular argument off. Sadly, it doesn't seem to take very much to get them going."

"Gee, the only thing I ever remember my parents arguing about was whether a colleague's paper on the current status of advanced mathematics in high schools had real merit or not. And that was really more of a debate than an argument," he recalled.

Sasha glanced across the room to where her mother was now stomping one stiletto-clad foot to emphasize whatever point she was trying to make, while her father was muttering in Portuguese, his face darkening in anger. "Lucky you," she sighed. "Meanwhile, living with these two was like being a permanent cast member in a telenovela. You never knew what drama was going to be enacted the next day. Ah, and then of course, their fights more often than not ended just like this."

Matthew followed the direction of her gaze to where Katya and Enzo were now locked in a passionate embrace, startled at how quickly they had made the transition from adversaries to lovers. But from the resigned expression on Sasha's face, this, too, was far from something new to her.

"Good thing they aren't staying here with you, like you originally suggested," she whispered to him. "Otherwise, my father would think nothing of carrying Mama off to the bedroom right about now. After they each discarded several articles of clothing first, of course."

His eyes widened as Enzo forcefully pushed Katya up against the wall, lifting one of her legs to wrap around his waist as he ground himself against her. And since Katya apparently didn't have a submissive bone in her body, she gave it back as good as she got, raking her long, blood red fingernails down her lover's back before biting down on his earlobe. *That* caused Enzo to smack her on the buttocks, which in return made Katya retaliate by biting his bottom lip this time.

"Cristo!" yelped Enzo, stepping away from the wall as blood began to trickle down his chin. "I've always sworn you were part vampire, Katya. Or maybe a witch. You're definitely crazy."

Katya glared at him, rubbing her abused posterior. "I don't like the spanking, Enzo," she snarled. "You know that. You watched that movie again, didn't you? The one where the man likes whipping women, or tying them up. If you ever try that with me, *you* will be the one who gets spanked. Ach, but knowing you, that would probably give you pleasure, wouldn't it? You like that sort of - "

"Okay, enough. Both of you," insisted Sasha, rising gracefully to her feet. "In case you've forgotten, today is my birthday. It's why Matthew arranged for you both to fly into town - first class no less - and reserved one of the nicest suites for you at the Gregson Hotel for three nights. And why he's taking us out to dinner tonight at one of the best restaurants in San Francisco to celebrate. So, please. Can you stop arguing for the next few hours so we can enjoy the evening? Please."

Enzo's features softened instantly, and he was at his daughter's side in the next moment. "My bebé," he crooned, cupping her cheek in his hand. "My lovely Sasha. Of course your mother and I will behave ourselves to honor your birthday. I will do my best to ignore that crazy woman during our dinner, so that we can all enjoy ourselves, yes?"

"Crazy!" screeched Katya. "*You* are the crazy one, Enzo! And you have been driving me crazy for almost thirty years. The first time you left me I should have never taken you

232

back. My life would have been much more peaceful if I had listened to Polina and married that nice Russian man who lived across the street from us in Paris."

Enzo smirked. "That old fool? You would have killed him after just one year - either by giving him a heart attack with all of your dramatics, or causing him to hang himself because he couldn't take any more of it. Katya, meu amor, I am the only man alive capable of handling you, and you know it. Now, no more arguing, hmm? Sasha is right. It's her birthday, and Matthew has been kind enough to make all of these plans so we could celebrate together. So now we celebrate, not fight. Agreed?"

The expression in Katya's green eyes was almost deadly as she glared at Enzo, but she merely nodded in response. "Yes. Agreed. Even if I want to break that vase over your head right now."

"Please don't," begged Matthew. "It's one of the few things I like in this place. And according to the bill from the decorator, that vase cost around five thousand dollars."

"For this?" Katya flicked a finger over the simple pottery urn disdainfully. "Hmm, I think maybe this decorator - how do you say it, Sasha - tore him off?"

"Ripped him off," corrected Sasha patiently. "Regardless, Mama, that's Matthew's business, not yours. Now, as soon as Papa wipes the blood off his mouth, we should leave for dinner."

Enzo grinned at his only child and obligingly dashed inside the guest bathroom to clean himself up a bit. During his brief absence, Katya wasted no time in unleashing a rapid fire stream of Russian at Sasha, and Matthew wryly assumed that the older woman was complaining loudly and bitterly about her on-again, off-again lover.

It had been quite a kick meeting Sasha's parents, he thought in amusement, and since they had arrived in town last evening he hadn't been bored for even a second in their presence. And while their personalities couldn't have been much different - fun-loving, gregarious, and easily amused Enzo, and the fiery-tempered, stubborn, and hard to impress Katya - the physical and emotional attraction between the couple practically gave off sparks every time their eyes met.

The more time he had spent in their presence, the more Matthew had marveled at just how different Sasha was in temperament and personality from either of her parents. She was most definitely her own woman, with her own unique set of values and beliefs, and if she hadn't born a noticeable physical resemblance to them, there was no way he would have believed them to be her parents.

Sasha and Katya were built along very similar lines - of medium height, small frame, and leanly muscled. Sasha's figure seemed a bit softer than Katya's, who was bordering on being skinny rather than slender. Matthew guessed the older woman was under constant pressure from the producers of her television show to look as thin as possible for the cameras, and judging from the way Katya watched her diet like a hawk he was willing to bet his hunch was right.

Without the spray-on tan she always applied for the television show, Katya's natural complexion was much lighter than the pale gold skin tone Sasha had obviously inherited from her father. Matthew suspected that Katya's carefully groomed mane of silky blonde hair owed most of its color these days to a bottle, though he had little trouble believing that the shade had once been her natural hue. And unlike her down-to-earth daughter, Katya loved clothes - expensive designer labels from what he'd been able to determine - like the sleek burgundy wool sheath dress and high heeled black leather ankle boots she was wearing now. Her gold earrings, chain necklace, and diamond studded bangle bracelet were discreet but obviously costly, and her strikingly lovely face was expertly made up. She looked glamorous and sophisticated, and much younger than her forty-nine years.

Enzo, on the other hand, with the streaks of silver in his otherwise black hair, and visible crow's feet at the corners of the green-gold eyes he'd passed on to his daughter, easily looked like the fifty-four year old man that he was - a man who had traveled the globe too many times to count, and who made it a point to live every day to its fullest. At the hotel suite last night, he'd confessed over an after dinner drink to Matthew that he had admittedly drank too much, partied too hard, and seduced too many pretty girls over the years, but that the only real regrets he had in his well-lived life revolved around Katya and Sasha.

"I should have been there for both of them more," he'd lamented drunkenly. "I should have forced that hard head Katya to marry me when we found out she was pregnant, should have chained her to my side. And we should have made a real home for our little girl, instead of carting her around the world with us like a piece of luggage. That was why, when she insisted on living with my sister-in-law, I stood up for her against Katya. My Sasha - she deserved

those years with Linda after everything her mother and I put her through. She's a good girl, my daughter, you know?"

"I know," Matthew had assured him. "She's kind and compassionate and never judges people. She has the patience of a saint, and the disposition of an angel."

Enzo had grinned wickedly. "In other words, not a thing like me or Katya! I used to wonder sometimes if the babies were switched at birth, and we got the wrong one. Sasha is so calm, so gentle, while her mother and I are like the hurricane and the tornado meeting up. And my daughter is the most important thing in the world to me, Matthew. I may not call her or see her as often as I should, but I think of her every day. And wish all the time that I'd done things differently."

"Well, she turned out just fine under the circumstances," Matthew had told him. "I think that Sasha is the woman she is today because of the way she grew up. So - thank you, Enzo, because I happen to love your daughter just the way she is."

"Love, eh?" Enzo had regarded Matthew a bit warily, running a hand through his unruly mane of dark, curly hair, the same sort of curls Sasha had. "Hmm. Sasha tells me that you already have a wife, no?"

"No." Matthew had given an emphatic shake of his head. "That is, not in any way that still matters."

He had explained what the current situation with Lindsey was, an explanation that had seemed to satisfy Enzo and assure him that Matthew's intentions toward Sasha were all above board.

"My Sasha needs a good man in her life," Enzo
had confided. "She's too independent, too afraid of
commitment. But it's a good sign that she wanted me and
Katya to meet you. Sasha has been alone too much in her
life already, so I'm happy that she has someone like you
to take care of her. And you're a good man, I can tell.
You take care of your woman and her parents, and Sasha
tells me you're a very good father as well. You can always
tell the measure of a man by how he treats other people,
Matthew. And by the quality of the alcohol he provides for
his guests."

Enzo had winked then, toasting Matthew with his
nearly empty glass of a very expensive Cuban rum, before
downing the rest in a quick gulp.

Enzo sauntered out of the bathroom lazily, his hands in the
pockets of his tailored black trousers, whistling cheerfully.
He slipped an arm around Katya's waist, and made a big
show out of planting a sloppy kiss on her cheek. She, in turn,
merely glared at him, letting him know in no uncertain terms
that a temporary truce might have been called between
them, but that the war was far from over.

After several glasses of a very expensive French
champagne, however, Katya was in a much better mood,
and actually laughed and smiled throughout dinner. At
Sasha's gentle urgings, Katya even ate heartily of her food,
which she admitted was delicious.

"You have good taste, Mathieu," Katya acknowledged,
pronouncing his name in the French manner, more like mat-
tue. "Aleksandra told me the dress and shoes she is wearing

this evening were a gift from you. A big improvement from what I usually see her in. She looks beautiful tonight, truly lovely."

Enzo reached across the table and picked up Sasha's hand, bringing it to his lips. "You mean more beautiful than usual, Katya," he corrected. "Because our daughter is always lovely, no matter what she's wearing. Though I must agree with your mother, bebé. That dress is quite spectacular. Excellent choice, Matthew."

Matthew merely acknowledged Enzo's compliment with a smile and toast of his champagne flute. Not for anything would he admit to having enlisted the help of Tessa Gregson in choosing an outfit for Sasha this evening, given the fact that he knew absolutely nothing about women's clothing. At least, he consoled himself, he'd asked one of Sasha's closest friends for assistance, instead of relying on a sales clerk or personal shopper. And after initially protesting that he had spent far too much on her, and that she was perfectly capable of buying her own things, Sasha hadn't been able to resist the gorgeous sage green silk gown. It had a halter neck and was cut low in the back, with a satin waistband and close fitting skirt. But what she had loved the most about the dress had been the subtle butterfly print patterned into the delicate silk fabric, and in the end hadn't been able to resist wearing it tonight.

He caressed the nape of her neck now, a nape that had been bared by the almost careless way she'd pinned her curls up this evening, holding them in place with a pair of clips adorned with green dragonflies. She'd kept her makeup minimal, but had done something subtle with her eyes and lips, and her pale gold skin glowed beneath the recessed lightning over their table.

Sasha smiled up at him, her hand covering his where it still rested on the back of her neck. "Pretty good massage technique there," she teased. "Maybe I should start teaching you a few things. That way you can return the favor and give me a massage once in awhile."

Matthew pressed a kiss to her temple. "Anytime, sweetheart. Though there's no possible way I could ever return all of the favors you've done me."

She flicked the diamond and emerald drop earrings that had been another birthday present. "I'd say these are a pretty expensive form of payback."

He waved a hand in dismissal. "I'm not talking about gifts or money, Sasha. What you've done for me has no monetary value, can't be bought or paid for. You gave me my dignity back, my self-worth, and gave me a reason to wake up and look forward to the day ahead - something I hadn't done for a long time. So a few small material things are no comparison to the things you've given me."

Tears shimmered in her eyes as she cupped his cheek in her hand, pulling his face towards hers until their lips met in a brief, tender kiss. Across the table, Enzo cleared his throat until Matthew glanced up at him a bit guiltily.

"Sorry," he mumbled. "Couldn't help myself. As you said, she looks lovely this evening, more so than usual."

Sasha gave her father a look of disbelief. "Honestly, Papa? You of all people are objecting to one tiny kiss in public? It's a wonder I wasn't warped for life watching you and Mama go at it almost every time we were out somewhere."

239

Enzo grinned wickedly. "We were very naughty, weren't we, Katya? Ah, do you recall the time we almost got kicked out of that club in Madrid? Or when the waiter at that café in Brussels told us we were making the other diners uncomfortable? And then of course there was that incident in Mexico City when - "

Katya clamped a hand over his mouth before he could finish his sentence. "Enough, Enzo," she commanded in a tone that made Matthew sit up a little straighter. "Yes, I'm sure Mathieu gets the message that you and I were silly, romantic fools in our youth. Fortunately, we've finally grown up. Well, at least I have." She bolted down the rest of her champagne, smiling her thanks when Matthew refilled it. "Good God, I'm going to be fifty next year. And Sasha will be thirty a year from today. We're all getting old, I'm afraid."

"Speak for yourself," retorted Enzo, topping off his own flute. "You are as young as you feel, meu amor. And you look fantastic for your age, much prettier and in much better shape than a girl half your age. Hotter, too."

He nuzzled her neck then, and made to slide his hand up under her dress until Katya very firmly removed it, and gave him another of those icy glares.

Matthew frowned as he did some quick calculations in his head, and realized uneasily that he was actually closer in age to Katya than he was to Sasha. At forty-one, he was nine years younger than the mother, but eleven years older than the daughter. He'd never thought about the difference in age between himself and Sasha before, largely because she was so mature and composed for her age, something of an old soul. And eleven years really wasn't all that much, he

240

reasoned. After all, there was a full fifteen years between Ian and Tessa, and he'd never met a couple who were crazier about each other than the two of them.

As dinner drew to a close, it quickly became apparent that for Enzo at least the evening was really just beginning. Sasha had warned Matthew that her father could turn into a real party animal at times, and evidently celebrating his daughter's twenty-ninth birthday was one of those occasions. Fortunately, Matthew had arranged for a driver this evening, having already witnessed the previous night how much Enzo could drink, and fearing that there would be pressure to keep up with him tonight. Sasha had arranged for a substitute to teach her Sunday morning yoga class, wanting to spend as much time as possible with her parents during their brief visit, so she somewhat reluctantly went along with Enzo's suggestion to go dancing.

Once inside the exclusive dance club - a place that would have been otherwise impossible to gain entrance to had Matthew not given the doorman a very sizeable tip - Enzo wasted little time in pulling Katya out on the dance floor. As they waited for their drinks to be served, Matthew let out a low whistle of admiration as he watched Sasha's parents more than keep up with the throngs of much younger couples out there dancing.

"Well, it's obvious that your mother's a pro at this," he commented. "But your father isn't half bad himself."

Sasha smiled. "Papa has more enthusiasm than actual skill, but he loves to dance and party. My mother has taught him some steps over the years, enough so that he can twirl her around the floor, but he prefers to let the music take him over and improvise. And of course that drives her crazy, which typically results in another argument."

Matthew shrugged. "As much as they bicker, it's pretty damned obvious that they're crazy about each other. But I get why they would have major issues living together for more than a few days."

She gave a delicate little shudder. "More like hours than days, I'm afraid. And it's definitely a case with those two of 'can't live with you, can't live without you'. I just hope that one of these days they'll finally find a way to cohabitate peacefully. As Mama said earlier, neither one of them is getting any younger."

Their drinks arrived then - a white Russian for Matthew, and a small glass of sherry for Sasha. They clinked glasses in a silent toast before each taking a sip.

"Thank you for arranging all this," she told him earnestly, taking his hand in hers. "Flying my parents into town, setting them up at the hotel, taking us all out to these wonderful meals. And of course for all the beautiful gifts, which once again were far, far too much."

He interlaced their fingers, resting their hands on her thigh. "It was my pleasure," he assured her. "You deserved to have a fabulous birthday. And even though I would have preferred to spend it alone with you, I'm happy to have shared this time with your parents. Even if your mom keeps giving me the evil eye. Have you told her exactly who I am, by the way? More specifically, how much money I have?"

"God, no." Sasha shook her head emphatically. "First of all, even if I explained it to her in three different languages, she would have zero idea of what it is you do for a living.

242

Believe it or not, she's even more inept at technology than I am, can't even figure out how to use an ATM. But she would definitely understand money. And if she knew exactly how rich you were, she'd be nagging me every single day to - well, you know."

Matthew grinned teasingly. "What? Make a commitment to you? Move in with me? Or convince me to make an honest woman out of you?"

She paused before replying, taking another small sip of her sherry. "All three, I suppose," she said reluctantly. "She tells me all the time that I'm getting older, that I should settle down and get serious about my future, that teaching yoga and doing massage isn't a real career, blah, blah, blah. I can't tell you how many quote unquote 'nice Russian boys' she's wanted to set me up with over the years. Of course, the fact that *she's* never felt the urge to get married and settle down is immaterial."

He had grown quiet at her words. "And what is it that *you* want, Sasha? Do you want to get married someday, maybe have children? We've never really discussed a future together, you know. And yes, I realize that I'm not exactly in the ideal position to do so at the moment, given that my obnoxious ex is still refusing to sign those divorce papers. But I do want to make a commitment to you, I do want to continue having you in my life. And while I can't offer you marriage right now, I'd love nothing better than to have you move in with me."

Sasha stiffened, and her hand suddenly grew slack in his. "Matthew - I'm not ready for something like that. It's too soon."

"We've been together for four months," he chided gently.

"Yes, and that's the longest any relationship I've ever been in has lasted until now," she declared. "I've never lived with anyone, never made a commitment of any sort to anyone, and have never really considered getting married. So, please. Believe me when I say it's too soon to talk about any of that stuff. Can't we just go on the way we've been doing?"

Matthew picked up her hand in his and studied it carefully, tracing a finger along her lifeline. "Do you care for me, Sasha?" he murmured.

"Of course I do," she replied immediately. She cupped his face between her palms, starting intently into his eyes. "I care for you very deeply, Matthew. As a friend, a lover, a person."

He smiled a bit sadly. "You don't mention love. Is that because you don't love me, or because you don't believe in such things?"

His question visibly took her aback, and she stared at him in silence for long seconds. "I - I don't know," admitted Sasha. "I mean, I believe that love exists between partners, have seen it with my own eyes - Tessa and Ian, Julia and Nathan, Julio and Chad. Even my parents, though theirs is much more of a love-hate relationship. As for myself, I'm just not sure I know what it feels like. Romantic love, that is. Of course, I love my parents, my Aunt Linda, my family. But what I feel for you is much different, Matthew. Maybe it's love, but maybe it's just affection. How do you know the difference?"

Matthew lowered his lips to hers. "Like this," he whispered, just before taking her mouth in a lingering, blistering kiss.

When he lifted his head a considerable amount of time later, it was to find Sasha staring at him with wide-eyed wonder, her lips swollen and trembling from his passionate kiss.

"*That*," he told her, "felt like a hell of a lot more than just affection, didn't it? And for me at least, I know exactly how I feel. I've been in love with you for a long time now, Sasha. I haven't said anything until now, since I know how skittish you are about relationships and all. But I'm crazy about you, want to spend every minute I can with you, and I'm going to keep trying to convince you to move in with me. And one of these days you're going to agree."

"M-maybe," she whispered tremulously, reaching almost blindly for her glass of sherry.

Matthew was prevented from pursuing the subject further by the return of Enzo and Katya at that moment, but he couldn't help the very satisfied grin that he flashed Sasha's way, letting her know in no uncertain terms that he wouldn't give up until she eventually agreed.

"HE'S A NICE BOY, ISN'T he? Well mannered, respectful, smart. And apparently he likes animals, too. That alone would give him high marks in my book."

Sasha grinned at her aunt. "Are you referring to Casey or Matthew? Because that could describe both of them. Especially at the moment."

The two women laughed as they watched Matthew and his son playing an enthusiastic game of fetch with the three dogs currently residing with Linda. OJ the cat was curled up

245

contentedly on Sasha's lap, while at least three other cats prowled through the cottage.

Sasha, Matthew, and Casey had made the drive to Stinson Beach in time to join Linda for a delicious lunch of homemade green chilé cheese enchiladas, Mexican rice, and a salad. Linda was Mexican by birth, but had emigrated to New Mexico as an infant and had grown up in the Taos area. After college, she had set off to explore much of Central and South American, looking for inspiration for her art, and it had been during a trip to Brazil that she had met Joaquim Fonseca. Theirs had been a passionate but relatively short-lived marriage, given that Joaquim was very much a ladies man and hadn't let a little thing like wedding vows stand in his way. Linda had returned to the States after the divorce, and eventually found her way to Marin County. She rarely traveled these days, claiming that it was just too much of a hassle, and too difficult to find someone to take care of all of her animals. But Sasha suspected that Linda's broken heart had never really mended after the bitter divorce, and that she'd retreated to this corner of the world to lick her wounds.

And Stinson Beach was an ideal place to retreat from the world, with its pristine beaches, funky beach town vibes, and peaceful, laidback attitude. Weekends in the summertime were something of a challenge, given the large crowds who flocked to town, but Linda typically just shrugged them off and kept close to home on those days.

"I see you survived last weekend with your parents," remarked Linda.

Sasha nodded. "They were both on their best behavior,

actually. I think some of that had to do with the royal treatment Matthew arranged for them - a five star hotel suite, meals out at some of the top restaurants in town, spa treatments, pretty much the works. It would have been in bad taste on their part to have one of their epic fights, very ungrateful of them under the circumstances."

"And how did they like Matthew?"

"Well, you know my father," replied Sasha drily. "I doubt there's too many people in this world he doesn't like, and especially not when there's free booze around. And of course it's just the opposite with Mama - there are very few people that she actually likes. But she was relatively gracious with Matthew, and I think at least that he impressed her. With my mother, that's about the best you can hope for."

"Hmm." Linda took a sip of the tea that she had just brewed for them a few minutes ago. "So Katya doesn't know just how rich Matthew is?"

"No. I mean, it had to be pretty obvious to both of them that he's wealthy, given everything he did for them last weekend. But I don't think either of my parents have a clue that Matthew is one of the forty richest men in this country. And as far as I'm concerned that's not necessarily information they need to know."

"I agree," replied Linda. "Especially Katya. Good Lord, she'd be pestering you three times a day to marry the man. Or at least move in with him."

Sasha grew pensive as she continued to watch Matthew and Casey toss tennis balls to the three dogs. "He's asked me to do that, you know," she said solemnly. "Move in with him, that is."

"Ah, I wondered when that might happen. And I'll just assume from the look on your face that you haven't said yes."

Sasha shook her head. "I told him it was way too soon to discuss something like that. I'm happy with our relationship the way it is right now, no need to rush into anything."

"And of course, because he's crazy in love with you, he isn't pushing you," observed Linda. "He won't want to risk scaring you off. But you won't be able to keep him at an arm's distance forever, niná. Sooner than later he's going to want more from you, and you'll have to make a decision."

"I know." Sasha sighed, stroking the marmalade cat's fur until he purred. "And I won't even ask how you know that Matthew's in love with me. He told me for the first time last weekend."

Linda gave a careless wave of her hand. "It's completely obvious, Sasha, in the way he looks at you, the tone of his voice, how he treats you like a lady. He's a good man, niná, hard to imagine you'd ever find one better. And judging from the way he gets along with that boy, he's a good father, too."

"The best," agreed Sasha. "He and Casey have a wonderful relationship, and Matthew is so proud of him. I just wish things weren't so difficult with his daughter."

Sasha had confided to her aunt that Hayley had begun opting out of spending weekends with her father, claiming she had a friend's party to attend or that she didn't feel well or that she had a school-sponsored weekend trip she really wanted to go to. Sasha had seen the hurt look on Matthew's face each time his daughter had found some excuse not to see him, and her heart had ached for him. She had suspected that the real reason Hayley didn't want to spend the weekends with her father was because of Sasha's presence, and had assured Matthew it didn't bother her in the least to give him time alone with his children. Matthew had resisted her offer at first, then grudgingly agreed, but even given the assurance that Sasha wouldn't be joining them hadn't changed Hayley's mind.

"She's obviously going through some stuff right now," *Matthew had acknowledged. "What I have no idea, since* *she won't confide in me, even when I take her out to* *dinner and it's just the two of us. But Hayley needs to get* *over whatever bug crawled up her butt and grow up. She* *also needs to start accepting the fact that you're a part of* *my life now, and while I appreciate your offer to not come* *over when she visits, that's not a long term solution. I'll ask* *Casey if he's got any ideas about what's up with his sister,* *but I doubt that will shed any light on the matter. Hayley's* *just got to work through whatever's bugging her, I guess."*

Linda's eyes narrowed in irritation. "Seems to me that what his daughter really needs is a good kick in the ass. I can just imagine how your own mother would have reacted if you'd pulled that kind of crap with her."

Sasha gave a delicate little shudder. "I wouldn't have dared to try. I just hope for Matthew's sake that Hayley comes around sooner than later."

Matthew and Casey joined them a few minutes later, both flushed and sweaty after cavorting with the dogs. Linda poured them each a glass of homemade lemonade, made with the lemons that grew in her garden, and the four of them simply sat for awhile, enjoying this late February afternoon. The sun was out, with nary a cloud in the sky, but since it was still officially winter the air temperature remained crisp.

"We should head back pretty soon," Matthew said regretfully. "Weekend traffic on the Golden Gate Bridge is always heavy, and Casey still has to get in some studying for a big test tomorrow."

"Of course," agreed Sasha. "Just let me get my things and we can head out."

The big orange cat made a sound of protest as Sasha set him down on the floor, but promptly settled his fluffy body inside one of the pet beds scattered around the cottage.

As Linda gave Sasha a hug good-by, she whispered in her ear, "Don't wait too long to tell Matthew you feel the same way. Ah, and don't deny it, niná. I can tell by the way you look at him that it's love, even if you don't think so. Don't always overthink everything, Sasha, okay? You don't always have to be logical or practical. For once in your life, just let your emotions rule you."

Sasha mused over Linda's parting words for the rest of the evening, and if Matthew noticed her preoccupation he chose not to comment on it. Still mostly full from lunch at Linda's, they had a light dinner before Matthew drove Casey home, with Sasha remaining behind at the condo. She always refused to accompany Matthew when he picked up or dropped off the kids at their home in Hillsborough, oddly reluctant to see the place where he'd once lived with Lindsey. She had surmised from bits of conversation with Casey that the place was enormous, more of an estate than simply a house, with all sorts of amenities like a swimming pool, tennis court, and outdoor kitchen. The thought of seeing such extravagance up close filled her with a sense of unease, and gave her cause to worry that perhaps Matthew might one day regret giving all of that up. She knew that she would never be happy living in that sort of luxury, that a simple, modest lifestyle was all she really needed to be content.

During his absence, she ran through a yoga sequence that she planned to teach in class tomorrow, but then found herself at loose ends. At Matthew's encouragement, she'd brought some of her things over to the condo to make it feel more like home - books, CD's, a favorite afghan, clothes, toiletries. But the large, ultra-modern condo still didn't feel particularly homey to her, and Sasha worried that it never would. Matthew had never discussed his plans for after the divorce was finalized, so she had no idea if he planned to continue living here long-term. She hoped not, because while the condo was spacious and elegant, with expensive furnishings and fixtures, it continued to feel cold and impersonal to her.

The front door opened then, and a weary looking Matthew trudged in. She could tell immediately that something was troubling him, and was at his side in an instant, tugging him over to the sofa.

"What's wrong?" she asked quietly, her fingers automatically beginning to massage the nape of his neck.

He groaned, closing his eyes and letting his head fall back against the sofa as she continued to work on his tense muscles. "Lindsey," he rasped. "I've told you that I never go inside the house when I pick up or drop off the kids, just so I can avoid seeing her. Well, this time she was waiting in the driveway when I pulled up, so I couldn't duck her. And Lindsey was in full-on bitch mode, let me tell you, ranting and raving about how I was neglecting Hayley, how moody she was, how depressed. Lindsey blamed all of it on the fact that you and I were together, that Hayley was just devastated that I'd found someone so quickly. It's all bullshit, of course, meant to make me feel guilty. I pointed out to Lindsey that you offered to stay away on the weekends I have the kids, and that I make it a point to have dinner alone with the two of them once a week. But she insisted that wasn't enough, that I was being insensitive to poor Hayley's feelings, and that I should care more about my daughter than I do about you."

Sasha's fingers stilled in his scalp. "I'm sorry she said such terrible things to you," she said somberly. "You know none of that is true, Matthew. But if you think it would help your relationship with Hayley to stop seeing me, I - I'd understand. Truly I would."

"No!" Matthew bolted to an upright position, grasping her by the shoulders as he did so. His eyes were wide and almost frantic. "God, don't even suggest that, Sasha! I love my kids, God knows I do, and I'd do anything to make them happy. But I deserve to be happy, too, and since you make me happier than anyone I've ever known, there's no way in hell I'm giving you up. Lindsey's just trying to make trouble is all."

"You're sure?" she asked uncertainly. "I don't ever want to come between you and your children, or make you have to choose."

"I know you don't," he assured her gently. "You don't

have it in you to be that sort of person. That's just one of the reasons I love you so much."

She hesitated, knowing instinctively that *this* would be the perfect time to tell him - when he was upset and feeling guilty and in dire need of reassurance and support. Impulsively, before she could think about it too much, Sasha straddled his lap, looping her arms around his neck.

"And the fact that you're such a wonderful father is just one of the reasons I love *you* so much," she confessed, her voice barely above a whisper.

Matthew stared up at her in wonder, his hands threading into her wild mop of curls. "You - you do?" he murmured in disbelief. "Are you sure?"

Sasha laughed. "I think so, yes. I mean, I don't have anything else to compare it to since I've never had a relationship that lasted this long before. But I'm pretty sure that I - oh!"

He tumbled her onto the sofa, then swiftly divested her of her yoga clothes and panties, leaving her naked beneath his fully clothed body. Sasha gasped as he kissed and caressed her with a passion and domination that he'd never exhibited before, as though her confession of love had awakened a long-dormant beast inside of him. He was aggressive and demanding, and most definitely the one in charge of their lovemaking tonight.

His lips traced a path between her breasts, then tugged a nipple between his teeth as he fondled the other breast almost roughly. His mouth continued its downward path over her rib cage and belly, then lower still. He spread her thighs apart, and at the first lick of his tongue along her slit, Sasha clutched handfuls of his short, spiky hair, her hips lifting off the sofa in reaction.

"God, that's good," she panted, as he continued to eat her out, his tongue flicking repeatedly over her clit as he added two fingers to the mix. With his lips sucking on her clit, and his fingers thrusting in and out of her body with rapid pumps, he brought her to a stunning, powerful climax, the inner muscles of her vagina spasming in reaction.

Her body was still humming, her head still spinning crazily, as Matthew swept her up into his arms and carried her into the master bedroom. He set her down reverently in the middle of the big bed, and she watched in something of a daze as he began to undress. She turned into his arms eagerly as he joined her on the bed, burying her face against his neck.

"That was perfect," she murmured in his ear, even as her hand drifted down his midsection to find his fully erect cock. "So perfect that I'm not sure I'll be able to return the favor satisfactorily."

Matthew shook his head, even as he emitted a long, low groan as she began to stroke his penis. "Sweetheart, everything you do to me is way, way more than just satisfactory," he hissed through clenched teeth. "And none of this returning favors stuff, okay? In fact, as much as I'd love to have that pretty mouth sucking me off, I need to be inside of you right now. Need to feel a part of you. Like this."

He rolled her beneath him, then thrust inside of her in one deft movement. She could feel how aroused he was, how needy, and knew that the sex would be hard and fast and maybe even a little dirty tonight, and she welcomed it all.

254

Sasha wrapped her legs around his waist, digging her heels into his buttocks as she silently urged him to go deeper, harder, faster, until they were fucking like wild things - her nails lightly scoring his back, his teeth nipping the flesh between her shoulder and neck, his hand gripping her hips so tightly he was practically lifting her off the mattress.

This orgasm was so intense that Sasha thought perhaps that she might have fainted for a few minutes, and she was breathing so hard afterwards that she was nearly gasping for air. Matthew remained imbedded inside of her, and she could somewhat numbly feel the hot rush of his semen trickling down the insides of her thighs. Tenderly, she brushed her fingers through the damp strands of his hair, trailing a series of kisses along his brow and temple.

"I love you," she whispered softly against his ear.

He lifted his head then, as if with a great effort, and grinned. "For real? I mean, you didn't just tell me that earlier because you felt sorry for me or anything?"

Sasha rolled her eyes. "No, Matthew. I never say anything I don't mean, remember? So if I tell you that I love you, it's because it's true. And I'm sorry it took me awhile to tell you. I guess - well, this is all new to me, you know? I'm still not sure about this whole relationship thing, or if I'm doing it right."

"You're doing everything exactly right," he assured her, his fingers tracing a path up and down her spine. "And don't forget I don't have a whole lot of experience with relationships myself. Lindsey was really my only serious girlfriend, and that didn't turn out so well in the end. So we'll figure this out together, okay? As long as we're honest and open with each other, the rest will just fall into place somehow."

She sighed, tucking her head beneath his chin. "There's still the problem with Hayley. I've got a feeling she's not going to be happy - or make things easy for you - until you and I stop seeing each other."

"Tough," declared Matthew firmly. "I love my kids, but I love you, too. And Hayley will come around eventually. Trust me."

He kissed her then, and she sensed he didn't want to think about the situation with his daughter again tonight. But even as she kissed him back, Sasha knew the problem with Hayley wasn't going to go away that easily.

chapter thirteen

March

"**I CAN'T REMEMBER THE LAST** time I've seen you look so happy, Matt. And I'm fairly certain the person responsible for that is talking to your mother right now."

Matthew grinned at his father. "You've hit the nail on the head, Dad. Sasha has been good for me. In a lot of ways. I'm glad that you and Mom seem to be getting along with her so well."

Wade Bennett clapped his oldest son on the shoulder affectionately. "Well, why wouldn't we be? She's a delightful young woman, Matt, very kind and soft spoken. And as different as night and day from - well, you know."

Matthew nodded. "Lindsey. It's okay for you to say her name, Dad. And I couldn't agree with you more. Life with my ex was always stressful, always chaotic, and always tense. I feel like a completely different person with Sasha in my life. I know that after working for twelve hours I can come home to find her here, and all the stresses of the day just disappear the second she smiles at me. I think I've needed someone like her for a long time."

"I think you've needed someone like her your entire life," corrected Wade. "I know you did the right thing by marrying Lindsey when she got pregnant, but she was never the right

257

woman for you, son. And I admire you for sticking with her for so many years, for trying to do right by the kids. But it killed me a little inside each time I saw you with her, saw how much she demeaned you and took you for granted. You're too good a person to put up with that sort of treatment, Matt, and especially from your wife."

"It took me almost twenty years to realize that, Dad," admitted Matthew. "And you're right. If it hadn't been for Hayley and Casey, I probably would have bailed a long time ago. Hell, if Lindsey hadn't been pregnant I doubt we would have ever gotten married, or stayed together more than a few months. I just wish she'd quit playing her little games and sign those damned divorce papers."

"What does your attorney have to say on the matter?"

Matthew sighed in frustration. "Since Lindsey has officially contested the divorce, the only options at this point are to try and reach a settlement, or to take her to court. And since certain facts would most likely be brought up during a trial, I'm putting that option off as a last resort."

"Hmm." Wade took a sip of coffee before setting the mug back down. "I assume these facts have to do with Lindsey's, ah, *extracurricular* activities?"

"Yeah. Except, as I've told you, her idea of extracurricular activities don't include belonging to the French Club or the debate team," replied Matthew dryly. "And as much as I'm willing to do almost anything to finally be free of her, I can't take the risk of the kids finding out certain things about their mother. Like it or not, Lindsey is still their mom, and I refuse to say anything negative about her to them."

"That's admirable, Matt," commended Wade.

"Unfortunately, there may come a time when she forces your hand to the point where you no longer have a choice. Can't your attorneys keep all that stuff sealed?"

"You'd like to think so. But I fear those sort of juicy details have a way of getting leaked, especially considering who I am. The media would love to get hold of a story like that, and the kids would suffer as a result. So for now at least I'm going to continue trying to reach a settlement with Lindsey."

Wade shook his head in disbelief. "What more can she possibly want? When you told me you were willing to give her half of everything you own, I thought for sure she'd sign on the dotted line without a moment's hesitation. How greedy can one person be?"

Matthew blew out a frustrated breath. "I don't think it's all about the money at this point. It's her pride and her ego, too. Lindsey can't stand the fact that I was the one to leave her. She's always thought she was too good for me, you know. That a nerd like myself should have been grateful that someone like her ever noticed me in the first place. My moving out and filing for divorce knocked her a few rungs off that pedestal she's always placed herself on, and she's trying to find a way to climb back up."

Wade inclined his head to the other side of the living room, where his wife Maureen was deep in conversation with Sasha. "And I'll bet the fact that you've found someone else - especially someone who's more than a decade younger than she is - really sticks in her craw."

"Probably. I certainly haven't tried to rub it in or anything like that. Especially since Lindsey continues to blame my relationship with Sasha for why Hayley is so moody and depressed."

Wade gave a hoot of laughter. "Moody, I'll go along with. But depressed?" He shook his head. "Nothing wrong with Hayley that taking her car keys and that damned cell phone away for a few weeks wouldn't fix. That sort of discipline sure helped cure your sister of the nasty disposition she developed when she was sixteen."

"Jackie?" asked Matthew curiously. "How come I don't remember her acting like that? Granted, she was always a bit of a pest when she was younger, and then a total smart ass when she started getting higher grades than I did at her age. But I never remember her being a sullen brat like Hayley's been lately."

"You were probably away at college or grad school at the time," surmised Wade. "But trust me, she was hell to live with for a few months. Just ask your mother if you don't believe me. It was her idea, actually, to take Jackie's car keys away, as well as restrict her internet access. Nothing like instilling some parental controls to fix a bad attitude real quick."

Matthew chuckled. "Yeah, I could see how that might motivate my sister. But while your idea has merit, there's no way I could make it stick. Lindsey would just override anything I tried to do, insisting that what Hayley really needs is for me to move back home and be part of the family again. I can't believe that after being separated for all this time Lindsey is delusional enough to think I'd ever move home again."

"I hate to say it, son, but I'm afraid she's not going to leave you a choice pretty soon. You're going to have to force her hand, which means going to trial. Maybe if you prepared the kids ahead of time, told them the general facts, you could spare them the worst of it."

"Maybe," agreed Matthew hesitantly. "But, you know what? Let's forget all that bullshit for the moment. You and Mom are only here in town for a few days, so let's enjoy every minute we have together, okay?"

Wade gave a thumbs-up. "You got it, Matt. I'm going to go help myself to seconds. This is all delicious."

Matthew had been thrilled when his parents had asked if they could spend the week off they had for Spring Break with him in San Francisco. Hayley and Casey were also off school this week, and Lindsey had unceremoniously announced a month ago that he was in charge of the kids this week while she jetted off to the Caribbean for a getaway with her girlfriends. Instead of booking his parents into a hotel for the week, Matthew had insisted they use his bedroom while he slept in the spare twin bed in Casey's room here at the condo. That meant Sasha wouldn't be able to spend the night at all this week, especially since she still insisted on staying at her own place when he had the kids.

But he had been adamant about her meeting his parents, assuring her that they would adore her as much as he did, and she'd reluctantly agreed to join them all for dinner a few evenings ago. As expected, Wade and Maureen had taken an instant liking to Sasha, and persuaded her to come along on additional outings. It was Friday morning now, and Matthew had ordered in brunch before their outing to the Muir Woods National Monument. He was officially on vacation this week, though he'd been fielding emails and phone calls on a daily basis, and had even snuck in a couple of video conferences.

When you were the CEO, he supposed with a sigh, you were never really on vacation. Still, he was grateful for any time he could spend with his family, and wished that his brother and sister had also been able to make the trip.

Over the years, and especially since he'd taken the company public and entered the billionaires club, Matthew had done his utmost to help out his parents and siblings. He'd bought his brother and sister each a house, and when his parents had stubbornly insisted on staying put in their own home, had had it extensively remodeled for them. All of his family members had new cars, and the boat he had purchased for his parents was Wade's pride and joy. There had also been numerous vacations he'd treated them to, and very generous birthday and Christmas gifts. And because they were all reluctant to let him do more than what he already did, Matthew had secretly set up trust funds for his parents, brother, and sister, so that they would always be financially secure.

While his father re-filled his plate with the sumptuous brunch buffet that the caterers had set up on the dining room table, Matthew sipped his coffee as he observed the four other people in the room. Casey was chatting animatedly with his grandmother and Sasha, happily chomping on a plate of bacon at the same time. At one point he offered Sasha a piece, who gave a little shudder in response, causing Casey to grin mischievously. Maureen seemed to genuinely like Sasha, and they had had several conversations so far about the merits of herbal remedies and supplements versus traditional prescription drugs. Matthew had been surprised at the extent of Sasha's knowledge, and had asked why she'd never finished obtaining her certification as an herbalist.

She'd given a half-hearted shrug. "I'm not sure I really know the answer to that. At the time, money was something of an issue, though I guess I could have borrowed it from one of my parents or applied for a loan. But I think it was just taking too much time away from the other things I loved - my yoga classes and massage practice - and I had to make a choice. I managed to learn quite a lot in the classes I did take, however, and I still attend workshops and lectures occasionally to keep up with things."

"If you ever decide that's something you'd like to pursue, you know that money wouldn't be an issue, right?" he had told her. "I would happily finance that for you, Sasha, so all you have to do is ask."

"Thank you," she'd replied gently. "I appreciate your offer, Matthew. But I'm very happy with my life just as it is right now. I don't like complications, and I go to great lengths to keep things simple and stress free. So, thanks but no thanks."

Matthew's gaze narrowed now as it fell on Hayley, who was curled up sullenly in a corner of the sectional sofa, fixated as usual on her cell phone. She'd griped loudly about having to get up so early this morning, and even more so about traipsing around in "some damp old woods". She had barely eaten, and aside from greeting her grandparents with a sulky "good morning" hadn't spoken a word.

He debated what his father had told him earlier - about taking away Hayley's phone for awhile in the hopes of teaching her a lesson. And the more he thought about it, the more he decided the idea had real merit. So when the time came to leave about a half hour later, he deftly plucked the phone from his daughter's hands and shoved it in the back pocket of his jeans.

Hayley was visibly shocked. "Dad? WTF? Is this some sort of stupid game? Give me my phone back!"

Matthew shook his head. "No. At least not until we return home later. You need to spend some quality time talking with your grandparents while they're here. They fly home on Sunday, after all, and you've barely spent any time with them. Besides, I doubt there'll be any cell phone signal or internet reception in Muir Woods. That way you can be sure to fully enjoy the beauty of nature."

"Are you insane?" screeched Hayley. "That is the dumbest thing I've ever heard! I need that phone, Dad. I'm expecting an important call from Sierra."

Matthew shrugged. "Seriously? It can't be that important, Hayley. Sierra can leave you a message and you can call her back later. Today is about family time."

Hayley threw up her hands in frustration. "Screw that. I'll just stay here then and use one of your computers to Facetime."

"My computers?" asked Matthew, chuckling. "You don't mean the computers that I've very carefully password protected, do you? Each one a different and equally complex password. Oh, and then there are the security questions you'd need to answer if you somehow managed to crack the password. And since the questions are all very, very advanced mathematical equations, I don't think that's going

264

to be possible."

She glared at him evilly. "This is so unfair," she hissed. "I should have gone along with Mom on her trip. That way I'd at least be having some fun right now, instead of getting dragged along to boring old museums and hikes in the woods. Ugh!"

"Your father's right, pumpkin," assured Wade cheerfully, calling Hayley by the nickname he'd always used for her. "Your grandmother and I hardly get to see you these days, so why don't you leave that silly phone alone for a little while and talk to us instead?"

Maureen draped an arm around her granddaughter's shoulders. "Why don't I go with you and help you pick out something to wear, hmm?" she suggested, glancing at the pajamas Hayley was still wearing. "And then we'll go have a lovely morning walking in the woods. Maybe on the way home we can stop for a late lunch at that sushi restaurant you were telling me about the other day."

"Maybe," mumbled Hayley sullenly, but she allowed Maureen to steer her in the direction of her room. Then her scowling gaze fell on Sasha, who had quite intentionally remained quiet during the entire incident, before asking her father in a haughty tone, "If today is supposed to be family time, then why is *she* coming along?"

Sasha's green-gold eyes widened in alarm, and she clutched her tea mug a little tighter. Maureen shook her head in dismay, while Wade opened his mouth to protest, until Matthew held up a hand to forestall him.

"Because I choose to have her along," he bit out angrily. "Because it makes me happy to have Sasha with us. And like it or not, Hayley, Sasha is here to stay. So you'd better start getting used to the idea, and you had definitely better start minding your manners around her. Now, go with your grandmother and get ready. Otherwise, you're not too old for me to hire a babysitter for you."

Hayley had paled visibly at her father's tirade, and looked defeated as she let Maureen shepherd her to her room. Casey tactfully announced he needed to finish getting dressed, and made a beeline for his room. Wade gave Matthew's shoulder an encouraging squeeze.

"You did the right thing, Matt," he assured him. "That little girl is definitely getting too big for her britches, and needs to toe the line. And being deprived of her phone for a few hours is nothing. Especially considering how rude she was to this beautiful lady here."

Sasha offered Wade a weak smile. "You're very kind. But I don't ever want to come between Matthew and his children. Or make trouble for him. I - I really think it's for the best if I don't go with you today."

"No!"

Matthew and Wade uttered the denial simultaneously. In seconds, Matthew was at her side, taking the mug from her trembling fingers and wrapping his arms around her.

"I wouldn't give Hayley the satisfaction," he declared. "My father's right. It's time she learned that she can't have her own way all the time. And that rudeness simply won't be tolerated. You've gone out of your way to befriend her, Sasha, to be kind to her. And there have been far too many times when you've backed out of dinners or breakfasts or outings because you were afraid it would anger or upset

Hayley. That ends now. She needs to start accepting the fact that you're a part of my life, and that her little snit fits aren't going to change that. So, please go with us, hmm?"

Sasha nodded. "Okay."

Wade grinned and gave a celebratory fist pump, his hazel eyes twinkling behind the same pair of horn-rimmed glasses he'd been wearing for thirty years. "Excellent news!" he declared. "I would have been so disappointed if you didn't join us, Sasha. And don't worry about Hayley, hmm? I was just reminding Matt earlier that his sister Jackie acted up in a similar fashion when she was a teenager, and she worked through it pretty quickly. I'll bet it will be exactly the same thing with Hayley. Next thing you know, the two of you will be the best of friends!"

Sasha smiled politely at Wade's enthusiasm, but Matthew could tell from the wariness of her expression that she was every bit as doubtful about his father's prediction as he was.

"WELL, IT SOUNDS LIKE CASEY had a great time at your father's this past week. What about you, Hayley? Did you have fun?"

Hayley gave her mother a look that was part sneer, part disbelief. "Seriously, Mom? I spent an entire week surrounded by not one, but four science and math nerds. I felt like I was trapped at a Geekfest with no way out. Does that sound like I had any fun at all?"

Casey cheerfully dunked an egg roll into sweet and sour sauce, just one of the dishes that Lindsey had ordered from their favorite Chinese restaurant for dinner. "I had a lot of fun," he declared, biting off half the egg roll at once. "It's always great to see Grandma and Grandpa. And the new show at the planetarium was awesome! And Grandma and Grandpa had never been to the Disney Museum, so it was like seeing it all over again."

Hayley rolled her eyes as she nibbled on a snow pea. "Like I said, it was just one big Geekfest. Meanwhile, *you* got to stay at a five-star resort right on the beach, sleep late, get massages, and drink margaritas all day. Now, that's *my* idea of the ideal vacation. I should have gone along with you, Mom. I might have actually had some fun that way, as well as having an awesome tan right now."

Lindsey paused before replying, not willing to admit out loud that bringing Hayley along on vacation this past week would have definitely put a cramp in her style. In addition to lazing around the beach for a good part of the day, Lindsey had also treated herself to a whole array of spa treatments, bought a dozen new outfits at the designer boutiques in town, and hooked up with three different men - all of them gorgeous, and all of them anywhere from ten to twenty years younger than she was. Dragging her teenaged daughter to the Caribbean with her would have put a complete damper on what had been a fabulous getaway.

"But your brother is right, honey," replied Lindsey. "You hardly ever get to see your grandparents. They would have been so disappointed if you hadn't been there."

"Oh, please." Hayley gave her mother another of those scathing looks that made Lindsey long to slap her across the face. "Stop trying to dream up excuses, Mom. You just didn't want me along to spoil your fun is all. Instead, I had one of the worst weeks ever. Thanks a bunch."

Casey, who seemed to be the only one at the table who was actually eating, took seconds of the vegetable chow mein, orange chicken, and honey walnut prawns. "Well, I had a good time and so did everyone else - Dad, Grandma, Grandpa, Sasha. Hayley's just mad because Dad took her phone away for a few hours one day."

Hayley stuck her tongue out at Casey, but Lindsey didn't even notice. Not at the mention of *that* name.

"Sasha was there during your grandparents' visit?" she asked faintly.

Casey nodded as he poured a generous amount of soy sauce over his heaping plate of food. "Sure. Oh, not the whole time. She probably just had dinner with us a couple of times, and maybe brunch once or twice. And she went to the museums with us and to Muir Woods."

Lindsey scowled. "That sounds like a whole lot of time to me. She didn't sleep over, did she?"

"Oh, God, are we back on this?" asked Hayley in dramatic fashion. "No, Mom. She did not spend the night. She never does when we stay with Dad. I guess they have to get their fucking done some other time."

"Hayley!" exclaimed Lindsey in outraged shock. "Do *not* say those things in front of your brother!"

Casey grinned. "Relax, Mom. I have heard the word before, you know. And I'm fourteen now, not four, so I sort of figured that Dad and Sasha are, uh, having sex. But Hayley's right, she never stays overnight when we're at Dad's."

"But he introduced her to your grandparents," she fretted, almost as if she was thinking out loud. "He brought her along on family outings, the sort of things *I* should be doing with you. It's not right, you know. Not right at all."

Lindsey grew increasingly agitated the more she dwelled on the matter, enough that she refilled and drained her wine glass twice within a very short period of time. Sensing her discomfort, Casey quickly changed the subject and practically wolfed down the rest of his food, excusing himself shortly thereafter.

Hayley, meanwhile, was preoccupied as usual with texting one or more of her friends and barely spared her mother a glance, even as Lindsey began pacing back and forth through the kitchen, her high heels tapping out an almost frantic rhythm.

"He's getting more and more serious about her then."

Hayley heaved a sigh worthy of the grandest diva, and impatiently set her phone down on the kitchen table. "Yeah, seems like it. So what? It's not like you didn't hook up with someone on your vacation."

Lindsey waggled a warning finger at her smart-mouthed daughter. "Watch it there, young lady. You don't get to judge me. And don't forget our deal. You're supposed to be thinking of ways to break those two up, and help me get your father back. I haven't exactly heard any great ideas lately."

Hayley shrugged. "You really need to give this up, Mom. Dad seems happy, and even if he wasn't all gaga over Sasha - which I personally don't get, I mean she's got a good body and a pretty face and all but she's just sort of quiet and boring - I don't think he has any intention of ever coming back to you."

Lindsey was so angry she felt like picking up the takeout containers of Chinese food and hurling them at the closest wall. It would be oddly satisfying, she thought furiously, to watch the chow mein noodles slither down the wall, or the sweet and sour sauce cling to one of the kitchen cabinets.

"You're wrong," she bit out, her cheeks flushed from a combination of anger and too much booze. "I know I can get him back. We just haven't thought of the right approach yet. And since you don't seem interested in helping me, I'll have to call in the big guns. In fact, I'm going to go call her right now."

Lindsey flounced off a bit unsteadily on her stiletto heels, way past tipsy at this point, and fumbling with the speed dial on her phone at the same time, until she reached her home office. Whenever she needed a sounding board, or someone to take her part, or simply go out and party with, the first person she called was her closest friend Nicole Prince. Lindsey had first met the thrice-divorced Nicole almost ten years ago, when she'd been dropping off her then-stepdaughter at the same school Hayley was attending at the time. The two women had bonded instantly, and been BFF's ever since. Nicole, in fact, had been one of the three friends who'd just accompanied her on this recent vacation to the Caribbean, and she was well aware of Lindsey's dilemma.

"You're not going to believe this one," Lindsey burst out as Nicole picked up the call. "Now he's actually introduced the bitch to his parents. That sounds serious, doesn't it? Oh, God, Nikki, he's going to find a way to divorce me and then marry that - that yoga teacher. What am I going to do?"

On the other end of the line, Nicole's voice was calming,

sympathetic, and coldly calculating. "Here's what we're going to do. First thing tomorrow - well, after Pilates and our mani-pedis, of course - we're going to figure this out. We'll come up with a plan to lure Matt back to you. Or at least to get him back in the house. And be prepared, Linz - you might have to prepare yourself to fight dirty."

Even as she poured herself a tumbler of vodka from the well stocked liquor cabinet in her office, a slow, satisfied smile crossed Lindsey's face. "Honey, I learned how to fight dirty from the time I was four years old. If it means getting Matt to call off this stupid divorce and have him move back in here where he belongs, I say the dirtier the better."

chapter fourteen

April – Kauai

"Mmm. If this is an example of what the lifestyle of the rich and famous is like, then maybe I could get used to the idea over time."

Matthew laughed at Sasha's lazily uttered statement. "Yeah, there's really not much to complain about here, is there?"

"Here" was the posh Gregson resort on the Hawaiian island of Kauai, where he had brought her for a week's vacation. Ian had been more than happy to arrange for them to stay in the owner's suite, a privilege usually only reserved for members of the Gregson family, top executives of the hotel firm, and special guests like politicians, celebrities, or very close friends of the family. Matthew and Sasha counted themselves fortunate enough to fall into the latter category.

Sasha took a long drink of iced tea, then lifted her face skywards as a cooling trade wind provided momentary relief from the hot Hawaiian sun. "Tessa told me all about this place when she learned we'd be visiting. But her descriptions didn't do it justice. I think I could be awfully happy taking up residence here permanently. Oh, not necessarily in this suite, but on the island itself. From everything I've seen so far, Kauai is definitely my idea of paradise."

Matthew nodded as he refilled both of their iced tea

glasses from the pitcher that was being kept cool in a mini-fridge. One of the many amenities of the luxurious suite was an outdoor kitchen that included the fridge, a large gas grill, a separate wine refrigerator, and a prep sink. "I agree. I've spent quite a bit of time in Hawaii over the years, but never on Kauai until now. We usually stayed in Maui or Kona."

She pushed her gold rimmed aviator sunglasses higher up her nose. "Is that the reason you selected this island for our trip?"

"That might have contributed to the decision," he admitted. "I wanted this vacation to be something special for the two of us, to go somewhere neither of us had ever been. But Kauai also has a reputation for being quieter and less commercial than some of the other islands, and I liked that idea a lot. The privacy we've had here so far has been great. And this has easily been the most relaxing vacation I've had in almost twenty years."

"Better than all the family camping and boating trips you took growing up?" she inquired.

Matthew had fondly recounted those happy memories to her, and Sasha had heard additional stories from his parents during their visit to San Francisco last month. She'd smiled wistfully at the images their tales had conjured up, and had only been able to use her imagination to get the full picture. Her own frenetic childhood had been nothing like what Matthew had known, and for all of the exotic places she'd traveled to with one parent or the other, she would have gladly traded all of them in order to experience the sort of family bonding that he'd known.

He shrugged. "Different sort of relaxation. Back then it

was to have a break from studying and school. Now the stresses have definitely multiplied, and become almost too much to take at times."

"You know, I would have been perfectly happy to go camping or backpacking with you," she told him. "As much as I've enjoyed being pampered and waited on these past few days, a camping trip up in the mountains sounds pretty good, too."

Matthew grinned. "It's probably still a little cool for camping, especially considering how much snow we got in California this year. But I'll definitely keep your offer in mind for the future. Have you done much camping?"

Sasha nodded. "I wouldn't say a lot, but Linda loves to camp so I've been on several trips with her and a group of her friends. The very first time I went camping was the summer I was sixteen. God knows neither of my parents would have ever dreamed of doing something like that. I mean, can you imagine my mother sleeping in a tent? Or my father eating hot dogs and beans?"

"Not even remotely," he replied readily. "Though I'm just guessing they'd both like this place a lot."

"You'd be correct. My dad would be spending half his day in the water. He and his brothers used to do some surfing in Brazil when they were teenagers. Unfortunately, knowing my father, he'd spend the other half of the day drinking too much and flirting with every pretty female who walked by. While my mom would split her time between the spa and finding ways to pick a fight with my father. So for those reasons alone I'm very glad they aren't here with us."

"Me, too." He reached across their side by side padded

275

lounge chairs to claim her lips in a long, lazy kiss. "For a lot of reasons."

Sasha gave his heavily stubbled cheek a tender caress. In the four days they'd been here, Matthew hadn't bothered to shave and she found that she liked this new look of his and told him so.

"Yeah?" he asked, wiggling his eyebrows at her suggestively. "Like enough to make you want to jump my bones?"

She pushed her sunglasses down her nose low enough to give him a glare of mock severity. "You do realize that practically all you've talked about since we arrived is sex?"

His answering smile was both sexy and adorable at the same time. "That's because you've spent almost the entire time we've been here wearing either a bikini or nothing at all. How can you blame a man for thinking about sex constantly when he's got a gorgeous woman like you by his side?"

Sasha sat upright on the lounger, wrapping her arms around her knees as she pulled them tight against her chest. "Mmm, if I lived in a place like this year round I think I'd want to wear a bikini all the time. And I wouldn't really need shoes at all. And I think practicing yoga at sunrise each morning on this beach would be more than worth getting up so early."

Matthew, too, sat up, and gave her knee a squeeze. "Man, that would really be the life, wouldn't it?" he asked wistfully. "Imagine saying to hell with everyone and everything else and living on this island permanently. I'd sell the business, buy some land here and have a house built exactly to our specifications. We could swim and sail and go for hikes on the trails. Though I think you might need to wear shoes for the last one."

"I guess so." She grew silent for a few moments before reminding him, "But you're forgetting something here - your kids. If you lived here all the time, you wouldn't get to see them very often. And I'm just assuming Lindsey wouldn't agree to give you custody."

"You're right. But unfortunately not because she wants them with her. She'd actually love nothing better than to be footloose and fancy free, and to do whatever she wanted without having to be responsible for them. But she wouldn't agree to give me custody as a way to spite me. Besides, as much as Casey would love living here, Hayley wouldn't be able to survive for too long without being near a hair salon or Bloomingdale's."

Sasha placed her hand over his. "Well, no matter. After all, it's just a fantasy, isn't it? You've got a lot of other responsibilities besides your children. Responsibilities that you aren't supposed to be thinking about this week. Feel like a swim?"

He set aside their glasses before taking her by the hand, and then doing a slow jog through the sand until they reached the edge of the water. To Sasha, the biggest attraction of this suite wasn't the huge rock shower or the enormous king-sized bed or the round-the-clock private concierge service. Instead, it was the proximity to their own secluded stretch of beach, where they could swim and sun and relax to their hearts content without ever seeing another person. She had learned to swim as a small child during the times she spent with her father and his family in Brazil, and though she rarely had the opportunity to do so nowadays, Sasha still loved to spend time in the water. There were three different pools located here at the resort, but they had yet to make use of them, preferring instead to swim in the ocean.

Matthew was a strong swimmer, having spent so much of his youth vacationing on Lake Michigan, and was enjoying this opportunity as much as Sasha was. Given that this section of beach was located on a secluded inlet, the waves were considerably calmer. Sasha took advantage of the tranquil waters, flipping onto her back and simply floating for long minutes, closing her eyes against the glare of the sun.

It had been a long time since she'd had a real vacation, she thought. The quick visits she made to Katya in Los Angeles didn't really count, since they were so stressful and exhausting that she'd return home more worn out then when she'd left. And she had been so intent on building up her massage practice and increasing attendance at her yoga classes that she hadn't been to Brazil in almost five years. Of course, she had seen her father two or three times a year, but only when he visited her in San Francisco or accompanied her to L.A. And it had been even longer than five years since she'd been to Paris to see her aunt and uncle.

As she flipped over and began to swim slowly to shore, Sasha wondered if Matthew would be interested in accompanying her some day to visit her family in both Brazil and Paris, and decided she would find a way to pose the question during their stay here. Matthew seemed so eager to please her, to do things for her, that it was difficult to imagine him saying no, especially since she had yet to ask him for anything. That didn't seem to stop him, however, from buying her things anyway.

When he had initially made the arrangements for this trip to Hawaii, he'd offered to take her on a shopping spree so that she could select whatever she needed. And when she had refused, as usual, he had taken matters into his own hands.

She had met him for lunch at his office, something she'd only done a handful of times since they had started seeing each other. A couple of those times, when Matthew had been especially busy, they had eaten inside his office since he'd only been able to spare a few minutes.

Sasha had suspected something was up when she'd spied the huge smile on Elena's face. Matthew's PA had taken an instant liking to Sasha the first time they had met, especially when she discovered that Sasha spoke fluent Spanish. Elena would often speak to Sasha in Spanish, usually when she was expressing concern about how stressed Matthew was that day, or that he hadn't taken the time to eat breakfast. The two women had become good friends, with Elena cautioning Matthew repeatedly to "hold on tight to this one, boss, because you aren't ever going to get this lucky again."

This time, however, instead of sharing her latest concern about Matthew in Spanish, Elena had been grinning ear to ear, and almost fidgeting with barely concealed excitement.

"Hey, chica," she'd greeted. "Wait until you see the surprise the boss has waiting for you. It was just delivered a few minutes ago, and I have to confess I peeked in one of the bags."

Sasha had regarded Elena quizzically. "Well, I know it's not lunch since we're supposed to be meeting Ian and Tessa

Gregson today."

Elena had shook her head. "Not food, no. Go, look. And don't argue with him about accepting this, okay? He's so excited he reminds me of my kids when they were little on Christmas. So don't burst his bubble, chica."

Sasha had been even more confused after Elena's warning, and had entered Matthew's office warily - only to gasp in astonishment at the sight of half a dozen shopping bags piled on his sofa. The bags all bore the Neiman Marcus logo, and from the twinkle in Matthew's eye as he'd stood to greet her, Sasha had known that the bags were for her.

"Since you wouldn't let me take you shopping for our Hawaii trip," he'd told her as he picked up one of the bags, "I decided to do it for you. Well, I might have asked Tessa for the name of the personal shopper she uses, but I picked out most of this stuff myself. I, uh, hope you like it all."

"Matthew. I can't - " she'd begun to protest, until she had remembered the warning Elena had given her moments ago. And since she had zero desire to piss off the rather terrifying PA, Sasha had merely sighed as she'd begun to look through one of the bags.

He'd bought her everything and more than one could need for a week in Hawaii - bathing suits and cover ups, sundresses, shorts and tank tops, jeans and T-shirts, flip flops, espadrilles, trail running shoes, hats, sunglasses, beach bags. He had thought of absolutely everything, including three new yoga outfits and a beautiful robe of sage green silk.

"I won't tell you that this is far too much and that you really shouldn't have done this," she'd begun. "Especially since I'm guessing Elena is eavesdropping right about now and

280

will chew me out big time if I don't accept all of these things gracefully. So - thank you, Matthew. Everything is perfect."

She'd twined her arms around his neck and pulled his head down to meet her kiss - a long, leisurely meeting of lips and tongues. But, as she'd lifted her head, she had whispered in his ear, well out of Elena's hearing, "Even if it is way, way too much!"

Sasha smiled at the recollection now as she emerged from the surf. She was wearing one of the half dozen new bikinis Matthew had bought for her - a tropical print of yellows, oranges, and pinks with a strapless bandeau top and low-cut bottoms that tied on each hip. All of the price tags had been carefully removed from all of the things he'd bought her for this vacation, but Chad, who had helped her pack, estimated that just this one simple bikini had probably cost upwards of two hundred dollars. Sasha had been appalled at that revelation, and had half-threatened to return everything to the store and then donate the money to charity. It had been Chad who'd gently reminded her that buying her these things obviously meant a lot to Matthew, and it was his way of giving back to her for everything she'd done to help him. Sasha had uttered a sigh of resignation, and continued packing her suitcase.

She was toweling herself off when Matthew finished his swim and began to walk across the sand towards the suite's secluded veranda. Four days in the Hawaiian sun had already given him a tan, darkening his previously pale skin. He'd been a little self conscious on their first day here while stripping down to his swim trunks, admitting that he had spent precious little time outdoors over the past few months.

Her gaze traveled slowly from his stubbled face, then down to his naked torso. There was a sprinkling of light brown hair across his chest, just the right amount for her taste. He was lean and toned, with a defined six pack and chiseled biceps, but wasn't overly brawny or muscled. Thanks to the changes he'd made to his diet - he was practically a vegetarian by now and carefully limited his alcohol intake - his abs were flat and hard, and there wasn't a spare ounce of fat anywhere on his body. He reminded her yet again of a triathlete - strong and lean and super-fit.

As he reached for a towel, he met her gaze before breathing in sharply. There must have been something in the way she was staring at him - lust, admiration, desire - because suddenly those very same emotions were mirrored in his own eyes.

"See something you like?" he asked in a husky voice as he tossed the towel over the veranda railing.

Sasha stepped in close enough to place a hand on his chest. "There's a whole lot of things I see that I like," she replied suggestively, then tugged playfully on the waistband of his trunks. "And even more things that I can't see right now."

Matthew's hands bracketed her hips, holding her still as he rubbed his erection against the notch of her thighs. "I second that opinion. Though in your case this bikini isn't hiding very much." He bent his head until his lips touched the side of her neck. "You were right earlier. You should definitely wear nothing but bikinis ninety percent of the time. Especially since your body was specifically designed for them."

She groaned as he took her mouth in a long, searching kiss, while his hands roamed over her buttocks, belly, and torso - fondling, caressing, arousing. Moments later he took her by the hand and quietly guided her into the master bathroom, then turned on the taps in the rock walled shower while they stripped out of their bathing suits.

In a move that left her gasping, Matthew pushed her up against the shower wall, the hot water streaming over their naked bodies. His chest was flush against her back, effectively trapping her in place as his hands returned to explore the curves and hollows of her body.

"I love your breasts," he rasped in her ear, cupping the gentle mounds and tugging at the nipples. "They're the perfect size, the perfect shape. All natural, just like you."

"Ohhh." Her head fell back limply onto his shoulder as he continued to squeeze her breasts. "They - they aren't very big."

"They're perfect," he repeated. "Absolutely perfect. There's not one thing I'd change about them. Same thing with the rest of your beautiful body." His hands skimmed down the sides of her rib cage to rest on her waist, while his wet lips traced a sensual path from her neck to her shoulder blades. "And I love the color of your skin, especially after you've been out in the sun for a few days. It reminds me of a café au lait. Or dulce de leche. Delectable."

Sasha whimpered as one of his hands squeezed her ass, then slipped between her legs where she was wet and slick and impatient for his touch. Both of them gasped as he thrust two fingers deep inside of her vagina, her hips instinctively moving in sync with each pumping motion.

"I want you just like this," he growled, even as he began to position the tip of his cock at the entrance to her body. "All wet and hungry and willing. Let me, Sasha."

She gave a little cry of alarm as he pushed his way inside, burying his fully erect cock all the way to the balls. She had to stand up on her toes slightly to accommodate him as he began to pick up the pace of his thrusts, his hands on her hips holding her still for him. Her breasts were crushed up against the surprisingly smooth rock wall, the surface abrading her nipples just enough to make it arousing.

As usual, Matthew was a quiet lover, not one for dirty talk or saying much beyond a few whispered endearments or groans of pleasure. Sasha preferred it that way, content to let their bodies say what needed to be said. And when he brought her to orgasm, she didn't feel the need to announce it to him loudly, especially since it was more than obvious by her gasp of pleasure, and the way she shuddered against him over and over. He was a bit more vocal when he followed her over a few moments later, crying out in satisfaction as he emptied himself inside of her.

They took a short nap after their shower, their nude bodies cuddled up close against each other as they slept. It was late afternoon when they rose from the bed, and pulled on some clothes - Matthew a pair of cotton drawstring pants and a colorful luau shirt, and Sasha one of the sundresses he'd bought her, this one of blue chambray with a lace-up neckline and embroidered bodice. Since they were having dinner brought to the suite this evening, neither of them bothered with shoes.

As he placed a call to his kids, Sasha walked out to the

veranda to give him some privacy. Matthew had spent very little time checking his work email or returning any business related phone calls, but he'd made it a point to call Hayley and Casey every day since they had been away. It didn't bother Sasha in the least that he did so, and she had actually been the one to encourage him to call each day. As for herself, she realized somewhat guiltily that she hadn't once checked her own email or voice mail, and quickly retrieved her phone to do so now.

She was relieved to see that there were only a handful of emails to reply to, one each from her parents, Chad, Julio, and Tessa, all of them asking how she was enjoying her vacation. While Matthew continued to talk to the kids, Sasha quickly replied to each email, keeping her responses brief for the most part. To Tessa, however, she typed out a lengthier reply.

Thanks for checking in. We're having a wonderful time, and everything you told me about this place is 100% true! I've never stayed in anyplace even half as nice as this resort, and the suite is like some sort of tropical palace. As for Kauai itself, well, it sort of feels like home here. I know that might sound odd to you, given that I've never been anywhere near Hawaii before, but the minute I stepped off the plane everything just felt familiar.

The week is going by way too fast, and I wish we could stay a month! But Matthew is already going to have a whole lot to get caught up on when we return, and Serge and Morgana wouldn't be too happy if I was away more than a week. So we'll be returning to San Francisco on Sunday, and I'll be back in the studio to teach class on Monday morning.

My best to you and Ian and thanks again for arranging this stay for us. It's been truly magical.

Matthew finished his call a few minutes later, and came to join her on the veranda, carrying a glass of chardonnay for each of them. Sasha had admittedly been indulging herself far more than usual this week, having a glass or two of wine or a mai tai, eating sugary breakfast pastries, and enjoying dessert after dinner. Matthew had dismissed her concerns when she'd fretted about her unhealthy eating habits, insisting that both of them deserved a break from their usual daily routines.

"Mmm, this is good," she told him after taking a sip of the perfectly chilled wine. "Everything okay with the kids?"

He shrugged, taking a much more generous drink from his own glass. "Casey's doing great, as usual, while Hayley is - well, being Hayley. I think I might have managed to pry a whole ten words from her."

"I'm sorry," she sympathized, wrapping an arm around his waist and resting her head on his shoulder. "Hopefully she'll come around sooner than later."

"Hey, I'm not going to worry about it right now," he declared. "Hayley knows how to get in touch with me if she needs anything, and we'll be home in three more days. So let's forget about whatever teenaged drama is going on in her life and enjoy ourselves. Okay?"

Sasha nodded. "Okay." She took another sip of her

wine, then sighed with pleasure as she glanced up at the magnificent colors of the sunset. "I'm not sure what the best time of the day is over here - sunset or sunrise. They both have their appeal."

Matthew brushed a kiss on her temple. "You really like it here, don't you?"

"Oh, yes," she agreed fervently. "I was just answering some emails a few minutes ago, including one from Tessa, and I told her that the minute we stepped off the plane it felt like I'd finally arrived home. Out of all the places I've been to in the world, Kauai is definitely my favorite. Thank you for bringing me here, Matthew."

"My pleasure." He bent and kissed her on the lips this time. "I'm happy that you like it here so much. And that it feels like home to you in some way. I don't imagine you've known that feeling too much in your life."

"No. I mean, there were several places that were familiar to me, where I visited regularly - my dad's family home in Brazil, my aunt's flat in Paris, the little apartment my mother and I had in New York for a few years. But it wasn't until I moved in with Linda that I had a permanent place, somewhere to leave all my belongings and know I wouldn't have to pack them all up again in a few weeks."

"It must have been something of an adjustment for you, though," commented Matthew. "Especially attending a regular school for the first time."

"You have no idea," lamented Sasha. "I didn't know much about American customs or fashion, or how to go about making friends or talk to boys. And while I spoke English fluently, I had a noticeable accent, sort of a mesh of

Russian and Portuguese. Fortunately, the high school I went to included students from a wide range of ethnicities, so I never completely felt like an oddball. Still, it was hard fitting in for the first year or so."

He regarded her curiously. "Now that you mention it, I do detect traces of an accent every so often. I'm not sure I would have really noticed unless you mentioned it, though."

"I worked on perfecting my English a lot during high school," she acknowledged. "But my accent still appears from time to time."

"It's charming," he assured her. "Just like you are."

They were interrupted then by the ringing of the doorbell to their suite, and Matthew hurried to open the door for the wait staff. Dinner was set out on the veranda with quiet efficiency, complete with the lighting of candles and torches.

"Enjoy your evening, sir, madam," said one of the waiters as he discreetly exited the suite.

Matthew held out a chair for her, and Sasha smiled her thanks as he took the seat across from her. The wait staff had already filled their water glasses, and left the bottle of wine chilling in a metal bucket. Matthew topped off both their wine glasses, then clinked his against hers.

"Here's to night number four," he toasted. "Each one has been equally special, equally memorable."

"I agree."

Matthew picked up his salad fork, but paused a moment before taking a bite. "I hope you know," he told her quietly, "that you'll always have a home with me, Sasha. I know you get along well with your roommates, but that place isn't really your home." He squeezed her hand. "Have you given

288

any further thought to moving in with me?"

She gave a small nod. "I actually have, believe it or not. But I'm afraid I'm no closer to a decision now then I was the first time you asked me. I - I will think about it, though, Matthew. I promise. And thank you - for what you just said. About always having a home with you. That's one of the kindest things anyone has ever told me."

He picked up her hand and brought it to his lips. "Then take me up on my offer, Sasha. Move in with me. I know the condo isn't really your style, but I'd let you redecorate it however you pleased. And I don't plan on making that my permanent home, you know. One of these days, hopefully very soon, I intend to look for another place, a real home. A home that I hope you'll share with me."

Sasha fought back the sudden surge of panic that threatened to choke her, reminding herself to practice what she preached and take deep, calming breaths. The idea of making such a commitment to anyone, even to Matthew, wasn't something she felt capable of dealing with just yet.

But he looked so hopeful, so happy, that she didn't have the heart to completely dissuade him tonight. Instead, she merely gave his cheek a fleeting caress, and murmured, "I'll keep giving it some thought, okay? I promise. Now, let's eat. I see that you ordered way too much food again, so we'd better get started if I'm going to finish even half of this."

It was a deliberate distraction, and Sasha knew that Matthew was well aware of her diversionary tactics. He tactfully didn't press her further for an answer, but she knew it would only be a matter of time before the subject came up again. And the next time he would expect an answer.

chapter fifteen

Late April

"HEY, BOSS. SORRY THAT I have to make such a lousy day even shittier, but your ex is on the phone and trying to say it's an emergency. Now, I can sniff out a load of bull a mile away and I say she's full of it, but she's continuing to be a major pain in my ass. Which considering how big my butt is, you can imagine how much that must be hurting right now."

Matthew didn't know whether to laugh at Elena's outlandish remark, or throw up his hands in frustration. It *had* been a really, really lousy day, one of the worst in recent memory, wrought with one crisis or problem or delay after another. And no matter how many times he'd reminded himself to take deep breaths, or to practice the various relaxation techniques Sasha had taught him, nothing really seemed to help. He'd barely picked at the lunch that Elena had unceremoniously plunked in front of him, and was admittedly well over his modest quota of coffee for the day, which wasn't helping his stress level one bit.

Dealing with Lindsey and her drama was the very last thing he needed right now, but it wouldn't be fair to expect Elena to deal with his ex. Sighing in resignation, he instructed Elena to put her through.

He hadn't even said hello when Lindsey's frantic, almost hysterical voice filled his ear.

"Matt, you have got to do something about Hayley!" she pleaded. "She is so out of control these days that I have no idea what to do anymore! Swear to God, I'm ready to ship her out to a boarding school. Or a convent. Can you please come over tonight and talk to her, see if you can get her straightened out? I just can't cope with her by myself any longer, Matt."

Matthew rubbed his right temple, where a headache had begun to throb nearly an hour ago. "Can you calm down and stop yelling for a second?" he begged. "Now, is there something in particular Hayley has done to set you off? Considering that she's been a major pain in the ass for the last few months."

"What *hasn't* she done?" exclaimed Lindsey. "She argues with me over the tiniest thing, ignores me when I try to ask her questions, laughs at me when I tell her she needs to be home at a certain hour. She's secretive and rude, and is hardly ever home these days. I tried taking her car keys away more than once, but the little witch just has one of her friends pick her up or calls Uber, and then sneaks out one of the back entrances. She's cut classes at least five times this month, and I'm getting a little tired of taking calls from the school. And then of course, there's all the stuff I found when I went snooping in her room the other day."

The headache was quickly beginning to spread to the other temple as well, and he started searching around in his desk for some Advil. "I won't even ask why you decided it was a good idea to search around her room," he replied wearily.

"Well, it was a damned good thing that I did, Matt!" Lindsey burst out. "Not only did I find a packet of birth control pills and a box of condoms, but a plastic baggie of marijuana, too! I know she's been sneaking out of the house late at night, too, and stays out till all hours on the weekend. And she disabled the Find My Friends app on her phone so I don't have any way of tracking her. She is totally and completely out of control, and I'm not sure how much longer I can take this."

"Have you confronted her about what you found in her room?" he asked patiently.

"Are you out of your mind?" asked Lindsey in horror. "She'd freak out if she thought I was snooping around. And we already spend so much time fighting, that the last thing I want to do is set her off. Can't you talk to her, Matt? Tell her that this has to stop, that she needs to start obeying the rules and being more respectful? I'm so stressed out by all of this that I'm hardly sleeping at night. It - it's hard being solely responsible for two teenagers, you know."

Matthew ignored Lindsey's very pointed dig, refusing to let her make him feel guilty. "When we separated, I offered right from the start to let one or both of the kids live with me," he reminded sternly. "And I've repeated that offer multiple time, Linz. You were the one who fought me on that, who insisted that the kids wanted to keep attending their schools and be near their friends, even though we both know they would have made the adjustment easily."

"It wouldn't have been as easy as you think, Matt," she argued stubbornly. "And now I'm stuck here taking care of them while you're free to do whatever you like."

He was incredulous at her self-centered attitude. "Should I remind you that I work twelve to fourteen hour days, and often six days a week, so that I can support you and the kids in the very lavish lifestyle you all enjoy? And I seem to recall that I'm still paying the bills every month for a full-time nanny - who the kids certainly don't need any longer - so that you can go to Pilates or the spa or out to lunch with your girlfriends whenever you want. I'd say that between the two of us, Linz, you've got a helluva lot more free time on your hands than I do."

"I'm still the one who has to deal with all of this crap on a daily basis," she pointed out.

"I talk to Hayley and Casey every single day, no matter how busy I am or where I happen to be," he reminded her in a tight voice. "Plus, they know darned well they can call or text or email me whenever they need something and I always respond almost immediately. I have dinner with the two of them once a week, unless I'm away on business, and they're with me every other weekend. Or at least Casey is, since Hayley would rather party with her friends or get her nails done than spend time with me."

Lindsey sniffed. "It's because of that - that girlfriend of yours, you know. Hayley doesn't like to stay with you because she feels you care more about your girlfriend than you do about her and Casey."

"Bullshit." Matthew ground the word out fiercely. "Complete and utter bullshit. Sasha is more than willing to give me time alone with my children when they visit. And she never spends the night, as you already know after grilling Casey on the subject multiple times. And Hayley is well aware of that fact, so don't be using Sasha as an excuse. Now, look, I'm having the day from hell here, and I have to get back to work. I'll give Hayley a call tonight and have a long talk with her."

"That's not going to do any good," warned Lindsey. "But maybe if you came by the house after work you could spend some time with her. You could have dinner with the three of us, then take Hayley aside afterwards and lay down the law to her."

He hesitated before replying, not wanting to admit that he was supposed to be having dinner with Sasha tonight. "I guess I could come by," he agreed reluctantly. "But don't plan on my staying for dinner. I'm going to be here at the office for hours yet, so I might not get down there until eight at the earliest."

Lindsey's tone instantly brightened. "That would be great, Matt! I think it would really do Hayley some good to have you remind her of the rules. You are still the man of the house, after all, and I think she'll respect that. Thank you, Matt, you have no idea how relieved this makes me."

It was on the tip of his tongue to correct her, to remind her that he was *not* the man of the house in any way, shape, or form. But that would have provoked another argument, and he was so exhausted and stressed out already that continuing to fight with Lindsey was the last thing he wanted to do. He grudgingly told her he'd stop by the house this evening, and to make damned sure that Hayley stayed at home tonight.

He buried his face in his hands for long seconds after he ended the call, wondering wildly how much crappier this day could possibly get. A quick glance at his schedule showed that he had a conference call starting in less than ten minutes, followed by two more meetings, so he had precious little time to talk to Sasha.

Fortunately, she was in between massage appointments and picked up his call on the second ring.

"This is a surprise," she told him. "I usually don't hear from you during the day. Is everything okay?"

"No, it's a veritable nightmare, actually," he admitted. "I was already having one of the lousiest days on record when I got a phone call from Lindsey."

Briefly, he filled Sasha in on what had transpired during the call, while she quietly let him vent.

"Knowing Lindsey, she's blowing all of this way out of proportion, but I feel like I need to see for myself what's going on," he explained. "And I really, really hate to do this, especially since it's the one thing that's been keeping me going all day, but I'll have to bow out on dinner tonight. I'm so sorry, Sasha. I feel like a rat for cancelling at practically the last minute like this."

"Don't worry about it," she replied calmly. "It's just dinner, after all. And I agree that you should pay Hayley a visit and try to find out what's wrong."

He was instantly relieved - and deeply grateful - at her easy acceptance, but he'd already known that Sasha would be understanding and supportive. Matthew wondered if she even had an angry bone in her body, or if she was capable of uttering a single nasty word.

"Have I told you lately what an amazing woman you are?" he told her tenderly. "Or how much I love you? I don't deserve you, you know."

She laughed softly. "That debate could go both ways, you know. Honestly, though, I do understand. Besides, Serge and Morgana need someone to substitute one of the classes tonight since the regular teacher has food poisoning. They'll be relieved when I tell them I can do it after all."

Matthew felt slightly less guilty at canceling their dinner date at this news, since it meant she wouldn't be alone the entire evening. "Would you still be willing to spend the night at the condo? I shouldn't be back too late, especially since the kids have school tomorrow and I know I'm going to be dead on my feet sooner than later. But it would sure mean a lot to know you'd be waiting at home for me after what's probably going to be an ugly scene with Hayley."

"I could do that, yes," Sasha agreed easily. "The class ends at eight-thirty, so I'll just plan on heading over to your place afterwards."

"Use Uber or Lyft," he reminded her. "You know I hate the idea of you taking a bus anywhere at that time of the night."

He had insisted on setting up accounts with both ride services for her so that she didn't have to take the bus home after the evening classes she taught. When he wasn't out of town on business, or having dinner with the kids, he would pick her up himself. But on those occasions when he wasn't available, like tonight, for example, he was able to rest easy knowing she had a ride home.

"I know you do," she replied. "Even though I'd been doing it for years before I met you, and never had any problems. But I know how much you worry, so I promise to use one of the services."

"Okay." He glanced at the clock, realizing that his

conference call would be starting any minute now. "Look, I've got to go. But thanks again for being so understanding. And I'll get home just as soon as I can."

"Drive safely. I love you, Matthew."

He replaced the receiver reluctantly, unwilling to end the call. Talking to Sasha for even a few minutes always filled him with a sense of calm, and helped him focus his attention. He hated, really hated, the thought of not spending the evening with her as planned, and thought darkly that Hayley had better get her act together fast. Because he damned sure didn't want to have to re-schedule any other evenings like this anytime soon.

UNFORTUNATELY, THAT EVENING TURNED OUT to be just the beginning of a string of similar such occurrences over the next few weeks. He would give Hayley a stern talking to, telling her that she needed to be more respectful to her mother, stop cutting classes, cease and desist sneaking out of the house, and spend more time studying rather than partying or shopping. Each time Hayley would rather meekly agree, apologizing over and over for her bad behavior, and she would shed a few tears telling him how much she missed him. There were even a couple of instances where Hayley had tearfully begged him to move back home, to reconcile with Lindsey so that they could all be one big happy family again. It had broken Matthew's heart to deny his daughter's requests, telling her gently but firmly that couldn't happen.

"I know it's tough, honey, but you need to accept the fact that your mom and I are over," he'd explained each time. "And while I'm always here for you, Hayley, that doesn't mean I'm going to move back in. Even though your mother hasn't signed the papers yet, I consider the divorce over and done with, and I moved on months ago. Hard as it is, you need to find a way to do the same."

After each visit to Hayley, things would be quiet for a few days, and Matthew would keep his fingers crossed that *this* time he had finally gotten through to her. But then Lindsey would call yet again, sounding more hysterical and upset each time, and fill him in on Hayley's latest escapades. And she, too, began to hint that maybe if Matthew moved back in - at least for a few months - that it might be the trick to help Hayley through this bad patch.

Matthew had given a weary sigh. "Jesus, did Hayley put you up to this? Never mind, because my answer is the same. No, I am not moving back in. No, you and I are never getting back together. Yes, I am still pursuing this divorce and one of these days I'll find a way to get you to sign those damned papers. I will do whatever I can to help Hayley deal with her issues, but moving back to Hillsborough is definitely not one of the options. So drop it, Linz."

"Well, we have to figure this out sooner than later, Matt. I swear I don't know how much more of this I can take," she had wailed.

"Look, the kids have just about a month or so left in

the school year. I still maintain it would be much better for Hayley to transfer to a different school in the fall. It would get her away from some of those friends you insist are such a bad influence on her. There's a couple of excellent private schools here in San Francisco I've been researching that would be perfect for her - small class size, lots of individualized attention, that sort of thing. I think the change would be good for her. She could live here with me, and you know how much she likes San Francisco."

"No." Lindsey had been stubbornly adamant. "First, I doubt she'd agree. She's very close to her friends and it won't be easy to separate her from them. Second, what's she supposed to do when you're out of town on business for a week or two at a time? I'm not allowing my sixteen-year-old daughter to be on her own in a big city."

"Haven't you been telling me every single time you call that her friends are part of the problem?" he'd argued back. "This would take care of that problem nicely. As for the other, I'd have to hire someone to live in while I travel. Not a nanny, since she and Casey are both far too old for that, in spite of what you say. More like a companion or personal assistant, that sort of thing."

Lindsey had given a disdainful sniff. "And you're forgetting another reason why an idea like that would never work. Hayley can't stand your girlfriend, so you wouldn't be able to have her over anymore."

"Like hell I wouldn't," Matthew had replied sternly. "Hayley needs to make way more of an effort to get along with people. There is absolutely no reason why she shouldn't like Sasha, none at all. Sasha has been nothing but kind to Hayley, far more than she deserves. And before you say it, Linz, I am not taking sides here. Yes, Hayley is my daughter but that doesn't mean she's always right, or that I always have to take her side. Especially when she's acting like a spoiled brat when it comes to Sasha. So if she can't grow up and learn to treat people decently, and accept the fact that Sasha is a part of my life, then I suppose another alternative is a good boarding school somewhere."

"But I don't want to be separated from her!" Lindsey had wailed. "I'd hardly ever get to see her if she went away. And it's been lonely enough without you here, Matt. I can't imagine what it would be like without my baby girl."

Matthew had stopped himself just in time from asking Lindsey in a very scathing tone how she could possibly be lonely given the number of men she'd been sleeping with - more than ever according to the weekly reports he still received from the private detective. "Well, unfortunately, you can't have it both ways," he'd told her instead. "On the one hand you're constantly complaining that she's too much for you to handle, that you're going out of your mind trying to cope with her antics. And then when I offer up two different solutions, you argue bitterly against them both. Make up your mind, will you, Linz?"

Lindsey had started crying again, though to Matthew her tears sounded as fake as her tits. "I just don't know what to do," she'd cried. "This is too much for me to deal with alone, Matt."

"Well, I've already given you two ideas on how to handle Hayley. Here's a third - we send her to counseling. In fact, *when I was down there last week I might have threatened her with that possibility if she doesn't start behaving better. But maybe the threat should become a reality."*

Lindsey hadn't liked that idea any better than the others, and had finally hung up on him in something of a snit. It had occurred to him then - and certainly not for the first time - that this whole situation with Hayley was a set-up of sorts, intended to make him feel badly enough that he would cave in and move back into the house. But while Lindsey was more than capable of something so devious, Matthew couldn't believe that his little girl would be a willing party to that sort of deception. Besides, he'd reasoned, Hayley had been moody and withdrawn for almost a year now, even before he had filed for divorce, so her issues couldn't be blamed entirely on his moving out.

It had been a rotten month for sure, he thought now, running a hand through his hair tiredly. In addition to all of the drama with Lindsey and Hayley, there had been all manner of issues to deal with here at MBI - the release of a new product line, several speaking engagements that he'd agreed to, hiring a replacement for the company's longtime marketing manager who'd been lured to a rival firm. And that was on top of all of his usual obligations, meetings, and daily tasks.

The only thing - correction, the only *person* - who had managed to keep him sane during this very trying time had been Sasha. Whether she had been giving him a massage, taking a few minutes to meditate with him, making love with him, or simply letting him vent about how horrible his day had been, she had offered her support and understanding and love every single day. Matthew honestly didn't know how he would have survived these past weeks without her, and vowed anew that no one and nothing would compel him to give her up.

"This isn't working, Hayley. Whatever you've been telling your father hasn't done the trick. I just got off the phone with him, and he won't even consider the possibility of moving back in here."

Hayley glowered at her mother. "I told you this was a stupid idea," she reminded Lindsey. "And Dad is definitely not stupid. No matter how many times you whine and cry and beg him, he's not coming back to you, Mom. Honestly, don't you have any pride at all? I mean, you're in good shape for your age, and you obviously don't have any problems getting guys. So why are you still hung up on Dad? Frankly, he's a big dork. So go find some hot guy ten or fifteen years younger than you are, and have a good time with him. You know, like Dad is doing with Sasha."

Hayley's indifference to the matter, not to mention the careless reminder that Matt's girlfriend was so much younger than she was, only made Lindsey angrier and more determined.

"Good thing you don't have any ambitions to be an actress," she snapped. "Because you obviously suck at it."

Hayley scowled. "Sorry if I'm not Sandra Bullock or Cate Blanchett. I haven't exactly had any drama classes or anything you know. Let's just call this whole thing off, okay? I'm tired of all this bullshit. If you want Dad back that badly, figure out

302

how to do it yourself. I'm done with your stupid games."

Lindsey bristled with indignation. "I don't think so, young lady," she hissed. "Did I forget to mention that one of the solutions to your so-called problems your father mentioned involved shipping you off to boarding school?"

"You wouldn't dare," hissed Hayley.

Lindsey smirked. "Oh, I'd dare all right. In fact, I was just reading up on a wonderful school the other day, one that's guaranteed to have results with rebellious teenager. It's a lovely campus, out in the countryside in central Utah - no cell phones, no cable TV, no internet unless it's for homework. Oh, and since it's a Christian school, there are prayer services twice a day plus a wonderful Bible study group. I think it would do you a world of good, Hayley."

Hayley gaped at her mother in horror. "There is no possible way that Dad would ever agree to send me to a place like that," she whispered.

"Oh, but I wouldn't really need his consent," assured Lindsey. "I have primary custody of you and Casey, after all, and I can make those sort of decisions all by myself."

Hayley shook her head emphatically. "Dad would set his foot down and you know it. All I would have to do is call him."

"Really?" Lindsey arched a brow. "Be sure to tell him at the same time that all of these dramatics have just been an act on your part, then. That you agreed to act out in order to lure him back home. Bet he'll be really proud of you for that, Hayley. And not even a tiny bit disappointed."

Hayley chewed at her bottom lip uncertainly. "You wouldn't really tell him that, would you?" she asked in a quavering voice.

Lindsey's green eyes narrowed menacingly. "I won't if you agree to cooperate with me. If you fulfill your end of the bargain and do whatever has to be done to get him back."

"Fine." Hayley threw up her hands in surrender. "I'll go along with whatever nutty schemes you and your crazy friend Nicole have cooked up."

Lindsey smiled. "That's my good girl. Now, obviously what we've done so far isn't quite enough. So, speaking of Nikki, she and I will have to really play dirty now. I'm meeting her for lunch tomorrow, and knowing her she'll think of something good. There's a reason why she came out of all three of her divorces with a bucketload of money. Having the best divorce attorney in the state was only part of that."

Hayley shook her head. "I still don't get why this is such a big deal to you. Why can't you just let it go? Sign the stupid divorce papers and move on with your life. It's not like you still love Dad or anything. And please don't try and bullshit me otherwise, Mom. If you loved him so much, then why did you fuck every guy who crossed your path?"

"Watch your mouth, little girl," warned Lindsey. "And butt out of things that aren't your business. As for why I want your father back - I guess it's a matter of pride. I mean, can you even believe that *he* left *me*? When I first met your dad, he was probably the biggest nerd I'd ever seen, with those glasses, and jeans that were too short for him, and he'd practically trip over his own feet half the time. He was damned lucky I still thought he was kind of cute in spite of all that. And if I hadn't been pregnant with you, I would have broken things off with him sooner than later. He just wasn't my type, you know?"

304

Hayley rolled her eyes. "Is there a point to this? Because, believe it or not, I actually need to get some homework done."

"The point," replied Lindsey angrily, "is that your father had some nerve in leaving me! Like he's ever going to do better. And he's already taking that bitch Sasha with him to events, the ones *I* should be going to. Do you have any idea how humiliating all of this is? I miss going to those parties and receptions, meeting important people, and seeing my picture in the paper or online. If it wasn't for me pushing him, your father wouldn't even know any of those people. He'd just be some nobody, some small-time computer nerd working for someone else. He owes me, dammit, and I want my life back! And between the two of us, we're going to make sure I get everything that I deserve."

As Lindsey stormed out of the room, Hayley breathed a sigh of relief. Dealing with her mother had never been easy, but over the past few months it had become a living nightmare. Sourly, Hayley thought that maybe the boarding school in Utah didn't sound quite so bad after all.

"THEY'RE SO BEAUTIFUL, JULIA. JUST the most precious little angels I've ever seen. Don't you agree, Sasha?"

Sasha smiled serenely as Tessa cooed at the baby boy she was cuddling. "I do, yes. But I think it was almost a given that Julia and Nathan would have beautiful babies." She cuddled the other twin - she was fairly sure this one was Justin while Tessa held Noah - and stroked her knuckles over his chubby baby cheek.

Julia gave a little groan. "How come they're both calm as

305

can be when you two hold them, but they scream bloody murder when I pick them up?"

Sasha gazed at Julia sympathetically. "Probably because you're exhausted and stressed and frustrated, and the twins pick up on all those negative vibes. Whereas Tessa and I have only been here for a little while, and weren't up half the night tending to two babies. You need to cut yourself some slack, Julia, and you definitely need to take better care of yourself."

"I know." Julia sniffled miserably. "I'm a mess. I don't sleep more than an hour or so at a time, can't remember the last time I ate a meal sitting down, and I haven't washed my hair in almost three days."

"Well, Sasha and I can stay all day," soothed Tessa. "Since today is Friday, she isn't teaching and doesn't have any massage appointments. And my schedule is wide open, too. So just show us a couple of basics about changing diapers and such, and we'll look after the boys while you have some time to yourself."

Julia's weary expression brightened instantly. "You guys are the best!" she enthused. "I didn't think it would be this hard taking care of two babies alone. But I guess I got lulled into a false sense of security, given that for the first six weeks after they were born I either had Nathan at home with me, or one set of our parents staying over. And Lauren and Ben spent a week helping out after that. Now with everyone gone and Nathan back at work, I'll freely admit to being completely overwhelmed."

"Have you considered hiring a nanny?" inquired Sasha. "At least part-time?"

Julia nodded. "I more or less told Nathan that we either get some help or he's taking a baby with him to the office every day. I've been in touch with a couple of agencies and they're sending over some applicants next week. But it will probably be at least another two to three weeks before someone can start."

"I know Sasha has to work, but I'll try to come over a couple of times a week until you get help," offered Tessa. "Ian and I aren't due to leave on another business trip until the middle of May, so I'll do what I can."

"And I'm happy to come over on Fridays," confirmed Sasha. "I'll also ask my friend Freya if she knows anyone interested in the nanny position. She's the midwife I mentioned to you a couple of times."

"That would be great," enthused Julia. "I'd actually prefer to use someone who's a personal referral. At this point, though, I'm pretty desperate. Enough that I begged Anton to come over on his day off next week."

Tessa and Sasha exchanged a look of mingled surprise and alarm. They had both met Anton on several occasions, including Julia's bachelorette party and baby shower. He was married to Travis, who co-owned the architectural design firm with Nathan. Anton was easily excitable, more than a little prissy, and the mere thought of him changing a diaper or rocking one of the twins to sleep was almost comical.

"Look, why don't you go take a nice long shower or bath, and then I'll cook breakfast for all of us," urged Tessa. "After that, I suggest you take a nap. Maybe Sasha and I can take the boys out in their stroller for awhile while you're sleeping."

Julia gave each of her friends a fierce hug. "Thank you

both so much," she replied, unsuccessfully stifling a yawn. "At this point, I'm not sure what sounds the most appealing - the shower, a real meal, or a nap. Or in what order."

Sasha eyed the tangled mass of golden brown curls that Julia had piled messily on the top of her head. "I vote shower. Especially since I'm pretty sure those are crumbs in your hair."

Julia looked mortified at this revelation, and dashed off without another word to clean herself up.

Tessa's blue eyes were twinkling mischievously as she grinned at Sasha. "I didn't want to be the one to tell her that she had food in her hair," she admitted. "You know how Julia is about always having to look like she just stepped out of a fashion magazine. Though I'm guessing her priorities have changed in a big way lately."

"Yes." Sasha continued to gently rock her twin, humming a soft tune beneath her breath as she did so. She smiled to notice that the baby's eyes had drifted shut and he appeared to be asleep.

Both twins slept peacefully for over an hour, more than enough time for their harried mother to shower and dress and do her makeup, and for Tessa and Sasha to prepare a hearty breakfast. The three women sat around Julia's breakfast nook sipping coffee or tea, and enjoying a vegetable frittata, home fries, and fresh fruit.

"Mmm, I think I'm actually beginning to feel human again," sighed Julia. "Please, God, just let them sleep a tiny bit longer so I can finish my coffee."

Tessa smiled. "I think Sasha is like the baby whisperer or something. All she did was hum a tune or two and Justin was out like a little light."

"Maybe I should get you to record whatever it was you were singing," joked Julia.

Sasha shook her head. "That's only part of it. It was also the physical contact. But more importantly, the baby could sense that I was calm. And in my experience, calm begets calm. In other words, Julia, when you're calm the boys should be, too."

"You'd like to think so, huh?" asked Julia wearily. "Maybe I'll feel calmer after that nap. Are you sure you guys are okay with looking after the twins for awhile?"

"Absolutely," insisted Tessa. "Get some sleep and we'll take it from here. Between the two of us we'll manage the diapering, and you showed us where you left the breast milk in the fridge. Now get along with you, hmm?"

Barely able to keep her eyes open, Julia stumbled out of the kitchen sleepily in the direction of the master bedroom.

"I'll do the dishes since you did most of the cooking," offered Sasha.

Tessa shrugged. "No rush. Let's enjoy our tea before the boys wake up. I'm hoping we have a few more minutes. Plenty of time to catch up with what's been going on in your life."

Sasha took a sip of her tea. "The usual, I suppose - work, seeing Matthew as often as I can, calling my mother every Sunday."

"Ian and I really need to have the two of you over for dinner again soon," lamented Tessa. "It's just been a really busy spring, what with Ian's birthday last month and our travel schedule and my college classes. I know what would be fantastic! You and Matthew should spend Memorial Day weekend up at the beach house with us. You'd love it there, Sasha."

"That sounds wonderful," mused Sasha. "But I'll need to check with Matthew about his schedule, see if he's supposed to have his children that weekend. I'll ask him tonight when we have dinner."

Tessa had a thoughtful expression on her face. "How's that working out these days - the situation with his kids, that is. The last time we spoke you said that the daughter was being a royal pain in the ass."

Sasha smiled. "Actually, I think that was your assessment of the situation when I told you about Hayley. But to answer your question, things have actually gotten worse."

She told Tessa about Hayley's all-too-frequent outbursts lately, the frantic phone calls from Matthew's ex, all the times he'd gone rushing down to the house to deal with the newest crisis.

"Hmm." Tessa tapped her index finger against her chin. "You know, forgive me for saying this, but something smells really fishy about everything you just told me."

Sasha nodded. "I've thought the exact same thing, Tessa. But I don't dare share my concerns with Matthew. He feels so guilty as it is about his kids, even though I assure him all the time he's a great father. I can't even imagine his reaction if I suggested that Hayley might be making all of this up just to get his attention."

"You're right. Unfortunately," commiserated Tessa. "He might or might not believe you, but I fear he's going to have to come to that conclusion on his own. Just don't let that little witch drive a wedge between the two of you, okay?

Matthew needs you more than ever right now."

"I know. In fact," admitted Sasha, "I've been giving his offer a lot of serious thought lately - the one about moving in with him. And I never thought I'd say this, Tessa, but I think I'm going to take him up on it."

Tessa gave a little squeal of delight, and reached over to hug her. "That's fantastic news!" she exclaimed. "And I know Matthew will be insanely happy at your decision. In fact, maybe it will be the motivation he needs to get tough with his daughter. If you're right in your suspicion that she's acting out in order to break the two of you up, then moving in with Matthew would put a real damper on her little schemes."

"I thought about that, too. But it's not the reason why I'm inclined to take him up on his offer. It just feels like the right time is all."

Tessa nodded. "I agree. So when are you going to tell him?"

"Tomorrow night, I think. We've got tickets to the final ballet program of the season, and are going out to an early dinner first. I thought about telling him over dinner."

Tessa clapped her hands in glee. "Perfect timing! Oh, he's going to be so happy, Sasha. And I'm thrilled for both of you."

Before Sasha could reply, one of the twins began to fuss and then let out a low wail, quickly followed by his brother.

Sasha laughed softly. "What was that you were just saying about perfect timing? Guess the dishes are going to have to wait until later."

chapter sixteen

MATTHEW WAS WHISTLING CHEERILY AS he chose a suit, shirt, and tie from his closet, his mood about the best it had been in several weeks. For the first time in nearly a month, he hadn't felt the need to go into the office today - a Saturday - and had not only slept in but spent a good two hours at his health club working out. He had run into Ian there, and accepted his invitation to brunch after their workouts. Coincidentally, Tessa was attending Sasha's yoga class at the same time, and having tea with her afterwards.

He had spent the afternoon answering some emails, calling his parents, and Facetiming with Casey, who was away for the weekend at a school trip to Disneyland. And tonight he and Sasha had a special evening planned - dinner at a chic French Vietnamese restaurant, followed by a performance of the San Francisco Ballet. Sasha, with her dance background, was especially excited to be attending the performance, and had been looking forward to this evening for the past few weeks.

And he had every intention of making this a night to remember for her, especially since he felt like a heel for cancelling out of several dates lately. The frequent phone calls from Lindsey begging him to come and deal with Hayley's latest tantrum or episode of bad behavior had forced him to back out of dinner dates or quiet evenings at home with Sasha, and he was determined to make all of that up to her tonight. Of course, she had assured him multiple times that she understood his dilemma, that she wasn't the least bit angry or upset, and that she applauded his efforts to be a good father to his daughter. But none of her reassurances had done much to assuage his guilt, and he vowed that the next time Lindsey called he would be firm in his resolve not to go rushing down to Hillsborough.

Tonight during dinner he planned to ask Sasha again to move in with him. He hadn't brought the subject up since their trip to Hawaii, sensing that she still needed more time to think it all over. But he was becoming increasingly impatient to have her with him all the time, to wake up beside her every morning, and know that she would be here each night. And that included the weekends he had the kids.

Lindsey would have a royal fit about that part, of course, but he was more than ready to do battle with her if it came to that. Casey certainly wouldn't have any problem at all if Sasha moved in, since the two of them got along famously. He was even practicing yoga with her here at the condo, and had been over the moon recently when he'd been able to kick up into a handstand on his own. Casey also enjoyed visiting Linda at her cottage in Marin, and always looked forward to playing with her dogs and cats and the rest of her menagerie. He'd even started to hint about wanting a dog or cat of his own, something Lindsey had always been adamantly opposed to, and he'd asked if this supposed pet could possibly live here at the condo.

As for Hayley - well, she would have to get over her

issues in a big hurry and simply accept the fact that Sasha was moving in. Matthew was getting damned tired of his daughter's antics and the negative impact they were having on his personal life. Boarding school was beginning to sound more and more appealing, he thought dourly.

As if on cue, his cell phone buzzed with an incoming call, and he scowled fiercely to see it was from Lindsey. He hesitated for a couple of seconds before turning the volume control to vibrate as he continued to get ready. When he checked his phone ten minutes later, he was annoyed beyond belief to find a total of ten missed calls from Lindsey - literally one per minute - and sighed in frustration as he listened to the first voice mail.

"Matt, where the hell are you? Jesus, we've got a huge problem on our hands here. You are not going to believe what kind of a mess Hayley has gotten herself into this time. Call me right away, there is no way I can deal with this one by myself."

The second message was equally as dramatic, as was the third where Lindsey really started to lose it, weeping and becoming increasingly hysterical. But by the fourth message his annoyance with his ex quickly turned to concern as she revealed more specifics about the problem with Hayley.

"Would you please fucking pick up your phone, Matt? Look, I didn't want to tell you this over the phone, but since you aren't answering my calls, I guess I don't have a choice. Apparently Hayley is pregnant - yes, you

heard me right - pregnant! I went into her bathroom while she was still asleep looking for some tampons since I was out, and I found a used pregnancy test in her wastebasket - a positive test. I freaked out when I saw it and woke her up, and we had the screaming match from hell. So you have got to get down here and help me deal with this. This - oh, Christ - this is a fucking disaster!"

Matthew stared at his phone in horror, unwilling to believe what he had just heard. Surely this was just Lindsey being her usual over-the-top self, and there was some reasonable explanation for what she'd seen. Like maybe the test had belonged to one of Hayley's friends. Or she had misread the results.

But since he could hardly ignore a message like that, he returned Lindsey's call in resignation, bracing himself for the angry barrage he was sure to face from her.

"Well, it's about fucking time you called," bit out Lindsey, not bothering to even say hello. "Where the hell have you been anyway?"

"Taking a shower," he lied, already bristling at her confrontational tone. "I didn't realize I needed your permission for that. And FYI, ten messages in ten minutes is overkill even for you. One would have been adequate. Now, what the hell is this about Hayley being pregnant? How in God's name did that happen?"

"The usual way, I expect," spat Lindsey sarcastically. "And she's being extremely closed-mouthed about the whole thing, won't say a word to me. But I just walked by her room and heard her crying her eyes out. You've got to get down here, Matt. This is a huge, huge crisis!"

He cursed beneath his breath, running a hand through his hair until it stood up in messy spikes. "I thought you told me she was on the pill," he growled.

"That's what I assumed, too. But when I asked her about that, she said she stopped taking them because they were making her gain weight. Like having a baby isn't going to do that and a whole lot more."

Matthew was horror stricken. "For Christ's sake, she's not actually thinking of having the baby, is she? She's only a kid, just sixteen."

"Plenty old enough to get knocked up. As for the other, I have no idea what she wants to do since she refuses to talk to me. But she'll probably talk to you. How soon can you be here?"

He glanced at his dresser where the tickets to tonight's ballet were waiting to be placed in his jacket pocket. He closed his eyes, taking a couple of deep breaths before telling Lindsey, "I actually have plans for tonight, Linz. Plans that would be very difficult to cancel. Maybe I could just talk to Hayley on the phone for now, and then come down in the morning."

"Are you freaking kidding me?" screamed Lindsey so loudly that he had to hold the phone away from his ear. "Our baby girl is pregnant, she's crying and upset, and you can't come down because you have a fucking date? Once again, your whore is more important to you than your own daughter."

Matthew's control snapped. "How dare you!" he hissed.

"For you to call another woman a whore is the most hypocritical thing you've ever said, given that high priced call girls don't spread their legs as often as you do. And for you to call Sasha - the finest, most decent person I've ever known - such a disgusting term is beyond belief. So shut the fuck up about her, Linz, because you aren't even worthy of breathing the same air as she does. As far as Hayley is concerned, you know damned well that I've been there every single time you've called. I fail to see how waiting until the morning to deal with this is going to make any difference."

"Why don't you tell her that yourself, Matt?" jeered Lindsey. "Here, Hayley. Your father wants to talk to you."

He was caught completely off guard, not having anticipated that Lindsey would wash her hands of the matter and hand the phone off to Hayley. And there was no way he could prevent the tug on his heart when he heard his daughter's tearful, choked-up voice.

"Daddy?" she whispered, sounding far more like the little girl of six who had once followed him everywhere than the sullen sixteen year old of late. "I'm so sorry. I didn't mean for this to happen. And I'm so scared. Can you please come over? I really need you right now, Daddy."

Matthew scrubbed a hand over his face in abject frustration, quietly cursing his ex for intentionally placing him in such a despicable position. "All right," he agreed reluctantly. "Give me a few minutes to make a phone call, and then I'll be over. And be prepared, young lady, to give me some answers. I want to know how this happened, who the father of this baby is, and what your intentions are. Don't think for a minute that

317

you're going to dodge my questions. I'll see you soon."

Angrily, he tossed his phone on the bed after ending the call, wishing instead that he could throw it against the window. With jerky motions, he stripped off the suit and tie he'd taken such care in selecting, tossing the discarded garments carelessly on the bedroom floor. As he re-dressed in jeans and a T-shirt, the ballet tickets caught his eye again, and the reminder of what he had to do next made the gorge rise in his throat. Reluctantly, he picked up his phone and placed the call.

"Hi," greeted Sasha. "I'm almost ready. I can't tell you how much I'm looking forward to this evening. "

Matthew wondered helplessly what rotten thing he had done in his life to warrant this much misery. "I know, sweetheart. Believe me, I was, too. And you're going to hate me forever, but I'm going to have to back out of our date tonight. I'm so sorry, Sasha."

There was silence for several seconds on the other end, before she replied. "Oh. That's - well, kind of heartbreaking, for lack of a better word. Should I even bother to ask or just assume this has something to do with Hayley again?"

He was taken aback by the terse, almost angry tone of her voice, given that he'd never once seen or heard her getting upset. But he figured that even someone as tolerant as Sasha had her limits, and cancelling their plans this evening - the ones she'd been so excited about - might have pushed her just a bit too far.

"Yeah, it's about Hayley," he admitted tiredly. "It seems that she's pregnant. Lindsey found out accidentally and all hell is breaking loose right now. I tried to put this off, honestly I did, but she's sixteen years old and crying her eyes out, and I'd feel like the worst father ever if I didn't go sort this whole mess out tonight."

"Pregnant?" asked Sasha in disbelief. "She's just a little girl, Matthew. I mean, obviously she's old enough biologically to get pregnant, but emotionally - wow. I can't even imagine how upset you must be right now. What are you going to do?"

"Hell if I know," he acknowledged. "But I told Hayley that I expect answers - plenty of them - and I think she knows I mean business. Meanwhile, I feel like a heel - once again - for canceling on you tonight, Sasha. I know how much you were looking forward to this evening."

"I won't lie and say I'm not disappointed, Matthew. There was something really important I wanted to talk to you about over dinner, too, but I suppose that will have to wait. You'd better go see what the situation is with Hayley."

Matthew was both startled and shaken to realize that Sasha was crying, given the way her voice had broken on her last sentence. She was always the strong one, always the sensible one, and he had no idea of how to deal with her sudden vulnerability.

"Sweetheart." He massaged the back of his neck, feeling the muscles there already beginning to bunch up with tension. "I know there's no possible way I can make this up to you, and you should definitely be very, very angry with me right now. And I know I've had to say this way too often as of late, but I'm so sorry, Sasha."

She gave a little sniffle, obviously struggling to gain control of her emotions. "I know you are," she told him quietly. "But that doesn't make this any easier. You'd better go, I won't keep you any longer."

"Wait." He forestalled her before she could end the call. "Look, why don't you still go out to dinner and then the ballet? I'll call the restaurant and give them my credit card, you can order whatever you like. And I'll have the tickets messengered over to you on my way out. The concierge can take care of that. I realize it isn't the same thing, but maybe you could ask Julio or Chad to go with you. That way you can still enjoy your evening."

"You're right. It's not the same thing at all," she chastised him. "And Chad and Julio are in Las Vegas this weekend at a wedding. But I suppose I could ask one of the other teachers from the studio if she'd like to go to the ballet with me. She used to study ballet so she'd probably be interested. Not the dinner, though. That was supposed to be something special for us. I don't want to go if you're not with me."

"We'll go another time," he promised. "I swear to you, Sasha. And I *will* make this up to you, one way or the other. Look, you're right, I do need to go, but I'll make sure these tickets get delivered to you within the hour." He paused briefly before telling her in a husky voice, "I love you so much, Sasha. I hope you know that."

"I do, yes. Good night, Matthew."

She ended the call without echoing his sentiments,, and the disappointment in her voice was so heart wrenching that this time he wasn't able to suppress his anger and frustration as he hurled his phone against the wall.

"IT'S ABOUT GODDAMNED TIME YOU got here. Once again you've forced me to deal with all of this crap by myself."

Matthew didn't even spare his enraged ex a glance as he walked inside the foyer of the house. "In case you've forgotten, I'm not here for you," he retorted, walking briskly in the direction of Hayley's room.

Lindsey, however, stayed right on his heels, not an easy task considering that even inside the house she insisted on tottering around on those ridiculous stilettos. He wondered vaguely if she'd been getting ready for a night on the town, given her attire of short, tight black skirt, sheer gauzy white blouse, and wearing so much makeup that his fingernails would come away filthy if he raked them down her cheek.

Hayley's bedroom was an untidy mess as usual, but Matthew figured that was the least of her problems at this point. She was curled up in a fetal position on her bed, a fleecy throw pulled up nearly over her head, and her eyes were red and puffy from crying. She glanced up as he entered, and gave him a watery smile.

"Hi, Daddy," she whispered miserably, holding out her arms to him.

As he eased himself onto the bed and pulled her into a hug, it occurred to him that Hayley hadn't called him Daddy in years, probably not since her tenth birthday when she'd decided that wasn't cool anymore, and wondered for a moment at the timing of this sudden change.

"Hey, baby," he murmured instead, stroking his daughter's long, silky hair. "You doing okay?"

321

Hayley shrugged. "Not really, no. This has been kind of a shock, you know?"

Matthew gave a short, sardonic laugh. "Yeah, no kidding. I didn't even know you had a boyfriend, Hayley. Have you told him that you're pregnant? And who is this guy anyway? Your mother and I are going to need to get his parents involved, figure this whole situation out between us."

"No!" exclaimed Hayley. "Dad, no! I - I mean, oh, God, this is going to sound so awful, I'm not even sure how to say this. But I don't - oh, God - "

"What she's trying to say," interjected Lindsey tersely, "is that she doesn't know who the father is. You don't think I've been trying to pry a name out of her since I found that damned test, Matt?"

Matthew stared at his daughter in horror. "What does your mother mean you don't know who the father is? Jesus, how many boys have you had sex with, Hayley - two, three, more?"

Hayley's pale cheeks reddened. "This is so embarrassing," she groaned, burying her face in her hands. "Do we really have to talk about this now?"

"We sure as hell do!" boomed Matthew. "I told you, young lady, that I was going to insist on having answers to all of my questions tonight. There is no way you're going to wheedle your way out of this. Now, tell your mother and I who the potential father - or should I say fathers - of this baby are."

"I don't know their names," replied Hayley reluctantly. "And I'm not even sure what they look like. I met them at a party, had never seen them before, and haven't seen them since. I'm don't think they're from around here."

Matthew struggled mightily to keep his temper in check as he prodded further. "What party? When was this exactly?"

"About six weeks ago. And, well, I'm not exactly sure where the party was either. I mean," she added hastily at her father's look of disbelief, "I didn't notice where we were driving to. And Brianne didn't remember either. It was dark and raining outside, and no streetlights so neither one of us know where the house was. Somewhere up in the hills, maybe Los Gatos or Saratoga, around there. I don't really know that area very well, and it might not even have been there for all I know and - "

Matthew held up a hand. "Stop. You're rambling on and on and not making a lick of sense. First of all, who's Brianne?"

"She's Hayley's new friend," explained Lindsey. "She and her older brother just transferred to the school this semester, and since Hayley has a big crush on the brother she's sort of latched onto Brianne."

"Is he the one who got you pregnant?" demanded Matthew.

Hayley shook her head emphatically. "God, no! He's a senior, two years older than I am, and doesn't even know I exist half the time. But supposedly he was going to be at this one party that Brianne convinced me to attend, only he wasn't there after all. And, well, that party turned out to be a big dud, so when Brianne met these two older guys there who said they knew where a real party was going on, we went with them."

Matthew closed his eyes, pinching the bridge of his nose as he felt a headache coming on fast. "And you have no idea where this other party was, hmm?"

"No. We, uh, might have had a few beers at the first party, and smoked a joint," she confessed sheepishly. "So I was already kind of out of it during the drive. And all I remember about the second party was one of the guys who brought us giving me a drink. Next thing I know we're waking up in Brianne's room the next morning, and neither of us can remember how we got there."

He counted to ten beneath his breath, trying desperately to quell his mounting rage. "Are you trying to tell me," he asked in a dangerously low voice, "that you were date raped and haven't said a word about it until now? My God, Hayley, what the hell were you thinking?"

Hayley quavered in fear at this uncharacteristic display of anger from her normally placid father. "I - I guess I didn't think of it that way," she answered in a small voice. "Being raped, that is. I don't even remember any of it, to be honest."

"Of course you don't." Matthew exhaled sharply, shaking his head in disbelief. "Because those bastards drugged you, and then did whatever the hell they wanted while you were unconscious. Did they hurt you, baby?"

Hayley shrugged. "Not really. I mean, I had an awful headache after and was sick to my stomach. So was Brianne. But I didn't have any bruises or anything like that, if that's what you're asking."

"Why in God's name didn't you tell someone what happened, Hayley?" he asked incredulously. "If you had said something right away one of us could have called the police, taken you in for an examination. They would have taken a blood test, figured out what sort of drug you were given, and might have been able to track down those bastards.

324

Or at least where this party took place. What about the first party you went to? Did you ask anyone who attended if they knew who these two guys were?"

"Oh my God, Dad - no!" exclaimed Hayley, horror-stricken. "You really think that Brianne and I are going to admit to all of our friends that we were stupid enough to go off with some strangers and let ourselves get drugged? Do you have any idea what people would have said about us, the gossip that would have gone around? Brianne and I haven't even talked about it since that morning, we agreed it was best to pretend it never happened."

"Well, you can't exactly do that any longer, can you?" retorted Matthew. "Did these rapists have a first name? And what sort of car were they driving?"

Hayley shrugged. "Um, everything is still pretty hazy, but I think they told us their names were Brent and Greg. No idea at all about their last names. As for the car, maybe a Mercedes? Or a Lexus? It was a dark car, and really dark outside so I didn't pay attention."

Matthew blew out a frustrated breath, running a hand through his already mussed hair. "Okay. Speaking of feeling hazy, there's still a few things that I'm really unclear about here. So why don't you start over from the beginning, and we'll go through all of this step by step."

Hayley opened her mouth as though to protest his request, but he figured the look on his face must have quickly convinced her otherwise. With poorly concealed impatience, she took him and Lindsey, who was still hovering in the doorway, through the events from that night six weeks ago.

325

It was one of the weekends that she was supposed to have been with Matthew, but had refused to go because of the party, as well as Brianne's invitation to spend the weekend at her house. Since Casey would be with his father, Lindsey had taken the opportunity to fly to Palm Springs for the weekend with Nicole and another girlfriend. The party had been on Friday evening, at the home of a senior at their school, and the house had been packed with nearly a hundred partygoers, most of whom Hayley hadn't known very well. Despite the crowd, Brianne had declared the party "dullsville", and had eagerly latched on to the two guys who were probably in their early twenties, likely college students. Hayley figured they were party crashers, since word of this particular party had spread quickly among their circle of friends.

Already more than a little drunk and high, she had gone along willingly with Brianne and the two males, but had been too out of it to pay attention to where they were driving. She vaguely remembered entering a big house high up on a hill, where another, even bigger party was in full swing. One of the guys who'd brought them there handed her a drink of something that she had chugged down without a second thought. The next thing she remembered was waking up in the spare bed in Brianne's room the next morning, hungover and completely out of it.

"At first, I just figured I'd had too much to drink and passed out," she related. "But then when I went to take a shower, I realized that, uh, well, other stuff must have happened. Same with Brianne."

"How in the hell did you manage to get back to Brianne's

house if you were both so out of it?" demanded Matthew. "I hope to God neither of you tried to drive in that condition."

Hayley shook her head. "We actually took Uber to the first party. I, uh, guess Brent and Greg must have dropped us back home. I know we didn't take Uber because neither of us have a record of calling them for the return trip."

Matthew placed his hands on his daughter's shoulders, looking her square in the face. "When you realized what had happened, why in the world didn't you tell someone?" he asked solemnly. "I would have come for you immediately, and I'm sure your mother would have flown home right away. Were you just going to keep this to yourself for the rest of your life?"

Tears glimmered in Hayley's eyes again as she shrugged. "I was ashamed. And embarrassed," she admitted. "And I didn't want to make either of you mad at me for all the stupid stuff I did - getting drunk, going off with a couple of guys I didn't know. Brianne's parents would have gone through the roof if they'd found out, so we promised each other to keep quiet about it. I mean, I know it sounds real bad, but neither of us were actually hurt. Though the part about winding up pregnant really, really sucks."

"Well, I still want to call the police," declared Matthew, taking out the phone that fortunately hadn't suffered any serious damage after he'd flung it against his bedroom wall. "I doubt that they'll be able to do much at this point, with so much time having past, and you and Brianne not remembering anything. But they might have had reports about related incidents, and can tie them to the same suspects. It doesn't hurt to try."

"No, Daddy!" protested Hayley, snatching the phone from his hand. "Please, please don't call the police! I think I would die of embarrassment if I had to tell that story to someone besides you and Mom. And - and it upsets me to have to keep talking about it, you know? Can we please just let it be and go on from here? Even if by some miracle the cops found these guys, so what? It's not going to change the fact that I'm pregnant now."

"What about my feelings, Hayley?" demanded Matthew. "I want to find these two bastards and beat the crap out of them for what they did to my little girl. Do you blame me for feeling that way? Or at least trying to bring them to justice."

"Matt, not now, okay?" interjected Lindsey, who'd remained largely silent until now. "It's been a rough day for Hayley, and I think we should give her some space now. You're just upsetting her more by pushing this issue with the police. And I hate to say it, but it's not going to do any good at this point. It will just make you and I look like irresponsible parents, not knowing where our daughter was that night, or having her feel that she could trust us enough with the truth."

"Fine." Matthew threw up his hands in frustration. "I'll drop that part of it for now. But we still need to discuss this whole pregnancy issue, what you plan on doing about it. First of all, have you been to a doctor? Or are you just assuming you're pregnant based on the home test you took?"

Hayley glanced back and forth between her parents uncertainly. "Um, no. I - I haven't been to the doctor yet. Mom's going to make an appointment for me on Monday. But I'm positive that I'm pregnant, Dad. I've felt sick to my stomach and tired and all the other symptoms. And it wasn't just the one test. This is the third one I used and they've all been positive."

"Okay." He nodded. "Now, what do you intend to do about this? Your mother said that you were actually thinking of having the baby? Under the circumstances, Hayley, wouldn't you prefer to - "

"Have an abortion?" she burst out. "No, I don't want to do that, Daddy. I want to have the baby and raise it myself."

"What?" Matthew was both shocked and horrified at this revelation. "Hayley, you can't mean that. For God's sake, you're sixteen years old and can barely look out for yourself. How in the world are you going to take care of a baby? You still need to finish high school, and then go to college. And you won't have the baby's father to help out. I can understand why you wouldn't want to have an abortion, but surely adoption would be a much better solution. They have open adoptions these days, so you would know who the parents are and could keep in touch with them, still be a part of the baby's life. Don't you think that would be a much better idea?"

Hayley shook her head stubbornly. "No, that's not what I want. I don't want to give my baby away. And we're rich, we can hire a nanny or someone to look after the baby while I'm at school."

"Honey, I really think you're oversimplifying this whole thing," cautioned Matthew. "You have no idea what's involved with raising a child. And you're so young, Hayley. I can't imagine that you'd want to tie yourself down this way. I really, really think you need to give this some very careful thought and weigh your options more closely."

"That's exactly what I've been telling her," interjected Lindsey. "She's going to ruin her life if she has this baby. I have no idea how she's going to keep this hidden from her friends, or what kind of social life she can have with a baby. You should listen to your father, Hayley, and either terminate the pregnancy or give the baby up for adoption."

"No!" Hayley shook her head stubbornly. "You can't force me to do either of those things, Mom, in spite of what you told me earlier. Can I talk to Dad privately now?"

Lindsey glared at her daughter. "Fine. But if you somehow manage to convince him to let you have this baby, then he'd damn well better be prepared to do his part in helping to raise it. Because if you think you're going to dump a baby on me to raise, young lady, then think again."

Lindsey stormed out of the room, her heels clicking in a fast, furious patter on the wood floors. Hayley waited until her mother was out of earshot, then turned to Matthew with a look of desperation on her face.

"Daddy, you've got to help me!" she pleaded. "Mom has been having a fit ever since she found out I was pregnant, and she keeps saying she's either going to force me to have an abortion or ship me off to some school or home where I can have the baby in secret and then have it adopted. Please don't let her do that, please?"

"Shh, it's okay," soothed Matthew, as Hayley flung himself into his arms. "I promise I won't let her force you into anything. We'll work through this together, all right? It's going to be a family decision, Hayley, and we'll consider all the options."

She nodded, burrowing her head against his chest. "I knew

you'd stick up for me, Daddy. Mom has been so horrible to live with ever since you left, you have no idea. She's mean and selfish and hardly ever here. But she says she won't let me go live with you, especially since you have a girlfriend now, says that her lawyer would file some sort of order to prevent me and Casey from moving in with you. Can she really do that?"

"I don't know, baby," he told her, pressing a kiss to her forehead. "I'd have to talk to my lawyer about it. But is that what you really want? You've never once given me the impression that you want to live with me."

Hayley shrugged. "I don't really want to move to San Francisco, no. I mean, I like my school and all my friends and this house and all my things. But dealing with Mom on my own has been so hard. Couldn't you come back, just for a little while? I mean, I know you and Mom aren't getting back together, but couldn't you stay here for a few weeks? At least until we figure all this stuff with the baby out."

Matthew was visibly taken aback at this request. "Honey, I really don't think that would help this situation. Your mother and I are as good as divorced, you know, and I'm not sure how my living here is going to help anything."

"It would help *me*!" insisted Hayley. "Especially now when I'm so upset and trying to figure everything out. Please, Daddy?"

He hesitated. "Hayley, you've only got a few more weeks left of school before summer starts. As soon as you're through you can come and stay with me while we sort all of this out. And I guarantee your mother won't stop you."

Hayley sniffled loudly. "But I can't leave Casey here alone

with her. She's so mean at times, I wouldn't feel right sticking him with her."

Matthew shrugged. "He can come, too."

"No." She shook her head. "Did you forget he's signed up for summer baseball league? He has practice or a game almost every day of the week."

"Shit, I did forget." He heaved a sigh of frustration. "Yeah, that won't work. And I understand your concern about leaving him here with your mom. You're a good sister to worry about Casey that way, honey. Look, I'll - I'll give it some thought, okay? Maybe I could stay for a few weeks until we figure out what we're going to do. But don't start thinking this means your mother and I are getting back together. *If* I agree to stay, it's strictly temporary, okay?"

"Okay," agreed Hayley happily, giving her father an enthusiastic hug. "Thank you, Daddy, thank you so much! You have no idea how much this means to me, how happy you've just made me."

The kiss she pressed to his cheek made Matthew feel warm all over, and he hugged her back comfortingly.

"Do you think you could stay tonight?" begged Hayley. "You can use Casey's room. Or one of the guest rooms, of course. It would make me feel so much better. Please? That way we could talk about all of this some more, start figuring out what options we have."

"Tonight?" asked Matthew in disbelief. He'd been hoping to get back to San Francisco in time to spend the night with Sasha.

"Could you? Please?" asked Hayley in a woeful little voice. Tears began to track down her flushed cheeks, and her chin

332

wobbled as she visibly struggled not to weep.

He sighed for probably the fortieth time that night, fully aware that his daughter was manipulating him. But given the trauma that she'd endured, the terrible secret that she'd been keeping to herself for weeks, and the burden that was weighing heavily on her mind, he reluctantly agreed.

"Just let me go out to my car," he told her. "I always keep an overnight bag in the trunk for emergencies. But," he warned her, "this is just for tonight, okay? No guarantees about anything beyond this. I told you I would think about it and I will, but I've got a lot to consider before I make any decision."

"Okay. Thank you, Daddy. This means so much to me. You're the best dad in the whole world, you know?" Hayley asked as she gave him a ferocious hug.

But whatever warm feelings his daughter's gratitude had stirred up weren't nearly enough to ward off the much stronger concerns that overwhelmed him as he headed out to his car – in particular how in the hell he was going to break all of this to Sasha without breaking her heart in the process.

"I TAKE IT ALL BACK, Hayley. That was an Oscar worthy performance you just gave. Natalie Portman couldn't have done a better job."

Hayley gave her mother a pointed look. "Dad's going to be back in a few minutes, Mom. You might want to hold off on the gloating for now."

Lindsey grinned, looking like a cat who'd just swallowed a canary. "Oh, but he fell for it all hook, line, and sinker! Just like Nikki predicted he would. I really owe her big time, you know, for dreaming all of this up. She's even more devious and conniving than I am, and that's saying a lot."

"Whatever," replied Hayley, already tired of the charade she'd been coerced into acting out. "And Dad hasn't said for sure that he's going to move back in. Even if he does, he made it pretty clear that he had zero intention of getting back together with you. So I wouldn't be celebrating just yet."

Lindsey shrugged. "He'll give in to you, I know he will. Your father already feels guilty that he isn't here enough for you and Casey. You just need to keep putting the pressure on. All you need to do is get him to move back in. Leave the rest up to me. I guarantee that he'll be calling off the divorce and we'll be one big happy family again in no time."

chapter seventeen

THE CONDO WAS ALMOST EERILY quiet as she let herself in, and for a minute or two she wondered if Matthew was here or not. But then she heard the sound of a door shutting in another room, and set her bag down on the sofa as she waited for him to emerge.

Sasha had thought for a time about not coming over when he had texted her earlier this morning, practically begging her to meet him here after her class. She was still more than a little upset, and definitely hurt, after he had abruptly cancelled their evening out, an evening that was supposed to have been the start of the next phase in their relationship. It was totally out of character for her to be in such an unforgiving mood, but her level of tolerance had been sorely tested these past few months.

But she was here now, and struggling to keep an open mind and listen to what Matthew needed so badly to tell her. Sasha assumed he was going to apologize, and try to make up for the fiasco from last night in some way. And while most people she knew would have stayed mad for at least a week, it wasn't in her placid nature to make someone grovel and beg. Besides, she admitted with a sigh of resignation, she was in love with the man, after all, and it was awfully hard to remain angry with him for very long.

And when the man in question entered the living room a few minutes later, any remaining annoyance she might have felt towards him disappeared in a flat instant, replaced instead with concern. Matthew looked exhausted and more than a little disoriented as he gazed at her somberly. He had dark circles under his eyes, and hadn't shaved, and his hair was sticking up into wild, unkempt spikes. He wore a wrinkled T-shirt and a pair of baggy sweat pants that looked like something he might have owned since college.

But it was the look on his face that concerned Sasha the most - a look of both sorrow and regret - and her hands suddenly felt ice cold. She had become quite adept over the years at being in tune with other peoples' emotions, at being able to sense their feelings, and she knew immediately that something bad was troubling Matthew.

"Hi," she greeted uncertainly, struggling to keep her voice steady.

He didn't reply, simply crossed over to where she stood and took her into his arms. He buried his face against the side of her neck, breathing in deeply of her scent, and squeezing her so tight that she had trouble taking a breath. She forgot that she was supposed to be mad at him, that he was the one who ought to be comforting and consoling her right now, and instead stroked his back comfortingly, her slender fingers massaging the tight muscles at his nape.

Matthew gave a muffled groan. "God, that feels good. My whole body feels like one big knot right now. And that includes my brain. I keep hoping that I'll wake up, and realize the last eighteen hours or so have just been a really bad dream."

"That bad, hmm? Why don't we sit down and you can fill me in on what happened?" suggested Sasha, urging him in the direction of the sectional sofa.

"What happened." Matthew shook his head despairingly. "The whole damned world went to hell overnight, that's what happened. But I'll get to that in a minute. God knows it's the last thing I want to talk about. How are you, sweetheart? I can't even begin to tell you how sorry I am for standing you up last night. Or how grateful I am that you agreed to come over today."

"It's okay," she replied. "I know that you would have been there if you'd been able to."

"Did you enjoy the ballet?"

Sasha nodded. "It was wonderful, thanks. And Chandra, my co-worker, was over the moon that I invited her. Though, of course, it wasn't the same without you there."

"I know." Matthew expelled a long, frustrated breath, his head falling back wearily onto the sofa. "And if there was some way I could make it up to you, I'd be doing it right now. But I've got a feeling you aren't going to be in a very forgiving mood after I tell you what happened with Hayley last night."

His words sent a chill up her spine, for he sounded so sad, so defeated, that she could only gaze at him in bewilderment. "What are you talking about?"

Matthew took her hand in his, squeezing it tight as though he was hoping to borrow some of her strength. "Besides the shock of finding out that my teenaged daughter is pregnant, I learned last night that she was also date raped. It happened about six weeks ago, on one of those weekends she was

337

supposed to spend with me but begged off to go to a party instead. A party where she was drugged and had who knows what done to her. And that she doesn't remember a damned thing about, including the names or faces of the thugs who raped her and her friend."

Sasha's whole body froze at this revelation, and all at once the terrible memories that she'd worked so hard at suppressing for the past dozen years came rushing back at her, as though it had all happened yesterday. Matthew seemed unaware of her plight, oblivious to the fact that she'd begun to quiver in reaction, or that the hand he continued to clasp so tightly had quickly turned ice cold.

"She was too ashamed about what happened to tell Lindsey or me until yesterday," continued Matthew. "And she would have probably continued to keep the information to herself if Lindsey hadn't found a pregnancy test in her wastebasket."

Matthew told her additional details, about how upset Hayley was, and how Lindsey had been pushing her to have an abortion, or threatening to ship her off to some home for unwed mothers, but his words failed to register in Sasha's numbed brain. The whole situation seemed eerily unreal to her, and she struggled to ward off the panic threatening to consume her as she realized that the monsters she'd kept hidden away for so long had broken free from their imaginary prison cells.

"Hayley's convinced herself that she wants to keep the baby," Matthew was telling her. "Christ, she's barely capable of making herself a piece of toast. How the hell she thinks she can take care of a baby is beyond me. She's got it all figured out, though, it seems - insisting that we can just hire a nanny to watch the baby while she's at school since we can easily afford it. And I understand her reluctance to have an abortion, especially considering all the trauma she's already gone through, but I'm going to try to keep convincing her that adoption is a much more sensible solution."

She gave a brief nod, acknowledging what he had just told her, but didn't feel capable of speaking at the moment.

Matthew, too, seemed at a loss for words for long seconds, and she could tell that he was struggling mightily with whatever he was about to tell her.

"You're going to think I'm out of my mind - and believe me, I'm pretty sure I am - when I tell you this next part," he began slowly. "And if it wasn't for Hayley's sake, for helping her get through all of this, then I wouldn't have considered it for even a second. But - Christ, here goes. She begged me to move back in, at least for a little while, until we can figure all of this out. Apparently Lindsey has been horrible to her these past months, but Hayley has kept all of that to herself, and it isn't fair to expect her to keep dealing with her mother's hostility alone any longer. So, as dumb as it sounds, I'm going to do it. Strictly to help support Hayley, and only until she's got her head on straight."

Sasha felt as though she'd been slapped across the face and kicked in the stomach at the same time, and that all the air had been sucked out of her lungs. She stared at Matthew in speechless shock, her hand going limp in his.

"You're moving back to Hillsborough?" she whispered hoarsely. "Does - does this mean the divorce has been called off?"

"God, no!" declared Matthew fervently. "There is nothing on this earth that could ever compel me to reconcile with Lindsey. And I've made damned sure she and Hayley are both very well aware of that fact. I'll be using one of the guest rooms, and having as little contact with my ex as possible. And considering how many hours I spend at the office, I won't even be at the house very often."

"I see." Sasha drew her hand away, wrapping her arms around her torso as the chill began to slowly permeate her entire body, and she had to force herself not to start shivering uncontrollably. "Wouldn't it have been easier to have Hayley just move in here with you? I mean, if the purpose of your moving back to Hillsborough is to offer her support and protect her from Lindsey, I would think you could do both of those things just as easily from here."

Matthew gave a brief nod. "I agree. And believe me, I tried more than once to convince Hayley to just move in here with me. But she still has a few weeks of school left, and doesn't want to be away from her friends. And neither of us want to leave Casey there alone with his mother."

Sasha began to inch a bit further away from Matthew every few seconds. "When is all of this happening?" she asked dully.

"Today. This afternoon." He shut his eyes, pinching the bridge of his nose, a surefire signal that he had a headache. "I was starting to pack some stuff when you arrived. Sasha, I need you to understand that this has nothing to do with us, that there's no reason you and I can't still keep - "

She held up a hand. "Don't say anything more. Please. Because if you think for even one second that I'm going to agree to keep seeing you - to keep *sleeping* with you - while you're living in the same house with another woman, you've lost your mind. It was always bad enough that you were still legally married, Matthew. I never told you how much that bothered me, how I always felt uncomfortable about it. But at least you were legally separated, living apart, and had split up months before you walked inside my massage room that day. At least I could assure myself that I'd had nothing to do with breaking up your marriage, or that I was the reason you wanted a divorce so badly. But this - I'm sorry, but this is more than I can handle."

Matthew reached out a hand to cup her cheek, only to recoil in surprise when she turned away from him. "Sasha, I had no idea you felt that way," he replied, visibly shaken by her revelation. "Why didn't you tell me? I thought I'd made it very clear that I felt absolutely nothing for Lindsey any longer, and that our marriage was merely a technicality, something that her signature on a piece of paper would end in a second. And nothing has changed in that respect, not one damned thing. Living in the same house - on an entirely different floor, for that matter - and only on a temporary basis, hasn't changed my feelings about getting Lindsey out of my life for good."

Sasha shrugged. "You say that now, Matthew. But who knows what could happen after you've been living there a few weeks or months? I'm sure Casey will be thrilled to have you back home, and who could blame him considering how close the two of you are. And if Hayley is serious about keeping her baby, it's only natural that she'll need your help and support, especially if the father isn't in the picture. It will

341

become more and more difficult for you to leave her after the baby is born, and when she expects you to become a surrogate father to her child. So you can fool yourself into thinking that this is only temporary, Matthew, but I'm not seeing it that way."

He paled noticeably at her declaration. "Sasha, no. That's not the way it's going to play out. I promise you. I'm only going to stay there for a few weeks at most, until Hayley makes some decisions about the future, and I can make sure that everything's okay between her and Lindsey. Then I'm planning on moving back here, and putting extra pressure on Lindsey to sign those divorce papers. Please, don't give up on me. And don't shut me out. I'm not sure I'll be able to cope without your support."

"No." She stood then, holding onto the back of the sofa for support, since her legs felt wobbly. "I won't ask you to choose between us, Matthew. That wouldn't be fair of me, and I don't want to make things harder on you. But none of this has been fair to me, either."

He surged to his feet, taking hold of her shoulders before she could move away. "I know it hasn't, sweetheart," he replied in a husky voice. "You've been the kindest, most understanding, and supportive girlfriend a man could ever ask for. You've put up with all kinds of crap from me - not just with my kids, but with work as well. And you've never once complained, even though you've had every right to, and I've been sort of amazed that you've never said anything until now. But please - don't give up on me now, Sasha. Don't give up on us."

Sasha shook her head. "I can't do this, Matthew. I can't

share that much of you. And even though you wouldn't actually be with Lindsey, it would kill me to think of you living in the same house with her, no matter what the circumstances are. So, this - this is over between us. I understand your concern for Hayley, though I don't necessarily agree with the way you're handling the situation. And I won't give you an ultimatum, or force you to choose. Especially since you've obviously already made your choice. Now, I think I should get the things I've left here and then leave, so you can go back to your family."

She wiggled out of his grasp before he could stop her, then quickly but methodically began to gather up the various personal belongings she'd brought to the condo these past few months - clothing and toiletries, books and CD's, the cashmere throw she liked to wrap around herself while they watched movies.

Matthew watched solemnly as she piled all of her things neatly in one corner of the sectional, his eyes sad and shimmering with tears. When she'd placed the last of her things on top of the pile, it occurred to her belatedly that she had nothing to pack them in.

"I don't have any bags here at the moment," she murmured distractedly. "Could you possibly ask Xavier or one of the others to box these things up and have them delivered to my place?"

He nodded sadly. "I'll take care of it, if that's what you really want. Though I was sort of hoping that you would just stay here while I'm gone. Alone, if that's the way you want it. This could be your place, Sasha. Or I'm happy to find you an apartment or condo of your own, arrange to have it all furnished and get you moved in. It's the least I can do for you, some small way I can take care of you."

"I've been taking care of myself for a long time, Matthew," she reminded. "And while I appreciate the offer, I'd rather remain where I'm at. I'd better go now."

"Wait. Please," begged Matthew. "I don't want to part this way, to make this good-bye. And while I have no right to ask you to wait for me, to be patient while this whole fucked-up mess plays itself out, I'm - Christ, I don't know what I'm asking. I just know that the thought of losing you, of not being able to talk to you or hold you again, is killing me. You're the most wonderful thing to ever happen to me, Sasha, the very best part of me. And having to let you go right now is like cutting out half of my heart."

Sasha closed her eyes, willing back the tears that threatened to spill down her cheeks. "You know, I should have expected something like this. Those first few times you came in for a massage, I already knew how attracted I was to you. And I was also very aware of the fact that you were still legally married, and that your kids meant the world to you. I mentioned you to Linda once, admitted to her that I liked you a lot. And she warned me then that I was setting myself up for heartbreak, that a man would nearly always choose his children over another woman. I forgot along the way how wise a woman my aunt is, and how I've never known her to be wrong about anything. I should have heeded her warning back then, should have never become involved with you. Maybe if I had listened my heart wouldn't be breaking into a million little pieces right now."

She could no longer hold back the tears, and couldn't

summon up the will to resist when Matthew pulled her into his arms. She sobbed quietly against his warm, comforting chest, and didn't pull away when he continued to press soothing kisses along her temple and cheek, or when his hand rubbed her back. She wanted nothing more than to fall asleep in the shelter of his embrace, then wake in a few hours to find this had all been a horrible nightmare.

"This doesn't have to be over, Sasha," he pleaded, the desperation in his voice mounting. "Look, I don't expect sex, I understand the moral dilemma you're experiencing about that. But can't we at least be friends? It would mean the world to me to at least be able to call you on the phone, or see you for lunch occasionally. You've made me so happy, sweetheart, the happiest I've ever been. And while I'm well aware that I've never deserved you, I'm still selfish enough to want to keep you in my life in one way or the other."

"I can't," she whispered brokenly. "Please try and understand. I can't keep waiting for this to be over, and for you to come back to me, Matthew. I'd die a little inside each time you called or that we saw each other, and then not know when we could be together again. So, please. Just let me go, okay? I know it's going to be hard for both of us, but it will be so much harder for me to keep in touch with you, only to have my hopes smashed each time we talk."

Matthew had a look of such despair and sadness on his face that she very nearly caved in to what he was asking. But while it broke her heart to do so, Sasha remained firm in her resolve.

"I need to go," she murmured absently, looking around for her bag.

345

But he was still holding onto her fiercely, every bit as reluctant as she was to say good-bye. "I wish you'd let me do something for you," he pleaded. "Not just as a way to say thank you for everything you've done for me, but so that I wouldn't feel like such a heel right now. I could set you up in a yoga studio of your own, no expense spared. Or arrange for you to go back to school and finish your courses to be a certified herbalist."

Sasha shook her head firmly. "Thank you for your offer, but I'll have to turn it down. I've never had any desire to run my own studio, especially not after seeing how much work Serge and Morgana put in behind the scenes, what with paying bills and ordering supplies and dealing with leases. As for the other, I'll take a pass on that, too. It's just not something I feel an overwhelming need to do at this point in my life." She cupped his cheek tenderly. "And you don't need to make anything up to me, Matthew, or give me things."

Matthew grasped her hand. "I can't help feeling like I'm abandoning you, Sasha. That I *am* in fact choosing my children - my daughter - over you, just like Linda warned you. But you've got to believe me when I say that's not what's happening here. Not exactly, anyway."

"I know," she assured him softly. "You're just being a concerned parent, trying to be there for his daughter when she needs him the most. You've always been a wonderful father, Matthew, and Hayley is a very lucky girl to have you. I just wish my own father had been there for me under similar circumstances. Instead, he was half a world away in Australia performing at a Latin music festival."

He stared at her in bewilderment. "What do you mean by

similar circumstances? Were you ever pregnant?'

Sasha shook her head. "No, thank God. But I - I was date raped. When I was seventeen. And, unlike Hayley, unfortunately I remember the entire, horrific incident all too well. In fact, hearing about what Hayley went through just brought all of those terrible memories rushing back. So I do understand, all too well, why you feel the need to protect her and help her through this. Because I never had my own father to do the same for me."

Matthew recoiled in shock, as though someone had just used a taser on him. "Sasha – my God. Why have you never told me any of this before? Why am I just hearing this now?"

"Why do you think?" she replied faintly. "Because it's obviously traumatic for me to think about, much less talk about. I've pretty much tried to repress the memories for the last twelve years. And the only other person who knows about this is Linda. I've never told my parents what happened, and I never intend to."

He continued to stare at her for long seconds, until he took her completely by surprise as he scooped her up into his arms, and carried her with long, purposeful strides into the master bedroom.

"Matthew, don't," she protested weakly, as he deposited her on the bed.

But he paid her no heed, wrapping her up in his arms instead, and simply holding her for untold minutes.

"How did something so unspeakable happen to you?" he whispered against her curls.

Sasha hesitated, knowing that she could trust Matthew implicitly, more so perhaps than anyone she'd ever met

347

before. But twelve years of keeping this particular secret hidden away, of forcing the memories into the deepest, darkest corners of her mind, made her wary.

"I'd really prefer not to talk about it," she hedged.

"Please. Sasha, I've told you a whole lot of things about myself these past few month, shared things with you that I've never done with anyone else. I'd like to think that sort of trust goes both ways."

She felt a bit ashamed at his gentle rebuke, and sighed in resignation. "All right. But what I'm going to tell you never leaves this room, Matthew. My parents can never, ever find out. Do you promise?"

He entwined his fingers with hers, holding their joined hands against his chest. "With all my heart," he vowed.

"All right." Sasha exhaled sharply, knowing that this would be far from easy. "I've already told you how difficult it was for me to fit in during high school - how I looked and dressed differently from the other girls, the accent I hadn't managed to get rid of, and mostly not being familiar with American customs or trends. I was incredibly shy around most people, but especially boys. So when this one guy asked me out, I was so excited, flattered even. I barely knew him, but he was good looking and popular and had always seemed like a nice boy.

We went out about three times, and each time he got a little more aggressive, a little more demanding physically. It went pretty quickly from just wanting a good-night kiss to petting, and then he started putting the pressure on me to go further. I was still a virgin, of course, and had very little idea about sex. By the fourth date, he lost patience and basically just forced me against my will. He brought me to his home on the pretext of meeting his parents, but the house was empty when we went inside. And there was no one there to hear me scream when he - he raped me."

"I'll kill him," muttered Matthew in a deadly voice. "I will fucking rip him apart with my bare hands for what he did to you. Tell me his name, Sasha."

"No, Matthew. I'm not going to tell you. Violence has never solved anything, and it certainly wouldn't help in this case. And it was a long time ago, I've managed to get past it and get on with my life. Now, can you please let me go so I can leave?"

"Not yet." He tightened his arms around her, preventing her escape. "What happened after that? You called the police, I take it?"

Sasha gave a short, bitter laugh. "Given that his father was the local chief of police, and his mother some sort of high-priced defense attorney, that wasn't exactly an option. And he took great pleasure in reminding me of those facts while I was running out of his house, warned me that any complaint I made would just get dismissed. It made me wonder if he'd done this to other girls, knowing that his parents would always keep the truth hidden away. I got out of there as fast as I could, made it to a gas station on the main street, and called Linda. I'm not sure she's ever made the drive from Stinson Beach to Mill Valley quite so fast."

"And she agreed with you about not pressing charges?" asked Matthew incredulously.

"Not at first, no. But the more we talked the whole incident over, the more we realized that we needed to keep

349

it quiet. For my sake, more than anything else. I was having a difficult enough time fitting in and making friends at school, and if word had gotten out about the attack I would have been an outcast. Everyone would have taken his side, and the last thing I needed at the time was to be gossiped about and shunned. And then of course there would have been my parents to deal with." Sasha shook her head. "My father wouldn't have bothered with the police. He would have gone after the boy himself, beat him unconscious, and not given a damn about the consequences. The same way I'm sure you feel about the boys who did this to Hayley."

"Yes," agreed Matthew solemnly. "Except that it's not likely I'll ever find out their identities since she and her friend don't remember anything about them."

"I'm sorry," she consoled. "But as awful as it sounds, maybe it's better in a way that the girls don't remember anything about that night. Believe, me, there have been many times over the years when I wish I could have just forgotten it all."

"Your mother doesn't know, either?"

"God, no. In a way, that would have been worse than my dad finding out. Because my mother would have insisted I leave Linda's, that I obviously wasn't safe there, and she would have probably taken legal action to force me to return to her. And that was the very last thing I needed at the time. Having Linda there was the only thing that got me through it all. My parents would have meant well, but they would have made everything ten times worse if they'd known."

Matthew threaded his hands through her curls, holding her head still as he gazed at her fiercely. "I'm going to find out who this bastard is, mark my word, Sasha," he vowed.

"And when I do, I'm going to ruin him, one way or the other. There are multiple ways to exact revenge on someone without resorting to violence. He's finally going to pay for his sins."

Before she could offer up a further protest, Matthew's mouth was on hers, kissing her like he'd never kissed her before - with mingled anguish, passion, despair, and possession. At the same time, his hands were tugging at her clothes, pulling the long cotton skirt up above her waist, and tunneling beneath her tank top to cup her breast. Sasha whimpered half-heartedly in protest, too shaken by everything that had just happened to want sex. But Matthew's kisses and caresses spoke clearly of desperation, of overwhelming need, and in the end she let him take what he wanted.

When he sensed her surrender, his mood changed immediately, and he became the tender lover he could so often be. The kisses he placed along her cheek, the side of her neck, and her lips were soft and sweet, seductive and persuasive. He took more care as he undressed her, his hands reverent as they touched her bare skin. She shivered as he plucked at her nipple, then replaced it with the gentle lick of his tongue.

She sensed that he didn't want or expect her participation right now, that this was his way of giving to her, of taking care of her. And it felt like his farewell, as though with each sweeping caress and each hungry kiss he was trying to imprint the memory of her on his soul.

But even as she allowed him to control their lovemaking, Sasha couldn't help the low moan that escaped her lips as he thrust carefully inside of her. Nor could she resist wrapping her legs around his waist as his strokes gradually became deeper, faster, hungrier. And when she came, he swallowed up her groans with another deep, drugging kiss.

Her cheeks were wet with tears when Matthew found his release moments later, and the urge to stroke his back and hair comfortingly couldn't be suppressed. He kissed her tears away, whispering against her lips, "I will love you until the end of days, Sasha. Please don't let this be over with, sweetheart. Don't shut me out of your life. I know it's a lot to ask, but I'm begging you to be patient for awhile."

Regretfully, she shook her head. "Let's not do this again," she pleaded. "I can't bear it, Matthew. And now I really do need to go. Before I let you talk me into something that's only going to break my heart over and over."

He didn't try and restrain her when she got out of bed and walked inside the en suite bathroom to clean up. And when she returned to the bedroom stark naked, the look in his eyes was one of bleak sadness instead of the lust that would normally be there.

"What was it that you were going to tell me over dinner last night?" he asked hollowly as she began to pull her clothes on.

Sasha shrugged as she fastened her bra. "That's pretty much a moot point right now, so no sense in discussing it."

"Please." He sat up, the sheet falling away from his bare chest. "Just tell me."

She stepped into the long skirt, readjusting the elastic waistband once it was in place. "Matthew, let's drop it, okay?"

"No." He shook his head stubbornly. "Give me at least

that much, Sasha. I could tell that whatever you wanted to say last night had to be important, so tell me now. Please."

"Fine." She took a deep breath before expelling it slowly. "I was going to finally take you up on your offer - the one about moving in here with you. But, like I said, that's sort of a moot point now, isn't it?"

Matthew paled visibly, and his hands were trembling as he placed them on either side of his head. "And just when I think this situation can't be any more fucked up than it already is," he muttered bitterly. "Instead of just muting my phone yesterday afternoon, I should have turned it off. That way we would have kept our date, you would have told me you were moving in, and all of that would be resolved now."

Sasha looked at him sadly. "You know it's not that simple. Whether you heard the news last night or this morning about Hayley, you'd still be going to her now. Turning your phone off would have only postponed the inevitable for a few more hours."

She walked on bare feet back into the living room to get her bag and shoes, not glancing behind her to see if Matthew followed. She had her hand on the front door when he said her name, and she turned to look at him one more time.

"Take care of yourself, sweetheart," he whispered hoarsely. "I have no idea how I'm going to go on without you, but I realize now how selfish I'm being to expect you to put up with all this crap."

"You're not being selfish," she replied sadly. "I think maybe I'm being the selfish one. But I'm not strong enough to handle this, Matthew, not strong enough to have my heart broken night after night. I'm sorry it has to be this way, but it's the only way I know to save myself."

Matthew nodded sorrowfully. "I won't stop thinking about you for even a minute, Sasha. Or loving you."

She closed her eyes for a moment, summoning up the will not to have an ugly breakdown right here and now. "Same here," she whispered, before walking out the door.

JULIO KNEW THE MOMENT SHE walked through the front door that something was really, really wrong, and if Sasha had held out even a smidgen of hope that she could hide what had happened from her overly astute landlord, it was crushed into miniscule pieces within seconds.

"*Querida*," crooned Julio, already enveloping her in a comforting hug. "What's wrong, baby? Tell your big brothers what's bothering you."

In reply, Sasha let her bag slip through nerveless fingers to land on the floor of the foyer, then promptly sobbed on Julio's shoulder as though her heart was breaking - which it definitely was.

Once Julio had settled her on the living room sofa, sandwiched between him and Chad, Sasha tearfully choked out all that had happened. Her landlords let her talk, which was a small miracle for the chatty Julio, only offering her an occasional pat on the back or a low murmur of sympathy.

"I - I did the right thing, didn't I?" sniffled Sasha. "I mean, should I have stuck by him, waited to see how this thing played out?"

"Absolutely not."

"Possibly."

Predictably, the spouses had differing opinions on the situation, with Julio remaining adamant that Sasha had done the right thing, while Chad continued to ponder the matter more closely.

"Well, I can tell you right now, that if *my* man told me he was going to move back to the same house where his ex was still living, I would have told him to kiss my ass," declared Julio. "I don't care what he might have told you about how things have been over for a long time, and that he's only doing this for his kids. Bitch is still sharing an address with him, isn't she? Who knows how long it will be before she starts sharing other stuff again."

Chad thwacked his husband on the forehead with his open palm. "Very sensitive of you to bring that up right now," he chastised. "Don't listen to him, Sasha. He's been watching too many episodes of *Scandal* lately. As for your Matthew, there's no denying that he's crazy in love with you, girl. I'm sure it's killing him inside right now to have to do this, to have to make this choice. But I also understand your point. He's cancelled enough dates with you these past few weeks that even a saint would be pissed off and fed up."

Julio wrapped an arm around Sasha's shoulders and gave her a smacking kiss on the cheek. "She *is* a saint, Chad. And I don't blame her in the least for finally setting her foot down. Matthew could have dealt with the problem child without moving back in with *la familia*. He's feeling guilty right now, and responsible. And I'm guessing that little brat is taking full advantage of poor Daddy and putting the pressure on him. But something doesn't feel right about this whole thing, you know? I can't put my finger on it right now, but it will come to me eventually."

Chad exchanged a knowing look with Sasha. "Told you he's been watching too many soap operas. Speaking of which, we need to get your mind off of all this for awhile. How about we order in from that Indian place you love, and then we can watch one of your favorite movies?"

Julio made a face. "You know I can't eat curry," he complained. "It doesn't agree with me. And I can never read the little tiny subtitles on those French films Sasha loves."

Sasha smiled in spite of her misery. "I'll take pity on you, then," she assured Julio. "Especially since I need cheering up right now. Why don't you pick out a good comedy we can watch? As far as dinner is concerned, believe it or not, I'm actually in the mood for pizza and red wine."

Julio clapped his hands in glee. "Now you're talking, querida! Let me go see if I can pry Elliott out of his bat cave for a night so he can join us. And Sadie's at home for once. She has Sundays off from the strip club."

Chad shook his head. "For the fiftieth time - at least - Sadie does not work in a strip club. It's officially called a gentleman's club."

"Yeah, right," snorted Julio. "Call it what you like, but I know what I saw the one time I went to watch her perform, and the girls might as well have been buck naked for the little scraps they were wearing. And the guys didn't look much like gentlemen to me."

"Just go ask them if they want to join us," instructed Chad. "But don't tell them all the details, would you? I doubt Sasha wants all of her personal business shared with the whole household."

"Fine. What should I tell them then?" asked Julio with an exaggerated sigh.

Sasha's chin wobbled as she blinked back tears. "That I've got a broken heart," she whispered. "And that the only short term cure I can think of is eating something greasy and trying to drink away my sorrows. Both of which are always easier when you've got as many friends as possible around you."

chapter eighteen

June

MATTHEW WAITED IMPATIENTLY FOR THE single serve coffeemaker to finish brewing, almost desperate for his morning caffeine fix. In the nearly four weeks since he'd been living back here in Hillsborough, he had yet to have a good night's sleep, and most nights was lucky to get three or four hours. Last night had been no exception, and he didn't expect the situation to improve anytime soon.

He couldn't recall a time in his life when he'd been so unhappy, so depressed, and the only real bright spot in his daily existence was his son. The one upshot of living here again had been being able to spend more time with Casey, and that was practically the only thing keeping him sane. The two of them would have dinner out at least twice a week, and Matthew made it a point to attend as many of Casey's summer league baseball games as possible. And since school was out for the summer, Casey had more free time in the evenings to watch movies or quiz his father about computer programming. Matthew was more than a little astonished to realize just how smart his son was, how adept at figuring things out, even more so than he and his genius-level IQ siblings had been at the same age.

Hayley, meanwhile, seemed at times to completely forget

the fact that she was expecting a baby. She hadn't breathed a word about the pregnancy to any of her friends, and had sworn Matthew and Casey to secrecy. She didn't seem to have a care in the world otherwise, and went about her life as though nothing at all was different, or was going to change in a very big way within the next few months. She was always asleep when he left for the office, and slept in until at least noon on the weekends. Hayley was rarely home in the evenings, preferring to spend time going to the mall or the movies with her girlfriends, and she seemed impatient and bored to tears whenever Matthew tried to engage her in conversation.

But when he had commented in a sarcastic tone the other night that she didn't seem to care one way or the other if he was here or not, Hayley had given him a hug and a little kiss on the cheek, assuring him that it meant the world to her to have him back, and that she hadn't been this happy in months. Matthew hadn't been entirely convinced that she was sincere, however, especially when she promptly turned down his invitation to join him and Casey for dinner the following evening, claiming she'd already promised Brianne to go shopping with her.

The coffee finished brewing, and Matthew grabbed the mug almost desperately, not caring that he burned the roof of his mouth by gulping a third of the hot liquid down at once. It was one of those mornings, he thought caustically, that he wished he could hook himself up to a coffee drip and have the caffeine delivered right to his veins.

His thoughts drifted automatically to Sasha, as they did so frequently these days, and wondered if she was already up and about. He knew her to be an early riser, particularly on the days like this one when she taught a morning class, and he tried to picture her at the studio going through her own practice. He missed those mornings when he had woken early, only to find that she'd been up for more than an hour already, putting herself through a grueling routine. If he shut his eyes, he could picture her now standing in a one-legged tree pose, or dropping back effortlessly into a graceful backbend. Or simply sitting in a cross-legged lotus position, her eyes closed, and her hands in prayer at her heart. He had timed her once as she sat unmoving that way, and for more than five minutes she hadn't so much as flinched, deeply immersed in silent meditation. She had looked so lovely, so utterly calm and peaceful, that he'd been envious in a way – envious because he himself had never known that sort of serenity before. And now, because fate had dealt him this very unexpected hand, Matthew feared he'd never come close to feeling the way he had during his time with Sasha - happy, content, and loved.

He had finished his coffee and was in the middle of brewing a second cup for the road, when Lindsey tottered inside the kitchen, her high-heeled, marabou-trimmed bedroom slippers clicking loudly on the flagstone floor. Matthew wasn't sure what the most startling thing about her appearance was - the short, ultra-sheer black lace robe and G-string that was all she had on, or the fact that she was actually up and about at six o'clock in the morning. Her long, glossy hair was carefully mussed, and she was already fully made up, complete with false eyelashes and bright red lipstick.

He realized with a sickening sensation that Lindsey had dolled herself up, and risen at what was for her an ungodly hour, with the intention of attracting him. There was no other reasonable explanation for her provocative appearance, and especially now, when she knew he'd be alone and ready to leave for work. But rather than be aroused by her near-nudity, Matthew had never been more turned off in his life.

"Good morning!" greeted Lindsey cheerily, something else she never did. "I'm glad I caught you before you left. Would you like me to cook you breakfast?"

Matthew couldn't help himself from laughing out loud. "Is this some sort of a sick joke, Linz?" he asked sardonically. "I think the last time you offered to make me breakfast was when you were pregnant with Casey. Come to think of it, that's probably the last time you were awake this early, too. And, no. I'm leaving now."

He poured his coffee into a travel mug, ignoring the fact that Lindsey had sidled up next to him, so close that one of her breasts brushed against his arm – most assuredly a calculated move on her part. He jerked his arm away immediately, not bothering to hide his distaste, and received a displeased hiss from her in response.

"I don't have cooties, for God's sake," she replied huffily.

"Hmm. I wouldn't be so sure about that," he sneered. "I hope, given as much as you sleep around, that you get tested regularly for STDs."

Lindsey gasped. "That is incredibly rude of you, Matt. And I'll have you know that I've been completely faithful to you these past few months."

Matthew snorted in derision. "Why? It's not like I give a

shit who you fuck anymore. As long as you make damned sure the kids aren't aware of what's going on - and that you never bring your fuck buddies here to the house - you can screw whoever you want."

Her green eyes were shimmering with tears, and her pouty lower lip quivered. "You're so mean, Matt," she whispered. "I'm just trying to be nice to you, and all you can do is insult me."

He gave her a scathing look. "Is that what you call this little farce - being nice? Offering to cook me breakfast for the first time in over a decade, prancing into the kitchen half-naked, getting up before dawn so you can catch me before I leave for the office? Forget it, Linz. I don't need your idea of nice. I've got to get going."

He picked up his travel mug and laptop bag, and started to head out of the kitchen without a backwards glance when Lindsey called out to him.

"What time are you going to be home tonight?" she asked. "And is there anything special you'd like for dinner?"

Matthew reluctantly turned to face her, intentionally keeping his gaze averted from Lindsey's semi-nude body. "You're not really doing this, are you?" he asked her tiredly. "Pretending that we're all one big happy family again. I told you when I agreed to move back in temporarily that this was solely for Hayley's sake, to help her through this trauma she suffered, and figure out what to do about her baby. I am not here for you, Lindsey, and I have zero interest in interacting with you. I have the great misfortune of temporarily sharing a house with you, but that's as far as it goes. And to answer your question, I'm picking Casey up after baseball practice and taking him out to dinner. I invited Hayley to join us but apparently she already has other plans."

Lindsey made a big show of wiping away her fake tears. "Can - can I join you and Casey for dinner?" she asked hopefully.

"No, you can't," he told her bluntly. "And for Christ's sake, go put some clothes on, will you? Just because you're a whore doesn't mean you have to parade around the house looking like one."

He marched out of the kitchen before she could react to that bombshell, but he could only imagine the curses his ex was heaping on his head right now. Fortunately for his peace of mind, he'd stopped giving a damn about anything having to do with Lindsey a long time ago.

At this early hour, the traffic heading into San Francisco was light, and the Tesla Model X ate up the miles smoothly. As usual, he had a hectic day ahead of him, jam packed with meetings, conference calls, and reports to review. In fact, the only good thing about his entire day would be spending time with Casey this evening.

He couldn't even count on Elena these days to provide some much needed comic relief or sympathy here and there, considering how pissed off she was with him. Matthew shuddered to recall the day he'd fessed up to his terrifying PA that he and Sasha were over, and that he had moved back to Hillsborough temporarily. Elena had gone off on him, but since the entire rampage had been delivered in rapid, furious Spanish, he could only assume that she'd called him twenty different kinds of a fool. But nearly a month later, her displeasure was still evident, her attitude frosty and impersonal, and he basically tiptoed around her most of the time.

Not that he blamed her, thought Matthew with a sigh. He'd expected too much from Sasha, just assumed that she would always be gracious and understanding and supportive of all the demands on his time. But even someone like her had a breaking point, and his decision to move back to Hillsborough had been it for Sasha. Over the past few weeks, he had tried to imagine how he would have felt if the situation had been reversed, and knew that he would have reacted exactly the same way. No matter how many times Sasha might have insisted that she felt nothing for her ex, and that their relationship was definitely over, Matthew would have still been furious at the mere thought of her cohabitating with a man she had once had an intimate relationship with.

He longed to call her, just for the sheer pleasure of hearing her soft, melodious voice, but had stopped himself every time he pulled out his phone. And he'd fought off the urge to ask Tessa about Sasha, especially since he was well aware that both she and Ian weren't exactly happy with him at the moment.

His parents, too, hadn't been able to hide their dismay when he had called to tell them the news, and his father had come right out and asked Matthew if he'd thought this move out carefully. His mother, on the other hand, had inquired about Sasha, and expressed her disappointment that she and Matthew weren't together any longer.

It seemed that no one was especially happy about his current status, including himself. In fact, the only person who seemed blithely unconcerned about the havoc she'd created was Hayley herself.

Matthew frowned as he took the freeway exit for his office, thinking again that something just felt – well, *off* – about this whole pregnancy issue. For one, both Hayley and Lindsey were being extremely secretive and uncommunicative on the matter. He'd pushed for details about Hayley's visit to the doctor and what had been said, only for her to stammer and stutter uncertainly. Lindsey had answered for her instead, stating that Hayley was simply embarrassed to be discussing such personal details with her father, and that the doctor had given her a clean bill of health.

But it was when he'd insisted on accompanying Hayley on her next doctor's visit that she and Lindsey had both gone off. Hayley had been visibly startled, and looked at her mother in something of a panic, and then both women had babbled almost incoherently about all the reasons why that was a bad idea. Hayley had reiterated what Lindsey had mentioned earlier, insisting that she would be mortified to have her father along while she was being examined and talking about "female stuff" with the doctor. She'd practically begged Matthew to drop the subject, and very reluctantly he'd agreed – at least for the moment. He had vowed to himself, however, to pay much closer attention to what was going on with his daughter, and that very soon she was going to have to answer some tough questions about her future.

The office was nearly deserted when he arrived, and he was able to plough through a considerable amount of work - answering emails, reading over some reports, making notes for a speech he would be presenting at a conference next week - all before Elena arrived. He communicated with his pissed-off PA largely by electronic means these days, since she barely spared him a word. Even when she grudgingly deposited his morning coffee and breakfast on his desk – plopping it down hard enough for the coffee to slosh over a bit - she didn't say a word or smile. Matthew thanked her profusely, telling her how much he appreciated it, but all he received in response was a glare and a grunt.

His workday was as busy and stressful as usual, and since there was a lunch meeting with his staff scheduled, he didn't leave the office all day. By the time four o'clock rolled around, he was exhausted both mentally and physically, and was more than eager to head out to watch Casey's baseball game.

Matthew hoped like hell that Lindsey wouldn't decide to make an unannounced appearance at the game, as she had a couple of times so far. Normally she disliked attending the kids' sporting events, and had invented multiple excuses over the years to avoid them. And he knew it was a deliberate move on her part to all of a sudden take an interest in such things. Lindsey was taking full advantage of his presence at the house to try and insinuate herself into his life, and thereby convince him to reconcile. On more than one occasion, she had tried to act as though they were all one big happy family again.

He'd arrived home from work one evening last week to find nearly a hundred people milling about drinking and eating and lounging around the pool. Lindsey had teasingly chastised him about forgetting that they were hosting a party, and had promptly dragged him along with her to greet the guests. More than half the people there had been virtual strangers to Matthew, but there were others that he knew well and who had actually been good friends at one time. Awkwardly, he'd dodged questions about whether he and Lindsey were reconciled now, muttering that he was really here because of the kids, and that the living arrangements were temporary. Lindsey had glowered at him after overhearing a few such comments, and then accused him afterwards of embarrassing her and making her look like a fool in front of their guests.

Matthew had given her a scathing look. "Don't you mean your guests, Linz? I didn't invite any of these people here tonight. In fact, I had no idea you were hosting this party. Because if I had I would have spent the night at the condo. And a word of warning, hmm? If you try to pull a stunt like that on me again, I don't care who I offend or how pissed off you get. I won't get dragged into staying, and I also won't hesitate to tell everyone exactly why I'm living here again. Temporarily, of course."

Lindsey had reacted in mingled anger and panic. "You can be such a cold-hearted bastard at times, Matt," she'd snarled. "And don't you dare tell anyone about Hayley. She hasn't said a word about the baby yet to any of her friends, so if you spill the beans ahead of time she'd never forgive you."

He had thrown up his hands in frustration. "Christ, what's she waiting for - the baby's first birthday? She's not going to be able to keep her little secret hidden for much longer. Once she reaches the four month mark, she's going to start to show."

Lindsey had given a casual shrug. "Maybe not quite that early. Hayley's a tiny little thing, you know, and probably won't gain much weight. It could easily be her seventh month before she starts showing."

"Well, she's going to need to stop hanging out by the pool all day with her friends, or going shopping or out to lunch, and make some hard decisions. If she's serious about raising the baby - which I'm still dead set against - then she'll need to find a nanny at some point. And if she chooses adoption, the far better solution under the circumstances, we should be meeting with a lawyer now and interviewing adoptive parents."

But Lindsey had dismissed his concerns, stating that he was overreacting as usual. "She's got plenty of time for all that, Matt. Though I seriously doubt she's going to consider giving up the baby."

Matthew had stared at her incredulously. "Please tell me that you are not encouraging her to keep this baby," he had said, dumbfounded. "I'm amazed that you would be in favor of your teenaged daughter having a baby, especially since that would make everyone stop and think about how old you are. And for someone who works as hard as you do to look fifteen years younger, and who thinks it's the greatest thing ever when people mistake you for Hayley's sister, that's a little surprising."

Lindsey had seemed a bit taken aback, as though that had never occurred to her until now. "Well," she'd demurred, "that's not what's really important, is it? I mean, think of it this way - the baby might be just what we need to bring us all together. To have us all be one big happy family again."

He had burst out laughing at that point - actually, hooted would have more accurately described the noise - and given a shake of his head. "I never figured you to be delusional this way, Linz. So stop spinning your crazy fantasies, hmm? Hayley can have half a dozen babies, and it's not going to bring me back to you. I will always be here for my children, but so far as I'm concerned I no longer have a wife, and haven't for almost a year now. So if you're nudging Hayley to keep this baby as a means to keep me, forget it. You and I are over, done, finished, and there's nothing on this earth that's ever going to change that.

Once again, her green eyes had shimmered with tears, and her voice had sounded hurt. "Why can't you be nice to me once in awhile?" she'd pleaded. "Why are you always so mean, Matt? You never used to be this mean."

"And you never used to sleep with every hot young stud you chatted up in a bar," he'd replied lazily. "You reap what you sow, Linz. Never forget that. Now, you can have as many damned parties here as you like. Just try to give me a heads-up next time, hmm, so I can make other plans for the evening? And don't bother sending me an invitation because I have zero interest in socializing with any of your friends. Or you, for that matter."

That hadn't been the end of it, however, as he'd fully expected. When he'd announced plans to take Casey back to Wisconsin with him for a week to visit his family, Lindsey had hinted broadly about coming along. Matthew had quite bluntly told her that she wasn't invited, and moreover that she wasn't welcome at his parents' home any longer. She'd stormed off in yet another of her hissy fits, and he had hoped like hell that she had finally gotten the message.

Given her seductive, half-naked appearance in the kitchen this morning, though, he doubted that Lindsey would be giving up anytime soon. Fortunately, he knew exactly what she was trying to do, and resolved to go to even greater lengths than usual to avoid her completely.

He arrived at the baseball field just in time to see the first pitch thrown, and settled in to watch the game. Casey was the centerfielder for his team, and was usually always the leadoff batter given his excellent base running speed. Matthew cheered and clapped with the smattering of other parents watching, especially when Casey got a base hit, stole second, caught a long fly ball on the run, and then capped his game off with a double. His team won the game easily, and Matthew grinned to see how excited all the boys were as they congratulated each other on the win.

As he waited for Casey to gather up his things, Matthew couldn't help imagining Sasha here at the game with him, cheering his son on even though she wouldn't really understand most of what was going on. He chuckled to himself as he recalled a time when Casey had done his best to explain the basic rules of the game to Sasha, who'd been the first to admit she knew next to nothing about professional sports. Nonetheless, she had listened intently to Casey, asking him a question here and there, and he had been extremely pleased at her attention. Matthew scowled as he thought back to the game Lindsey had shown up at a couple of weeks ago, feigning an interest in her son that she'd never shown before. But instead of watching the game and making an attempt to cheer Casey on, Lindsey had spent almost the entire time checking her email or texting friends or touching up her makeup and hair. Matthew had thought sardonically that it was small wonder Hayley had picked up the same rude habits, considering what sort of a mother she had as a role model.

Dinner was a relaxed affair at a barbeque joint that was one of Casey's favorite places. He licked the sauce off his fingers as he ate a rib, then washed it down with a gulp of lemonade.

"How's your dinner, Dad?" inquired Casey as he speared a forkful of coleslaw. "You aren't eating much."

Matthew offered up an apologetic smile, and forced himself to eat a piece of brisket. "Dinner's great, as usual. Never had a bad meal at this place, have we? But I guess I'm just not all that hungry tonight. Too much stuff going on at work as usual."

Casey swallowed his food, then hesitated before continuing. "You, uh, seem kind of depressed these days, you know. Depressed and sad. Is it just work, or are you maybe missing Sasha?"

Matthew's head jerked up in astonishment. "Jesus, are you really only fourteen years old? Sometimes I feel like you're the adult and I'm the kid."

Casey grinned. "Well, you're the one who keeps telling me that I know way more about math and computers and programming than you did at my age. But it's pretty obvious that you aren't happy, Dad. And I'm sorry that you've got to go through all this. Especially since Hayley was always such a bitch to Sasha."

"Casey," warned Matthew. "What have I told you about using that word? And particularly about your sister. Not cool, buddy."

Casey shrugged, unconcerned. "Sorry, but it's true. And Sasha was always so nice to her. She was nice to everyone, you know? I miss her too, Dad. She was really cool, and I was just getting the hang of some yoga poses she was teaching me. Bummer."

"Yeah, you can say that again." Matthew set his fork down, even though his dinner was barely half-touched. "And you're right. I'm sad because I can't see her anymore. Or even talk to her on the phone. I wanted to keep in touch, maybe see her for lunch once in awhile, but she thought it was best to just call it quits. I asked a lot of her, you know, expected her to always be understanding. And that was wrong of me."

Casey drank down the rest of his lemonade, an uncertain expression on his face. "Uh, would you be mad at me if I told you that I still email Sasha sometimes? Like maybe once or twice a week. You know, just to say hi and all since she was nice to me."

Matthew chucked his son on the chin playfully, his smile warm. "Of course I wouldn't be mad. I think that's great of you to keep in touch. How- how is she?"

"Okay. She doesn't say much, you know, especially when it comes to email. But I think she's okay. Just - well, she sounds kind of sad, too. I'm guessing she misses you as much as you do her."

Matthew thought about Casey's words the rest of the

evening, fretting that his son was exactly right about Sasha also being sad. He longed to call her himself, or send her an email. Or, even better, to see her in person. But he refrained, wanting to respect her wishes, and knowing that he still had nothing to offer her, that his life was as screwed up as ever with no end in sight to the misery.

He watched a movie with Casey and Hayley, grimacing when Lindsey joined them - uninvited, of course - and made sure he sat as far away from her as possible. Afterwards, he spent an hour or so doing some research for MBI's next big project, before deciding to call it quits for the night and head for the shower.

As he emerged from the en suite bathroom a few minutes later, he frowned to notice the lights in the bedroom were dim, and wondered if a bulb had just burned out. But it quickly became apparent how the lights had suddenly grown so much dimmer, and who was responsible.

A stark naked Lindsey was reclining provocatively on the bed, a deliberately seductive smile on her crimson lips. Briefly, clinically, his gaze traveled over her nude body, and observed absently that she was even skinnier than usual, her ribs clearly defined. Her extreme slenderness made the overlarge breast implants look even more ridiculous, more out of balance. And made him feel more than a little sick to his stomach, the barbequed brisket churning in his stomach.

"Get the fuck out of here," he told her through gritted teeth, finding the robe she'd coyly draped over a chair and tossing it at her. "And cover up. I've never found the sight of pornography especially appealing."

Lindsey's mouth tightened at the implication that she

looked like a porn queen, but remained stubbornly nude. "You used to like all of this," she purred, cupping her breasts and tugging at the nipples. "When we first met, you couldn't get enough of my body. Don't you remember how eager you always were to fuck me, Matt? How you could barely last long enough to shove your big cock inside me? Mmm, we used to fuck like rabbits back then, you could go all night long. Want to see how well your endurance has held up over the years?"

"With you?" he scoffed, turning his back as he pulled clean clothes from his dresser. "Not in a million years. Now, get out so I can get some sleep. And don't pull a little stunt like this again, got it? Otherwise, I'll have a lock installed on the door."

But instead of leaving, Lindsey crept up behind him on bare feet and wrapped her arms around his waist, pressing the length of her petite body against his back. She began to slide one hand down towards his cock, which was fortunately covered by the towel he'd wrapped around his waist.

He clamped a hand viciously around her wrist, hard enough for her to cry out in pain. "What part of get out don't you understand?" he hissed. "I realize your multitude of lovers aren't in the habit of tossing you out of their bed, but then again we haven't really been lovers for a long time, have we? Not in any way that matters."

"Come on, Matt," she purred, rubbing her rock hard implants - he refused to think of those revolting *things* as breasts - against his back. "You must be horny as hell by now, it's been weeks and weeks since you've seen your little yoga teacher. And you may claim you don't love me

374

anymore, but you will absolutely love how I'm going to make your cock feel."

Enraged that she would dare to mention Sasha, he broke away easily from her clinging hold. "I would happily go without sex for the rest of my life before I ever touched you again," he bit out. "And," he added slyly, "how do you know I haven't seen Sasha? Since my living here doesn't have shit to do with you, that means I don't have to tell you a damned thing about my life. Now, for the last time, get the fuck out of my room."

Lindsey had paled at his taunt. "I don't believe you," she whispered. "You don't have it in you to be unfaithful to me."

He hooted in disbelief. "You mean like you do? I wouldn't be so sure of that, Linz. Besides, I never considered it as being unfaithful to you since in my mind we've long since been divorced. And now, since you seem so reluctant to leave, I'll do the honors."

He dressed quickly in the bathroom, making sure he bolted the door securely behind him, then grabbed his laptop bag, wallet, and keys upon his return to the bedroom. Lindsey still stood there in the middle of the room, though she'd thankfully pulled her robe back on.

"Where the hell are you going at this hour?" she asked in alarm.

"Well, there's no way I'm sleeping in this bed again until the sheets have been changed," he declared, "so I'll spend the night at the condo. And stay the hell away from me from now on, Linz. Not only don't I want you in my bed, I don't want you in my life, either."

Matthew was out of his room and down the stairs in a

flash, and within minutes he was behind the wheel of the Tesla. He drove much faster than usual, given that it was a crystal clear summer night with practically no other cars on the road, and that he was struggling to keep his rage under control. He was furious with Lindsey, furious with himself, furious with the world. It had been scarcely a month since he'd moved back to Hillsborough, but sometimes it felt like a year.

He made it to the condo in near record time, barely acknowledging the concierge as he strode briskly to the bank of elevators. Fortunately he hadn't moved all of his things out of the condo, and still had plenty of clothing, toiletries, and non-perishable food on hand.

He hadn't been inside the condo since that awful day last month when he'd watched Sasha walk out the front door, taking his heart along with her. And as he stood just inside the foyer he could still see her tear-stained face, could still hear her soft voice as she sadly bid him good-by, and his heart ached anew at the recollection.

He dropped his laptop case on the sofa, then impulsively pulled out his phone and pressed speed dial for the number he had yet to delete. It rang several times, and since he knew his name would appear on the caller ID on the other end, he doubted whether the call would even be answered.

But he was startled when Sasha accepted his call, her melodious voice merely saying his name in greeting.

"Matthew."

He recalled that she was one of the very few people who called him by his full name, nearly everyone else using the diminutive of Matt. And no one had ever said his name quite like she did, making it sound somehow like a caress.

"Sasha." He closed his eyes for a few seconds, sending up a silent prayer that she was actually talking to him. "God, Sasha. It's so damned good to hear your voice, sweetheart. And I know I promised I wouldn't call, wouldn't get in touch with you, but I - I just needed to hear the sound of your beautiful voice. Just this once."

There was silence on the other end before she gently rebuked him. "You shouldn't be calling, Matthew. You know this isn't right."

"Bullshit." He knew he had probably shocked her with his passionate declaration. "Being with you, talking to you, is practically the only right thing I've known for the last year. These last weeks have been total hell, sweetheart, complete torture. I miss you so much, need you so much. I - I'm at the condo right now, long story, but Lindsey pissed me off big time and I just couldn't stay at the house tonight."

"I see." She paused again before asking. "Was there a reason for your call, or did you just need to vent?"

He sighed, the slight edge in her voice noticeable even though she seemed as polite as ever. "I didn't plan to call you," he admitted. "Not that I don't fight off the urge every single day. It was just - this was the first time I've been back here since that day. And, well, all I can think about, all I can see, is the way you looked when you left that afternoon. It's the same image that's been haunting my dreams every night."

"It hasn't exactly been easy for me, either, you know," she replied. "And having you call like this out of the blue isn't making it any better."

"I'm sorry," he apologized. "I know I don't have any right to call you, to use you as a sounding board. I just miss you so damned much, Sasha. My whole life has gone to hell since that day you left. And while I know I shouldn't be contacting you this way, I just don't give a damn tonight. I want more than anything for things to go back the way they were, to be with you again. And I know that my daughter needs me right now, but I need *you* just as badly. Will you - that is, if I came to pick you up, or sent a car for you, would you be willing to come over for a little while? Just to talk, have a cup of tea. Please?"

"Matthew. You know I can't," she chastised him quietly. "So long as you're living in the same house with Lindsey, I just - can't. So please don't ask that of me. And please - don't call me again. I do love you, Matthew, but nothing has changed. I have to protect myself from getting hurt, and seeing you, even for something as innocent as a cup of tea, would just break my heart all over again."

He pressed a fist against his forehead, feeling the beginnings of a headache coming on. "Okay," he whispered. "I'll abide by your wishes and won't call you again. But I won't stop thinking about you, Sasha, or loving you. Or wishing that I wake up tomorrow morning and find this has all been one long nightmare."

"Good-bye, Matthew."

He stared at the phone for long seconds after she ended the call, not realizing he'd been crying until a fat tear plopped onto the screen.

chapter nineteen

Late June

"**You have no idea how** much I've missed mornings like this - getting my ass kicked for ninety minutes while sweating my brains out, and then rewarding myself with a cappuccino and a muffin. Not to mention hanging out with two of my very favorite people."

Julia took a sip of her foamy coffee drink, sighing in bliss as she swallowed, then broke off a piece of the oversized caramel chunk muffin she'd ordered.

Sasha eyed the muffin skeptically. "Since you're still nursing twins and obviously need the calories, I'll skip the nutritional lecture for once."

Julia shrugged. "Good. Because I wouldn't have listened to you, especially after the week I've had. Both of the boys had ear infections, and I swear I wanted to cry every time they did. Thank God for my part-time nanny. At times Alina is the only thing standing between me and a complete nervous breakdown. Be sure to tell Freya thank you again for the referral."

"I will." Sasha scooped up a spoonful of blueberries and Greek yogurt. "She was happy to help, and will be pleased to hear that Alina is working out so well."

Tessa smiled impishly as she sipped her tea. "Who knows?

Maybe I'll be needing a referral for a nanny one of these days. Maybe sooner than later."

Julia gasped in delight. "Omigod, are you pregnant? Tessa, that's fantastic news!"

Tessa shook her head. "Not yet. At least, it's probably too soon to tell. But I've stopped taking the pill, and Ian and I are definitely trying." She gave a very, very satisfied smile. "We're trying very, very hard. And very, very frequently."

This time Julia stuck her tongue out. "Quit rubbing it in, okay? I can't tell you how many times Nathan and I have gotten *this* close to making it happen, only to get interrupted by one or both of the boys. It's almost gotten to the point where we have to get a babysitter so we can sneak out to have sex somewhere."

Sasha's eyes twinkled in amusement. "It will get better," she said confidently. "Look at how much has improved in just two months - you have a part-time nanny, you're eating better - well, except for that muffin - and getting more sleep. And you're back to yoga. Patience is the key, Julia. And taking a few minutes to meditate every day helps, too. God knows it's one of the only things that's helped me cope as of late."

Tessa gave Sasha's hand a squeeze. "I'm so sorry," she replied sympathetically. "Here Julia and I have been prattling on about the wonderful things happening in our lives, and being totally insensitive to what you're going through."

"You're not being insensitive, Tessa," assured Sasha. "And I'd much rather hear about the happy things going on in your lives than dwell on my own misery."

"I wish I could think of some way to help," fretted Tessa.

all of the gifts and things he gave me and burn them. Most of the time, though, I'm just sad. And of course it didn't help when he called me a couple of nights ago."

She told her friends briefly about the late night call from him, and how he'd pleaded with her to meet with him.

"And I'll admit to being really, really tempted," confessed Sasha. "He sounded so unhappy, so upset, that all I wanted to do was comfort him and tell him everything was going to be okay. And then it dawned on me that I'd been doing exactly that from the very beginning of our relationship. I was always the understanding one, the one who never got upset or annoyed. So I stood my ground and asked him not to call me again. Because for once I was the one who needed comfort."

Tessa reached over and gave her a little hug. "Good for you," she murmured. "You're always doing nice things for other people, always being kind and supportive. And as much as I like Matthew and feel badly for the situation he's landed himself in, I think he needs to find a way out of it on his own. It isn't fair of him to expect you to keep supporting him and not giving the same back to you."

Julia waggled a finger in Sasha's direction. "Stand your ground, girl. Don't give in to him unless he's got those damned divorce papers signed. And for God's sake don't feel sorry for him. Tessa's right. You need to think about yourself for once, Sasha. And I think a trip to Paris is an excellent way to start."

Sasha thought back on her friends' advice during the bus ride back home. Taking a vacation to Paris was certainly tempting, and it would even be worth dealing with all of the family drama that would accompany the trip. Linda had also invited her along on a trip to Sedona, where she and some friends would be renting a house, and planned to hike through the red rocks and vortexes. Sasha had only been to Sedona once, and been enthralled by its magical, mystical beauty, so the temptation to accompany Linda on her trip was high.

There was also a week-long yoga retreat and teacher training near Lake Tahoe that she'd been asked to help teach, as well as Tessa's offer just today to use the beach house she and Ian owned on the Sonoma coast.

She needed to do at least one of those things, needed to get away for awhile where she wouldn't have too much time on her hands to mope and feel sad and lonely, and miss Matthew something fierce. Sasha knew that she'd fallen into a deep funk, and no matter how often she meditated, or how hard she pushed herself through an intense yoga practice, nothing seemed to be helping.

Even Julio was quickly growing frustrated with her, since the bulk of his efforts to cheer her up didn't seem to be doing the trick. He'd cheerfully accompanied her to art shows, a modern dance performance, and a poetry reading, and never complained once - though he had fallen asleep during the latter. He had watched movies with her, even the foreign ones with subtitles, and accompanied her on long walks and hikes. Chad, who fancied himself something of a gourmet chef, had cooked up a number of her favorite vegetarian dishes, and coaxed her to eat when her appetite had been lacking. And she'd even let the two of them drag her along to watch Sadie perform a brand new dance at the

chapter nineteen

Late June

"**YOU HAVE NO IDEA HOW** much I've missed mornings like this - getting my ass kicked for ninety minutes while sweating my brains out, and then rewarding myself with a cappuccino and a muffin. Not to mention hanging out with two of my very favorite people."

Julia took a sip of her foamy coffee drink, sighing in bliss as she swallowed, then broke off a piece of the oversized caramel chunk muffin she'd ordered.

Sasha eyed the muffin skeptically. "Since you're still nursing twins and obviously need the calories, I'll skip the nutritional lecture for once."

Julia shrugged. "Good. Because I wouldn't have listened to you, especially after the week I've had. Both of the boys had ear infections, and I swear I wanted to cry every time they did. Thank God for my part-time nanny. At times Alina is the only thing standing between me and a complete nervous breakdown. Be sure to tell Freya thank you again for the referral."

"I will." Sasha scooped up a spoonful of blueberries and Greek yogurt. "She was happy to help, and will be pleased to hear that Alina is working out so well."

Tessa smiled impishly as she sipped her tea. "Who knows?

Maybe I'll be needing a referral for a nanny one of these days. Maybe sooner than later."

Julia gasped in delight. "Omigod, are you pregnant? Tessa, that's fantastic news!"

Tessa shook her head. "Not yet. At least, it's probably too soon to tell. But I've stopped taking the pill, and Ian and I are definitely trying." She gave a very, very satisfied smile. "We're trying very, very hard. And very, very frequently."

This time Julia stuck her tongue out. "Quit rubbing it in, okay? I can't tell you how many times Nathan and I have gotten *this* close to making it happen, only to get interrupted by one or both of the boys. It's almost gotten to the point where we have to get a babysitter so we can sneak out to have sex somewhere."

Sasha's eyes twinkled in amusement. "It will get better," she said confidently. "Look at how much has improved in just two months - you have a part-time nanny, you're eating better - well, except for that muffin - and getting more sleep. And you're back to yoga. Patience is the key, Julia. And taking a few minutes to meditate every day helps, too. God knows it's one of the only things that's helped me cope as of late."

Tessa gave Sasha's hand a squeeze. "I'm so sorry," she replied sympathetically. "Here Julia and I have been prattling on about the wonderful things happening in our lives, and being totally insensitive to what you're going through."

"You're not being insensitive, Tessa," assured Sasha. "And I'd much rather hear about the happy things going on in your lives than dwell on my own misery."

"I wish I could think of some way to help," fretted Tessa.

so-called gentleman's club she moonlighted at. Nothing, however, had seemed to help for very long, and no matter how hard she tried to remain positive and upbeat, Sasha quickly found herself descending back into a funk. And she feared that getting out of town for a week or two wouldn't help her to stop missing Matthew, or cure the bad case of the blues she'd come down with.

She did smile, however, after arriving home and checking her phone for messages. There was a text from Elena, who had kept in regular contact with her, and had made no secret of the fact that she was good and pissed off at her boss. Rather than act supportive and sympathetic, Elena seemed intent on making Matthew's life as difficult as possible, as evidenced by this morning's text.

Hey, chica. Comé está? The boss looks like crap this morning but what else is new. And he's so out of it he doesn't realize that I brought him decaf instead of regular. He'll figure it out when he falls asleep at his desk after lunch. #Revengeissweet.

Sasha shook her head in reluctant amusement, feeling an odd sort of satisfaction that Elena was obviously taking her side, but also feeling sorry for Matthew at the same time. She tapped out a quick reply.

No revenge, please? At least not on my account. He actually needs you more than ever right now so please do what you can for him. Some caffeine would be a good place to start.

387

Her phone pinged with an incoming text almost immediately, and this time she couldn't help herself from laughing out loud.

OK, chica. But this is for you not him. Besides I already got my revenge for the day when I brought him a blueberry bagel and strawberry banana yogurt after he asked for sesame seed and vanilla. He must have been hungry tho since he ate them anyway.

Sasha made a mental note never to piss the fearsome Elena off, even as she tapped out another response.

Muchas gracias, Elena. Please take care of him for me. I'll feel better knowing that he has you to look out for him.

Elena's reply was quick and to the point.

OK, I'll do my best. Even tho I still want to punch him in the face.

As she continued to check her messages, Sasha was thrilled to see that Casey had sent her an email, complete with a photo of himself doing an arm balancing pose she'd taught him right before the breakup with Matthew. It touched her deeply that the boy continued to keep in touch, though he was careful not to mention his father or the situation with Hayley. She replied to his email cheerily, complimenting him on his progress, and offering up some advice on further mastering the pose.

The house was quiet, since all of her roommates were at work, or in Sadie's case school, and after showering and changing clothes, Sasha found herself at loose ends. She had to be back at the yoga studio in a couple of hours to meet a massage client, and then substitute teach a class, but felt oddly unambitious to do much until then. Normally she would read or do a little housework or gardening, but today she seemed to be suffering from an odd ennui.

It had been like this for her, she realized, for several weeks now, and she despaired that things were going to get better in a hurry. Listlessly, she ran a finger around the edges of the painting that Matthew had given her for Christmas, the one of a woodland fairy with gossamer wings and long, curly hair that he'd sworn looked just like her.

"I miss you," she whispered. "I didn't think it would hurt this much, that it would be so hard. I think about you all the time, and have to fight off the urge to call you. But it has to be this way, Matthew. No matter how much I love you, I can't be with you while you're living in the same house as *her*. My heart is already broken, and I'm pretty sure the rest of me would be, too, if I hadn't let you go."

Impatiently, she brushed away the tear that had trickled down her cheek, and resolutely headed out to the small garden at the back of the house to do some therapeutic weed pulling.

THE NEW STUDENT IN HER class looked oddly familiar to Sasha, though she knew they had never met before. It wasn't very often, in fact, that she had new students in her classes, since her regulars made sure to reserve their spaces days and even weeks ahead of time. But on weekday mornings like this one, the front desk staff would usually hold back a few spots for walk-ins, particularly during the summer when tourists abounded in the city. Sasha assumed that the unfamiliar woman had managed to snag one of those spots.

The dark-haired woman looked to be in her late thirties or possibly early forties, and was both slender and very well groomed. She shrieked money, lots of it, given her perfect makeup and glossy hair, expensive yoga attire, and the diamond stud earrings that were nearly as large as the rings on her wedding finger. But while she was undeniably trim and fit, except perhaps for her overly generous bust, she seemed to be having some difficulty keeping up with the demanding pace and flow of the class. She was frequently out of breath, and took numerous breaks to mop her brow or drink from her water bottle. Discreetly, Sasha brought over two of the cork yoga blocks that many students used in their practice, at least for poses that they struggled with.

"Here," Sasha murmured in a low voice to the woman, placing one on each side of her mat. "This should help. Revolved triangle is a difficult pose, so using the blocks can definitely help you there."

The woman stiffened noticeably as Sasha gently tried to adjust her posture, and pulled away. "I'm fine," she spit out through clenched teeth. "And I don't need the blocks."

Sasha was taken aback by the woman's obvious hostility, and instantly removed her hands. "Of course," she agreed easily. "It's entirely up to you."

She moved away then, puzzled by the angry green-eyed glare the woman had directed towards her, and went to help another student - this one smilingly grateful for the adjustment. Once in a great while Sasha would encounter a student like this woman - usually someone who was fit and trim and attractive, but who unfortunately also possessed a huge ego that rebelled whenever someone suggested they weren't doing something quite right. In most of those cases, she would tactfully back away and give the student their space, unless they were attempting a pose that could cause them real physical harm if done incorrectly.

Sasha had plenty of other students who both needed and welcomed her assistance and suggestions, and she was kept so busy for the duration of the class that she didn't give the hostile woman a second thought. It wasn't until the class was over, and students began to roll up their mats and filter out of the studio that Sasha paid her much heed. There was still this niggling little thought at the back of her head that she knew this woman from somewhere, or had at least seen a photo of her, but she couldn't quite put her finger on it - at least until the woman came right up to her, smiling smugly.

"So we meet at last," the woman began lazily, her green eyes reminding Sasha of a feral cat that Linda had adopted once - a cat that had hissed and spit and scratched if you got too close.

Sasha regarded her curiously. "You do look familiar. Have you attended my class before?"

The woman looked disdainful. "No, and I certainly won't be back. I'm actually not a yoga fan, I much prefer Pilates."

Sasha's spine stiffened, for Hayley had once said something similar. "You're Lindsey," she acknowledged, her voice sounding much calmer than she felt. "I see the resemblance to your daughter now. That's why you looked familiar."

Lindsey smiled smugly. "Most people think Hayley and I are sisters."

"Hmm. Well, once Hayley's baby is born, I'm guessing that won't be the case any longer. And let me wish you congratulations in advance. You must be so pleased at the thought of becoming a grandmother."

The smiled stiffened on Lindsey's face, and Sasha silently congratulated herself for thinking up such a pointed dig on the spur of the moment. She could picture both Julio and Elena giving her an enthusiastic high-five for so thoroughly putting Lindsey in her place.

"You think you're so fucking superior, don't you?" hissed Lindsey, her green eyes narrowing dangerously. "But don't forget, bitch, that *I'm* the one Matt's living with now, and the one who's still wearing his ring." She waggled the obscenely large diamond in Sasha's face. "He got tired of slumming it with you, and is back where he belongs - with his family. So your little scheme to steal him away has backfired big time."

"Steal him?" Sasha arched a brow in disbelief. "Just to clarify, when Matthew and I first started seeing each other the two of you had been legally separated for a few months already. And he also told me exactly why he's divorcing you. So I fail to see how I could have stolen him from you when he'd already been long gone."

Lindsey's otherwise pretty face looked ugly now, given the way her features had contorted with rage. "That's all in the past now," she snarled. "And the divorce isn't happening. Matt's back with his wife and children now, so hah hah - you lose."

Sasha gave her a sad smile. "Is that what you think this is, Lindsey - a game or a contest? There are no winners and losers here as far as I'm concerned. And if Matthew is happy, then that's all that really matters to me. Now, if you'll excuse me, I have to do some preparations for my next class. Oh, and speaking of classes - if you do decide to give yoga a try again, I'd strongly suggest you start with a beginners class. My classes are very advanced, and you're obviously not ready for anything that difficult."

She walked out the door gracefully, unhurried, though she was half afraid that Lindsey would hurl one of the yoga blocks at her head, or simply unleash a string of curse words at her. It wasn't until she reached the small studio and closed the door behind her that she expelled the breath she'd been holding for long seconds.

'Well, as Julio would say, that really sucked,' she thought to herself, even as she began to focus on her breathing, forcing herself to regain her composure and calm down.

Once again, Sasha turned to her personal yoga practice to find solace, to retreat to a place deep within her psyche where no one could touch her. By the end of an hour, she was sweaty and sore, but infinitely more serene, and she felt confident that she'd be able to put the ugly episode with Lindsey out of her head.

Her confidence was short-lived, however, as the co-owner

of the studio – Serge - approached her with a puzzled expression on his face a few minutes later. Sasha had been chatting with Willow at the front desk when her boss walked up, scratching his round, balding head in bewilderment.

"Hey, Sasha. You got a minute or do you have an appointment coming up?" he asked.

She shook her head. "Not for almost an hour. What's going on?"

Serge swept a hand towards the back of the studio. "Let's chat for a minute in my office."

Sasha followed him down the hallway into his office, not at all sure what he wanted to discuss, and equally unsure if she should be concerned at this unusual summons.

"I'll make this quick," began Serge. "One of your students - must be someone new, since I've never seen her before - complained about you. Said you were rude and disrespectful, and that your class was just about the worst one she's ever attended. I asked her three times if we were talking about the same person, and she insisted that it was you. So - talk to me. What the hell happened?"

Sasha pinched the bridge of her nose between her thumb and index finger, willing away the dull headache that was beginning to make itself known. "Was this woman petite and dark haired? Around forty years old?"

Serge nodded. "Yup. And with tits out to here." He cupped his hands in front of his chest, mimicking the size of Lindsey's breasts. "Fake as a three dollar bill, of course, but she makes damned sure you notice them."

Sasha heaved a sigh. "That's Lindsey Bennett. Matthew's ex - well, not so ex-wife nowadays. I didn't know who she

394

was until the end of class when she approached me to gloat about the situation. And I might have gotten a little testy with her about some things, but not during class."

Serge looked incredibly relieved at this news. "Ah, that explains a lot. The jealous ex, the hot young girlfriend. Sounds like she came here to check out the competition, and cause some trouble for you in the process."

"I'm hardly competition anymore, Serge," she replied sadly. "After all, Matthew's with her now, not me."

"Baloney." Serge waved a hand in dismissal. "He's with his kids, not his ex, from what you've told me. And while Mrs. Bennett is definitely hot, she's also a stark raving bitch. I'm guessing Matthew is hating his life right about now, and wishing he'd made a different choice." He enfolded Sasha in an affectionate embrace. "You're one in a million, kiddo, and Matthew knows it. He'll figure it out sooner than later, and beg you to take him back."

She shrugged. "I'm not convinced of that, Serge. And even if he did, I'm not so sure I'd want him back. I'm the complete opposite of my mother in almost every way except for one - I'm not a very forgiving person at times."

Serge patted her on the back. "But you're also a softie. So I'm pretty sure that you'd take Matthew back under the right circumstances. In the meanwhile, I'm glad you told me about his wife. I knew there had to be a reasonable explanation for her complaint, given that the only complaints I ever get about you or your class are about how tough it is to actually get into a class. I'm also going to tell Willow that Lindsey Bennet isn't welcome in this studio in the future. No one's allowed to insult the best yoga teacher I've ever known, and the most beloved one at this studio."

Sasha hugged her boss. "You and Morgana are like family to me, you know. And your faith in me makes up for that nasty encounter with Lindsey. Thanks, Serge."

"Anytime, kiddo. Especially since keeping you happy is very, very important to my business. I'm well aware that you could get a job at any other studio in the city just by walking in the door. So don't let that jealous bitch ruin your day, okay?"

But Serge's words did little to reassure Sasha, or make her forget the ugly scene with Lindsey. She was still shuddering over the encounter as she readied the massage room for her first client.

Her phone buzzed with an incoming call, and she glanced at the caller ID out of curiosity, given that she rarely got calls at this time of the day. The fact that it was her aunt Linda calling was even more unusual, since they typically communicated via email or text.

"I hope I'm not bothering you, niná," began Linda. "But I just heard some really shocking news and I needed to tell you before you read it somewhere else. It's - well, about Riley Cullen."

Sasha froze, not sure that she had heard Linda correctly, but unwilling to ask because hearing *that* name mentioned again just might send her a little over the edge.

"What about him?" she asked in a hollow voice. "I thought you and I agreed to never bring him up again."

"I know. And believe me, I wouldn't have mentioned him except for what I've just learned about him and both of his parents. Sasha, you know that old saying about how bad things happen in threes?" inquired Linda.

"I do. Just a superstition, though. One of many my mother believes in."

"Well, in this case, Katya would have been right. I just left Mill Valley, had to pick up some supplies at the pet store for my little zoo here, and it seems like the whole town is abuzz with what's been going on. Riley was arrested almost two weeks ago for embezzlement and tax fraud, and he's already been fired from the investment firm he was working for. His father has been relieved of his duties as chief of police pending an investigation into charges of corruption. And Mrs. Cullen is in danger of being suspended from the State Bar for something or other. What makes all of this so shocking is how it happened to all three of them at practically the same time."

Sasha knew without ever having to ask that this was no coincidence. And she was convinced that somehow Matthew had made all of this happen, just as he'd promised her. What was it exactly he'd said that night after she had tearfully confessed about being date raped by the vile Riley Cullen - "I'm going to ruin him, one way or the other". Somehow Matthew had discovered the identity of her attacker, likely using the clue that Riley's father had been the chief of police. It would have been a simple enough matter at that point to figure out who Riley was. What Sasha couldn't figure out, though, was how Matthew had brought all this about, how he had exacted revenge on the boy who'd destroyed her innocence and caused her so many nightmares over the years.

"That - that's weird, all right," acknowledged Sasha

faintly, not daring to share her suspicions that Matthew had somehow been the catalyst behind the Cullen family downfall.

"Well, I suppose that hardly matters, does it? What's important here, Sasha, is that justice is finally going to get served. That bastard unfortunately got away with what he did to you, but one way or the other he's going to answer for his evildoing. And I'm sorry I had to drag all this up again, or even mention his name. But I thought you deserved to know."

Sasha thanked her aunt for telling her, then chatted about other matters for a few minutes until it was nearly time for her client to arrive. She continued to stare at her cell phone for long seconds after telling Linda good-by, wondering if she had the nerve to make another quick call, or whether she should send a text or email instead. Impulsively, before she could change her mind or lose her nerve, she pressed the call button.

He answered immediately. "Sasha. God, I'm so glad you're calling. Where are you?"

"At the studio. And I've got a client coming in any second, so I can't talk long. But, well, I just heard about the - the Cullens. And I have to know, Matthew. Was it you?" she asked, her voice trembling.

There was silence on the other end for long seconds before Matthew replied. "I vowed to you that the man who hurt you would pay for his sins. And I always fulfill my promises, Sasha. Especially the ones I make to you."

She closed her eyes, her hand gripping the edge of the massage table for support as her legs began to shake. "I normally don't believe in revenge," she whispered. "I prefer to leave that sort of thing to my mother. But in this case - thank you, Matthew. For chasing away a monster that's been lurking in the back of my closet for too many years to count."

She ended the call abruptly, not trusting herself to remain on the line a second longer. Otherwise, she wouldn't have been able to stop herself from telling him how much she still loved him. And, as his wife had so cruelly pointed out a little while ago, loving Matthew wasn't Sasha's right any longer.

chapter twenty

Early August

"THANKS FOR THE RIDE, MRS. Fogerty! I'll see you at practice tomorrow, Blake. Hopefully it doesn't get cut short again because of the heat."

Casey waved good-bye to his friend and his mother who'd offered him a ride home. When today's baseball practice had been halted before noon because of the ninety-plus degree temperatures, Casey had started to call his mother so she could come and pick him up. But Blake had forestalled him, assuring Casey that his mom would be happy to drop him off since they only lived two blocks away.

It was just as well, thought Casey as he let himself in the house, since the likelihood that his mother would have actually been the one to pick him up was practically nonexistent. Lindsey would have insisted that their housekeeper Maribel picked him up, even though that wasn't one of her duties. Poor, good-natured Maribel, though, had a difficult time saying no to anything that Lindsey and Hayley asked of her, and ended up doing lots of little things outside of her regular responsibilities. The situation had only become worse since Matthew had set his foot down about employing a nanny for Casey and Hayley, insisting that they were both well past the age where they needed that sort of help.

Casey had agreed wholeheartedly, especially since he'd endured all sorts of teasing from his friends whenever he had been dropped off or picked up at school or other events by whoever the current nanny had been. And since he and Hayley were at school all day, the nanny had had very little to do most of the time, and precious little even when they were at home. Hayley had treated the succession of nannies like her personal attendants, asking them to get her a snack or tidy up her room or even do her homework for her.

He showered, changed into cargo shorts and a T-shirt, and then made his way downstairs to the kitchen. Not wanting to bother Maribel, whom he'd spied dusting in the living room, Casey made himself a sandwich. Unlike his high-maintenance mother and sister - both of whom insisted on being waited on practically hand and foot - Casey's needs were much simpler, and he had always been self-sufficient, even as a little boy.

After putting his dishes in the dishwasher, he ambled outside to see how hot it really was. A swim in the pool sounded awfully good, and he wondered how long he'd need to wait to digest his lunch. As he began to walk around the side of the house towards the pool, however, he froze in his tracks at the sound of raised voices. Unsurprisingly, his mother and sister were arguing again, something they seemed to do on a regular basis. Normally, Casey would have just ignored them and continued on his way, but his ears perked up in surprise at what his mother was saying to his sister.

"Hayley, for God's sake. How many times do I have to tell you? You can't just lounge around in a bikini anymore.

You're supposed to be almost five months pregnant, and you won't fool anyone this way. Especially since that bikini doesn't cover very much."

Hayley's voice floated around the corner, sounding both irritated and bored. "Relax, Mom. You and I are the only ones here right now. Casey won't be back until close to dinnertime, and Dad's still away on his business trip. Nobody is going to walk by and notice that I haven't gained a pound. In fact," she added happily, "I've actually dropped five pounds. My size 00 jeans fit perfectly now."

"You stupid girl!" hissed Lindsey. "No one is going to believe for a second that you're pregnant if you intentionally keep losing weight! Don't you dare wear those jeans around the house when your father's here. He's already too suspicious for my liking."

"Yeah, tell me about it," groused Hayley. "Before he left on his trip the other night, he cornered me for almost an hour asking a bunch of questions. And while I realize that Dad is a big nerd, making a two page list of stuff to ask me takes nerdiness to a whole new low. I thought I was going to faint or have a panic attack or something equally gross the whole time."

"Well, I hope like hell that you answered all his questions correctly," replied Lindsey in a threatening tone. "We're too close now to risk you screwing this up. What sorts of things was he asking you anyway?"

Hayley emitted a long-suffering sigh. "God, what didn't he ask me? He wanted to know what brand of pre-natal vitamins I was taking - thank God you bought me some, because he insisted on reading the label. Then he was pushing me to register for something called Lamaze classes, and offering to go with me to be my birth coach or some such crap. Eww, even if I really was pregnant, there is no way I'd want my father to be in the delivery room with me. How embarrassing and pathetic would that be? I mean, all the doctors and nurses would think I was some sort of loser, having my dad there instead of the baby's father."

"Hayley. Focus, for fuck's sake, will you?" chastised Lindsey. "That last part is sort of a moot point, isn't it? Since you aren't actually pregnant, that is. But you've got to keep this little act up for just a few more weeks. I'm getting closer and closer to convincing your father to call off the divorce. I just need to make sure he stays close by a bit longer."

"Really, Mom? Because it sure seems to me that Dad is spending more and more time away from here lately. Besides all of these business trips, I know he's been staying at the condo a few nights a week. That doesn't sound like you're making much progress to me," Hayley taunted.

"I don't tell you everything, Hayley," retorted Lindsey. "Some things are private between husband and wife. All you need to know is that things are coming along nicely."

"Whatever." Hayley yawned. "The only thing I want to know is how much longer I need to keep up this farce. I'm tired of having to wear layers whenever Dad's around, or put him off when he starts talking about interviewing nannies and choosing what room would be best for the nursery. I - I don't like lying to him, Mom. It isn't fair, you know? I wish now I'd never let you con me into this whole mess."

"Don't you dare cave in now, you little brat!" yelled Lindsey. "I can still ship you off to that boarding school in

Utah, you know. And after deliberately deceiving your father for almost three months, he won't want to have anything to do with you if he learns the truth. He'd probably sign the enrollment papers himself for that school as punishment. So don't stab me in the back at this point, Hayley, because you will sorely regret betraying me."

"Fine." Hayley's voice choked up a little. "But how much longer, Mom? School is going to be starting in a few more weeks, and there's no way in hell I'm wearing baggy clothes the first day back."

"Just a couple more weeks," begged Lindsey. "I swear to you. I'm *this* close to getting him back, I just need to wear him down a teensy bit more. Then this will all be over with, and you can go back to the way things were."

"And have you figured a way out of this whole mess yet?"

"Of course. Well, I have to give credit to Nikki, since all of this was her idea. But this is the plan. Your father has another business trip scheduled in about ten days, and he'll be gone for a week. During that time you're going to have a miscarriage. And of course he'll feel terrible about it, want to rush home to make sure you're okay, and obviously stick around to help you through the trauma."

Hayley snorted. "Jesus, Mom. I'm not sure which of you is more twisted - you or Nikki. What soap opera did she watch to hatch this ridiculous idea anyway? Or did she steal the idea from some sappy romance book?"

"Does it really matter?" snapped Lindsey. "The important thing here is to keep your focus for just a few more weeks. I realize your father is getting more and more suspicious, so you really need to lay it on thick, Hayley. The next time he asks you questions about the baby, for God's sake show a little more enthusiasm, will you? We're so close, don't blow it now!"

Hayley changed the subject then, asking Lindsey her opinion about a pair of shoes she wanted to buy, and Casey used the opportunity to very quietly tiptoe back inside the house. He knew instinctively that it was very, very important not to let on that he'd just overheard this extremely enlightening conversation, or that he had the slightest suspicion that Hayley had been faking this pregnancy thing from the very start. Or that their mother had apparently been the brains behind the whole charade.

As he made his way stealthily to his room, Casey realized that the revelation that Hayley had made the whole thing up wasn't all that shocking to him. Not that he'd really given it a lot of thought up until now, but it had seemed a bit odd to him that his pregnant sister looked skinnier than ever. And that she seemed totally unconcerned with the fact that she had gotten herself knocked up. And try as he might, Casey had never been able to envision his spoiled, selfish, airhead of a sister ever lifting a finger to take care of a demanding baby. He just wished he hadn't been so preoccupied with school and baseball and computer camp these past few months; otherwise, he would have likely been highly suspicious of the situation and maybe mentioned his concerns to his father.

'Shoot. I've got to tell Dad,' he thought to himself suddenly. 'And as soon as possible. Man, is he going to be pissed off when he learns the truth. Especially since he had to break up with Sasha because of stupid Hayley and her phony pregnancy.'

It certainly wasn't the sort of bad news that one wanted to break to someone via a text or email, and maybe not even a phone call. Plus, Casey couldn't take the risk that his mother or sister would overhear him. He feared that if they found out he was on to them they would spin another, even more fantastic story, and completely deny anything Casey might tell Matthew. No, he would have to find a way to get his father alone and tell him everything he'd just overheard.

Matthew was flying home from his business trip in Dallas later today, but Casey couldn't recall what time he was due in. He closed the bedroom door for privacy as he placed a quick call to his father's PA.

"Hey, Elena. How's it going?" he greeted.

Elena, who could frequently be grumpy with other people, was *always* nice to Casey. "I've had worse days," she replied matter-of-factly. "But this is a nice surprise to hear from you. Keeping busy over the summer?"

"Yup. Baseball league and computer camp. Hey, can you tell me what time my dad's due in today? And is he on the company plane?"

"Sure." Elena sounded a little wary, given that Casey rarely called her directly, but she was able to give him the information he wanted without a fuss.

"Thanks, Elena. I, uh, just needed his help with some computer stuff tonight. You know, for that camp I mentioned."

"Well, since his flight gets in around four this afternoon, I'd say he should have plenty of time to give you a hand. Nice to talk to you, Casey. And don't be a stranger, hmm? I haven't seen you or your sister in almost two years. Have your father bring you to see me sometime."

Casey readily agreed, anxious to get off the phone and start figuring out the next steps in his plan. He had almost two hours to get to the airport terminal where the private plane his father was traveling on would be landing, which should be plenty of time. The tricky part of this plan was going to be sneaking out of the house without his mother or sister noticing he'd returned from baseball practice so early.

But he received the break he needed a few minutes later, when his mother sent him a quick text, informing him that she and Hayley were going out to a late lunch and then shopping, and that Maribel would pick him up from practice. Casey breathed a sigh of relief, then watched discreetly from his bedroom window until he saw his mother's Aston Martin pull out of the driveway, his sister ensconced in the passenger seat. He waited a full fifteen minutes after they left before putting the next part of his plan into motion.

He snuck out of the house using one of the numerous side exits, the overwhelming heat of the day momentarily sucking the air out of his lungs. He walked around the block, staying out of sight, then used the Uber app on his phone to summon a car. After dismissing their last nanny, Matthew had set up accounts for both Casey and Hayley with the car service so that they would never have to worry about getting a ride when they needed one.

While he was waiting for his ride, Casey texted Maribel, telling her that he was going to Blake's house after practice and that she didn't need to pick him up after all. He was glad that he'd found a shady spot to stand while waiting for his ride, since the temperature was now in the high nineties, and wished he had taken the time to grab a bottle of water.

Fortunately, the car arrived right on schedule to pick him up, and if the driver thought it a bit odd that his passenger was a fourteen year old boy he didn't offer up a comment. Casey drummed his fingers on the seat impatiently as they encountered several pockets of traffic on the drive to the airport, and fidgeted as the minutes continued to count down until his father's flight was due to arrive in.

The Uber driver left him off at the terminal where Matthew's flight would be landing, and Casey dashed off to wait for him in the arrivals area, hoping that it was the correct spot. It had been awhile, probably close to two years, since he had accompanied his mother and sister here to the airport to pick up Matthew, and while the waiting area looked mostly familiar, he wasn't entirely sure.

But a short time later, Casey breathed a sigh of relief as he spied his father trudging wearily through the terminal. Matthew looked both exhausted and depressed, and Casey now knew beyond a shadow of a doubt that he'd done the right thing in coming here this afternoon. Gleefully anticipating his father's reaction to the news he was about to share, Casey practically jogged ahead to meet him.

DESPITE DRINKING AT LEAST THREE cups of very strong coffee so far today, Matthew was visibly dragging as he forced himself to keep walking through the airport terminal. He'd left for Dallas three days ago, and kept up a whirlwind schedule for the duration of his trip. He rarely slept well when he traveled on business, usually too wired up to

408

be able to fully relax, and this trip had been no exception. He was looking forward to sleeping in his own bed tonight, even though it meant locking his bedroom door to keep his overly amorous ex out of his room.

Lindsey had continued to throw herself at him shamelessly, despite his stern and downright hostile admonitions that she would be the very last woman in the world he'd ever be attracted to again. And with each pathetic attempt to tempt or seduce him, Lindsey had seemed increasingly desperate, almost panic stricken that her wiles simply weren't working.

He was really going to have to do something about this whole fucked-up situation, and soon - like any day now. He was frustrated as hell with Hayley and her apparent disinterest in anything having to do with the baby she was carrying. He felt like shaking her at times, anything to shock her into action and start facing reality. His daughter seemed blithely unaware of just how much her life was going to change in a few more months, and Matthew's doubts continued to increase about the wisdom of Hayley keeping this baby. He made a mental note to ask his divorce attorney for a referral to an adoption agency, fully intending to steer Hayley more firmly in that direction. It would be the best solution for everyone involved, especially the baby. In fact, he might as well place that call right now while he was thinking about it.

'No time like the present, I always say,' he thought to himself, taking his phone from his jacket pocket and scrolling through the contacts list. But before he could press the number for his attorney, he heard a familiar voice calling out to him.

"Dad! Hey, Dad, over here!"

Matthew glanced up in astonishment to see Casey waving at him frantically. Instantly alarmed, because he couldn't fathom why his son would be waiting for him here at the airport if there wasn't some sort of emergency, he hurried over to where Casey was waiting impatiently.

"Hey, buddy," he greeted, pulling his son in close for a hug. "What's going on? Must be something big for you to meet me like this. Is your mother here, too?"

Casey shook his head. "Nope, just me. I, uh, got your flight info from Elena and took Uber here. Mom doesn't know I'm here, she thinks I'm still at baseball practice."

Matthew eyed him warily. "And why aren't you there? Are you in some sort of trouble, Casey?"

"No, nothing like that at all. I swear, Dad. And practice ended early today because it's like a hundred degrees outside. A couple of the guys almost fainted from the heat yesterday, so Coach made us stop before lunchtime."

"So why all the secrecy, hmm?" inquired Matthew as he steered Casey towards the exit, where a driver employed by MBI would be waiting to pick him up. "It's pretty obvious you don't want your mother to know you're here, so what gives?"

Casey gave a furtive glance around, as if to make sure no one else could hear what he was about to say. "I, uh, sort of overheard some stuff that Mom and Hayley were discussing. They didn't know I was home, and after hearing what they were talking about I knew I had to tell you as soon as possible."

"Why didn't you call me then? You didn't need to come all the way out here to meet me," rebuked Matthew gently.

Casey shrugged. "You'll understand when I tell you. It's -

well, you're going to be really ticked off, Dad. And I thought it was better to tell you in person. Besides, I didn't want one of them overhearing me."

Matthew frowned. "Okay, now you're starting to worry me a little. What exactly did you overhear, Casey?"

Casey grimaced. "Maybe we should wait until we're inside the car before I tell you. Because you're gonna be really, really mad."

Matthew sighed. "Just tell me. I promise I won't lose it."

"Hayley isn't really pregnant. She's been faking the whole time. And not only does Mom know but I think she was the one who thought up the idea in the first place."

Matthew froze in place, even as his driver pulled up to the curb. "You must have heard them wrong, buddy," he said faintly. "Your mother is capable of a lot of things, but something like this seems way beyond even her warped mind. And I can't believe that Hayley - my little girl - would willingly go along with something so cruel."

"Nope. It's all true, Dad. Look, the car is here. Let's get inside and I can tell you all of it. From the beginning."

Numbly, Matthew obeyed his son's urging and slid inside the backseat of the Town Car. Once he and Casey were both inside, he pressed the button to raise the privacy panel so that they could speak freely without the driver overhearing them.

Matthew turned to his son, trying desperately to keep his simmering anger from reaching the boiling point. "Now, tell me all of it, Casey. From the beginning. And don't leave anything out."

He listened in growing disbelief and fury as Casey patiently and thoroughly relayed the conversation between Lindsey and Hayley. And even then Matthew still couldn't believe it was really true, questioning Casey over and over on specific points. But after nearly twenty minutes of this, he leaned back in his seat wearily, closing his eyes as he scrubbed a hand over his face.

"Jesus." He shook his head in disbelief. "And you know what the worst thing about all of this is, Casey? Not the fact that your mother and sister cooked up this elaborate charade, but that I was stupid and naïve enough to fall for it. How the hell could I have been so dumb?"

"It's okay, Dad." Casey squeezed his shoulder reassuringly. "It sure sounds like the two of them spent a lot of time dreaming all of this up. And I guess Mom had help from Nikki."

Matthew grimaced. "Yeah, that might explain some things. Nikki is the queen of lies. That's how she swindled so much money out of her ex-husbands. But I should have been smarter than that, Casey. Jeez, I've got a Mensa-level IQ. You'd think I would have known better."

Casey grinned. "You were the one who told me that brain smarts don't always equal street smarts."

Matthew chuckled, despite the burning anger he felt at having been so thoroughly deceived. "Yeah, I seem to remember that. And *you* are probably the smartest person I've ever known, buddy, despite the fact that you're only fourteen. More like fourteen going on fifty, in my opinion. And I owe you big time, Casey. I can't tell you how much it means to me to finally realize the truth."

"So what are we going to do now, Dad?"

Matthew grinned. "So it's "we", is it? Glad to have you on board, buddy. And as far as our next steps, I think we should grab a bite to eat somewhere and discuss our strategy. Are you hungry?"

Casey gave him a look of disbelief. "Dad, do you really have to ask that question? This is me, after all. I'm *always* hungry."

He rumpled Casey's hair. "That's what I figured." He lowered the privacy panel, then directed the driver to take them to one of Casey's favorite restaurants, a place where the burgers were greasy, the beers ice cold, and the air conditioning would be on full blast. It sounded like the perfect place to plot strategy with his son on what their next moves should be. And, for the first time in months, Matthew was actually hungry. Starving, actually, enough that ordering two giant burgers was starting to sound like the best idea he'd had all day.

"Hey, Dad," ventured Casey somewhat timidly, as the driver exited the freeway. "Does this mean that you and Sasha can maybe get back together? I know you miss her a lot."

"Maybe," mused Matthew. "But it's a little premature to start thinking about that, buddy."

In actuality, the possibility of getting Sasha back had been nearly the first thing that had crossed his mind after Casey had blurted out that Hayley's pregnancy was all a lie. But he couldn't get too far ahead of himself, he thought cautiously. He was going to have to tread very carefully over the next day or so in order to bring this whole ugly mess to a head, and use the opportunity to kill two birds with one stone.

And right after they settled into a table and ordered their

food, Matthew took out his phone and placed a call to his attorney after all - except that the purpose of the call was no longer to inquire about potential adoption agencies. Instead, it was to share the good news that he'd finally figured out a way to force Lindsey to sign those damned divorce papers.

chapter twenty-one
February

"**WELL, THIS IS SO NICE,**" gushed Lindsey. "I can't remember the last time we all sat down to dinner as a family. I hope it's just the first of many more nights like this."

Matthew didn't offer up a reply, simply taking a sip of his iced tea as he observed the others at the table. Casey was tucking into his meal hungrily, since very little seemed to affect his appetite. Hayley, predictably, was merely picking at her food while texting one or more of her friends at the same time. Only Lindsey looked happy, her features practically glowing at this opportunity to have everyone together. And Matthew was willing to bet that she was silently congratulating herself on finally getting the results she'd plotted and schemed for these past months. He was pissed off enough - not to mention vengeful - to let her go on believing that for a few more minutes. After all, it would be that much more satisfying to see the look on her lying, deceitful face when he confronted her with the truth.

Lindsey had been ecstatic when he'd called her earlier today and said he'd be home to have dinner with her and the kids this evening. She had almost squealed with excitement, in fact, and Matthew had felt more than a little repulsed at her enthusiasm. She had made a big show out of asking him what he'd like for dinner, and then promised to cook everything herself.

Matthew wasn't the least bit fooled, however, and knew very well that the chicken parmigiana, Caesar salad, and garlic bread had been prepared by Maribel. But the food was admittedly delicious, and he took two helpings of everything. Ever since Casey had met him at the airport yesterday afternoon, food had quickly sounded appetizing again. And life - *his* life, in particular - suddenly felt like it was truly worth living once more.

But he still had to let all of this play out, had to slowly, one by one, reveal all of the cards he currently held in his hand. And if getting Lindsey's hopes up, if letting her believe that she had finally won him back, only to demolish it all in one fell swoop was cruel, it was no less than she deserved.

Matthew caught Casey's eye as the boy reached for another slice of garlic bread, and gave a slight, almost imperceptible shake of his head. Casey glanced back down at his plate, practically shoving the whole piece of bread in his mouth at once. But Matthew knew that his son had received the signal loud and clear - to stay out of what was about to unfold until the time was right.

Over greasy burgers, fries, and milkshakes late yesterday afternoon, father and son had rather gleefully plotted how they would handle the situation with Lindsey and Hayley. Casey had wanted him to confront his mother and sister the second they arrived home, but Matthew had cautioned his son to be a little patient.

"There are other things at stake here, Casey. Things

416

that I've got my attorney checking into for me even as we speak. And until I hear back from him, which will probably be tomorrow morning, then you and I need to keep our cool. Your mother isn't going to get away with what she's done, and I'm keeping my fingers crossed that I can use all of this as leverage to finally get that divorce."

Casey had nodded, but a wistful expression had crossed his face. *"I know. It must have really sucked for you these last few months, Dad. But at least it was cool having you back home for a little while. I'll miss you when you move back out."*

"Hey." Matthew had rumpled his son's hair affectionately. *"What if you moved out, too? I can tell my attorney that one of my new conditions is that I insist on having custody of you."*

Casey's face had lit up. *"Really, Dad? You'd really want me to live with you?"*

Matthew had reached across the table and given him a fierce hug. *"It would be a dream come true for me,"* he'd replied somberly. *"Though it would mean you'd have to live in San Francisco, and change schools. Think you could handle that?"*

Casey had shrugged. *"I'm starting high school in a few weeks, so I'd be at a new place anyway. And, yeah, I'd have to make new friends and stuff, but I'd be okay with that. It would be worth it in order to live with you all the time, Dad."*

Matthew had blinked back tears. *"Consider it a done deal, then. We'll have to move fast, get you enrolled in a new school, and I'll probably have to offer up a few bribes* or call in some favors to get it done. But one way or the other it'll happen."

Casey had slurped his milkshake loudly. "Mom won't be happy about it," he observed.

"Like I care?" Matthew had snorted. "And believe me, by the time I'm done with her, your mother will be the unhappiest woman in the state of California. But it's what she deserves. Now, let's go over our story one more time, okay?"

"What should we do after dinner?" inquired Lindsey cheerfully. "It's early yet, and since the kids are still on summer break maybe we can go see a movie together. It's been ages since we've done something fun like that."

Lazily, Matthew took another drink of his iced tea. Unlike Lindsey, who'd been guzzling wine all during the meal, he had declined any alcohol, wanting to keep his wits sharpened for what was about to unfold.

"Actually, I was going to suggest that you take Hayley shopping for maternity clothes tonight," he drawled, observing his daughter very carefully to gauge her reaction. "After all, honey, it's about time, don't you think? How much weight have you gained so far - ten, fifteen pounds? Perfectly normal, of course, for being almost five months pregnant, but it's pretty obvious that you just can't wear your regular clothes any longer."

Matthew had to force himself not to smirk, and hoped that Casey was doing the same, as he watched the expression of mingled shock and furor that crossed Hayley's face. Lindsey paled noticeably beneath the layers of heavy makeup on her face, and he knew his words had definitely hit a sore spot.

"Omigod, Dad!" shrieked Hayley. "How can you say something like that? I have *not* gained anywhere near that much weight! In fact, I've actually lost a few - uh, I mean..."

Hayley's voice trailed off as she realized her flub, and she glanced anxiously at her shell-shocked mother for guidance. Lindsey was quite obviously flustered, and quickly tried to cover up Hayley's blunder.

"You're embarrassing her, Matt," chided Lindsey. "You know Hayley doesn't like to talk about anything having to do with her pregnancy around you."

"Hmm. Could that be due to the fact that she isn't actually pregnant, and never has been?" inquired Matthew calmly. "And that the two of you, along with your so-called friend Nicole, have cooked up this entire series of lies for the sole purpose of getting me to call off the divorce?"

Lindsey and Hayley both gasped simultaneously, with Hayley once again looking at her mother in a panic.

"Are you out of your mind, Matt?" exclaimed Lindsey in feigned outrage. "How can you even suggest that we'd make up something like that? Of course Hayley is pregnant, almost five months along now. Why would you think otherwise?"

"Because I heard the two of you talking a couple of days ago," chimed in Casey. "You were out by the pool and arguing about how much longer Hayley had to keep up the pretense. And she said this had to all be over with by the time school started because there was no way she was going to wear baggy clothes on the first day back. And then you told her that during Dad's next business trip she'd conveniently have a miscarriage, and it would all - "

419

"Shut up!" Lindsey screeched, surging to her feet and storming over to where Casey sat. "You deceitful, lying little brat! How dare you eavesdrop on me! You take that back right now, admit to your father that you made all that up, or I'll - "

She had raised her hand menacingly, and started to bring it around as though she intended to slap Casey across the face. But Matthew forestalled her, gripping her wrist so tightly that she yelped in pain. And there was real fear in her eyes when she saw how furious he was.

"Don't you dare," he warned her in a dangerous voice, "ever even consider laying a hand on either of my children. I'd have you charged and arrested for child abuse before you could blink an eye."

Lindsey glared at Matthew first, then at Casey. "He had no business listening in on a private conversation," she muttered sullenly. "He should have had the courtesy to let us know he was home."

Matthew gave a hoot of laughter. "Why? So that your web of lies wouldn't have become unraveled? You would have liked that, wouldn't you, Linz? Or if Casey had just kept quiet about what he'd heard and let your deception unfold according to plan. Fortunately, at least one of my children can be counted on to do the right thing."

Tears were already streaming down Hayley's cheeks, and she was basically blubbering as she pleaded, "Daddy, please listen to me. I didn't want to do this, I swear! But Mom forced me, she threatened - "

Matthew held up a hand to silence her. "Save it for now. I'll get to you in a few minutes, young lady. And believe me, you've got an awful lot to answer for. But right now, I need to make sure your mother fully understands the consequences of what she's put me through these last few months."

Lindsey lifted her chin mutinously. "You still aren't forcing me to sign those damned divorce papers, Matt," she insisted. "This changes nothing."

"Oh, I beg to differ, my soon to be ex-wife," he retorted. "You see, as soon as Casey told me everything he'd overheard between you and Hayley, I called my attorney. And he's positive that a judge would easily grant me a divorce after hearing the way you coerced our daughter into lying so blatantly, *especially* about being date raped. You'd be considered an unfit parent, and I could even get full custody of both kids if I wanted. However, I'm only taking Casey with me at this time. It's going to take some time for me to forgive Hayley for her part in all this."

Lindsey looked like she was going to be sick to her stomach. "You - you can't take Casey," she protested weakly. "I won't let you."

"I can and I will," corrected Matthew. "And there's not a damned thing you can do about it. If you think I'd leave him alone here with you for one more night, you're crazier than I thought. He's already packed up most of his stuff, and it's in the car. Along with my things, by the way. We'll be going back to the condo tonight, and we've already found a great high school for him to attend in San Francisco."

Lindsey shook her head, sinking back onto her chair as though afraid her legs would give out from under her otherwise. "Fine. He can go with you. For now." She glared at her son again. "I'm so pissed off at the little tattletale right

421

now anyway, I'm not sure I could stand having him anywhere near me. You've ruined everything, Casey. *Everything.*"

Casey shrugged, clearly unfazed by his mother's anger. "Maybe for you," he replied nonchalantly. "But I'm happy to be going with Dad. And the new school I'll be attending is super cool. And what you and Hayley did was really mean, Mom."

"I did it for us, Casey!" Lindsey screamed. "For you and Hayley. So that you'd have your father back here where he belonged."

Casey shook his head. "No, Mom. I think you did it for you. Because you were mad that Dad left you. And even madder when he started seeing Sasha. You just wanted Dad back because he bruised your ego, and because he was happy without you. You wanted him to come back so you could get revenge, not because you cared about me or Hayley."

Lindsey's green eyes narrowed dangerously. "On second thought," she hissed, "maybe I won't care if you leave. You ungrateful, backstabbing brat. How dare you - "

"Enough!" demanded Matthew. "Leave my son out of this, Lindsey. He did the right thing, and there is no way I'm going to allow you to keep verbally abusing him. In fact, Casey needs to finish packing a few things, don't you, buddy? Why don't you go take care of that? We'll be leaving shortly."

Casey didn't need to be told twice, and fairly ran out of the kitchen where they'd been having dinner.

Matthew glanced back at a sullen Lindsey. "How long did you two honestly think you could keep getting away with this?" he asked, shaking his head in disgust. "Not only

422

did you make Hayley lie about being date raped, you were going to make her pretend she'd had a miscarriage as well? Jesus, you are one sick bitch, you know that? Now, I strongly suggest you give your attorney a call first thing in the morning and set up an appointment to sign those divorce papers. My attorney has already let her know what's been going on, and she's reluctantly agreed that you no longer have a leg to stand on."

"Well, sounds like I'll just have to get a new attorney then, doesn't it?" declared Lindsey. "Because there is no way I'm signing those papers, Matt."

He shrugged. "Fine. Have it your way. I believe I already mentioned that your signature is no longer required. Based on your appalling actions of late, a judge will grant me a divorce with or without your consent. Of course, it would be easier and quicker if you'd finally cooperate and sign, but one way or another our marriage is finally going to be over with."

"Then take me to fucking court!" she challenged. "Because I'm not going to sign anything willingly."

"You might change your mind when you go over the revised settlement terms," replied Matthew rather matter-of-factly. "Let's call it a bit of extra motivation for you to make this easier for all of us. Effective immediately, each day that you refuse to sign, the amount of the settlement decreases by a hundred grand. That works out to three million a month, Linz. So I'd really urge you to reconsider, given your spending habits. That's a lot of money to lose while we're waiting for a judge to grant me a divorce. My attorney said sometimes these cases can drag on for a few months. Think about it, hmm?"

Lindsey pounded her fist on the kitchen table, causing the dishes to rattle precariously. "Fuck that!" she hissed. "You can't do that, Matt!"

"Ah, I beg to differ," he taunted. "Call your attorney and ask her, Linz. I think you should start practicing your signature as soon as possible."

Lindsey stormed out of the room, her phone in hand, leaving Matthew to face his teary-eyed, trembling daughter.

"Daddy, I'm s-sorry," sobbed Hayley. "I know how angry you must be right now. But Mom made me do it, I swear. I never wanted to lie to you, but she didn't give me a choice."

"I'm not angry, Hayley," he replied stoically. "At least not with you. But I am disappointed. Terribly disappointed that you could willingly participate in something like this. And knowing your mother, I'm convinced she forced you into this. But you should have confided in me, Hayley. Should have told me what she was up to. Do you honestly think I would have allowed her to send you off to some boarding school without my consent? I'm hurt that you had so little faith in me."

Hayley flung herself at him, wrapping her thin arms around his waist as she wept against his chest. "I didn't think it would ever get this far. Mom was convinced that the two of you would get back together right after you moved back in. But when that didn't happen, things just got more involved."

"Didn't you ever hear that old saying "oh, what a tangled web we weave when first we practice to deceive"?" he murmured. "Basically, it means that once you start lying you can't stop. Otherwise, everyone will realize that you were

424

lying all along. Now, be honest with me for once, Hayley. What was the real reason you chose to go along with your mother's crazy scheme?"

Hayley kept her gaze downcast, too ashamed to meet his eyes. "I - I guess maybe part of it was that I was, well, jealous of Sasha," she admitted reluctantly. "I didn't like it that she obviously meant that much to you. And I sort of hated the fact that she was so perfect. No matter how much of a bitch I was to her, she was always nice, always understanding. And somehow that made me feel bad about myself, like admitting that I wasn't a very nice person."

"You weren't," agreed Matthew without hesitation. "At least not to her. And you're right. Sasha made every effort to be your friend, to get along, and you froze her out each time. And because of your little games, you've managed to destroy my relationship with her, Hayley. You know, I hadn't been happy with your mother for a long time. I'll accept the blame for part of that, but it was largely her fault that our marriage went to pieces. When I started seeing Sasha, I felt happier than I had in years. Now that's all gone, thanks to you and your mother."

"I'm sorry, Daddy," she sniffled. "I wish I could make it up to you somehow."

Matthew shook his head, taking a step back. "I don't see how that's possible at the moment," he said sadly. "Look, Hayley. You know I'm always here for you. You can call or text me if you need something. But, well, I think that it's going to take a little time for me to process all of this, to forgive you, and until then it's probably best if we don't see each other. I'll call you in a few days, okay?"

425

Hayley nodded sadly. "Okay. I - I wish none of this had ever happened, Daddy. That I called you the first time Mom started talking about the idea."

He pressed a farewell kiss to her forehead. "Me, too."

"I'M AFRAID THERE ISN'T MUCH food here at the moment, buddy. We'll have to go shopping sometime tomorrow and stock up."

Casey shrugged unconcernedly. "No big deal, Dad. I know where all the places to eat are around here, so I can fend for myself for a day or two."

Matthew grinned, rumpling his son's hair affectionately. "Yeah, you sure can. But you won't have to keep doing that any longer. You and I are a team now, Casey. And you're never going back to live with your mother. I should have insisted on getting custody of you when I first left your mother. But at the time I didn't want you to have to leave your friends, or change schools during your last year at middle school."

"It's okay, Dad. Besides, if I hadn't been living with Mom, I would never have overheard her and Hayley talking. So I guess it's all working out for the best."

"Seems that way, huh?" agreed Matthew as he deposited a load of bags in Casey's room. Someone from the building staff would be delivering the rest of their things any minute now since they hadn't been able to carry everything in one trip.

"Hey, Dad?" asked Casey timidly.

Matthew smiled at his son reassuringly. "What is it, buddy?"

"When are you going to let Sasha know? I mean, that

you've moved back here. And about Hayley and everything."

Matthew's smile froze on his face. "I don't know, Casey," he admitted quietly. "I'm not even sure how to begin a conversation like that. And I'm sort of terrified that she won't want to have anything to do with me again. I wouldn't blame her, frankly."

"Nah." Casey waved a hand dismissively. "She'll come around, I know she will. She's not the sort of person who holds grudges, you know?"

"Yeah, I know." Matthew sighed. "But it's more complicated than that, buddy. I promised myself that I wouldn't get in touch with her again until I had those signed divorce papers in hand. It isn't fair to Sasha otherwise. So let's hope that your mother's greed outweighs her vindictiveness."

Casey's eyes, so like his father's, twinkled mischievously. "You could always change the terms of the settlement again, make it a million dollars a day she loses out on if she doesn't sign."

Matthew whooped with laughter, clapping his son on the back. "I think maybe you should re-think becoming a computer engineer, Casey. You'd make a hell of a divorce attorney instead."

chapter twenty-two

"WHEN PEOPLE TALK ABOUT THE glow pregnant women get, I'm very sure they were referring to you, Tessa. I don't think I've ever seen you look so beautiful."

Tessa was indeed glowing as she smiled with pleasure at Sasha's compliment. "I *feel* like I'm glowing from the inside out," she agreed. "And everything I read about morning sickness and having no energy and all the other symptoms just haven't materialized yet. Julia says I'm a freak of nature, and that it isn't normal to be two months pregnant and not feel even a little bit awful."

Sasha shook her head. "Nonsense. No two women will experience the same symptoms when they're pregnant, so it's not surprising that you're feeling so much different than Julia did." She winked teasingly. "And knowing Julia, she's probably just jealous that you seem to be sailing through these early weeks so easily, while she had a tough time of it."

Tessa's blue eyes twinkled mischievously. "Julia can be a bit of a drama queen at times," she acknowledged. "But I think she's right that I might be something of a freak by feeling so wonderful."

"Enjoy this special time in your life," replied Sasha encouragingly. "But even though you feel good, you need to be careful not to overdo it, hmm? I'm glad to see that you were hydrating all during class, and taking things a little easy. You're strong and fit and should easily be able to keep doing this class up through your final trimester. But listen to your body, Tessa. And if it's telling you to back off, then do so. Morgana teaches a wonderful pre-natal yoga class here, and by your seventh month that's something you might want to consider."

Tessa sighed. "Careful, or you'll start to sound like Ian. He's already so overprotective of me I feel like I'm living in a glass bubble at times. And I know the further along I get in this pregnancy the worse he's going to get."

Sasha gave her friend a little squeeze on the shoulder. "Enjoy it," she advised. "Your husband is so devoted to you, Tessa, that it almost brings a tear to my eye to watch him around you. He'll be the same with your child."

"I know." Tessa nodded. "Especially if the baby is a girl. And Ian has made his wishes very well known - he really wants this first one to be a little girl."

"Well, your husband does seem to get whatever he wants," teased Sasha. "He wanted you for a long time from what you've told me, and his patience was finally rewarded. So if Ian wants a daughter, I'm thinking he'll get one."

Tessa smiled. "I know it's too early to tell, but, well - what do your vibes tell you? About the gender of the baby, that is."

"Hmm." Sasha studied Tessa carefully, then placed her palm gently over Tessa's tummy. "You don't have even the tiniest baby bump yet, so there's no way to predict how you'll be carrying. And while I usually can't pick up anything about the baby's aura until at least the fourth month, I am feeling some distinctly feminine vibes already. So I would say the chances are quite high that you're going to have a girl. Does that make you happy?"

Tessa nodded enthusiastically. "Of course! Though unlike Ian I'd be perfectly happy with either a boy or a girl. And since I hope to have at least three or four children, at some point I'm bound to have one or more of each gender."

"You're going to be a wonderful mother, Tessa," assured Sasha warmly. "Your baby is going to be a very lucky little girl. Or boy," she added hastily. "I can't say for certain yet that you're having a girl. And I already know that Ian isn't a believer in my vibes, as you call them. Like most men, he's a skeptic about that sort of thing."

Tessa grinned. "But that's why it will be so satisfying to prove that you were right all along! Maybe then he'll be a believer."

"Perhaps. Now, will I see you again before you head off to Italy?"

Tessa and Ian were departing within the next few days for a two week vacation at his family's villa in Tuscany, a trip that was an annual tradition for the Gregsons.

"We're flying out on Friday afternoon," confirmed Tessa. "So I'll be here for your Wednesday morning class for sure, and maybe on Thursday evening as well. Julia's coming on Wednesday, and wants to have breakfast afterwards if you're available."

"I think so, yes. I'm pretty sure I don't have a massage appointment until after noon that day."

Tessa gave her a hug good-bye, then had to dash off to a doctor's appointment. Tessa had lingered after class for a few minutes to chat, and now the big studio was completely empty. Another class was due to start here in less than twenty minutes, so Sasha began to gather her belongings up.

But as she went to pick up her bag, she froze at the sound of an achingly familiar voice coming from the doorway.

"Uh, hello? The girl at the front desk said it would be okay for me to come in."

Sasha turned around slowly, not sure if she should feel annoyed, angry, or merely impassive at the sight of the only man she'd ever loved - and the only one who had thoroughly broken her heart - hovering uncertainly in the doorway.

Even though it was a work day, Matthew was casually dressed in jeans and a white chambray shirt, the sleeves rolled up to expose his leanly muscled forearms. His face was lightly stubbled, but at least his hair had been neatly combed and slicked back. He looked tired but oddly serene at the same time, and he was smiling at her hopefully.

Sasha crossed her arms over her chest and regarded him impassively. "Actually, there's another class starting in here within the next few minutes so I was just about to leave."

"Oh." Matthew glanced at the thick manila envelope he was holding. "Um, okay. Well, can I buy you a cup of coffee, then? I mean, tea. I know you don't drink coffee, that was just a figure of speech."

"Matthew," she rebuked. "You aren't supposed to be here. You know that."

"Please." He raised his eyes to hers, and she couldn't help the little lurch her heart gave when she saw the desperation in his gaze. "I've got something to tell you, Sasha. Something really important. And I know I don't have any right to ask, but can you please just hear me out for a few minutes? Please?"

Sasha heaved a sigh. "Fine. But I have a client coming in for a massage in less than an hour, so coffee - rather, tea - is out. We can talk in the massage room for a few minutes."

Matthew didn't argue, merely followed along willingly behind her as she headed in the direction of the massage rooms. Once inside, Sasha flicked on the lights and stored her bag as Matthew closed the door behind them.

He was looking around the small room with a wistful expression on his face. "I can't believe it's been almost a year since the first time I set foot in this room," he recalled. He glanced at the massage table longingly. "God, I could really use a massage right about now."

Sasha frowned. "Please tell me that you've been having regular massages since - well, since the last time I gave you one."

Matthew shook his head. "It wouldn't have been the same," he told her earnestly. "And it wouldn't have felt right. Plus, the last thing I've had time for is looking out for myself."

"I can tell," she admonished him. "You've lost weight, and I'm just guessing you haven't been eating right."

He shuddered. "You'd be revolted if I told you what my diet has been like as of late. But that isn't why I'm here."

"I didn't imagine that it was," replied Sasha calmly. "So you'd best tell me then, hadn't you?"

"Yeah." Matthew fumbled with the metal clasp of the manila envelope he'd been carrying around. He drew out a thick packet of papers and held them out to her. "This is why I'm here. I wanted to show you this in person."

Reluctantly, Sasha took the papers from him, refusing to meet his eyes. Just being this close to him brought back all of the emotions she'd been trying so hard to repress these last few months - not just the hurt and anger she had felt when he'd gone back to his family, but all of the good memories, too. She missed being with him, missed talking to him about how his day had been, or gently lecturing him about taking his vitamins or making sure he got enough sleep. And she really, really missed falling asleep in his arms after he'd made love to her so tenderly that it had brought tears to her eyes. Being near him this way, close enough to smell the soap he'd used to shower with this morning, brought all of those emotions surging to the surface until they threatened to overwhelm her. She took a deep, calming breath before glancing at the papers, which looked to her inexperienced eyes to be some sort of legal document.

"I don't understand. What exactly is this? Am I supposed to read all of these pages or something?" she asked half-jokingly.

"No." Matthew shook his head. "Just the first and last ones will suffice."

Sasha looked at the top sheet more carefully this time, and three words jumped out at her - "Decree of Divorce". Slowly, not permitting herself to get her hopes up, she flipped to the last page as Matthew had instructed.

There were two signatures there, both notarized and dated a few days ago. She recognized Matthew's bold, almost indecipherable scrawl, and then gave a soft gasp when she realized the second signature was Lindsey's.

"I just picked the papers up from my attorney a little while ago," Matthew told her somberly. "Lindsey finally gave in and signed them late last week. After some extra added persuasion, that is."

Sasha's hand was trembling a little, and she quickly handed the document back to him before it fell. "What - what sort of persuasion?" she asked faintly.

Matthew gave a wry grin. "The sort Lindsey understands best - the financial kind. I changed the terms of the divorce settlement after certain, ah, developments occurred. She stood to lose a hundred thousand dollars for each day that she refused to sign. And when she realized I was dead serious on the matter, she caved. The divorce will be final in about six weeks."

She wrapped her arms over her torso, suddenly feeling chilled despite the warmth of the massage room. "What about Hayley?" she murmured. "I thought the whole reason for you moving back to Hillsborough was to help her get through her pregnancy."

He snorted. "What pregnancy? Those developments I just mentioned? Turns out that Lindsey and Hayley concocted this very elaborate web of lies about the date rape and the pregnancy, even about how Hayley was acting out and being rebellious. A web of lies very carefully woven with the intent of trapping me inside of it. Lindsey was so desperate to get me back, to reclaim her place as Mrs. Matthew Bennett, that she had the nerve to coerce Hayley into going along with her warped plans."

Sasha stared at him in horror. "She lied to you about everything?" she whispered. "My God, Matthew. I knew Hayley could be, well, difficult, but I never thought she could be that cruel to her own father. I'm so sorry. I can't even imagine how much that sort of betrayal hurt you."

Matthew nodded. "Yeah, it sucked big time. Doing something so twisted is vintage Lindsey, so it didn't surprise me to learn she was the mastermind behind everything. But to learn my own daughter was a willing participant in ruining my life - well, like I told Hayley, it's going to take me some time to forgive her. Even if she was strong-armed into cooperating."

"I had this feeling - no, never mind." She shook her head. "It's not my place to say anything, especially since I can tell you already feel awful about this."

He placed a hand on her forearm. "No, please. Tell me. I know you well enough to realize that your feelings and premonitions are usually always right. What were you about to say?"

Sasha couldn't resist touching him a second longer, feeling an overwhelming rush of empathy for what he had endured at learning his own child had betrayed him. She placed her hand over his, giving it a comforting squeeze. "I couldn't help but be a little suspicious of Hayley's story. I never said anything to you at the time, didn't want to sound like I was bitter or resentful. But, well, something just felt off about the whole thing. If for no other reason Hayley didn't seem like the sort of person who would ever consider going through with a pregnancy under such circumstances. She's a bit too much on the self-centered side for that. But it wasn't my business, and I figured that you knew your daughter far better than I did."

Matthew snorted. "I thought I did," he muttered. "But it seems like I didn't know her at all. And I'll admit to having plenty of my own doubts about her, especially as the weeks went on and she acted like nothing had ever happened. I guess I just didn't want to face up to the possibility that my own child - the little girl who used to idolize me and follow me everywhere - could do something so despicable. It isn't a very good feeling to realize how wrong you were about someone."

He looked so sad, sounded so dispirited, that the instinct to offer him comfort took over. She wrapped her arms around his waist, resting her head on his chest, and whispered simply, "I'm sorry."

Matthew's arms tightened around her like a vise, squeezing her so tight she had to gasp for breath until he loosened his hold a bit. He buried his face against the side of her neck, not speaking, but she could feel the desperation in his embrace, sense the loneliness and sorrow he'd been feeling, and she willingly, silently, offered him the comfort he so badly needed.

"God, I've missed you," he rasped in her ear. "So damned much, Sasha. Not one day has gone by that I didn't regret what I'd done, that I didn't wish I was back with you. I haven't had one truly happy day since the last time we were together, and I'd more or less given up on ever being happy again. But I knew I couldn't come back to you, couldn't try to win you back, until I was finally free of Lindsey. And now I can truthfully say that I'm a free man. And that I'm bound and determined to get you back, no matter what I have to do. Please, please tell me that it's not too late."

"Matthew." She eased herself away from him, feeling overwhelmed all of a sudden by his nearness and his passionate declaration. "I - I can't tell you something like that right now. I mean, you've taken me by complete surprise here, and this is the very last thing I expected to hear today. You need to give me some time to absorb all of it, to think everything out. These last few months have been awful for me, too, you know. And while it's good news that your divorce is finally going to happen, at the same time you can't just expect me to forget everything you've put me through. I need some space to deal with this, to think it over. And to decide if being with you is really what's best for me."

Matthew cupped her cheek in his hand, his gaze both shocked and pleading. "Sasha, you don't mean that. Look, I didn't expect that you'd just welcome me with open arms. I know how much I hurt you, how much I put you through even before I moved back to Hillsborough. But don't shut me out, please? Give me a chance to make it all up to you, to show you how much you mean to me. I've never loved anyone the way I love you, never felt like I belonged with someone like I do with you. And I always thought you felt the same way."

"I did. I do," she corrected. "And it's not my feelings for you that are the issue now. And what's happened these past few months isn't even my main concern. I'm - well, frankly, I'm just not sure that I'm cut out for a long-term relationship. With anyone. You and I never really had the opportunity to discuss what happened to me back in high school, considering that I sort of sprung the news on you as I was walking out of the condo."

"You're right. We didn't," he agreed somberly. "And while I understand how traumatic that must have been, you should have told me long before that day. I thought we were closer than that, Sasha. I for one feel closer to you than I have to anyone else in my life. I suppose it isn't the same for you, though."

"It's not that," she was quick to assure him. "And I did wind up telling you eventually. You know something about me that only one other person in the world knows, something not even my parents know. I'd say that speaks volumes about the extent of my trust in you, Matthew. I'm sorry I didn't tell you before that day, but talking about what happened - about Riley - just wasn't something I did. I tried so hard for so many years to just forget what had happened, to suppress the bad memories, that even for you I couldn't bear to dredge them up again. I don't expect you to understand, but I also never intentionally tried to hide the truth, either."

"I get that," replied Matthew gently. "But I'm not sure where you're going with this, Sasha. You were telling me that you didn't think a long-term relationship was your thing. Are you trying to say that what that fucktard Riley did to you has messed you up in some way?"

"Maybe," she whispered uncertainly. "What he did certainly made it hard for me to trust anyone. He betrayed my trust in the worst possible way, stole my innocence, and made it all but impossible for me to feel comfortable in a relationship for very long. But it's more than that, Matthew. I mean, look at my life, the way I was raised. My parents would flit in and out of each other's lives several times a year, never staying faithful to the other for very long. It's not like I've had a great example to follow, you know. Or had the chance to see what a committed, meaningful relationship is supposed to look like. Maybe I'm destined to be like the two

438

of them - never settling down, never making a permanent commitment to someone. I'm not sure I'd be very good at it. And after what you've gone through with Lindsey these past years, you deserve someone who can give you that sort of promise and devotion. I just don't know if that person is me."

"Well, I sure as hell do!" declared Matthew fiercely, yanking her back into his embrace. "I think I knew when we spoke for the first time at Ian and Tessa's wedding that you were this incredibly unique and special person. And I wished then that I had someone like you in my life. Someone who'd show me kindness and compassion and just love me for who I am, and not for the material things I could give them. And you don't have to make a commitment to me, Sasha. I won't ask you for that, won't pressure you into any sort of permanent relationship. Even though you were on the brink of moving in with me before I screwed everything up. That offer still stands, by the way. Except that we'd have an additional roommate."

At her inquiring look, he explained that he'd insisted on getting custody of Casey, and that his son would be living and going to school in San Francisco now.

Sasha smiled fondly. "I'm so pleased for both of you," she told him earnestly. "He's a wonderful young man, so kind and genuine. Just like his father. He, um, has kept in touch with me over these past few months. I hope that's all right with you."

"Of course it is. And I already knew that the two of you were in contact with each other. Though I asked him not to say anything about these new developments to you, since I wanted to be the one to tell you."

439

She nodded. "I was sort of wondering why I hadn't heard from him, but figured he was just busy. And, well, if I ever decide to revisit the idea of moving in with you, having Casey there would just be a bonus."

Matthew looked relieved. "I figured that you'd feel that way. And Casey is probably the most self-sufficient kid you could ever want. He's actually cooked dinner for me these last few nights, gone to the grocery store by himself, did the laundry. Having him with me has been a joy. And having you move in would make both of us very, very happy. Casey said to tell you that, by the way."

"Tell him thank you. And I'll think it over, I promise. But I honestly don't know if I'm capable of making that sort of commitment now, Matthew. I realize that I was ready before all of this drama happened with Hayley. But now - well, as you may have surmised, it's difficult for me to trust people. And - "

"And I broke that trust," he finished sadly. "I broke your heart. But I'll do whatever I have to do in order to convince you that will never happen again, Sasha. It's why I just showed you those divorce papers. Lindsey is out of my life for good. And my relationship with Hayley is going to need some serious repair work. She needs to regain *my* trust, needs to prove to me that she can be responsible and honest. Most importantly, she needs to accept that you're a part of my life and that I will never, ever allow her to treat you rudely again."

Sasha hesitated for long seconds before replying. Matthew was swiftly starting to break down all of the defenses she'd erected around herself these past few months, telling her all of the things she'd longed for him to say, and tempting her to simply say yes. But old habits tended to die hard, and she needed time - and space - to ponder everything she'd just learned.

"I can't give you an answer right now," she stated with determination. "I need to think about all of this, meditate on it, work through it in my own way. So, please. Give me the room I need, all right?"

Matthew looked as though he was about to argue the matter further, but then gave a weary sigh and raked a hand through his hair instead. "All right," he consented reluctantly. "I know I screwed up big time, and that I'll have to win your trust back. If it makes any difference to your decision, I'm planning to look for a new home here in the city. Someplace in a residential neighborhood, maybe closer to Casey's school. I realize the condo doesn't have much personality, and that you've never really liked the place. I feel the same, by the way."

"I'm glad to hear that. And whether or not it sways my decision, I think it's the best thing for you and Casey. A chance to make a fresh start."

He gripped her almost desperately by the biceps. "A chance for all of us to make a fresh start," he reminded her. "Please give me that chance, Sasha. Please. I've been so lost without you, so unhappy. These past few months have been the worst of my life, and I know it's all my fault. Let me make it up to you, sweetheart. I'll get on my knees and beg if I have to."

Sasha shook her head, clasping his face between her palms. "No, Matthew. Don't ever do something like that. I have no desire to punish you, and there's nothing to make up. You had what you believed was an impossible choice

441

to make, and I don't blame you for wanting to take care of your daughter. If there's anyone to blame, it's your ex. And it sounds like you've already made her pay the price, in more ways than one."

Matthew pressed a kiss to her forehead. "I'll give you the time you need," he promised. "So long as you promise that you'll at least consider coming back to me."

"Yes. I promise. I don't know how long it will take me to decide, or what my ultimate decision might be. But I do promise to think about it and - mmm!"

He cut off what she was about to say next by kissing her long and hard, walking her backwards until she was pressed up against the wall. He kissed her with a hunger that spoke of desperation, as though he could coax the answer he wanted from her that way. Sasha groaned beneath the pressure of his mouth on hers, the way his tongue parted her lips and tangled with hers. She had missed him, too, missed the intimacy they had shared both in and out of the bedroom, missed being held in his arms this way. For a few precious minutes she let herself forget everything that had happened, that he had chosen to walk away from her, and all of the heartbreak that had ensued following his departure. For now she kissed him back fervently, letting her hands rove over his shoulders and back, then slide down to caress his buttocks. She didn't resist when his hand cupped her breast, his thumb teasing the rock hard nipple. And she offered no protest when he hooked her leg around his waist, allowing the swell of his cock to rub against the notch of her thighs.

Matthew's lips traveled down the side of her neck, then back up to her ear, where he muttered hoarsely, "God, I want you! Feel what you do to me, Sasha, how crazy I am for you. Please, sweetheart. Please. It's been so long, not since that last night at the condo. Let me love you."

His hand cupped her between her legs, his thumb rubbing against her clit through the thin cotton fabric of her yoga pants. Sasha gasped, well aware that she was perilously close to coming right then and there, and she swiftly took hold of his wrist, pulling it a few inches away from her overly sensitized body.

"No," she gasped raggedly. "Not here. And definitely not now. You promised me space, Matthew. You promised me time. Please don't pressure me. And especially not with sex."

He was breathing heavily as he reluctantly stepped away from her, his forehead and upper lip damp with sweat. "I'm sorry," he muttered. "You're right, I'm not being fair. I - it's just that I want you so damned much, Sasha. I've dreamed of you, ached for you. But hard as it is – as hard as I am right now - I'll leave you alone. At least until you have an answer for me. But don't ask me to give up hope, Sasha. Or to stop loving you. Because neither of those things is ever going to happen."

Matthew gave her one last, hungry kiss before he practically ran out of the room, as though he didn't trust himself to remain locked inside with her one minute longer.

Sasha slumped against the wall, too shaken by what had just happened to think straight for a minute or two. It was only a quick glance at the wall clock that set her in motion, realizing that her massage client would be arriving in less than ten minutes. Fortunately, the room was more or less ready, and she would have a few more precious minutes to compose herself.

But she found it nearly impossible to concentrate over the course of the day, and chastised herself for booking so many appointments today. She'd been doing that a lot lately, loading up her schedule with massage appointments and substitute teaching other yoga classes. She had even agreed to temporarily teach a class on Friday mornings – the one day of the week she had always insisted on having off – while the regular teacher was recovering from a badly sprained ankle. Keeping as busy as possible had been one of the ways she had tried - mostly without success - to cope with her loneliness and sorrow these past few months.

It was late afternoon before she had a break, taking a few minutes to drink some water and eat a snack of almond butter and apple slices. Sasha took out her phone, the one Matthew had given her last Christmas, and scrolled through the somewhat scant list of contacts stored there. She felt the overwhelming need to talk to someone about what had happened earlier with Matthew, to ask their advice about what to do next.

She immediately eliminated her mother, since Katya would insist that she spit in Matthew's face and tell him to go to hell. And knowing how busy Julia was with her twins, Sasha didn't feel right bothering her. Tessa would provide a good sounding board, though Sasha hesitated to call her, knowing that she and Ian were close to Matthew. The last thing Sasha wanted to do was make Tessa take sides.

Instead, she called Linda, the one person she knew could be counted on to give practical, sound advice. Linda had always been there for Sasha, especially during the most turbulent times of her life, and today definitely fell into that category.

Her aunt was delighted to hear from Sasha, if a bit surprised. After her trip to Sedona, the one Sasha had regretfully declined to join her on, Linda had headed to New Mexico to visit family, and was staying with her sister in Taos for a few more days.

"So what gives, niná?" inquired Linda. "I know you wouldn't be calling me here unless there was something wrong."

Sasha sighed. "I never could fool you when something was bothering me. Guess that hasn't changed, huh? Matthew came to see me today, Tia. With signed and notarized divorce papers in hand."

"Ah." Linda's tone of voice indicated she now knew exactly why Sasha had called. "And he wants you back, of course. But you're hesitating. Why?"

Sasha told her all of it - how Hayley and Lindsey had devised their elaborate hoax, then how Casey had found out about the ruse and told his father; how Matthew hadn't hesitated to turn the tables and use Lindsey's deception against her as leverage to finally get his divorce; and how Matthew had offered to get on his knees and beg Sasha to return to him.

Linda chuckled. "You should have taken him up on his offer, Sasha. At least to see if he would have really done it."

"You know I don't have it in me to be vindictive that way, Tia," admonished Sasha. "As it was, I was awfully hard on him. But not for the sake of being mean. I honestly, truly don't know if I'm ready for a relationship like that."

445

"You were ready a few months ago," chided Linda. "You were all set to move in with him, take the next step in your relationship. And then all hell broke loose with his daughter. Matthew must be so hurt by what she did."

"Yes. Hurt and disappointed. It's going to take some time for the two of them to rebuild their relationship. But he's a good father, and loves both of his children very much. Eventually he and Hayley will make their peace and figure out where they go from here."

"In the meanwhile, where are *you* and Matthew going from here?" asked Linda pointedly. "And what's your real reason for holding back, niná? Is it because you're that pissed off at him, or are you just afraid of getting hurt again?"

Sasha shut her eyes, gently massaging her temple. "Maybe a little of both," she admitted. "Though more the latter than the former. It's hard to stay angry at Matthew for very long, you know. Especially since seeing him today made me realize how much I still love him."

"Then I fail to see the problem, Sasha. If you love the man, then go be with him. Have some trust in your love, and in human nature. I know that what happened to you back in high school made it almost impossible for you to trust people. But not everyone is a rotten louse like that family. By the way, I understand additional charges have been filed against Riley. Seems like you weren't his only victim, and now that his parents can't protect him and get charges dismissed, some of those other women are coming out of the shadows and speaking up. He'll be in jail for decades."

Sasha knew she should have felt a sense of satisfaction, or relief, but instead she just felt numb at hearing this news.

"It's what he deserves," was all she said in response.

"Yes, it most assuredly is," stated Linda. "Just like you and Matthew deserve to be happy. Together. Both of you have had your share of bad times, but it doesn't have to be that way anymore. He's a good man, Sasha, and he's crazy about you. So open your heart to him, hmm? And don't allow what happened more than a dozen years ago to keep controlling your life. It's time to move on, niná, and you'll never find anyone better than Matthew to do that with."

Linda's parting words kept repeating themselves in Sasha's head for the rest of the evening, and she knew deep down that it was perhaps the purest truth she'd ever heard. But despite that realization, she was still no closer to making a decision then she'd been earlier today.

chapter twenty-three

SASHA COULD FEEL THE SLIGHT trembling in her biceps as she continued to hold the challenging *eka pada galavasana* or flying pigeon pose. The advanced arm balance posture called for her to bend one leg at an angle, then rest the shin on her triceps, before lifting the other leg off the floor. It required both arm and core strength, as well as tremendous concentration. She held the pose for long seconds before gracefully dismounting and stepping back into downward dog.

She had been so focused on holding the pose that she hadn't heard the door to the small studio opening, and it wasn't until someone began applauding that she realized she wasn't alone. A bit annoyed at this interruption, she glanced sideways to see Willow hovering in the doorway.

"Sorry for staring," the front desk clerk offered cheerily. "but that was truly amazing to watch. I'm not sure any of the other teachers here can even attempt something like that."

Sasha sighed, and slowly rolled up to a standing position. "Flying pigeon isn't as difficult as it looks, it just requires a lot of focus. What's up?"

Willow offered up an apologetic smile. "Sorry to interrupt you, I know how involved you get when you're practicing alone. But there's someone asking for you up front, and I thought you'd like to know."

Sasha frowned. "A massage client? I don't have any appointments for at least a couple of hours."

"Nope, definitely not a client. He's, um, younger than most of your clients or students. And definitely a cutie. Want me to send him on back?"

Sasha grabbed a towel and began to blot the sweat off her face and upper chest. "No, that's okay. Just give me a minute to grab my things and I'll be right up."

Willow gave her a thumbs up, then headed back towards the front desk. Sasha quickly turned off the music before dropping her phone into her bag, then grabbed her towel and water bottle. She had stashed her sweater and shoes back in the massage room prior to her class this morning, and padded on bare feet up towards the lobby area, puzzled as to who her mystery visitor might be.

Casey was grinning broadly as he watched her approach, waving a hand in greeting. "Hi, Sasha! Thought I'd surprise you."

She deposited her things on one of the chairs in the lobby before enfolding Matthew's son in a hug. "Well, mission accomplished - I'm surprised. Also a little on the sweaty side. Sorry."

"It's okay." Casey hugged her back enthusiastically. "And you don't sweat nearly as much as I do after a baseball game."

Sasha smiled at him fondly. "Well, you haven't seen me after a two hour class held in a ninety-five degree room. Now, to what do I owe this very nice surprise? Shouldn't you be in school?"

He shook his head. "School doesn't start until next Wednesday, so I have a few more days of summer break. I'm sorry I haven't been by to see you until now, or even emailed you. But things have been sort of crazy, you know?"

"I do, yes. Your father came by to see me earlier this week to let me know what's been going on. I don't suppose your visit today has anything to do with that?" she inquired knowingly.

Casey looked adorably guilty, and so much like his father that Sasha's heart ached just a bit at the sight. "Um, maybe," he demurred, looking down awkwardly at his feet. "I mean, I wanted to see you, too, of course. But, well, do you think maybe we could talk for a few minutes? I could buy you some tea. Or lunch, whatever you like. My treat, of course."

"I think that sounds like the best offer I've had all week," she replied teasingly. "Let me grab my things and we can head out."

As Sasha retrieved her sweater and flip-flops from the massage room, she couldn't help but be a little suspicious as to the timing of Casey's impromptu visit. She didn't want to believe that Matthew had been the brains behind this, and that he had encouraged his son to try and persuade Sasha into coming back to him. Matthew had acted desperate enough a few days ago to use any means necessary to change her mind, but given what had just happened with Hayley and Lindsey, she didn't think he would copy a page from their book and coerce his son to help him out.

As she re-joined Casey in the lobby, Sasha realized with some surprise that she was actually hungry. She and Tessa often had a light breakfast together after these morning

450

classes, but Tessa was busy with her last minute packing for Italy and hadn't been able to stay after class today. Sasha had worked up something of an appetite during her own intense practice, and ordered a grilled vegetable panini and a bowl of tomato soup at the little café she'd suggested to Casey. Being the typical teenaged boy he was, Casey's meal was nowhere near as healthy as hers – a towering mushroom and Swiss burger accompanied by a huge plate of fries.

He grinned at her as he unapologetically dunked a fry in ketchup. "I hope it doesn't gross you out to look at this. I mean, I know you don't eat meat or junk food."

She shook her head as she reached for her glass of iced herbal tea. "It's fine, Casey. I don't expect everyone to eat the same sort of diet I do. Though from something your father said the other day, it sounds like he's reverted back to his unhealthy eating habits."

"Yeah, maybe a little," admitted Casey. "And that's just one of the reasons you really, really need to take him back, Sasha."

"Ah." Sasha regarded him with a half-smile. "I was wondering how long it would take you to get around to that particular subject. I mean, there was only so long we could discuss your new school and what team you think is going to win the World Series - whatever that is. Should I assume your father doesn't know you came to see me today?"

"Dad has no idea I'm here," assured Casey. "And if I had even mentioned the idea to him, I'm guessing he would have told me no."

She took a bite of her sandwich. "And yet here you are," she pointed out.

"Yeah." Casey sighed and sipped his Coke through a straw. "Dad - well, he's been through a lot these past few months. Actually, make that these past few years. Even before he and Mom broke up I could tell he wasn't happy. He works so hard, and has so much responsibility at his job. And he always felt guilty that he couldn't spend enough time with me and Hayley. Mom nagged at him all the time about that, like it was totally his fault, and she wasn't very nice to him. And then, well, I guess you know about all of her, uh, boyfriends."

Sasha arched a brow in surprise. "Your father might have mentioned something about that," she replied carefully. "But what do you know, Casey?"

He shrugged casually. "Enough. I mean, I don't know any details or names or anything gross like that. Eww. But Hayley made some comments about it after Dad moved out. At first I didn't really understand what she was talking about, but after she explained it sort of made sense. Like why Mom wasn't home very often, and liked to go away with her friends on the weekend all the time."

"I'm sorry you had to find that out," Sasha consoled him. "Hayley probably shouldn't have repeated those things to you, especially since you're only fourteen."

"It's not a big deal." Casey swallowed a hefty bite of his burger. "I just felt bad for Dad. And knowing about Mom helped me understand why he wanted to get a divorce. I mean, part of being married is making a commitment to the other person, isn't it? I guess my mother stopped taking that commitment seriously."

"Have you spoken to your mother since you moved in

with your dad?"

He nodded at Sasha's question. "Once or twice. She's not very happy with me right now, so we didn't talk very long. Mom sort of blames me for everything that happened, says I shouldn't have been eavesdropping."

Sasha squeezed his hand fiercely. "Do *not* let her blame you for any of this," she insisted. "It's not really any of my business, but she and Hayley should be ashamed of themselves for lying about something as serious as a pregnancy. And for deliberately trying to manipulate Matthew. You did exactly the right thing in telling your father what you overheard, Casey. I'm sure he feels the same way."

"Yeah, pretty much." Casey grinned mischievously. "In fact, he was so grateful for me telling him the truth that he bought me a brand new laptop for school. Top of the line, too, with every feature you can imagine. If you come by the condo for dinner tonight, I'll show it to you."

She smirked at him knowingly. "I like how you just snuck that last part in there, Casey. Very smooth. Unfortunately, I'm not about to fall for it."

"Please, Sasha." Casey had dropped all hint of teasing or pretense, and was about as serious as she'd ever known him to be. "I know you're mad at my father right now, and you should be. But do you think you can please forgive him, and give him another chance? Dad's a really good guy, and I know he's crazy about you. You'd make him so happy if you came back to him."

Sasha shook her head. "It's not that simple," she explained gently. "And there's more involved than what happened a few months ago. I understand why he felt the need to move

453

back into the house, why he wanted to help your sister - even though it turns out she didn't actually need his help. There's – well, part of it has to do with me, Casey. Because of some stuff that happened to me when I was younger, I have a hard time trusting people. And while I know your father is sorry for what happened, it doesn't make it easier for me to trust him again."

"He was really, really unhappy when the two of you split up," Casey blurted out. "About as sad as I've ever seen him. And I started feeling guilty after awhile. Because as great as it was having him back home again, I didn't want my dad to be sad. And he's still not really happy. I mean, he likes having me around, and he's totally relieved to be away from my mom again. But I don't think he'll ever really be happy again unless you come back to him."

She closed her eyes briefly, scolding herself for letting Casey's pleading sway her feelings this way. "Casey, you need to give me some time, okay?" she told him a bit more sternly than she had intended. "It's only been a few days, after all. And it's wonderful that you care about your father so much, he's so lucky to have a son like you to look out for him. But this isn't an easy decision for me to make."

"Why not?" challenged Casey, who was obviously not going to back down quite so easily. "I thought you loved my Dad."

"I do, of course. But there are other things to consider, to - "

"No." Casey gave a stubborn shake of his head. "That should be the only thing to consider. You and Dad love each other. You make him happier than anyone in the whole world. He was miserable without you, hardly ate, didn't sleep, didn't take care of himself. You have to go back to him, Sasha. Please."

"Casey," she protested. "Don't put all of this on me. Please. Of course I love your father, and want the best for him. But I've got myself to consider, too, and what's best for me."

"Dad is the best person in the whole world!" declared Casey. "He'll do anything for you, Sasha. And he needs you so much. Look, my mom wasn't - well, very nice to him. She never did stuff for him or looked after him or took care of him the way you did. He was always trying to make her happy, giving her stuff, and letting her have her way. She made him really, really unhappy, so he deserves someone now who's going to make *him* happy. Please don't put him through this. My dad deserves to be happy more than anyone I've ever met. And being with you makes him happier than anything."

Sasha sighed, holding up her hands in silent surrender. "You've made your point, Casey. And believe me, no one wants your father's happiness more than I do. Matthew is the most wonderful, amazing man I've ever known, and the months we were together were the happiest I've ever been. It's just - I just need a little more time to be sure."

"You don't have to make a decision yet," coaxed Casey. "Just come over tonight and have dinner with us. Seven o'clock. I'll tell the concierge that you're coming over so he can send you right up. Look, you don't have to give me an answer now, okay? Think about it this afternoon. But seeing you would make my dad smile again. And he hasn't been doing much of that lately."

She scowled at him. "You really have the art of the guilt trip down, don't you? I'll think about it, Casey. That's all I can promise."

455

He grinned as though it was his birthday, Christmas, and a trip to Disneyland combined. "You'll be there. I can tell. You can't stand the thought of hurting someone's feelings or knowing that they're sad. And my dad is so, so sad without you, so - "

Sasha placed a hand over his mouth. "Okay. Quit while you're ahead, kid. Now, no more trying to con me into coming over. Let's finish our lunch, and I'll consider your invitation this afternoon."

Casey obeyed, but he seemed entirely too pleased with himself for Sasha's liking. He abided by her wishes, though, and didn't bring the subject of Matthew up again, even when they went their separate ways after lunch.

Once again, Matthew was all she could think about that afternoon during two massage appointments, and then while she was running errands. She put away the groceries and other things she'd bought, then started a load of laundry. The big, multi-storied house was empty, since her other roommates were at work, and for once Sasha wished that Julio was around to give her some unwanted advice. She wondered if Tessa's flight to Italy had taken off yet, if there was still time to give her a quick call. She mused the wisdom of calling Linda for the second time in five days, since she already knew her aunt would urge her to go to Matthew. She was almost desperate enough for advice to call her mother, even though she would regret that move as soon as she made it.

But Sasha knew that this was a decision only she could make. No amount of advice or opinions from her family or friends - not even Casey's appealing pleas - could make it for her. She was going to have to do some intense soul searching, and do it fast, since seven o'clock was quickly approaching.

MATTHEW EYED HIS SON WITH mingled curiosity and concern. "You okay there, buddy? You're acting kind of weird tonight, almost like you're worried about something."

Casey laughed nervously. "Um, no. Everything's okay, Dad. I'm just anxious for the food to get here is all. As usual, I'm starving."

Matthew shrugged, even though he was far from convinced that all was well. "Whatever you say. The food should be here any minute. And if you're that hungry there should be plenty of snacks in the kitchen."

Casey shook his head, and resumed pacing around the living room, as he'd been doing on and off for the last twenty minutes or so. "I'm good. I don't want to spoil my appetite for the pizza. You know that Amici's is my favorite."

"Yeah, I know. Though ordering two extra larges plus a medium might be overkill, even for you," joked Matthew.

Casey gave another nervous laugh. "Leftovers. Pizza always tastes better the next day."

Matthew rolled his eyes. "You're going to have enough leftovers for about three days. And what's with ordering a Margherita? You usually only eat pizzas with meat, meat, and more meat on top, not tomatoes and cheese."

"Just sounded good for a change. Oh, cool. Sounds like it's finally here."

Casey practically flew across the room at the peal of the

doorbell, leaving Matthew to chuckle at just how hungry his son must be. It had been wonderful to have Casey living here with him, a dream come true to be together again. Matthew reflected on just how much his life had changed in a scant two weeks - his long-contested divorce from Lindsey was finally going to happen; he had permanent custody of his son, something he should have fought for from the start; and he'd begun to make discreet inquiries about the possibility of selling his company. There was only one more thing - correction, one more *person* - who was missing from the picture in order to make his happiness complete. He knew he had to be patient, to give Sasha the time she'd begged for, but it was hard, so damned hard, when all he wanted was to have her by his side, to hear her soft, sweet voice say his name.

"Hello, Matthew. I hope you don't mind my joining you this evening. But, well, I was invited, after all."

Astonished, his gaze flew in the direction of that voice, and his heart immediately starting beating double time when he saw Sasha standing just inside the entryway. Her multi-hued hair curled riotously about her face, those green-gold eyes sparkling with silent mischief. She wore a floaty cotton sundress of blues and lavenders, a dress he recognized as one he'd bought for her during that blissful vacation to Kauai. As usual, she'd slipped off her shoes the moment she'd walked through the door, and he wanted to drop to his knees and kiss her bare, dainty feet in adoration and gratitude.

"Sasha. My God, you're really here. How - why?" he asked, vaguely aware that he was babbling.

She smiled, that lovely, warm, serene smile that he'd missed so much. "I told you - I was invited. By your new roommate. Is that all right with you?"

In answer, he surged forward until he was close enough to swoop her into his arms, lifting her up until her feet left the ground. She made a small sound of surprise, but merely looped her arms around his neck, holding on tight as he twirled her around in a circle.

"Do you really have to ask?" he murmured as he carefully set her back down. He gave her a soft, sweet kiss, not daring to do more for fear he wouldn't be able to stop. Then he gave his son an inquiring look. "The pizza order makes more sense now - both the quantity and the vegetarian one."

Casey grinned. "I wasn't sure she was going to show up, you know. Though I did my best to convince her at lunch today. Guess my guilt tripping worked, huh?"

Sasha rumpled his hair playfully. "It didn't hurt, kid. But in the end I just decided to follow my heart. And it led me here, to the person I was always meant to be with."

Matthew looked from Casey to Sasha and then back again, a perplexed expression on his face. "Sounds like this is going to be a very interesting dinner conversation. Speaking of which, that must be the pizza."

Casey waved him off, and went to answer the door for the second time in as many minutes, leaving Matthew to turn to Sasha, cupping her cheek tenderly.

"Does this mean you're back for good?" he asked urgently. "That you've decided to give me another chance?"

She gave a quick but decisive nod. "Yes, that's exactly what it means," she whispered. "We have a lot to talk about,

Matthew, but at least I'm willing to start the conversation."

"Thank God." He gave her another fast, hard squeeze before taking her by the hand and leading her over to the dining room table.

Matthew intentionally kept the conversation lighthearted and casual during dinner, a fact that Sasha seemed grateful for. As usual, she proved to be a good listener, especially when it came to Casey. Matthew didn't miss the way his son's face lit up with pleasure when Sasha demonstrated a real interest in his stories, asking him specific questions that indicated she'd been paying close attention to what he'd said. Lindsey had always been too wrapped up in her own selfish agenda to bother much with either of her children, though at least she and Hayley had had more in common - fashion, makeup, celebrity gossip. For the life of him, Matthew couldn't imagine his ex listening patiently as Casey almost giddily described the new school he would be attending, and what classes he would be taking. The thought occurred to him that Sasha, who'd yet to have children, had far more of a maternal instinct than Lindsey, the mother of two teenagers.

He refilled her wine glass, causing her to glance up and meet his gaze. She smiled her thanks, picking up the glass of her favorite pinot noir, and taking a small sip. They had yet to discuss anything personal, or have even a minute just to themselves, and still every time their eyes met it felt like a caress, a promise of what was yet to come this evening.

Fortunately, Casey seemed well aware of his father's need to be alone with Sasha, and after dinner he tactfully retreated to his room, claiming that he was scheduled to play *League of Legends* with a group of his friends. Matthew typically didn't encourage him to indulge in online video games, but he was more than happy to send Casey on his way this particular evening.

While he and Casey had been clearing off the dining table, both insisting that Sasha didn't lift a finger, she had taken the opportunity to slip out to the balcony. It was where Matthew found her a few minutes later, her curls being gently tossed by the late summer evening breeze as she leaned over the railing.

"I've missed this view," she murmured as he came to stand beside her. "It's the condo's best feature, in my opinion."

He smiled. "I agree. And it will be tough to find a comparable view from the houses I've started to consider."

Sasha turned to look at him, her expression definitely interested. "You're really serious about this, aren't you? About moving out of this place and into a real home for Casey."

"Yep. Ian gave me the name of the realtor he used when he first moved to San Francisco, and I hope to start looking at some places next week. And while those places may not be able to offer a view like this one, they'll have plenty of other features to make up for it. Including a much larger space where you'll be able to do your yoga practice. *And* a separate massage room."

She couldn't hide her delight at this pronouncement. "Really? It sounds like you're looking for an awfully big place."

He shrugged. "Nowhere near as big and impersonal as the house in Hillsborough. But maybe somewhere along the lines of Ian and Tessa's place. In fact, the realtor tells me there are several homes for sale within a few blocks of their house. Would you like that, Sasha - to live so close to your friends?"

"Of course," she replied easily. "But you should be more concerned with what Casey is going to be happy with. After all, this is mostly for his sake."

"Not entirely," corrected Matthew. "Granted, the neighborhood is less than a ten minute drive from his new school, and there's a park and shops and restaurants nearby. But Casey will be off to college himself in four years, so there's more to consider than just his feelings. Besides, he's such an easy kid that he'd be happy living most anywhere. As for me - well, anyplace that makes you happy, Sasha, is where I'd want to live."

She gave a slight shake of her head. "Don't make this about me, Matthew. My feelings shouldn't factor into a decision like this."

"Why?" he inquired lazily. "It's going to be your home just as much as mine or Casey's. In fact, I insist that you come along with us when the realtor shows us some properties next week. If you're going to live there, it should be a place that you feel you can be happy in. Besides, aren't there certain vibes that a house gives off? The kind that tell you if you're going to like it there. I was sort of hoping that your gift of sensing auras might help when it comes time to buy a home."

Sasha regarded him with a quirk of her brow. "What you're describing sounds more like *feng shui* to me, something I definitely have no background in." She grew silent then, turning back to look out at the city skyline. "And I haven't made a decision yet about moving in with you, Matthew. I'm willing to take the first step, to try and work things out. But that doesn't mean I'm going to pack up my things and move in overnight."

He gave a sigh of resignation. "Yeah, I sort of figured that might be the case. But I'm more than willing to take things slow if that's what you need. And I'm just grateful and happy to have you with me no matter what the terms."

"Thank you," she told him, leaning her head on his shoulder. "I need stability in my life, Matthew, need things to be calm. And that is definitely a holdover from my childhood, when nothing was stable or remained the same for very long. So I need some time now to make sure that my whole world isn't going to be torn apart again."

His arm went about her shoulders, hugging her close against his body. "Take all the time you need," he whispered. "Just as long as I can be part of your life in some way. But I still want you opinion about the new house - you know, just in case you decide to move in someday."

"Okay." Sasha grinned up at him. "That actually sounds like fun. As you know, I've never really had a home of my own, just Linda's place and for a few years a little apartment I lived in with my mom in New York City. I'm not sure I'd know what to do with so much space."

"It doesn't have to be as big as Ian and Tessa's place," he assured her. "In fact, I'd like something smaller and cozier myself. Just as long as it has character and feels like a real home - not like the mansion down in Hillsborough, and definitely not like this condo. Besides, living here in the condo won't be an option for much longer."

"Is the company thinking of selling it?" asked Sasha.

He shook his head. "No, I would imagine given its location it will be a valuable asset to whoever buys the company. I - I haven't told anyone else, just the attorney who's begun to look into the matter for me. But I'm dead serious about getting out, Sasha. I don't want to spend even one more year working my ass off and not enjoying the benefits of all that hard work. I fully intend to sell MBI as soon as possible, and spend a lot more time with you and my kids and on myself. God knows I have enough money to live on for more than ten lifetimes, so that certainly isn't an issue. And I'll probably do some consulting work or public speaking now and then. But my first priority is going to be focusing on the things that mean the most to me - and you're at the very top of that list."

Her eyes shimmered with happy tears as she impulsively flung her arms around his waist. "That's wonderful news!" she exclaimed. "You've worked so hard for so many years, Matthew, that you deserve a break. And if you do feel the need to go back to work someday, it will be on your terms, and doing what makes you happy. Maybe you'll even have time to start doing yoga."

He grinned at her teasing comment. "I'd have to start with the Yoga for Inflexible People class. And I know for a fact that I'd never, ever be able to attempt some of those crazy poses you can do. But I'm looking forward to doing a whole lot of things I never have time for. Though I'm afraid all of that will have to wait awhile. Even after my attorney finds a suitable buyer for the company, there'll be months of negotiations and contracts and other legalities before I'm officially unemployed."

"At least it's a start," she replied encouragingly. Then, more soberly, she asked, "Was this the same attorney who uncovered all the details on the Cullens?"

"No. That would have been the firm of private investigators I use for various purposes. The same PI's who spent over two years following Lindsey and her legion of lovers around. They're discreet, efficient, and know exactly where to look for useful information. They had the dirt on the Cullens in less than seventy two hours. After that it was just a matter of alerting the proper authorities about what they'd found out, and the rest just unfolded on its own."

Sasha nodded, seeming to be satisfied with that explanation. "Okay. And while I've never considered myself a vengeful person, always believed it was better to forgive and forget, I'm glad that Riley in particular is finally going to pay the price for what he did. Maybe that makes me a bad person, but for once I don't seem to care very much."

Matthew rubbed her back soothingly as she rested her cheek against his shoulder. "It makes you human, Sasha," he corrected. "And hopefully it also gives you some satisfaction, some sense of closure. There was no possible way I was going to let that bastard get away with what he'd done. I didn't give a damn that it was a dozen years ago. What he did was still bothering you, still having a negative effect on your life. It needed to be dealt with, and he needed to be brought to justice. So, it's over and done with now, and you don't need to think about it ever again. Okay?"

"Yes." She brushed her lips against his stubbled cheek. "Thank you, Matthew. For giving me that peace of mind that's eluded me for so long. And for being so protective. I'm not really used to that, you know."

He gave a low growl, already highly aroused at being this close to her, and her sweet kiss only stoked the fires that had been building in his lower body all evening. "Well, get used to it, sweetheart," he warned her. "I know you've got this independent streak a mile long, but I fully intend to take care of you in every possible way from now on."

"Speaking of taking care of things," she whispered naughtily. Her hand slid down past his belly, then gently palmed his rigid cock. "It sure feels like it's been a very long time since you, ah, took care of this."

"Jesus." Matthew's head fell back helplessly as she began to stroke him persuasively through his jeans. "A really long time. Like, ah, M-May. The - the last time you and I were together."

Sasha pressed her small, firm breasts against his chest, her teeth nipping teasingly at his earlobe. "Then you and Lindsey - you weren't tempted even a little?"

"Hell, no!" he bellowed. "To even think of touching that slut turns my stomach. And being with *any* other woman after what you and I had together, Sasha - well, that's just sacrilegious, blasphemous. I would have spent the rest of my life alone if I couldn't have you, sweetheart."

She kissed him, a long, searching kiss that he quickly took control of. She gasped beneath his lips as he picked her up easily, then carried her back into the condo and straight to the master bedroom. He wanted to ask if it had been the same for her - if there had been no other men during the months they'd been apart. But he quickly forgot what it was he'd wanted to say, forgot pretty much anything except maybe his own name, as she pulled the floaty, feminine cotton dress up over her head, and stood in the middle of the bedroom clad in just a bra and panty set of dainty blue lace.

Her pale golden skin fairly glowed in the dimly lit bedroom, just a small corner lamp providing a bit of illumination. She was as slender and graceful as ever, looking every bit like the dancer she had once been, and she was so exquisite that this time he did give in to his instincts and knelt at her feet. Sasha made a sound of surprise as he wrapped his arms around her upper thighs, resting his head on her stomach. Her hands drifted up to tenderly stroke the back of his neck.

"I just want to hold on tight," he confessed. "Tight enough that you can never leave me again. Being without you these last few months has been the worst time of my life, Sasha. Please, please say you'll stay. And especially tonight. I can't remember ever wanting anything this badly, or needing someone like I need you now."

"Matthew, I…"

But whatever she might have been about to say was pre-empted when he yanked her panties down past her ankles, then promptly buried his face between her thighs. Their groans of pleasure rose up simultaneously in the room, and Matthew had just enough presence of mind left to glance over and make sure he'd shut the door firmly behind them. And then his only focus was on Sasha, making sure he gave her every pleasure, took care of her every need, using his lips and tongue and fingers in that endeavor. He lavished attention on her, practically worshipped her body, until she was panting and crying out, desperately seeking release.

"Please," she begged in a husky voice. "Inside of me, Matthew. Please. I want it to be mutual. I want it to be powerful. I want *you*."

They fell on the bed together, a tangle of limbs and lips, breaking apart only long enough to pull the clothes from their bodies, until their naked forms were fused as one. Matthew cursed loudly and vividly as she took firm hold of his cock and guided him inside her, then swiftly wrapped her legs around his waist, urging him to go even deeper.

"Ah, God," he rasped, each thrust of his cock inside of her hot, wet pussy more forceful, more determined than the one just before. "God, I've missed this, missed you! Nothing has ever felt this right before, Sasha, never felt this perfect."

She pulled his head down to hers, silencing him with another deep, searching kiss. She spoke to him instead with her body, her back arching off the mattress to meet each thrust, her hands sliding down his back to grasp his ass. She urged him on wordlessly, their lovemaking becoming increasingly frantic, and nearly out of control, until he felt the inner muscles of her vagina begin to spasm around his cock. The start of her orgasm in turn triggered his, and despite his resolve to make this first time back with her last, he lost complete control, lost himself as he came more powerfully than he ever had before. His entire body shook as he emptied himself inside of Sasha's tight, welcoming body, hard enough that the headboard slammed up against the wall noisily.

He collapsed on top of her much smaller, slighter body afterwards, so dazed by what had just happened that he wasn't even aware of his actions. It was only when she began to wiggle out from under him, gently easing him off of her, that he groaned and quickly rolled to his side.

"Sorry," he mumbled, reaching out an arm to tug her in close. "I didn't hurt you, did I?"

"Of course not," she assured him, her index finger tracing over his lips. "But I might have come up with a suggestion for this new house you're planning to buy."

"Oh?" He propped himself up on an elbow, gazing down at her with interest. He took it as a very, very good sign that she was voluntarily bringing up the subject of house hunting. "What might that be? A swimming pool? Sauna? Herb garden?"

Sasha laughed. "Not that all three of those things don't sound amazing, of course, but what I was really going to suggest was that you make sure the place has excellent soundproofing. I, ah, think we were pretty loud right now. I just hope we didn't put on a show for Casey a few minutes ago."

"Nah." Matthew waved away her concerns. "First of all, his bedroom is clear on the other side of this place. Second, if he's playing video games online with his buddies I guarantee he's using headphones. Specifically, these very high tech ones with a built-in microphone. And as loud as those games can get, he wouldn't have heard a thing coming from this room. But I get your point. One of the criteria for this new house might be having the master suite on a different floor than the other bedrooms. After all, if I'm going to have all this extra time on my hands after selling the company, I can't think of a better way to spend it than locked away with you in our bedroom."

"Hey, you're not playing fair here," she protested weakly.

469

"You're supposed to be giving me space, letting me figure out if I'm ready to move back in with you, and where we go from here. Instead, you keep tempting me with talk of this veritable dream house, with all these incredible features that I can't even imagine existing in the same place at once. And that's not even counting the way you just made love to me. That was - extraordinary, Matthew. It brought tears to my eyes. And made me ache just a little. Right here."

She picked up his hand and brought it to her heart, which was beating at a pace almost as erratic as his own. He cupped her breast reverently, teasing the small, dark red nipple deliberately.

"That ache you feel?" he whispered, bending his head to brush a kiss over her heart. "That's love, Sasha. I know because I'm feeling exactly the same thing right now. But it's a good ache. One that will always remind us of how much we love each other. And as for not playing fair." He grinned devilishly. "All's fair in love and war, sweetheart. And if I thought for one moment that there was a way I could tempt you into moving in with me, I'd do it in a flash. So tell me. What could I do for you, buy for you, that might sway your decision?"

Sasha pretended to think the question over carefully, tapping her finger on her chin thoughtfully. "Well, as you know, stuff like clothes and jewels and cars don't interest me much. And you've already offered to include a yoga room and a sauna and an herb garden in whatever house you buy. That just leaves one thing, really, that might tempt me into saying yes - a beach house in Kauai," she added jokingly.

Matthew immediately surged to a sitting position, then

grabbed his phone from the nightstand and began tapping out a text.

Sasha regarded him curiously. "Who are you texting?"

He winked at her, his grin nearly splitting his face. "My new realtor. To see if he can find us a place in Kauai as well as here in San Francisco."

She jackknifed to a sitting position, peering over his shoulder at his phone. "Matthew!" she protested, when she glimpsed the text he'd just sent. "I was just teasing, you know. I wasn't serious about buying a place over there."

Matthew set his phone down, then tumbled her back onto the pillows. "I am," he stated firmly. "In fact, I can't think of anything I'm more serious about. Well, except for you, maybe. And I think a second home in Kauai is a fantastic idea. That week we spent there was one of the best times of my life. If we had a place of our own, we could go there whenever we wanted."

Sasha wound her arms around his neck. "As bribes go, that's a pretty extravagant one. Most guys I know would probably start with sending flowers or an expensive dinner or maybe a weekend away somewhere."

He shook his head. "I know that sort of thing doesn't work with you. No, buying a house in the place you said felt like home to you from the first time you stepped off the plane – that's not a bribe, Sasha. It's a promise."

471

epilogue

June — Island of Kauai, Hawaii

"EXACTLY HOW EARLY DID YOU get up this morning? You've obviously been doing yoga down at the beach again, and it's barely seven a.m."

Sasha turned as her husband emerged sleepily from the main house onto the wide, covered verandah where she'd been watching the waves for the last ten minutes. Their home here in the Hanalei Bay area of Kauai afforded them both spectacular views and easy beach access, two of the "must-haves" on their wish list when they'd begun searching for properties.

She gave him a quick kiss as he joined her at the edge of the verandah. "A little after five, I guess. It's hard for me to sleep late at this time of the year since the sun rises so early. And we have a busy day ahead of us, since my parents want to drive down to Poipu today."

Matthew snorted. "If that's your idea of a busy day, then I think we've already spent too much time here. You're starting to think like a Hawaiian after just a couple of weeks."

She grinned. "Come on, admit it. You kind of love that idea, don't you? As far as spending too much time here, you've earned it, Matthew. You could spend the next two years here and not have it be enough time."

He yawned, stretching his arms wide as he lifted his face to the early morning sun. "I won't argue with that idea," he admitted. "Though I suppose Casey will have to go back to school at some point."

She linked her arm through his, resting her head on his bare shoulder. "Well, we have weeks and weeks before that happens. And a pretty long guest list of people visiting us over the next couple of months. So let's enjoy it, hmm?"

Matthew pressed a kiss to her forehead. "I will. I *am*. It's still taking me a little time to get used to the idea that I'm officially unemployed. After all, it's been less than a month."

He had completed the sale of MBI a scant three weeks ago, after months of negotiations and complex paperwork. Matthew's main priority in finding a buyer for the company had been ensuring that all of his employees would remain in their current positions, with zero layoffs or staff reductions. He had also agreed to retain his position on the Board of Directors, as well as take on various consulting projects on occasion.

With Casey still finishing up his freshman year of high school, this was the first opportunity they'd had to get away since the sale of MBI had been finalized, and they had arrived at their beach house in Kauai just three days ago. The beach house that had been Matthew's wedding present to his new wife.

He'd grinned sheepishly upon presenting her with the deed to the house she'd fallen in love with at first sight. "I'll freely admit to having stolen this idea from Ian," he had joked. "He bought that house of theirs on the Sonoma coast for Tessa as a wedding gift. But while this might not be a very original idea, it's a darned good one. Don't you agree?"

Sasha had laughed, hugging the deed against her. "I absolutely agree! I knew the minute I saw this place from the road that it would be the one. And as soon as I walked through the front door I could feel all of the good vibes surrounding us. I know you think it's silly to believe that a house or an object can actually talk to you, but I felt like that place was calling me home." She had kissed him then, her green-gold eyes shining. "I love that house. And I love you for giving it to me. And I already know that we're going to have many, many happy times there."

They had been married in March, on the first day of spring. Sasha had declared it was the perfect time to marry, since the Spring Equinox was a time for rebirth and renewal, and, in Matthew's case, a second chance at love. Their wedding had been a simple affair - at her insistence - with fewer than fifty people in attendance. And despite Katya's attempts to interfere with the plans, the wedding ceremony had been held outdoors, on a Mount Tamalpais ridgeline in Marin County. The weather had been clear and unseasonably balmy, the views breathtaking, and the guests had been regretful when they had been ushered inside the luxury inn for the start of dinner.

Enzo had beamed with pride when he'd given his daughter away, while Katya hadn't been able to stem the flow of tears that trickled down her cheeks. The two of them had been on their best behavior that day, having vowed to get along for once since it was their only child's wedding, and they had thrilled the guests with their dance skills. Polina and Maxim had flown over from Paris, and Enzo's brother Joaquim from Brazil. Linda, too, had called a truce with her undeniably charming ex for the day, and had even danced with him a time or two.

A heavily pregnant Tessa had been Sasha's matron of honor, while Matthew's brother Patrick had handled the duties of best man. The elder Bennetts had been thrilled to welcome Sasha into their family, and Maureen had whispered to her that *this* time they had actually looked forward to seeing their son get married.

All of Sasha's former roommates had been at the wedding, along with several of her co-workers at the yoga studio. A few of Matthew's employees had also been invited, including a beaming Elena. And of course, both of Matthew's children had been there - an overjoyed Casey and a subdued but accepting Hayley.

It had taken months for Matthew to rebuild his frayed relationship with his daughter, the hurt he'd felt at her betrayal long lasting and not easy to forget. Sasha had insisted on giving him time alone with Hayley the first few times they had seen each other, not wanting to push the girl too hard. Gradually, the ice had begun to thaw between father and daughter, to a point where Matthew had felt comfortable enough to include Sasha in their outings.

Sasha had been surprised at the changes in Hayley from the last time they'd met. Hayley had actually been polite, and responded to Sasha's attempts at conversation. The two women still had a ways to go before Sasha would term their relationship friendly, but the hostility and rudeness Hayley had always demonstrated in the past was no longer an issue.

Of course, part of the reason for her change in attitude could be credited to Katya. At Christmas dinner - the first big event that Matthew and Sasha had hosted in their new home in San Francisco - Katya hadn't bothered to hide her displeasure with Hayley's bouts of moodiness and continued obsession with texting and emailing. Katya's admittedly short fuse had reached the end of its rope, and she'd rather loudly reprimanded Hayley right at the dinner table. And while Hayley had been visibly startled at the rebuke, she had rather meekly put her phone aside for the rest of the evening.

Katya had taken Hayley under her wing after that, and it seemed that her particular brand of tough love was exactly what the moody teen needed. By the end of the holiday week, Katya had Hayley enthralled with stories about all the celebrities she'd met on *Beyond Ballroom* over the years, and Hayley had begged Sasha to take her along the next time she visited Katya in L.A. And while Sasha still considered her relationship with Hayley to be a work in progress, it continued to improve on a regular basis.

It had helped, of course, when Sasha had urged Matthew to take his daughter on a tour of college campuses during Spring Break, insisting that the two of them needed some alone time. And when they had moved into the charming Queen Anne Victorian home a scant three blocks from the Gregsons' place, Sasha had encouraged Hayley to pick out the décor and furnishings for the bedroom that would be hers whenever she visited. It had been particularly important to Sasha that Hayley considered the new house her home, especially since Lindsey had already declared her intention to sell the Hillsborough mansion once Hayley went off to college. According to Hayley, her mother then planned to move somewhere "more exciting", like Los Angeles or New York. Matthew had muttered "good riddance" under his breath at learning the news, though he had long ago cut off any contact with his ex-wife.

Sasha loved their place in San Francisco, even though it was very different than the rustic beach house here in Kauai. The Victorian in the city's Pacific Heights neighborhood featured numerous windows that let in a ton of natural light, original hardwood floors, beautifully detailed crown molding, and the house felt cozy and charming despite its three levels and numerous rooms. The house in the city had also felt like home the instant she'd walked across the threshold, and she'd known immediately that this was the place for them.

Casey was thriving at his new school, had made lots of new friends, and had just wrapped up a very successful baseball season. He was over the moon at the idea of spending almost the entire summer here in Kauai, and had already persuaded Matthew to let him take surfing lessons. Hayley would be joining them at some point during the summer, along with Matthew's parents and siblings for a week or two at a time.

One of the main selling features of the beach house had been the two separate guest cottages on the property. Owning a vacation home in one of the most beautiful places on earth had quickly made Matthew and Sasha extremely popular with their family and friends, and they were expecting visitors almost every week this summer – Chad and Julio, Serge and Morgana, Elena and her two sons, in addition to Matthew's family members. Sasha just hoped that her parents wouldn't end up trashing the cottage they were occupying for the next ten days if they started fighting with each other as they so often did.

"Speaking of guests," drawled Matthew. "Things have been pretty quiet with your folks so far. Then again, I might have removed most of the breakable items in their cottage."

She laughed softly. "That's never stopped my mother before. If she's angry enough at my father she'll throw most anything in reach at him - an apple, her shoe, a book. But you're right - so far, so good. I think it would be hard to get upset about anything in a place as beautiful and peaceful as this. My mother seems as relaxed as I've ever seen her, while my dad is either swimming or drinking, just like I predicted."

He rubbed her upper back, bared by the low cut of her yoga top. "It's good for them to spend some time together, for the three of you to do so. Your parents are getting a little too old for all the drama, don't you think? Maybe if they're thrown together often enough they might actually consider getting married."

Sasha's laugh deepened. "I dare you to say that to my mother's face," she teased. "Just make sure there aren't any heavy objects close by that she can throw at your head, though."

Matthew winced. "Okay, you've convinced me. No more talk of another wedding in the family."

She sighed, propping her elbows on the veranda railing and gazing back out at the ocean. "I used to wish all the time when I was growing up that they would finally get married and settle down," she admitted. "That the three of us could be a real family. It took me a long time to realize that my parents are happier this way. That no matter how much they fight and how many times they leave each other, somehow they always find their way back. Though my father did tell me recently that he's tired of all the touring and traveling, and is thinking of retiring soon. *And* that he might decide to settle in Los Angeles afterwards. Of course, he hasn't broken that bit of news to my mother just yet. I think he's waiting for her to be in the right mood. He could have a very long wait on his hands."

He chuckled. "That's for sure. And speaking of retiring - has Serge stopped sending you emails begging you to change your mind?"

"Not yet. But at least he's sending them less frequently. And I haven't retired completely, Matthew. I'll still be teaching class one day a week and doing workshops once a month, as well as having private sessions at my beautiful home studio. Have I told you recently how much I love that space? And how much I love you for having it all redone?"

Matthew had insisted on dedicating nearly half of the lower level of their San Francisco home as a space where Sasha could both practice yoga and continue to do massage for a select number of clients - including him. The room was spacious and well lit, with beautiful bamboo floors, and painted in Sasha's favorite shade of sage green. And most recently it was where she'd patiently begun to guide him through his own yoga practice, something he finally had time for since finalizing the sale of MBI.

Sasha had agreed to cut back on both her teaching and massage schedule so that she had more time to spend with her new husband, and also be free to travel frequently. And while she certainly didn't need the income, she had felt an obligation to her devoted students and clients not to quit either of her jobs entirely.

He grinned down at her. "I think you might have mentioned something along those lines a few days ago. But, hey, I'm good with hearing you say it on a regular basis."

She pressed a kiss to his bare arm. Having just stumbled sleepily out of bed, Matthew was clad only in a pair of loose fitting cotton board shorts, and was shoeless, just like Sasha. It was a tradition, after all, in Hawaii to leave one's shoes by the front door. In fact, the only person who insisted on wearing shoes indoors was Katya, but at least she'd left her four-inch stilettos back home and had settled for jeweled flip flops instead.

"I love you," murmured Sasha, her hand caressing the lean muscles of his biceps. "And I'm really loving this new look of yours – no shirt, no shoes, no shaving. Not to mention the tan you've managed to acquire in less than a week. Happiness looks good on you, husband."

He pulled her into his arms. "Happiness *feels* good, too. Happiness and no stress for the first time in two decades. Though it's something of a temporary break, you know. At some point I need to get serious about the foundation."

Even after signing away half his net worth to Lindsey as part of the divorce settlement, Matthew had still been left with a sizeable fortune. A fortune that had nearly quadrupled after selling MBI. It was a staggering amount of money, one that Matthew knew he'd be hard pressed to spend even a small percentage of in his lifetime – especially given Sasha's general disdain for material things. When he'd suggested the idea of starting a foundation of some sort with a good portion of the money, she had overwhelmingly supported it.

"I know. But you can do that on your own terms, at your own pace. And not just yet. You deserve a good long break. And this is the perfect place to have one," she reminded him, sweeping an arm around to indicate their current surroundings.

He nodded, resting his chin on the top of her wild curls. "Couldn't think of a better place. Though as long as you're by my side, I'd consider anyplace in the world to be paradise."

Sasha rubbed her thumb over his heavily stubbled chin. "When did a self-professed nerd get to be such a romantic?" she teased.

Matthew captured her hand and pressed a kiss to the palm. "When I was lucky enough to meet you," he replied softly. "You realize that today is almost two years exactly since Tessa and Ian's wedding? The day you scolded me for drinking too much booze, coerced me into dancing with you, and then begged me to take better care of myself?"

Sasha thought for a moment. "You're right. Their anniversary is in two more days. I'll have to send Tessa an email congratulating them. Though I expect she's preoccupied with her little Gilly these days."

Sasha's instincts had been proven right yet again when she had predicted Tessa and Ian's baby would be a girl. Gillian, named after Tessa's late mother, was about six weeks old, and the prettiest baby Sasha had ever seen. Cuddling

481

her best friend's daughter had stirred up maternal instincts that Sasha hadn't believed she possessed. But she'd been pleasantly surprised when broaching the subject with Matthew to discover that he was more than open to the idea of having a baby.

"Not quite yet, though," he'd cautioned. "I'd like to have some time to just enjoy ourselves, enjoy this sense of freedom. But maybe within the next year we can revisit the subject. I wasn't around nearly as much as I would have liked to be when Hayley and Casey were small, so the thought that it would be completely different with a new baby is awfully appealing. And I know you'd be a wonderful mother, Sasha – kind and patient and devoted. Because that's the way you are with everyone you love."

His sweet, lovely words had made her choke up just a little, and she had given him a heartfelt kiss in response. "That's because most everyone in my life is so easy to love," she'd replied teasingly. "Especially you. And I love the idea of having a child together. Maybe next year, like you suggested. After all, there's really no rush, is there? You and I have all the time in the world now."

It began to rain just then, a light, fleeting summer rain that would be over almost as soon as it had begun. And though they were protected by the roof of the veranda, Matthew still urged his wife inside.

"Come on. We should start getting breakfast together. Casey will be up before too long, and you know how hungry he is first thing in the morning."

Sasha followed him across the wide veranda, pausing at the entrance to the house. Like many homeowners in Hawaii, they had followed with tradition and chosen a name for their house. Matthew had even commissioned a local artist to hand paint the small wooden sign that had been hung just to the right of the front door.

Sasha traced a finger over the sage green lettering that spelled out the name she and Matthew had chosen, a name that represented not just this beautiful house but the beautiful life they were making together – it was called *Serenity*.

The End

Dear Readers,

I hope that you've enjoyed getting to know Sasha and Matthew, and taking this journey along with them. When I first began writing the Inevitable series, I never envisioned these two characters together, mostly because they were such different individuals, who lived very different lives.

But eventually their story began to take shape in my head, and the idea for Serenity came together. This was a bit different than some of my previous books, as the relationship between Sasha and Matthew is more tender, and perhaps a little less passionate and sexual than say Julia and Nathan's, or Tessa and Ian's. But there is no denying the great love and need they have for each other, and how in the end they helped each other overcome difficulties and demons from their past.

Just one more book to go now in this series – Stronger – which will be the story of Cara and Dante (who were introduced in book three of the series, Shattered). I'm taking a very short break and then will be diving right into Stronger. Angela and Nick will also be featured in this final book, and you will get to see how their relationship has progressed since the end of Shattered. I think you are all going to adore Cara, and alternately love and hate Dante at various points in the story.

After Stronger, I'm toying with the idea for a brand new trilogy, one that's a little more fun and light hearted, and each book a standalone.

Thank you all for your continued support, and your words

of kindness and encouragement! It keeps me going on those down days when I read a bad review, or suffer from a bout of writer's block. Please be sure to keep in touch, I always love to hear from you.

Happy Reading!
Janet

SOCIAL MEDIA AND CONTACT

Email - janetnissenson@gmail.com

Website/Blog - www.janetnissenson.com

Facebook - @JanetNissensonAuthor

Twitter - @JNissenson

Goodreads - www.goodreads.com/janetnissenson

Pinterest - @janetnissenson

Instagram - @janetlnissenson

ADDITIONAL TITLES BY THIS AUTHOR

THE INEVITABLE SERIES:

Serendipity (Book #1 – Julia and Nathan's story)

Splendor (Book #2 – Tessa and Ian's original story)

All You Need is Love (Book #1.5 – the Serendipity sequel)

Shattered (Book #3 – Angela and Nick's story)

Sensational (Book #4 – Lauren and Ben's story)

Serenity (Book #5 – Sasha and Matthew's story)

COMING SOON:

Stronger (Book #6 – Cara and Dante's story)

THE SPLENDOR SERIES:

Covet (Book #1)

Crave (Book #2 – same book as Splendor [Inevitable #2] but with a dozen new/additional scenes)

Claim (Book #3)

Printed in Great
Britain
by Amazon